Readers Love Kerry

'All Kerry Barrett's books are brilliant'

'I love Kerry Barrett's books and this one
is no disappointment'

'Highly recommended'

'I just loved the way Kerry took us effortlessly from
one era to another'

'Immediately bought another Kerry Barrett book -
great writer!'

'Brilliantly written gripping loved it'

KERRY BARRETT is the author of eight novels, including the *Strictly Come Dancing* themed *A Step in Time*, and *The Girl in the Picture*, about a crime novelist who solves a 160-year-old mystery.

Born in Edinburgh, Kerry moved to London as a child, where she now lives with her husband and two sons. A massive bookworm growing up, she used to save up her pocket money for weeks to buy the latest Sweet Valley High book, then read the whole story on the bus home and have to wait two months for the next one. Eventually she realised it would be easier to write her own stories . . .

Kerry's years as a television journalist, reporting on *EastEnders* and *Corrie*, have inspired her novels where popular culture collides with a historical mystery. But there is no truth in the rumours that she only wrote a novel based on *Strictly Come Dancing* so she would be invited on to *It Takes Two*.

When she's not practising her foxtrot (because you never know . . .), Kerry is watching Netflix, reading Jilly Cooper, and researching her latest historical story.

Also by Kerry Barrett

The Could It Be Magic? Series
Bewitched, Bothered and Bewildered
I Put a Spell on You
Baby, It's Cold Outside
I'll Be There for You
A Spoonful of Sugar: A Novella

A Step in Time
The Forgotten Girl
The Girl in the Picture
The Hidden Women

The Secret Letter

KERRY BARRETT

ONE PLACE. MANY STORIES

HQ
An imprint of HarperCollins*Publishers* Ltd
1 London Bridge Street
London SE1 9GF

This paperback edition 2020

First published in Great Britain by
HQ, an imprint of HarperCollins*Publishers* Ltd 2020

ISBN: 9780008331016

MIX
Paper from
responsible sources
FSC C007454

This book is produced from independently certified FSC™ paper
to ensure responsible forest management.

For more information visit: www.harpercollins.co.uk/green

Printed and bound by CPI Group (UK) Ltd,
Croydon, CR0 4YY

To the strong women in my life who are the living embodiment of Deeds Not Words: my fabulous aunts, Pauline and Norma; my godmother, Linda; my second mum, Les; and of course, my amazing actual mum, Dorothy.

Prologue

Esther

December 1910

I picked up the letter I'd written and read it over to myself. I knew he'd never see it, but it made me feel better, just putting my feelings down on paper. Putting everything that had happened behind me.

'Sometimes the fight is part of the fun,' I'd written. I smiled sadly. That was exactly how I felt, and why everything had gone so wrong between us; there had just been no fight.

Picking up my pen again, I signed the letter with a flourish and then wafted the paper, waiting for the ink to dry. I wouldn't send it. There was no need. But I wanted to keep it somewhere safe, somewhere I could find it if I ever needed to remember why I'd done what I'd done.

I glanced round my small bedroom, looking for inspiration, and my eyes fell on my fabric bag, stuffed under the bed. I pulled it out and opened it and found inside the wooden photograph frame holding the only photograph I had of my former love. Perfect. But first I had to change something else. On my bedside table was my journal and tucked inside was a photograph of myself. It had been taken at a recent suffragette rally and vain as it sounded, I loved the way it made me look. I had my chin raised slightly and a flash of fire in my eyes. I looked like a woman to be reckoned with.

Smiling, I opened the back of the picture frame and took out the photograph that was in there. Should I throw it away? No, he was part of my past no matter how horribly things had ended. Instead I put it into the bag and pushed it back under the bed. Then I put the photograph of myself into the frame, folded up the letter and put it in an envelope, carefully tucked that behind the photo and fixed the back on securely. I proudly stood the photograph on my bedside table. I would keep that picture with me, wherever I ended up, and every time I looked at it I would remember that I had been made stronger by everything that had happened.

'The fight goes on, Esther,' I said to myself. 'The fight goes on.'

Chapter 1

Lizzie

August 2019

I stared at the building where I would spend most of my time for the next year, or even two, with a mixture of hope, fear and resentment.

'Just a few months,' I whispered to myself. 'Just a few months, and then you can get back to normal.'

I pushed my sunglasses up on top of my head so I could see better and squinted in the brightness. It was an old-fashioned school building. The sort of building that in London would have been converted into luxury flats years ago. It had black iron railings, a paved area at the front with hopscotch markings and two entrances, over which in the stonework was carved "boys" and "girls". I knew that at the back was a more modern extension, but staring at the front I felt like I'd gone back in time.

My stomach lurched with nerves and I took a step backwards, lowering my sunglasses again like a shield.

'Chin up, Lizzie,' I told myself sternly. 'You've got this.'

But I wasn't sure I did have it.

It was mid-morning but it was quiet. No one was around and I was glad. School didn't start for another ten days though I'd come to Elm Heath early so I could move into my new house, get settled in, and generally find my feet a bit. It was very different here from my life in Clapham and I knew it was going to take some getting used to.

I took a deep, slightly shuddery breath as I thought about my ex-husband, Grant, who was – as far as I knew – still living in leafy South-West London. Predictably, he'd managed to emerge from the disaster of the last couple of years smelling of roses despite being asked to leave Broadway Common School before he was pushed. Never had the phrase "men fail up" seemed truer than when I'd discovered he'd walked into a fancy job in some think-tank, advising local councils on education policy and was earning more now than he'd ever done as a head teacher. Which was ironic considering one of the many, many things he'd done wrong was being creative with some of the school budgets.

Under my sunglasses, I felt a tear start to dribble down my nose and I reached up with one finger to wipe it away. I had to stay strong or I would fall apart. And yes, it wasn't fair that I'd been treated with suspicion too, even though an investigation had proved that I hadn't been involved in Grant's misdemeanours whatsoever. But it was harder to prove I didn't know anything about it, because while he was head of the huge junior school, I was in charge at the infants' school next door. And as I'd soon discovered, no one really believed that I was innocent, despite what the official reports said. I'd waited for Grant to clear my name – to speak out on my behalf. But I was still waiting. Because as it turned out, Grant telling everyone I knew nothing would have effectively meant admitting he'd done all the things he was accused of. So instead he stayed quiet.

With the trust gone in our marriage, I'd found myself moving back to my mum's house at the ripe old age of thirty-eight. And with the trust gone in my job, I'd resigned and applied for new posts all over the place – just to get away from London.

'And here I am,' I said out loud, still looking at Elm Heath

Primary. Elm Heath was an ordinary school. It wasn't a super, high-performing school; it was just a normal, nice-enough village primary. And that made it the perfect school for me to prove myself.

There was no doubt everything that had happened had left me needing to show the teaching world that I still had it, and I thought Elm Heath would give me that opportunity. As far as I could see, it was just a bit old-fashioned. The last head teacher had been in her job for yonks, and she'd been quite resistant to change. I thought I could drag the school into the twenty-first century, revitalise it, get my mojo back and then go back to London and to normality. Albeit a Grant-free normality.

I forced a small smile. This was just a blip, I thought to myself. Just a small hump in the road of my career. And perhaps a slightly bigger hump in the road of my personal life because despite everything he'd done, I still missed Grant. I missed being part of a team. The Mansfields. Grant and Elizabeth. A double act. A "you two". Now it was just me.

Sighing, I picked up my bag. I'd moved into my tiny terraced house yesterday – my whole life reduced to a few boxes of books – but it was still chaotic and I had a lot to do to get sorted before term started. I really should get on with it.

As I turned to walk away from the school a voice shouted from the playground.

'Ms Armstrong? Yoo-hoo! Ms Armstrong!'

I ignored it for a split second and then looked back over my shoulder as it dawned on me that I was Ms Armstrong. I'd applied for this job in my maiden name – part of my plan to be "me" instead of Grant's other half.

Across the playground, a short woman – perhaps ten years older than me – came barrelling towards the gate.

'Wait!' she called. 'I'll let you in!'

I groaned as I recognised her from one of my interviews. It was Paula Paxton, the deputy head. Grant would have said she was the perfect mix of overenthusiastic and underachieving. Though she'd been very nice to me when I met her before, I just wasn't really in the mood for company.

'Ms Armstrong,' she panted as she unlocked the gate. 'I saw you from my office and thought you would want to come in rather than lurk outside. So I said to myself, I said "Paula, run downstairs and let her in – she doesn't want to be lurking outside," and I raced downstairs and then when I saw you pick your bag up, I thought I'd missed you.'

Faced with such jollity, I winced. Despite how nice Paula had seemed at my interview, I wasn't sure I could deal with her kindness today when I was feeling fragile. She saw my reaction and she paused while opening the iron gate.

'I'm babbling,' she said. 'I always babble when I meet new people. I'm sorry.'

I managed a weak smile. 'Don't be,' I said.

She reached out and took my bag from me.

'Coffee?'

I smiled more genuinely this time. 'Coffee would be great.'

I followed her through the echoey corridors of the school. Generally, I disliked schools out of hours. They needed the children to make them feel alive, I always thought. But today, I appreciated the quiet stillness of the building. It was cool inside, no fancy air-conditioning could compete with hundred-year-old thick stone walls.

I was wearing a vest top, cropped jeans and Havaianas that flipped and flopped loudly down the hall. Paula Paxton was dressed for work in a neat wrap dress with court shoes and – I thought – nude tights. It was thirty degrees outside, and it was the summer holidays, so I wondered if she dressed like that all the time. On the beach. At the gym.

'God, I'm so hot,' she said, over her shoulder. 'I've been to a funeral.'

Oops.

'Sorry,' I muttered, feeling horrible for having had nasty thoughts about her. Paula waved her hand at me.

'Nah, don't be. It was some client of my husband's firm. I only went so I could bring the car home afterwards because I need to go to the supermarket later, and I could have got the bus, but I'll have a lot of bags . . .'

I smiled and she stopped.

'Babbling again,' she said. 'Here are the offices.'

She opened a door on her left. It was an original, thick with paint and with a wobbly window on the top half.

Inside was a sort of reception area with seating and two desks for the secretaries I assumed. Beyond it were two more doors, similarly old-fashioned, one marked "head teacher" and one marked "deputy head teacher".

'I'm on the left,' she said. 'I teach as well, obviously, so I don't use my office much. But I have the coffee machine. Milk and sugar?'

After suffering in too many staffrooms where the only refreshments on offer were clumpy catering tins of instant, I was pleasantly surprised to hear there was a coffee machine. I smiled.

'Just milk, please. I'll just have a look at my own office if that's okay?'

'Hold on,' she said. She opened the top drawer of one of the desks and pulled out a key.

'This is yours.'

I wondered if there was any point in keeping a key just centimetres away from the door it unlocked but I didn't say anything. Instead I simply unlocked the door.

'I'll fire up the Nespresso,' Paula said. 'Well, it's not a real Nespresso, because they're so expensive. It's just the Marks and Sparks version, but I find it's just as good . . .'

She trailed off, much to my relief.

'Just come in when you're ready.'

I nodded and, taking a deep breath, I went into my new office.

It was pretty bare. There was a big desk by the window, a round table, and two empty bookcases. On one wall there was an old-fashioned black and white photograph of a young woman wearing what I thought was Edwardian dress, and a fierce expression.

'You're going to have to go,' I told her out loud. 'I can't have you looking down on me so disapprovingly.'

My voice bounced around the empty room.

Suddenly overwhelmed by everything, I sat down at my new desk and put my face in my hands. This was my last chance to save my career and start again but it just seemed like a huge task. Was this going to be a massive mistake?

Chapter 2

Lizzie

I sat like that for a few minutes, wallowing in my misery over my new life. None of this was my fault, I thought. I was just another one of Grant's victims, like the parents he fooled, and the kids he let down, and whose SATs results he faked, and the PTA whose funds he siphoned off. Though that bit had never been proved, and like I said, he'd never actually admitted the rest – just insisted it was all a misunderstanding. I took a deep breath and rubbed my eyes, trying to pull myself together. I couldn't fall apart now, not with Paula Paxton in the next room.

'Excuse me, Ms Armstrong,' a voice said, making me realise that Paula Paxton wasn't in the next room; she was in my room, clutching two mugs of coffee.

I forced my head upright and tried to smile. But my neck felt weak and my smile weaker.

'Oh dear,' Paula Paxton said. 'Oh dear.'

She put both mugs on the desk and in two strides was next to me. Tentatively, she touched my arm.

'Feeling a bit overwhelmed?' she said.

Her kind voice almost made me fall apart. With super-human strength I managed to nod, without looking at her.

'I know what happened,' she said. 'In your last job, I mean. You don't have to explain.'

Of course she knew. She'd been in my interviews; she must have read my application. Knowing she knew made me feel oddly relieved and embarrassed at the same time. I couldn't bear her feeling sorry for me. It was the sympathy and the sad faces and the tilty heads asking 'how ARE you?' that had made life in London so completely awful.

Paula rubbed my arm gently and then went round the other side of the desk and sat down opposite me. She pushed one of the mugs towards me and picked up the other one.

'I think I should tell you just how thrilled we are to have you here,' she said in a conversational tone. 'I've read all the things you've written in *Teacher* magazine. And I was actually at your training day in Brighton.'

This time I did manage to meet her eyes.

'Really?'

Grant had been the face of our schools. We worked together but he was the driving force. He was the one doing the Tedx talks, and writing for the broadsheet education supplements about his views on education policy, and his approach to helping young children learn. He was outspoken, handsome and funny, and he really knew his stuff, so he was very media friendly. He'd even been on *Question Time* once. In fact, I thought it was his profile that had led him to make the bad decisions he'd made. Education is a long game and seeing children through their years at school can sometimes feel like an age. Grant couldn't wait for results, and so he had to fiddle them, because he couldn't be seen to be failing. Apart from in our marriage, of course. He didn't care about that going wrong.

But I'd been passionate about what we were doing, too. I'd written a few articles for a teaching mag; I'd done a couple of seminars at training days. And it seemed Paula Paxton knew all about them.

Now she smiled at me. 'Ms Armstrong . . .'

'Lizzie,' I said. 'Please call me Lizzie.'

'Lizzie, Elm Heath Primary needs a boost.'

'I know.'

'I've worked here for twenty years,' Paula went on. 'My daughter came here. It's such a lovely school. We were just so thrilled when you took the position.'

I smiled at her across the top of my coffee mug. It was nice to hear after so much bad stuff.

'You're so inspirational,' Paula was saying. 'You have such wonderful ideas about putting the children first in everything.'

I felt a very small flush of pride. 'Really?' I said. That had always been my focus.

Paula smiled at me again. 'I read some of your husband's articles too.'

'Ex-husband.'

She bit her lip. 'He's more about winning.'

I'd taken a mouthful of the rather good coffee while she was talking and now I swallowed it all, making me cough.

Still spluttering, I laughed for the first time in what seemed like weeks. It sounded slightly strange. 'That's Grant in a nutshell.'

Paula grinned at me, then taking advantage of the friendlier atmosphere between us, she leaned forward. 'Was it awful? Your break-up?'

I shrugged. 'You know when people say something's ended not with a bang but with a whimper? It was like that, really. He let me down professionally and then – boom – it all just crumbled.'

'That's almost worse,' Paula said and again I was surprised by her insight. I nodded, feeling another rush of self-pity and, sensing my mood, she smiled again.

'I've organised a barbecue for you to meet all the staff,' she said. 'My house, tomorrow evening.'

'Oh I'm not sure . . .' I began. I was still finding my feet in Elm Heath and I wasn't sure I was quite ready to meet my teachers.

Paula waved her hand. 'It's all arranged,' she said. 'I'm only round the corner from you – I'll send someone to collect you on the way so you don't get lost.'

I blinked at her, astonished. She'd arranged a party for me and she knew where I lived? In London I'd be suspicious of such overly friendly behaviour, but here it just seemed . . . nice. I thought briefly of boozy staff parties at the Three Crowns in Clapham High Street and then shook my head to clear the memories. My life was different now and I had to get used to it. And if it was totally overwhelming, then I'd stay an hour, make an excuse of doing more unpacking or something, and scarper.

'Thank you,' I said, smiling. 'That's very kind.'

'I'll leave you to it,' Paula said. 'Could I ask you to rinse out your mug and put it back in my office when you're done?'

'Of course.'

She got up and turned to go. 'Feel free to make the office your own,' she said as an afterthought. 'If you need more bookshelves, or chairs just let Jeff the caretaker know.'

'Thanks,' I said again. I glanced round. It was a bigger office than the one I'd had in London and I was sure I could make it my own. My eye was caught by the portrait on the wall. 'Paula, who's that woman in the picture?'

She smiled. 'That's Esther Watkins,' she said, proudly, as though it needed no further explanation.

I screwed up my face. 'Sorry, I don't know who that is.'

'She founded Elm Heath Primary back in the early twentieth century,' Paula said, as though she was reading from an information card at a museum. 'We're actually one of the oldest schools in the county. Esther Watkins dedicated her life . . .'

'Maybe we should move her picture,' I said hurriedly, interrupting her before I got treated to a lecture about a sour-faced spinster who probably thought children should be seen and not heard.

Paula looked horrified so I backtracked immediately.

'I mean, maybe she needs to be seen. We could put her in the main office, perhaps. Or in the corridor.'

'Perhaps.' Paula sounded doubtful. 'I've always thought it was nice that she's in here. This would have been her office at one time, you know?'

I knew when I was beaten. I'd move grumpy Ms Watkins when I was settled in and had a quiet moment to myself.

'I'll see you tomorrow then,' I said to Paula.

She grinned at me, obviously pleased she'd convinced me to leave Esther Watkins where she was.

'I'll send someone round to get you about sixish.'

'Sounds great,' I said, forcing away the nerves I was feeling at being "presented" to all the staff at once. 'Lovely.'

Chapter 3

Lizzie

What did one wear to a village barbecue? I wondered, looking at my small selection of clothes later. When my life had fallen apart, I'd put most of my belongings into storage while I holed up at my mum's house. And then, when I'd moved down to Elm Heath in the middle of deepest, darkest Kent, I'd realised I didn't need all the stuff I'd accumulated over the years – it just reminded me of better times – so I sold it all, except for a few boxes of books.

Now I had what might be called a capsule wardrobe. A very small capsule wardrobe. I decided to go casual, so I pulled on the pair of cropped jeans I'd been wearing at school yesterday and a floaty vest with little flowers on it, and put a cardigan in my bag in case it got chilly later.

I was, I discovered when I was trying to draw a straight line with eyeliner, ridiculously and shakily nervous. What if everyone knew what had happened in London and they all thought I'd been involved? What if none of them wanted to work with me? What if – I gasped aloud and jabbed myself in the eye with the eyeliner pencil – they'd all wanted Paula to be the new head and were resentful that I'd got the job?

With one eye watering, I wiped off the mess I'd made of my make-up and instead just dabbed on some lip balm. They'd have to take me as I was. I brushed my hair, then went downstairs to my tiny kitchen and took the bottle of Prosecco I'd bought out of the fridge. If all else failed, I'd bribe them with bubbles.

I was ready and waiting when the doorbell rang, but it still made me jump because I was so edgy. I took a deep breath, plastered a smile on my face and opened the door to find a woman maybe five years younger than me on the doorstep. She had bright blonde hair in a high ponytail and freckles and looked like a cheerleader in an American teen film.

'Hello, I'm Lizzie,' I said, then I paused. 'Lizzie Armstrong.'

She grinned at me, showing neat, white teeth. 'I'd worry if you weren't,' she said. 'Paula sent me to fetch you. I'm Pippa Davis. I teach years one and two.'

I relaxed, slightly, in the face of such friendliness. 'Nice to meet you Pippa,' I said. I picked up my bag and the bottle. 'Shall we go?'

Paula was right, she did live just round the corner. I wondered if it was going to be odd living on top of all my colleagues and – more importantly – my pupils. Though we'd lived fairly close to our school in London, catchment areas were so small we didn't have students as neighbours. This was going to be totally different.

'Everyone's so excited to meet you,' Pippa said as she bounced down the side of Paula's large detached house – I remembered what she'd said about her husband having clients and wondered briefly what he did – and into the big garden, me trailing behind like a sulky teenager.

'She's here!' she sang. 'Lizzie's here!'

The garden was full of people, chatting and laughing, but as Pippa made her announcement, they all fell silent and as one they turned and stared at me. I felt sick. I'd not wanted to arrive with a huge fanfare, like this.

'Hello,' I squeaked. 'Hi.'

Everyone chorused hellos and Paula rushed up to us and gave me a hug that surprised me.

'So pleased you could make it,' she said. 'Come and meet everyone. Pippa, can you get Lizzie a drink?'

My head spinning, I took the glass Pippa handed me and drained it without even looking at the contents.

'So, Pippa you've met,' Paula said. 'And her best friend is Emma, who's our school secretary. She keeps us all organised. They both went to Elm Heath Primary together – isn't that lovely?'

'Lovely,' I echoed.

I could hear Grant's mocking voice in my head. He'd roll his eyes at the thought of people growing up here, marrying their childhood sweetheart, and staying put. 'It's so English,' he'd say with a sort of superior chuckle. 'So white, straight . . . vanilla.'

I thought of Broadway Common School where we had kids speaking more than thirty languages, celebrated every festival going, worked hard to include the kids with two dads in Mother's Day and the ones with two mums in Father's Day, and I wondered if I'd miss that diversity.

'This is Nate – Mr Welsh – who teaches years five and six,' she said introducing a man about the same age as Pippa and Emma, who'd no doubt gone to school with them too.

I shook his hand. 'Pleased to meet you,' I said.

Nate stifled a yawn. 'God, I'm sorry,' he said in horror. 'That was so rude.'

Paula looked at him with genuine affection. 'Nate's a new dad,' she said.

'Congratulations.' I smiled at him. 'Is your wife here?'

Nate looked at me with a hint of mischief in his eyes. 'My husband Marc is over there with our baby, Leia,' he said.

I turned to see an athletic man, a bit older than Nate, expertly bouncing a baby on his knee, while holding a bottle of beer and chatting to another man.

I screwed my face up. 'Sorry,' I whispered, feeling a tiny flush of triumph. Ha, Grant! I thought. Village life is interesting.

Nate chuckled. 'Don't be. It must be hard for you coming from London where people aren't as liberal.'

He was joking, I thought. But I blushed anyway.

Nate introduced me to another teacher – Celeste – who was a dead ringer for a young Michelle Obama, right down to the enviable upper arms. I slid my own bingo wings into my cardie as I spoke to her, feeling self-conscious and not just about letting myself believe that everyone in Elm Heath was a boring stereotype.

Paula's husband Chris was on the barbecue and their daughter Chloe, who was in sixth form, handed out drinks. It was all very pleasant, just a bit – overwhelming. Trying to make a good impression on so many new people was hard work.

Needing a moment to myself, I slunk across the garden to an empty deckchair and sat down. To my left, Paula's husband Chris was flipping burgers. He was engaged in what seemed to me to be a fairly heated discussion with the man who'd been talking to Nate's handsome husband. The other man was shorter, stockier, and more dishevelled than Marc, but also very attractive in his own way.

Both Chris and the other man looked quite cross and I was intrigued. I leaned slightly to the side and tried to eavesdrop on their conversation.

'I think you're being unrealistic,' Chris was saying. 'Idealistic.'

The other man frowned. He looked worried. 'I thought perhaps, I could just see it as business . . .'

'Are you the new headmistress?' a voice at my elbow said, interrupting my earwigging. I turned to see a small girl – year three, I guessed with my expert eye – with a gap-toothed smile and wonky bunches.

'I am,' I said.

She fixed me with a serious stare. 'Are you a nice headmistress or a strict headmistress?'

I thought about it. 'Could I be both?'

'S'pose.'

'Then I will be both.'

'You don't look like a headmistress.'

'Why not?'

'You look like a mummy.'

I smiled, a genuine, not-nervous smile. 'Do I look like your mummy?'

'My mummy is dead.'

I stopped smiling. 'I'm sorry.'

The little girl grinned at me. 'I have a daddy.'

'That's nice.'

I shifted awkwardly in my seat. Obviously, I considered myself to be good with kids, but I was off my game this evening and this small child was unsettling me.

'What is your name?' she asked.

'Ms Armstrong. What's yours?'

'Cara,' she said, frowning. 'What is Mizzzzzzz?'

'It's a title, like Mrs or Miss.'

Cara shook her head, her lopsided bunches bouncing. 'I think you're getting muddled,' she said kindly, patting my hand. 'Miss means you haven't got a husband or a wife, and Mrs means you have. Mizzzzzz is just pretend. Do you have a husband or a wife?'

I swallowed. 'No, I don't have a husband.'

'Do you have a wife?'

'No.'

She nodded. 'Then you are a Miss,' she said, speaking clearly like I was elderly and hard of hearing. 'MISS.'

'Cara, are you being a nuisance?'

The attractive man who'd been talking to Chris was standing in front of us. He flashed me a smile and for a split second I felt a flicker of interest and not just in his conversation. He was wearing a rumpled T-shirt and jeans and his hair was sticking up, but there was something about him that I liked.

18

'I'm chatting to MISS Armstrong,' Cara said. 'She is the new headmistress and she is nice and also strict and she doesn't have a husband or a wife.'

I felt myself flush as the man raised an eyebrow at me. 'Strict, eh?'

Urgh. 'I have my moments,' I said. Where on earth did that come from? Was I flirting?

The man put his hand on Cara's head. 'We need to go, angel,' he said. 'It's late.'

'But Daddy, it's a party.'

'And now it's finished.'

Cara rolled her eyes and I couldn't help but chuckle.

'Nice to meet you, MISS Armstrong,' the man said. 'I'm Danny Kinsella, by the way.'

'Are you a teacher?' I said, running through the list of names Pippa had bombarded me with in my head.

'God no. Just a friend of Paula and Chris.'

'And a daddy,' Cara said.

He smiled down at her. 'And a daddy.'

'See you at school then, Miss Armstrong.'

He waved at me, and he and Cara wandered off down the side of the house and out on to the road. I stared after them feeling slightly off-balance. There was definitely more to life in Elm Heath than I'd imagined.

Chapter 4

Lizzie

I was at school at the crack of dawn on the first day of term. I had always been an early riser, and when I was nervous I could never sleep.

I thought I'd be the only person there, but Emma was already in the office.

'Morning,' she sang. 'Ready for action?'

I grimaced. 'As I'll ever be.'

She put a hand on my arm. 'You'll be great. Cup of tea?'

'Yes please.'

Emma headed to the corner of the reception area where there was a sink, a little fridge and a kettle and busied herself finding mugs.

'I'll let you get on,' she said over her shoulder as she filled the kettle. 'Some things arrived for you. I've put them all on your desk.'

I thanked her and headed into my office. I'd come in every day for a couple of hours and made it more homely. I'd put books on the shelves, and brought in my stationery. But Esther Watkins still glowered down at me and the whole room was still pretty bare. At least it had been. Now there was a stack of post on my desk, a huge bouquet of flowers, a box of chocolates and two bottles in shiny presentation bags.

'Oh my God,' I breathed. 'What's all this?'

Emma had come up behind me, holding my tea. 'Everyone's very pleased you're here,' she said. 'The big card and the chocolates are from the staff, but I think all the other bits are from parents.'

She handed me the mug. 'I'm going to go and check all the classrooms,' she said. 'See you in a little while.'

Overwhelmed, again, I sat down on the chair and stared at the pile of gifts. I couldn't believe how welcoming everyone was being. It was not what I'd expected and I almost felt guilty that they were being so nice when I was seeing this job as a step on my road back to normal life. A means to an end, rather than an end in itself.

I took a deep breath and a swig of tea and started opening the cards. They were all full of lovely good luck messages.

'Wishing you and Elm Heath Primary lots of luck for the future,' one said. 'Love Sarah, Gary, Olivia (y6) and Rosie (y4).'

'Let's hope this is an exciting new chapter for Elm Heath Primary,' read another. While another said, in a child's hand writing: 'Hello Mrs Armstrong! From William, Luke, Charlie and Emily.' The kids had all signed their names individually and drawn little pictures of themselves and it was so adorable I could forgive them calling me "Mrs Armstrong".

There was even one from Danny and Cara Kinsella. 'Good luck, MISS Armstrong,' Danny had written, which made me smile even while I prickled with irritation. 'See you soon.'

I arranged the cards on the shelves, put the wine to one side to keep for drinks with the staff on Friday – I thought we'd probably need them – and opened the big card from the staff.

They'd all written personal messages to me, telling me how much they were looking forward to working with me, and how they thought this was the start of good times for Elm Heath Primary. I felt guilty all over again as I read them, given that I was approaching this job as a sort of gap year. A sabbatical. A way of pressing the reset button after a blip in an otherwise high-flying teaching career, no matter how many sweet pictures the kids drew, or how many messages of support the staff shared.

'Don't look at me like that,' I said to Esther Watkins as she stared down at me.

I drained my mug of tea and turned my attention to the flowers. They were peonies – my absolute favourite and very hard to come by in early September.

With a slight sense of misgiving, I pulled out the envelope that was tucked inside the cellophane wrapping and slid my finger under the flap to open it.

'Queenie,' the card read. I winced at the stupid nickname that I'd not heard in a long while. 'Missing you fiercely but wishing you lots of luck. Gx'

My stomach twisted. How could he do this? I was just getting to the point where I didn't think about him every hour of every day and now he'd wormed his way in again.

'Sod off, Grant,' I said out loud. I screwed up the card and threw it in the bin, then reached in and took it out again.

It had been such a shock when I'd discovered the extent Grant had gone to in his career. The risks he'd taken and the questionable practices he'd employed and not even for the good of the kids, simply to make himself look better – for his own gains. I'd been shocked by his deception, and by the fact that he'd not been the person I'd thought he was.

And then I'd been shocked all over again at how easily he'd sacrificed our marriage. His only concern was looking after himself; I didn't seem to count for anything. It had been a long, hard year for me, living with Mum, coming to terms with what had happened, applying for jobs and having to explain why I'd left London over and over again. But it looked like Grant didn't appreciate that at all.

'Sod. Off,' I said again. This time I ripped the card up into tiny pieces, shredding it on my desk like ironic confetti.

A knock on my door made me jump and I swept the bits into the bin, just as Paula stuck her head round.

'Morning! The kids are about to arrive,' she said. 'Thought you might like to stand in the playground with me while they come in?'

I didn't really. I wanted to hide in my office and pretend I wasn't there, but I knew the sight of all the children would boost my spirits. I glanced at the cards on my shelf – I also knew the parents would be expecting to see me.

'Absolutely,' I said. 'Let's go.'

* * *

When the kids were all safely in their classrooms, I felt much happier. They'd all been so excited, skipping into school, shouting greetings to their friends. Cara had arrived, gripping the hand of an older woman I assumed was her grandmother, and gave me a cheery wave.

'They're a good bunch, by and large,' Paula said as we strolled back to the office together. She taught reception and the littlest children weren't starting until next week, so she was donning her deputy-head hat today.

'I'm looking forward to seeing them all together in assembly later.' I paused. 'There aren't many of them,' I said carefully. 'I knew the school was small, but . . .'

Paula bit her lip. 'I noticed that too. I knew numbers were dwindling but . . .'

'More so than you expected?'

Emma looked up as we entered but didn't interrupt, obviously sensing the tone of the conversation.

'I think so. It's hard to tell in the playground.'

'I'll have a look,' I said. 'I should have admissions from the county by now. Come with me.'

Paula followed as I went into my office, sat down, and opened my emails. I was used to lots of movement in the days before term started; London had a population that was always changing with people arriving and leaving often, so getting final admission numbers at the last minute didn't faze me in the slightest.

I found the right email and clicked on it. It was automatically generated by the council and had a list of pupils who had been withdrawn before the start of term. I scanned the names – there were about twenty of them. I turned my screen round so Paula could see.

'Oh bugger,' she said. 'That's four year sixes, a handful of year fours and fives, and lots of year threes.'

'And you have eight starting in reception next week?'

Paula nodded.

'How many do you normally have?'

'About twelve,' she said. 'Sometimes as many as fifteen.'

'Is there a waiting list?' I said, knowing the answer. Paula just laughed without humour.

'Where are they all going?'

She shrugged. 'The big primary in Blyton, I imagine.' Blyton was the nearest town and had a newly built primary school.

'It's quite a distance.'

'It is, but it's a good school. It's a modern school with lots of bells and whistles. Some parents obviously think the journey is worth it.'

I picked up a pen and tapped out a rhythm on the desk, thinking. 'What went wrong here, Paula?'

She sighed. 'I think we all got a bit set in our ways.'

I met her eye. 'All?'

'As you know, the old head was quite old-fashioned,' she said diplomatically. 'We're looking forward to you shaking things up.'

I smiled, even though I had that knot of anxiety and guilt in my stomach again. I didn't mind shaking things up, but I hadn't had any idea that pupil numbers were falling so fast. It didn't sound good, to me. 'Any ideas about what we should do?'

'Lots,' Paula began, then paused as Emma knocked on the door.

'There's a phone call for you, Paula,' she said. 'Lily Johnson's mum. She says Lily's been having nightmares about starting school and she wonders if you can pop in and see her?'

Paula smiled. 'Bless her,' she said. 'I'll sort it out. Sorry, Lizzie.'

She went off to take the call, leaving me marvelling at the thought of a teacher popping into to see a nervous four-year-old before she started school. It was a privilege, I thought, to be able to look after the kids like that. This was a lovely school.

Above my desk, Esther Watkins looked down at me, her expression unreadable.

'Oh, shut up,' I said.

Chapter 5

Esther

April 1910

I flinched as the huge metal gate clanged shut behind me. After everything that had happened, I was jumpy and nervous. Would that stay with me? I wondered. I thought it probably would. I was changed forever now.

Beside me, was my friend Minnie, looking shrunken and pale. She stumbled and I caught her arm.

'Easy, there,' I said.

'Anyone coming for you?'

She shook her head.

'Me neither. I'll walk with you.'

We were both unsteady on our feet. Both feeling the effects of a few weeks in prison. We'd been on hunger strike and had suffered the horrors of being force-fed shortly before we were told we were being released early. But Minnie had been inside longer than me. She was feeling it more. I looked at her in concern, hoisted my bag on to my back and offered her my arm. She hung on to me in a fashion very unlike my independent friend. I thought about just how long the Holloway Road was. I wasn't sure she would make it.

We took a few steps forward and I looked back over my

shoulder at the prison behind us. It was a huge, grey stone building, squatting like a giant slug on the side of the road.

'Where are you going?'

She shrugged. 'Dunno. I lost my digs. You?'

'Home,' I said, though the word felt strange in my mouth. 'Back to my mother.'

'You never talk about her,' Minnie said. 'She a suffragette, is she?'

I laughed out loud for the first time in weeks. 'No,' I said. 'She's . . . disapproving.'

We shuffled along a bit further and then paused as a hansom cab drew up next to us.

'Minnie Gantry and Esther Watkins?' the cabbie asked, leaning out of the window. His horse stamped its foot, eager to get going.

'Yes?' I said, cautious. I had no money and I doubted Minnie had any either.

'Mrs Pankhurst sent me to see you home,' he said. 'Jump in.'

I was still wary. 'We have no means to pay you.'

'All done.'

I exchanged a glance with Minnie. 'Minnie has nowhere to go.'

'I got an address here, from Mrs P,' he said. 'Are you getting in or not?'

I helped Minnie inside then followed. She slumped in the corner and I thanked our lucky stars – and Mrs Pankhurst – that the cab had shown up when it did.

I'd only been inside Holloway for a few weeks, but as soon as my cell door had clanged shut on that first awful night, I'd put pen to paper and started writing about my experiences. I'd always written letters, since I was a child. I never sent them, just wrote them – to school friends who'd wronged me or who'd helped me, to my mother when she annoyed me, to the king, to teachers I liked, to characters in the books I read. And even to my father when he died. So when I went to jail, it seemed obvious to start writing about it. And this time I sent the letters and Mrs Pankhurst wrote back, asking for more. I'd only met her once or twice but I felt like I knew her – and perhaps she felt the same because she was obviously looking out for us.

I must have dozed off myself because it felt like just a couple of minutes before we were pulling up outside my mother's terraced home in Wandsworth. I didn't even remember crossing the river.

Bleary-eyed, I sat up. 'Good luck, Minnie,' I said. 'I hope we meet again.'

She gave me a sleepy smile, without opening her eyes. 'And you, Esther. Our paths are bound to cross soon.'

I thanked the driver and slid out of the cab, clutching the bag that contained my meagre belongings. At the front door, I took a deep breath, bracing myself, before I knocked.

It took an age – or perhaps it just felt that way – before my mother answered.

'You're back are you?' she said.

'I am.'

She left the door open and walked away back to the lounge, I supposed.

'There's no food,' she said over her shoulder.

'Not hungry.' I paused. 'Can I have a bath?' I felt grubby and dusty, covered in prison muck.

Mother looked round at me, her mouth a pinched knot of disappointment. 'Do what you like,' she said. 'You always do.'

I went up the steep steps to my bedroom. It was tucked under the eaves in the roof of the house, cramped and uncomfortable. My narrow bed was neatly made with clean sheets and a blanket and I managed a tiny smile; it seemed Mother hadn't completely given up on me.

Looking at my bed, I was suddenly overwhelmed with tiredness. It wasn't easy to have a proper night's sleep in prison. Sharing a cell with other women, the cries and sobs and shouts that carried on long into the wee small hours, and the discomfort of the hard beds all made for an unpleasant experience. Which was the point, I supposed.

I pulled off the dress I was wearing, which still smelled of Holloway, and balled it up. I knew I wouldn't throw it away – I didn't have the luxury of having so many clothes that I could afford to discard them on a whim – but I didn't want to wear it for a long while. I couldn't sleep while I was so filthy, though, so I plodded back downstairs and heated some water for the bath, my arms aching with fatigue as I filled it.

It was chilly in the back room and I didn't linger in the tepid water. I washed my body and my hair, which had got long while I was away. There was no sign of my mother. I guessed she was reading, either in her own room or in the lounge. She obviously didn't want to speak to me, and I couldn't blame her really. This was hard for her. Everything was hard for her.

Until my father had died, we'd had a good life. Not affluent, not by any means. But we'd lived well enough. He was a clerk, working for a firm of solicitors, and my mother had been a tailoress and after I came along she took in mending and made dresses from home. They were so proud of me when I got my job as a schoolteacher. I thought my father would burst.

But just two years later, he was gone and so was all our money – thanks to his gambling habit. A habit he'd kept secret from my mother and me, but which had left us with debts to pay. Faced with poverty, we'd had to move to this house – I looked round as I dried myself off with a thin towel – this cramped two-up, two-down, where we could hear everything the neighbours said and did, and which my mother hated. It was our lack of options, as two women with no man providing for us, while clearing up the mess that he'd left behind, and my rage over that helplessness, that had led me to the women's suffrage movement. And the friends I'd made there had become my family while my mother grew ever more distant.

With heavy legs, I climbed the stairs to my room. Mother's

door was firmly shut, so I didn't call goodnight. Instead I simply pulled my nightgown on over my head and slid beneath my sheets, ready for sleep.

Tomorrow, I thought, I would speak to Mother and clear the air. I would explain what Mrs Pankhurst and the other women were trying to do and make her understand how important it was. How vital it was that women like me and Mother had some agency over our own lives, and how allowing us to vote was just the start of that.

I reached down into my bag and felt about for the battered old notebook I wrote in. I would start by writing her a letter, I thought. I just needed to get her to listen . . .

* * *

I woke with a start a clear twelve hours later, my notebook still on my lap with just "Dear Mother" written at the top of the page, to the sound of the front door closing and the murmur of voices.

Sitting up in bed, I strained my ears to hear. It sounded like Mrs Williams, the headmistress of the school I taught in. But it was Saturday, and I'd been planning to visit her myself later to explain I was back and ask her for my job back.

Why was she here?

Quickly, I threw on a dress and shawl and twisted my plaited hair up on the back of my head, then as quietly as I could, I tiptoed down the stairs and sat at the bottom, to hear what was being said.

'I'll wake her,' Mother said. 'We can't leave you waiting.'

'She must be very tired after her . . .' Mrs Williams tailed off.

'Well, yes,' said Mother awkwardly.

I felt like shouting: 'Prison! I am tired because I have been in prison for six weeks and I couldn't sleep.' But I resisted. An outburst like that would hardly help the situation. And I feared it needed help because the only reason I could imagine for Mrs

30

Williams arriving on our doorstep on a Saturday morning was not good.

Slowly, I stood up and made my way into the lounge.

'Good morning, Mother,' I said. 'Mrs Williams.'

Mother stood up. She was twisting a handkerchief in her hands, winding it round her prominent knuckles. 'I will make tea.'

Alone with Mrs Williams, I sat down on the edge of a chair. 'What brings you here so early?'

Mrs Williams gave me a disbelieving glance. 'You don't know?'

'I was hoping I might be mistaken.'

She shook her head. 'I came to tell you we can no longer employ you at Trinity School,' she said.

I closed my eyes. 'Mrs Williams,' I began. 'Could I just explain . . .'

'I'm afraid not.' She stood up. 'We cannot employ criminals at our school.'

'I'm not a criminal,' I said. 'I was a political prisoner.'

She looked at me in disdain. 'You engaged in a criminal act.'

'I smashed a window.'

'And that is illegal.'

'Yes, but . . .'

'Your employment is terminated,' she said. 'And I feel I must tell you that you will be similarly unwelcome at every school in London.'

'Surely not every school?' I said, sulky like one of my pupils.

'Every school,' Mrs Williams said. 'Every one.' She picked up her shawl and glared at me. 'Please thank your mother for the tea but I have to be on my way.'

She spun round and stalked out of the room as I sank back against the chair. Why did I cheek her? Why didn't I throw myself on her mercy, apologise, and beg for my job?

A creaky floorboard made me look up. Mother was standing there, her face drawn. She had dark circles under her eyes and I felt a flash of guilt that I'd caused her more pain.

'You have to leave,' she said.

I stared at her.

'Now,' she continued. 'I can let your room out if you go. I can't afford for you to be here. Not now you have no job.'

'I'll get another job.'

'Not soon enough. No one will take a chance on you. Not now. Not after this. It could take months before you're earning again.'

My eyes were hot with tears. 'Mother, no.'

'Esther,' she said. 'I've found a lodger already.'

'Where will I go?'

She looked down at me and suddenly her sad face seemed full of menace. 'I don't know, Esther,' she said. 'And I don't much care.'

Chapter 6

Esther

It took just minutes for me to pack. I had so few belongings nowadays that my whole life fitted into a carpetbag.

I went downstairs, my bag thumping against the walls, and found Mother in the kitchen, washing up.

'I'm going now,' I said.

'Goodbye.' She didn't look at me.

'Do you want me to send word of my new address?'

She shrugged. 'Whatever you see fit.'

Without another word – what else was there to say? – I turned and, with my shoulders hunched, I left the house. I walked a little way along the street and then stopped. I was at a loss. I had no idea where to go. Not even which direction to walk in.

I supposed I should try to find a job first and then a room? Or would it make more sense to find a room first? I had picked up a few coins from my drawer at home, but it wouldn't go far. I wasn't even sure it would be enough to cover any rent up front. Would landladies want rent up front? I had no idea.

Hauling my bag on to my shoulder, I wandered through the narrow streets of Wandsworth, unconsciously heading back towards Stockwell and the home where I'd grown up. Another family lived there now. A family with lots of children to fill the rooms where I'd played by myself as a child. A family with a mother who was loving and full of laughter – like mine had once been – and a father who really was the sort of man everyone believed him to be, and not secretly gambling away his family's future.

I walked along the side of the park towards our old house. It wasn't far from here that I'd first met Mrs Pankhurst's daughter, Christabel.

I'd been walking home one day, over a year ago, and just like today I'd taken the long way round because I'd wanted to see our old house again. I'd walked down an alleyway where the back gardens of the houses on our former street met the back gardens of the next road along, but what I'd found was a group of women. A large group actually. They were all gathered in the street, staring up at a woman who was leaning out of the window of a house on the corner and talking.

The houses were tall here – proud, I'd always thought – and the woman was small so she was using the window as a stage. It was clever.

I'd stopped just where I was and listened, mesmerised. She talked about how women's views needed to be represented and stated that she believed all women who paid taxes should be allowed to vote. I found myself nodding along, as her words struck a chord with me. It was as though this woman knew exactly how I was feeling. About how helpless I'd felt since my father's death, how frustrated I was that I had no agency over my own life, and how absolutely furious it all made me.

And then she said something that resonated with me – with the anger I felt inside.

'We've been polite for forty years,' she said. Standing in the street, I snorted. My mother was polite. She was too polite. She just went about her business, struggling through life and trying to keep her head above water, never arguing because it was unladylike. Never saying a bad word about my father, even though he'd left us with nothing.

Above me, the woman was still speaking. 'We've signed petitions and asked nicely and nothing has changed,' she said. 'It is time to adopt vigorous methods.'

The women below her all cheered and the speaker carried on. 'I believe the tide is turning,' she said.

'Coppers,' someone near me shouted. 'Clear away.'

The woman disappeared back into the house and dropped the open sash window with a thud. The crowd melted away in seconds, leaving me lurking in the alleyway next to the back gate of my old house. I'd been so gripped by the woman's words I'd not even registered where I was standing. There were shouts from the street ahead and I saw a policeman run past. I frowned. What did they care if some women gathered together to share their thoughts? I wondered. Why were they so scared?

In front of me, the gate to the house opposite opened and the woman who'd been speaking peered out. She was elegant and well dressed and looked nothing like the sort of person who should be hiding from the long arm of the law.

'It's fine,' I said. 'The police are on the main road.'

She smiled at me, but as she stepped into the alleyway we heard a man shout: 'These houses have back gates. Check down the alley.'

Her eyes met mine and without thinking I, Esther Watkins, who'd never done a thing wrong in my whole life, reached behind me and opened the gate to my old house.

'Here,' I said. 'There's a shed. The coppers won't look there.'

She paused for a second, obviously sizing me up, then having decided she could trust me, she darted across the alleyway and into my old back garden. I'd played so many games here as a child it was strange to be back and for a second I felt dizzy as the memories flooded into my mind.

I sent up a prayer thanking God it was cold and drizzly and the children of the house were warm inside and not playing on the lawn, and I hurried the woman along the edge of the garden and into the potting shed.

She'd taken off her gloves and hat and shaken her head.

'I thought I was a goner there,' she'd said. 'Thank you.' She stuck her hand out for me to shake. 'I'm Christabel Pankhurst,' she said.

And that was the beginning.

Now, standing in the shadow of my old family home, I felt suddenly more positive. The suffragettes were a sisterhood, I thought. The Women's Social and Political Union – the proper name for the group of women who'd become the suffragettes – was led by Mrs Pankhurst and her daughters. We were all family as they were. The suffragettes were the reason I'd gone to jail, and the reason I'd lost my job, and I knew without a shadow of a doubt they would help me now.

With new-found energy, I lifted my chin and strode out on to the main street. I'd find Mrs Pankhurst, I thought. She'd know what to do.

The only problem I had was that I wasn't completely sure where Mrs Pankhurst lived, or where I could find her. I had an inkling she was based in East London but I had no real idea where and I didn't fancy wandering the streets until I stumbled upon a suffragette. Chewing my lip, I gazed up at the houses and tried to remember which window I'd seen Christabel speaking from. Could I knock there and ask if the occupants knew where I could find Mrs Pankhurst? They had to be sympathetic if they'd allowed her daughter to make a speech from their house. But I wasn't completely sure which of the identical sashes it had been – nor which window belonged to which house.

Unsure and nervous about intruding, I decided instead that I would head to Kennington. I'd been to several meetings at a house there, where a very active suffragette lived. I'd knock there and ask for directions to Mrs Pankhurst's house.

I glanced back over my shoulder at the home I'd grown up in. That life was all gone now. I may have been thrown out on to the streets by own mother and lost my job but I was part of something. Something bigger than just me . . .

'OOF!'

I gasped as the ground came up to meet me and all the air was pushed out of my lungs. I'd tripped over something and now I was sprawled face down on the pavement, the contents of my carpetbag scattered across the stones in front of me and to the side and no doubt behind me too.

Carefully, I pushed myself up to sitting. My cheekbone was grazed and my nose was bleeding.

'Oh, blimey,' I said. 'What now, Esther?'

A man, hurrying along, stepped over my legs without looking down at me and then trod, with his mucky boots, on one of my underskirts that was lying in an undignified heap on the ground.

I opened my mouth to shout at him but instead of angry words, all that came out was a sob. And once one sob had been released, I found I was powerless to stop the others. I sat on the pavement outside my former family home, bloodied and bruised, with my belongings strewn into the gutter, and I cried.

'Need a hand?'

I looked up, sniffing loudly. A young man stood there, his arm outstretched to help me. I grasped his hand and stood up, wincing as I did so. My cheek was sore and so, I discovered, was my arm.

'What happened, Miss?'

'I tripped, I think,' I said, putting my fingers to my nose to see if it was still bleeding. 'I fell and my bag split.'

He pulled a handkerchief out of his pocket and gave it to me.

'For your nose,' he said. 'I'll pick everything up.'

'Thank you.' I was grateful to him for coming to my aid and for the handkerchief, which seemed to have stopped the bleeding.

He scooped up my dresses, and a book that was in the gutter, and helped me put them all back in my bag.

'I'll let you get those bits,' he said, gesturing with his head towards my underwear and avoiding my eye.

Quickly, I gathered them up and stuffed them in too. 'If I hold my bag in my arms, nothing can fall out,' I said.

He smiled at me. He was rather nice-looking, I thought, with dark blond hair falling over his forehead and a mischievous glint in his eye.

'Very enterprising,' he said.

'I try my best.'

'Where are you off to?' the young man asked. 'I'm just on my way to Lambeth Police Station. If you're going that way, I can walk with you. Make sure you don't come a cropper on the way.'

My stomach twisted in alarm. 'The police station,' I said, trying to sound light-hearted. 'Are you in trouble?'

'Good Lord, no,' he said, raising his eyebrows high on his forehead. 'No, I'm a constable.'

He sounded proud and I forced myself to smile.

'How nice. No uniform?'

'I'm not officially working today, and actually, I'm based over in Whitechapel usually, but I have to pop in.'

'I'm going the other way,' I said hurriedly, though the quickest route to the house I was planning to visit would take me straight past the police station.

'Then I'm afraid I have to say farewell,' the man said.

'Thank you for helping me. Someone stepped over me, before you stopped.'

'I can well believe it.'

He grinned at me again and I felt a tiny curl of interest in my lower belly.

'I'm Joseph,' he said. 'Joseph Fairbanks.'

'I'm Esther W . . .' I stopped myself just before I told this eager young constable my real name – the name that appeared on my criminal record – and pretended to dab my nose again while I desperately looked round me for inspiration. My eyes fell on the painted bricks of the house opposite. 'Esther Whitehouse,' I said.

'It's very nice to meet you,' Miss Whitehouse,' he said. 'I hope our paths will cross again one day.'

'Likewise,' I said politely, though inside I felt uncomfortable.

How awkward it would be for him to find out the young woman he'd helped was fresh from jail and an enthusiastic suffragette? I wouldn't want to put him in that position. No, I thought, it would be easier for everyone if I never saw Joseph Fairbanks again.

Chapter 7

Lizzie

September 2019

The first big event of the school year was, I discovered, the Elm Heath harvest festival. This was all new to me. At my last school our harvest festival had been pretty low-key. We'd sing about ploughing the fields and scattering, and the parents would send their kids in with a donation for a local foodbank.

But at Elm Heath, it was a Big Deal.

'We're a farming community,' Paula explained. 'At least we were. Things have changed a lot but there are still pupils who live on farms. It's an important part of life in Elm Heath.'

I nodded.

'Sounds interesting,' I said. 'What happens?'

What happened, I discovered, was the school ran the whole show, apart from the traditional thanksgiving service at the church. Elm Heath Primary was the focus for a week of festivities. There was scarecrow making, and a corn-dolly workshop – I didn't know exactly what a corn dolly was but I didn't tell Paula. I thought I'd just google it later. There was a concert with folk dancing, which the kids then performed at the nearby care home for elderly people. And there was a country fair at the weekend, in the school playground, where locals would sell produce and crafts. It all sounded very wholesome, and a million miles from Clapham.

'It's a lot of work,' Paula said apologetically. 'I can't believe I didn't mention it before now.'

'It's fine, honestly.'

I was actually quite pleased to have more to fill the hours when I wasn't at school. Though I was enjoying being back in the swing of school life – more so than I'd anticipated, truth be told – I was finding life on my own to be, well . . . a challenge.

More than once I'd thought about calling Grant and changed my mind. I didn't want to open that can of worms, not after the way his flowers had unsettled me. I didn't miss him exactly. It just felt odd doing this all by myself. When I had been head at Broadway Common Infants, Grant was just across the field in the junior school ready to offer advice (and opinions) whenever I needed. I'd never been in charge alone before. And, of course, I was going home from school to my little cottage, which was cute and homely – if not really to my taste – but echoed with emptiness. I was lonely; that was the truth.

* * *

So for the next couple of weeks, I threw myself into organising the concert. I found songs that even the littlest reception child could sing, and worked out cool dance routines for the sulkiest of the year-six boys. Considering we'd only had a short while to sort it all out, it was a triumph. They performed for their parents, and for the elderly residents at the care home, and on a makeshift stage at the country fair on the Saturday.

'Are you crying, Miss Armstrong?' Cara Kinsella, who was dressed as a corn-on-the-cob with yellow tights, a yellow T-shirt and her face painted to match, eyed me suspiciously.

'Noooo,' I said, subtly wiping away a small tear. The kids had all worked so hard and it had been lovely.

'Maybe you have hay fever,' she said helpfully. 'Daddy has hay fever.'

'That's probably it,' I said.

'Do you want a toffee apple? My grandma has been making them.'

She took my hand and dragged me through the throngs of people in the playground. There were all sorts of stalls, selling jams, bread, vegetables, sweets and even a few Christmas decorations though it was only late September.

'Here,' she said in triumph depositing me in front of a stand with brightly coloured bunting. 'My grandma.'

Cara's grandma was the woman I'd seen dropping her off on the first day of term. Up close, she was elegant with chic greying hair, wearing a simple shift dress. She smiled at me.

'You must be Miss Armstrong.'

'I am,' I agreed. 'Are you really Cara's grandma?'

'I'm Sophie Albert,' she said in a voice that had the faintest hint of a French accent.

'Grandma is my mummy's mummy,' Cara explained. 'That's what a grandma is. Grandma, can Miss Armstrong have a toffee apple?'

'Of course.'

She handed me an apple covered in thick red toffee and wrapped in cellophane and waved away my attempts to pay.

'Please, we're friends now,' she said.

'Thank you.'

She nodded at the chair next to her. 'Sit down,' she said and obediently I did, feeling suddenly very weary.

'You must be tired after organising that wonderful performance.' She smiled at Cara who bounced up and down on her yellow feet.

'Did you like my bit, Grandma? When I said about looking after the trees?'

'I loved it.'

Cara saw one of her friends across the playground and darted off to speak to him while Sophie sat down next to me.

'She has a lot of energy.'

'She's wonderful.'

'So like her mother was at that age – it fills me with joy even as it breaks my heart.'

Remembering what Cara had said about her mummy being dead, I wasn't sure what to say so I just gave what I hoped was a sympathetic smile.

Sophie looked distant for a second, then she focused on me again.

'We are all very excited to have you here,' she said. 'Do you think they will close this school?'

I was disarmed by her way of saying exactly what she thought. 'Erm,' I began. 'I'm not sure . . .'

She waved her hand. 'But things are going wrong,' she said. 'Look how few children are here now. Look how they all go in their cars to the fancy school in Blyton.'

'Well, yes, but . . .'

Sophie took my hand. 'My husband went to this school, and so did my daughter,' she said to me. 'And now my grand-daughter. And ask anyone here, they will tell you the same.' She gestured with her arm, taking in the whole school, and maybe even the village. 'Imagine if we didn't have this,' she said.

I shifted on my deckchair and gave the rows of toffee apples my attention, instead of Sophie. 'I'm not sure there's anything I can do,' I muttered.

'Psssht,' she said. 'Of course there is.'

'Is she roping you in to sell toffee apples?'

It was Danny. Despite myself, I sat up a bit straighter wondering if I had mascara smudged beneath my eyes.

'Sophie,' he said.

'Hello, Danny.'

Was I imagining it, or did Sophie's face suddenly look harder? More pinched?

'We've mostly been chatting,' I said, trying to lighten the atmosphere that I sensed between Sophie and Danny. 'Not done much selling.'

'I've been telling Miss Armstrong that she can save Elm Heath Primary.'

Danny smiled at me, a cheeky smile that gave me that unsettled feeling again. 'I imagine you're good at just about everything, MISS Armstrong,' he said. 'But I think this one might even be beyond you.'

Sophie glared at Danny – there was definitely tension there – and he ignored her, looking at me instead.

'But you never know,' he added.

'It's not closing,' I said, knowing my words were empty because the lack of pupils spoke for itself. Danny just shrugged and Sophie looked away across the playground to where Cara was running round with her friends who were both dressed like pumpkins.

'Cara's over there,' she said bluntly.

Danny looked like he was going to say something then he shut his mouth instead. After a second he opened it again.

'Nice seeing you again, Ms Armstrong.'

I was faintly disappointed that he'd used my correct title.

'Thank you for the good luck card,' I called as he wandered over the playground towards Cara. He raised his hand to show he'd heard.

Sophie was looking at me, her brow furrowed.

'He's a tricky one,' she said. Was she warning me off? There was really no need. I was hardly in the market for romance.

I didn't get a chance to respond because one of the pumpkins was suddenly at my elbow. It was a little boy from Cara's class whose name was Hayden. Or Jayden. Or perhaps Cayden.

'Miss?' he said.

'Yes?'

44

'Cara said she thought you were a bit sad, Miss.'

I wasn't sure what to say. I looked at his little orange face, all earnest and worried, and smiled.

'I'm not sad.'

He shrugged. 'Thought this might cheer you up.'

He reached out his hand. In his palm was a corn dolly. I'd never got round to googling them, but instead I'd watched the kids making them. They'd twisted and wrapped corn into little shapes to make their creations. This one was a simple circle with a red ribbon bow.

'Thank you,' I said, genuinely touched at the gesture. 'You're so kind.'

'That's lovely, Jayden,' Sophie said, obviously realising I was struggling to get his name.

'It really is. I'll put this in my office at school and it will make me smile every time I look at it.'

'Miss, I made one for you too.'

On my other side was a little girl dressed as Elsa from *Frozen*, which had no direct link to harvest as far as I could tell. She pushed a corn dolly into my hand.

'Thank you, Elsa,' I said and she beamed at me.

'I did one as well.' Cara was there, in her yellow get-up, brandishing her corn dolly, which was plaited like her hair.

I took hers too. 'These are all wonderful,' I said.

And suddenly I was surrounded by children, all giving me their corn dollies – the little creations they'd all worked so hard on.

'Miss, they'll bring you good luck,' they told me. 'They're lucky.'

I took each one, gathering them into my lap and trying not to show the children how overwhelmed I was by their kindness.

Then the parents started handing me their dollies too. Some of them were like tiny works of art – the dried corn twisted into heart and star shapes, or made to look like little ladies with fronds of corn forming their skirts.

'Good luck,' they each said as they handed them over.

By the time they'd finished I reckoned I had a hundred or more of the dollies heaped in my lap, and tears streaming down my face.

'Thank you,' I said over and over. 'Thank you.'

I wasn't sure what to do next. I couldn't stand up because my knees were covered in corn and slightly alarmingly I couldn't seem to stop crying either.

Luckily, like a guardian angel, Paula appeared behind the group of children and parents.

'Let's take all these to your office, shall we, Ms Armstrong?' she said.

Sophie handed her a linen bag and together we carefully put all the corn dollies inside.

'Come on then,' Paula said, like I was one of her reception children. 'Come on, Lizzie.'

I blew a – slightly snotty – kiss to the children as I followed her into school feeling like something important had just happened. Perhaps I wasn't planning to stay at Elm Heath forever, but I knew without a shadow of a doubt that I had to do my best to reverse the trend of children going to Blyton and do everything I could to make sure the school stayed open.

Chapter 8

Lizzie

'I can't believe they did this,' I said later. I was sitting at Paula's kitchen table with an enormous glass of wine and the corn dollies all spread out in front of me. 'I can't believe they gave them all to me.'

'It really was something,' she said. She picked one of them up and showed me. 'Look, this one is like a peacock's tail.'

I admired it.

'They're all wonderful. I'll ask Jeff if there is some way we can display them in my office.'

Jeff was the school caretaker and a very creative handyman to boot.

'He'll come up with something, I'm sure,' Paula agreed.

I picked up Jayden's corn dolly – the little circular twist of corn tied with a ribbon – and smiled. 'So they symbolise luck?'

Chris was rummaging in a kitchen drawer, looking for a take-away menu.

'Luck,' he said without glancing up. 'And fertility.'

I swallowed a gulp of wine as I laughed.

'Well I'll just take the luck, thanks.'

'I can't find the blasted menu,' Chris said.

'I don't suppose Deliveroo delivers here?' I said hopefully. I'd

47

been looking forward to a curry since Paula suggested it earlier on, after my corn dolly experience.

'Noooo,' said Chris doubtfully.

I picked up my phone and found the app, then I showed them how it worked.

'So you choose what kind of food you want, then pick a restaurant, and then you scroll through and add what you want to your basket . . .'

I tailed off, aware both Chris and Paula were staring at me.

'I'll just call Nish on his mobile, instead of calling the restaurant,' Chris said. 'He won't mind. What do you fancy, Lizzie?'

'Chicken biryani?'

'Done. Usual for you, Paula?'

She nodded and Chris pulled out his phone and went into the hall to make the call. I heard him laughing with the person on the other line.

'Living in a village is very different from living in London,' I said to Paula. 'It's strangely both harder and easier.'

She grinned at me. 'You'll get used to it,' she said.

'I am starting to, I think.'

'You've not got much choice, now.'

I looked at the piles of corn dollies on the table. 'Do these mean that I'm one of you now?'

'Definitely. You might never leave.'

The idea didn't fill me with horror, much to my surprise.

Chris had come back into the kitchen and was topping up our glasses.

'You'll like Nate's husband,' he said.

'Marc?' I remembered seeing him at my welcome barbecue.

'He's the son of a friend of Sophie's, or a distant relative, or something like that,' Paula said, leaning forward in a conspiratorial way. 'He came to work on some project nearby . . .'

'He's a surveyor,' Chris put in. 'Or is he an architect? Something along those lines.'

48

Paula tutted at his interruption. 'He stayed with Sophie for a few weeks, met Nate and boom! That was it.'

Her mentioning Sophie made me think of the expression on her face when Danny had approached the toffee apple stall earlier.

'What's the story with her and Danny?'

'Similar,' Chris said, misunderstanding. 'He works in finance, and the company he works for provides investment for public sector initiatives . . .'

'Oh Chris, shush,' Paula said. She looked at me through narrowed eyes. 'Why do you want to know?'

I drank some wine. 'Sophie was all smiley until he appeared,' I said. 'Then she looked annoyed and wouldn't really talk to him.'

Paula nodded and Chris topped up my glass.

'I was good friends with Isabelle – Sophie's daughter,' Paula said. 'I was older than her, but we both liked the same kind of music and we got to know each other that way. We were always in touch but we reconnected after Bella graduated from university.'

'I'm sorry,' I said. 'You must miss her.'

Paula gave me a small smile. 'I do,' she said. She took a deep breath. 'Paula met Danny at uni. They stayed in Manchester afterwards and set up home together. It was a mistake really. They weren't love's young dream. They were always breaking up and she'd come home, then go back to him five minutes later. She left him for good when Cara was a baby.'

'How did she die?'

'Ovarian cancer it was,' Paula said. 'Nasty stuff. Anyway, she got sick, and he, to be fair to him, came when she needed him. He started spending more time with Cara and when Isabelle went into the hospice, Cara moved in with Danny. I think he's really stepped up and he's a wonderful dad now.'

'But Sophie's not sure?'

'I don't think she can forgive him for making Isabelle's life so miserable when she only had a short time to live it.'

I nodded. 'That's really sad.'

The doorbell rang, letting us know our dinner had arrived, and our talk of Danny and Sophie was forgotten.

On Monday morning, I went into school feeling full of beans. I'd really enjoyed the weekend and I was more positive and excited about the days ahead than I'd been for months. A year, even.

Until, after morning assembly, when I sat down at my desk and opened an email from the head of the council's education department, a woman called Denise Deacon, asking me to ring her, urgently.

'Uh-oh,' I said out loud. 'This can't be good.'

I dialled the number on the bottom of her email and she answered straight away.

'I'm not going to beat around the bush, Lizzie,' she said when I'd introduced myself and we'd exchanged a bit of small talk. 'As far as pupil numbers and budgets are concerned, the council can't justify keeping Elm Heath open any longer.'

My stomach lurched and for one terrifying moment, I thought I might throw up all over my desk. I took a deep breath and tried to control my voice. 'I see.'

'It's no secret that admissions are falling and with financial cuts the way they are, well . . .'

'Times are tough,' I said, sounding weak and quavering. 'How long do we have?'

'They're looking at the end of the academic year. But I wanted to speak to you first because I thought it was important that you know it's not definite. The axe is being sharpened but it's not yet fallen.'

I was heartened – slightly – by that news. We still had the rest of this term, and two more, to change the council's mind. If they were open to their minds being changed of course.

'What can we do to stop this closure?'

She sighed. 'That's the million-pound question, isn't it? I wish I knew the answer because Elm Heath is a lovely school.'

'It's an important school.'

There was a pause at the other end of the line. 'Listen, Lizzie,' she said. 'I think your best bet is to prove the school plays a vital role in the community. Maybe that it's more than just a school; that it provides services that can't be found elsewhere.'

'Like what?' I said, at a loss.

'No idea, you'd have to get creative.'

I tapped the end of my pen on my desk. 'We've got no breakfast or after-school club here,' I said. 'They were really well used at my old school.'

'That's exactly the sort of thing that I mean,' Denise said. 'As things stand, the kids can get the education they're getting at Elm Heath from Blyton Primary. And the council have put a lot of money into that school – it's in their interests to up the pupil numbers there.'

I snorted, but I was still thinking. 'We had a police station at my old school. Like a community thing where the kids got to know the local bobbies. Obviously, things are a bit different round here, but it could still work? Or what about using the school hall for fitness classes? I bet there are local Zumba teachers and whatnot.'

'It's a start,' said Denise.

I was on a roll, scribbling ideas down as I spoke. 'Did you ever see that TV show where they took little kids into a retirement home?' I said, thoughtfully. 'What about inviting some local people to afternoon tea with the children?'

'These are all great ideas,' Denise said.

'But?'

'But I'm worried they don't go far enough. You need to think about what makes Elm Heath unique.'

'It's very old,' I said.

'Well perhaps you can show that it's of special historical interest. Anything that makes it important.'

'More important than giving kids a good education?' I said, slightly sulky that she'd dismissed all my ideas.

She gave a small, humourless laugh. 'Quite,' she said. 'If you can come up with something then perhaps there's a chance.'

'Fine,' I said. 'Then that's what we'll do. As well as all that other stuff.'

We ended the call and I sat for a second, thinking. So the axe was swinging above our heads after all. What had started as a project to save my career was suddenly a project to save a school. Was I up to the task? Was it worth it?

I glanced at the pile of corn dollies on my shelf, waiting for Jeff to put up a display for me.

'We could do with a bit of that luck now,' I muttered. I'd have to call a staff meeting, let everyone know what was going on. Urgh. Maybe I should buy some wine, to help the news go down a bit easier?

'What would you do, Esther?' I looked up at the photograph that I'd not yet managed to move. 'Would you roll over and let them close the school or would you fight?'

Esther looked at me, her expression fierce, and I looked back at her, and a tiny idea took seed. She founded this school, I thought. Maybe she had a story we could use. Get us some publicity.

I studied her photo. She was staring, unsmiling, at the camera wearing a severe black skirt and high-necked white blouse with a sort of flouncy cravat-type creation. Her chin was lifted and she looked snooty, to my twenty-first-century eyes. She didn't look like she was the type to put up a fight about anything.

I opened my laptop and typed Esther Watkins and teacher into the search engine then blinked in surprise at the first entry, which seemed to be a court report from a newspaper dated 1910.

'Esther Watkins, aged twenty-one, schoolteacher, sentenced to ten weeks in Holloway Women's Prison for public disorder offences,' it read.

'That can't be right,' I said to myself. I glanced over at the photograph where our Esther's names and the dates 1889–1970 were written on the frame. I added up in my head. If our Esther had been born in 1889 then she would indeed have been twenty-one in 1910.

'Well, well, well,' I said. There was obviously more to Esther Watkins than I'd imagined. I felt a small flicker of excitement followed almost immediately by crushing disappointment. An ex-con's story was hardly going to prove that Elm Heath was a vital part of the community, was it? I was just going to have to come up with something else.

Chapter 9

Esther

1910

I walked the long way round to the house, clutching my bag to my chest as I tried to remember the name of the suffragette who lived there. Agnes, I thought. I couldn't recall her surname. It was a long walk up the hill from Stockwell, and when I eventually found the house, hot and bothered and with my cheek throbbing, Agnes wasn't in.

I pulled the bell and heard the noise echoing round the empty house and then, completely out of ideas and energy, I sat down on the stone step. I'd wait, I supposed, until she came home. It wasn't as though I had anywhere else to go.

Leaning against the iron railings I found my eyes closing but I forced myself awake. I may have been on my uppers but I wasn't about to start sleeping in the street like an urchin.

'Are you waiting for me?'

I looked round to see a woman, older than me – in her thirties I guessed – hurrying up the stairs. She looked vaguely familiar.

'I've seen you at meetings,' she said now. 'I'm Agnes Oliver.'

'Esther,' I said, standing up. 'Yes, I was hoping you could tell me where I could find Mrs Pankhurst.'

'Oh, heaven knows, that woman is never around when we need her.'

Faintly amused by the woman's sense of entitlement, I smiled. 'She is often busy.'

'We're all busy,' Agnes said. 'She wants me to put together this blessed newspaper and it's all well and good, but when I'm spending all the hours God gives me on that, she forgets I've also got three children who need looking after. And she promised she was going to find me a governess but has she? No, she has not . . .'

Without stopping to think, I interrupted her tirade. 'She has,' I said. 'Found you a governess, I mean.'

Agnes blinked at me and I stuck my hand out for her to shake.

'It's me. I'm Esther Watkins and I'm a schoolteacher. At least I was.'

'What happened?'

I screwed up my face and took a chance. 'I lost my job because I was in Holloway.'

Agnes nodded slowly. 'The school won't have you back?'

'No.'

She was looking at me, sizing me up, I guessed. I tried to stand up straighter, aware that I was not at my best, and tucked a stray strand of hair behind my ear.

'What happened to your cheek?'

'I tripped over a tree root on my way here.'

Agnes nodded again, her eyes never leaving my face.

'Is it a live-in position?' I said, hoping beyond hope that it was.

'I would prefer it to be live-in but if that's a problem, we can discuss it. Did Mrs Pankhurst not explain all this when she told you about the position?'

'I must have forgotten,' I lied. 'So much has happened.'

'Hmm,' she said. For a moment, I thought I'd made a big mistake and that this wasn't going to be the answer to my prayers but then she clapped her hands together.

55

'You'll be perfect,' she said. She gripped my arm tightly. 'Could you possibly start today?'

Relief flooded me. 'I could.'

'Wonderful. I can get you a cab and we can collect your things.'

'I have all my things,' I said, gesturing to my carpetbag. 'I don't have much. And, well, I can't go home because my mother is of the same mind as my former headmistress.'

Agnes's face softened. 'Doesn't approve?'

'Not in the least.'

The familiar frustration and rage that I felt when I thought of my mother began to build.

'We lost everything when my father died because of mistakes he made,' I said through gritted teeth. 'We had to sell the house. But still she thinks women are supposed to suffer and that this is just the way it shall be.' I took a breath. 'Sorry.'

Agnes shook her head. 'Don't apologise,' she said. 'We all have our reasons for finding our way to each other.'

She picked up my battered bag. 'Now, shall we go in?'

She unlocked the large front door and I followed her inside. I hadn't even asked how many children I would be teaching. I hoped it would be two quiet little girls rather than four boisterous boys, but I felt I couldn't ask because I'd pretended that I knew all about the job.

'Edie?' she called. 'Edie?'

A woman wearing an apron came rushing through the hall from the back of the house. 'I was hanging out the washing,' she said. 'Have you been knocking?'

'Not at all,' Agnes said, peeling off her gloves. 'This is our new governess, Esther. Esther, this is Edie our housekeeper.'

Edie and I nodded hello to each other.

'Are the children here?' Agnes looked around her as though she expected them to appear in a puff of smoke.

'Went for a walk with Mr Oliver.'

'I shall go and find them.'

Edie showed me to my room while Agnes went to find the children. My bedroom was on the top floor alongside another room with bookshelves crammed with books, a blackboard, and a low table. The windows looked out over London.

'What a marvellous view,' I said. 'I can't imagine the children ever want to do schoolwork when they could be looking at the rooftops.'

'Mr John always wants to do his schoolwork,' Edie said as I sent silent thanks upwards for a scholarly pupil. 'The girls don't apply themselves so much, so I've heard.'

I wondered how many girls there were. 'Remind me of how old they all are,' I said casually.

'John's ten, Meg's eight and Pearl's almost seven,' she said. 'They're nice kids most of the time. Just don't let them run rings round you.'

I smiled. 'Don't worry about me. I can give as good as I get.'

She looked at me with a critical eye. 'Yes, I reckon you can. Though right now it just looks like you could do with a good dinner and an early night.'

I nodded, almost moved to tears by her kind words, which seemed ridiculous. It was just such a long time since anyone had said anything nice to me.

'Go and meet the children, then come into the kitchen for some food,' Edie said. 'You'll soon settle in here.'

She was right. Within a week I felt like I'd been there forever. Agnes and her husband – who was also called John – were kind, the children were welcoming, and I was so grateful to have a roof over my head and money in my pocket that I thanked my lucky stars every day that I'd bumped into Agnes on her doorstep.

On my first Saturday with the family, Agnes knocked on my bedroom door.

'I know it should really be your day off but I have some jobs to do for Mrs Pankhurst,' she said. 'And Christabel is breathing down my neck, too. Could you possibly take the children to the park?'

'Of course,' I said. I had nothing else to do, though I was itching to get back to meetings. 'What sort of jobs do you have to do?'

'Lord, I almost forgot you were one of us,' Agnes said, pleased. 'It's mostly frightfully dull newsletter bits but I can show you this afternoon, if you like? And I have a meeting this evening – would you like to come along?'

I was thrilled. 'Yes please,' I said. 'I'm feeling a little out of touch.'

'You can tell us all about your exploits in jail,' Agnes said.

I picked up my shawl. 'I'm not sure about that,' I said. 'But I'd like to come, thank you.'

After a delightful morning with the children, who were really a lovely bunch, I tracked Agnes down in the dining room. She was sitting at the table, a typewriter in front of her. She was surrounded by reams of paper and looking flustered.

'Oh, Esther, thank goodness,' she said. 'Can you help me?'

I pulled out another chair and sat down. 'I can try.'

'Christabel and I want to get this all to the printer next week, but we're missing a few pages, and I need to fill them.'

She looked up at me and gasped in delight. 'Of course!'

'What?' I said, warily. I may only have known Agnes for a week but I was already getting to understand her spontaneity didn't always work out for the best.

'You have to write something about your time in jail.'

'Really?'

'I heard a whisper that you were the one writing to Mrs Pankhurst about her experiences in Holloway,' she said. 'Is that true? I heard the letters were wonderfully detailed. Evocative.'

I bowed my head, embarrassed by the praise.

'Come on, Esther,' Agnes urged. 'You're educated and witty, which is more than I can say about some of the writers we have contributing to the paper. Don't tell Christabel I said that.'

I smiled briefly but then shook my head. 'I'm not sure, Agnes.'

She took my hand. 'You've been through an ordeal,' she said, her reading glasses slipping down her nose. 'I believe it would be good for your own peace of mind to share your experiences.'

I nodded. 'That is true. It always helps me to write things down.'

'It would certainly be good for others to read about them. So they're prepared, if needs be.'

She pushed the typewriter towards me.

'You want me to do it now?'

She held out a piece of paper and slowly I fed it into the typewriter.

'I shall do my best,' I said.

Agnes smiled at me. 'That's all I can ask.'

Chapter 10

Esther

The next day should have been my day off again but after church I found I couldn't settle to anything. It was a glorious spring day and I wanted to be outside so I put my book to one side and went to find the children to see if they wanted a walk.

The idea was met with a great deal of enthusiasm so we all pulled on boots and hats, and went out to the park. They liked going to the ponds to see the ducks so we headed in that direction, the children running ahead and me walking more sedately behind, feeling the weak sun on my face and revelling in the fresh air. I felt at peace, for the first time in weeks, and also determined.

Last night's meeting had been astonishing. I'd spent the afternoon writing about my time in Holloway and when Agnes read what I'd written, her face had gone pale.

'How awful,' she'd said.

'It was certainly no fun but I didn't have it bad, compared to some. I had only just started my hunger strike when I was released so I'd only suffered being forcibly fed once. But believe me that was enough.' I'd felt bile rise in my throat at the awful memory and had to take a moment to swallow before I could carry on. 'My friend Minnie went through it twice and it was much worse the second time. She was in a bad way.'

'Well, I'm very pleased you are sharing your thoughts,' she'd said.

And at the meeting she had stood up and introduced me.

'This young woman is Esther Watkins,' she had said. 'She was recently in Holloway and I would like her to tell you all a little about her experiences there.'

I'd spoken slowly at first about prison. I'd told them about the women I'd met, and how we were treated.

'I still dream I'm there,' I'd said. 'I wake up in the morning not sure where I am. And I think about the women I met in there all the time. I wonder how they're getting on – the ones who stayed longer – and I find myself looking at the clock and thinking they'll be sending round supper now. Or wondering if Mrs Flintoff has recovered from her cold, or if Miss Bolton has managed to sleep through a whole night without a bad dream.'

'Are you frightened you'll go back?' one woman had asked me.

I'd thought for a moment. 'No,' I'd said. 'I don't want to go back but if I have to, then I will. Because this is important. Women are not second-class citizens, to mop up men's mess and do their bidding. Not any more.' I'd looked around the room at the women. 'They're the ones who are scared,' I'd said. 'Not us. They're scared that giving us a voice means things are going to change. And they're scared because they know we're right.'

Some of the women had cheered and suddenly I'd felt bolder.

'I'm frightened of going to jail again, but I'm not stopping.'

They'd cheered again and I'd sat down feeling buoyed up by their support. I was a part of something, I'd thought. A part of something very important.

But later in the meeting, while someone else was talking, things had taken a turn. I was suddenly aware of a flurry of noise and movement at the back of the hall as women got to their feet.

'Is there a problem?' the woman on stage had called. But no one had answered. I'd stood up, trying to see what was wrong. Next to me another woman had shrieked.

'Rats,' she'd gasped. 'There are rats in the hall.' She'd clambered on to her chair and others followed.

At the back of the hall, someone had thrown the doors open and women had begun streaming outside.

Bewildered I'd looked round and saw to my horror that the woman on the chair was right. There were several large brown rats scuttling along the floor in the hall. They were darting this way and that under the chairs, while women had held their skirts up, trying to avoid them.

Agnes had been next to me, looking disgusted.

I'd clutched her arm. 'Shall we go?'

'Please.'

We'd both hitched up our skirts and – grateful that we were sitting towards the back of the hall – we'd made a dash for the door.

Outside, and across the road, we'd shaken out our skirts.

'Ugh, I feel dirty,' Agnes had said. 'How on earth did that happen? We've used that hall often and never seen vermin before.'

'Someone put them there,' a passing suffragette had said, still holding her dress up above her knees. 'Heard about it happening a few times in Manchester.'

'Who would do such a thing?' The hatred we drew was nothing new, but it still shocked me every time I experienced it.

She'd shrugged. 'Coppers?'

'Miss Whitehouse?'

Startled out of my memories of the rat-infested meeting, I almost ignored the voice behind me, until it said again: 'Miss Whitehouse?' and I remembered the false name I'd given the young man who'd helped me to my feet last week.

I turned to see Joseph Fairbanks – I found I had no trouble remembering *his* name – grinning at me. My heart – my foolish heart – gave a flutter as I looked at his handsome face and I cursed myself inwardly. All this talk of women being equal to men, and there was I going giddy at the first sight of a crooked smile and friendly blue eyes . . .

'How lovely to see you,' Joseph said.

For the first time I noticed he was wearing his police constable uniform, holding his hat under his arm, and I felt a rush of something. Fear? Trepidation? My only dealings with constables had not been good and the horror of the rats in the meeting was still raw. Despite Joseph's smile and handsome face, and my absolute certainty that he was a good man unlike some of the others I'd come across, I found I wanted to spin on my heels and run away.

But instead, I nodded politely. 'Likewise.'

'Enjoying the spring sunshine?'

'Indeed.'

'It seems a shame to walk alone,' he began, but he stopped as Meg skipped up to me.

'Esther, we have found a patch of daffodils, which means winter is truly gone now – come and see.'

She tugged at my skirt and I smiled down at her, happy both at her enthusiasm and that she had given me an excuse to leave.

'One moment, Meg,' I said and she darted off again.

'Not alone then?'

I smiled, properly this time. This truly was a nice man. Not someone to fear. Someone, in fact, I felt I liked although we'd only met recently.

'I'm a governess,' I said. 'I'm not sure I am ever alone.'

Joseph laughed and his whole face lit up. 'I've got four brothers,' he said. 'I know how that feels.'

'I should go and admire the daffodils.'

'And I should get to work.'

We smiled at each other again and I felt a pull towards him. I may have been twenty-one years old, but I'd never had a romance. Some of the girls I'd known at school were married already but I'd been so busy dealing with my father's death and the mess he'd left behind and then getting involved with the WSPU, that I'd not really had time to think about finding myself a suitor.

'Until next time,' he said.

He sauntered off down the path, spinning his hat on his hand as he went.

I watched him go, thinking – somewhat wistfully – that if things were different, and he wasn't a policeman and I wasn't, well a criminal in the eyes of the law, then perhaps we could have spent some time together.

But instead, I went to find Meg and the daffodils, which were indeed very lovely and I thought about what to say to Agnes if Meg mentioned me chatting with a constable in the park.

We'd not been home five minutes before Meg brought it up, just as I knew she would. She was a bright little girl and she was endlessly fascinated by people.

'Esther was talking to a friend in the park,' she said to her mother as she wrestled off her boots. 'A man.'

Agnes looked at me with raised eyebrows. 'A man? Is that so?'

I braced myself, waiting for her to say he was a policeman. Like me, most of the suffragettes did not think much of the constables who were a thorn in all our sides. Agnes would not be happy about me chatting with one, I thought. Especially after last night.

'Yes,' Meg said looking rather too pleased with herself. Here it came. She was surely about to announce he had been wearing a uniform. But it seemed that wasn't what had interested my charge about my exchange with Joseph Fairbanks – she'd been watching me instead.

'Esther did laugh a lot, and she tilted her head on the side when she talked so the whole world must have looked the wrong way around.'

'Meg,' I said, embarrassed, but Agnes just chuckled and Meg was undeterred.

'And Esther's cheeks were all red like they are now.'

I put my cool hands to my face. She was right, the wretched child. My cheeks were flaming.

'Edie has made lunch for you all in the kitchen,' Agnes said, dropping a kiss on Meg's head. 'Go on.'

The children raced off for their food and I busied myself gathering their boots to take upstairs.

'Oh leave all that for now,' Agnes said. 'Come and have tea and tell me all about this handsome chap you've been chatting to.'

To my surprise, I discovered I had quite a lot to say about Joseph.

'I met him the other day when I fell over on my way to Mrs Pankhurst's house,' I told Agnes. 'He picked me up and brushed me off.'

'He picked you up,' she repeated, delighted.

'He did.' I paused. 'He was nice. Another man stepped over me and trod on my petticoat but he stopped to help.'

'A gentleman.'

'Handsome, too.'

'So that's why your cheeks were red,' she teased and I felt myself blush again.

Agnes clapped her hands. 'It's like a fairy story,' she said. 'You fell over and he fell in love.'

'Heavens, Agnes, no. You are getting ahead of yourself.'

'Don't pretend you're not interested.'

I tried to look indifferent but I failed. 'He's nice,' I admitted. 'I like him.'

'I knew it!'

'But this is all stuff and nonsense,' I said. 'Nothing will come of it. Goodness, I'm so busy with the WSPU business, and the newspaper, and the children . . .'

Not to mention the fact that he was a policeman and there was no way a constable could even entertain the idea of romance with a woman like me. No way at all. I shook my head vigorously.

'No,' I said. 'I am committed to the cause.'

'Some men are allies to the cause,' Agnes pointed out. 'My John, for one.'

'Your John is a treasure. But he is far from the norm.'

I wondered if it was possible that PC Fairbanks could be a secret supporter of women's suffrage. Perhaps. He seemed to be such a nice chap. Surely he would be able to see the reason behind our arguments? Though that didn't mean he could suddenly start spending time with suffragettes.

'Anyway, whether he is an ally or not, I have no time for male attention.'

'Really?' Agnes said, disappointed.

I was firm. 'Really.'

Chapter 11

Lizzie

2019

I knew that telling the staff that the council intended to close Elm Heath Primary would be terrible. I thought it would be one of the worst things I'd ever had to do.

When the shit hit the fan in Clapham it had been bad, but at the start I'd been absolutely certain that it was all a big mistake and that Grant would never have done the things they said he'd done.

Of course, I'd been wrong, which had made the whole thing even worse, but I didn't know that at the beginning, even if I started to have some niggling doubts later on.

But the way I'd felt that day when Grant told me he'd been suspended while they investigated some "inconsistencies'" was nothing compared to the way I felt just imagining the expressions on the faces of the Elm Heath staff.

And so, I decided not to tell them.

'They'll just start looking for another job,' I reasoned with myself. 'Or they'll blame me and make things difficult. It's better if they don't know yet.'

Instead, at the end of the school day, I took Paula into my office and shut the door on Emma, who was pretending to be absorbed in putting her coat on and absolutely not listening to what we were saying.

'What's all this?' Paula said, looking alarmed. 'Bad news?'

'The worst.'

The colour drained from her face and she sat down heavily, looking like the air had been knocked out of her.

'They're closing Elm Heath?'

I nodded.

'I never thought they'd actually do it.'

'It's not definite yet.' I was eager to reassure her, because I couldn't bear to see how bereft she looked. 'That's why I'm only telling you for now – not everyone else.'

She shrugged. 'What can we do? I know how these things work – once a decision has been made, it's made.'

'Not necessarily,' I said, but my protests sounded weak to my own ears. 'I spoke to Denise Deacon at the council and she said it wasn't signed off yet. It's not official.'

Paula looked up at me, a tiny glimmer of hope in her eyes. 'What exactly did she say?'

I thought for a moment. 'She said it was a shame and she wished the school could stay open. I got the impression she's on our side, thought she couldn't really say so outright.'

Paula nodded. 'And?'

'She said we had to be creative and prove that Elm Heath was a vital part of the community, or that it was of special interest. We've got some time – and I've had a few ideas.'

'Hit me,' Paula said.

I found my scribbled notes and took her through what I'd come up with so far and she listened intently, her mind obviously racing with her own ideas.

'My friend Joanna is a personal trainer,' she said. 'I bet she knows loads of fitness instructors who might want to use the hall. I'll put the word out. If we're smart we could get someone hiring it every evening and that will definitely help the budget.'

I nodded, pleased she'd got on board so fast.

'And I absolutely love the idea of bringing the kids and the elderly people together.'

'I don't think that will be a money-making idea really but it will prove we're important in the community, which is also part of the plan.'

'And the after-school club will do both,' Paula said triumphantly.

'I hope so. I'm surprised you don't do one already.'

She grimaced. 'Like I said, we got a bit stuck in our ways. We'd need someone to run it though.'

'I had an idea about that, too.'

'You're on fire today.'

I grinned. 'What about Sophie Albert?'

Paula clapped her hands. 'That's a fabulous idea. She knows all the kids anyway, and she's got her DBS checks because she's often helping out at school things.' She thought for a moment. 'And I think I'd ask Celeste to coordinate from our side. She's very organised and she is keen to have a new challenge. Might encourage her to stay.'

'Great,' I said. 'That's sorted then. I'll chat to Celeste and Sophie. Could you and Pippa take on the afternoon teas for the elderly people? Maybe speak to some daycentres or whatever? If they work well with the little children, we can extend it to the older ones.'

'On it,' Paula said.

I ran my fingers through my hair. 'I just hope it works,' I said. 'Denise seemed to think it was a start rather than a solution. She sounded quite downbeat about it all.'

'I really believed that once we had you at the helm we'd be fine,' Paula said, almost to herself.

'I did worry that this was because of me. That the axe is falling while I'm here, because of what happened,' I admitted out loud for the first time, my mood going from positive to negative in record speed.

'At your old school you mean?'

I nodded.

'Absolute rubbish,' Paula said firmly. 'They were fully up to speed with everything that happened when they offered you the job.'

'I s'pose,' I muttered.

Paula fixed me with the stern glare that made unruly children quake. 'You need to stop feeling guilty about something you didn't do.'

'I s'pose,' I muttered again.

There was a pause. I played with the edge of the desk, wondering what to say next.

'What did you mean when you said interest?' Paula said.

'Pardon me?'

'You said we had to prove the school was of special interest. What kind of interest?'

'Well, Denise suggested historical, because I mentioned how old it was,' I said. 'But anything I suppose.'

'Right,' Paula said, fire in her eyes.

'Do you have an idea?'

'What about Esther?' she said, gesturing to the photograph on my wall.

'I'm a step ahead of you there. But that's not going to work.'

'Why not?'

'Because,' I said. 'I googled old butter-wouldn't-melt Esther Watkins and discovered she was a criminal, that's why.'

Paula stared at me. 'I don't think so.'

'Google doesn't lie.'

She raised an eyebrow at me.

'Okay, Google sometimes lies, but the dates match up. I'm pretty sure it's the same woman.'

Paula didn't speak; she just looked so upset that I felt bad all over again.

'Look,' I said. 'Let me do a bit more research. Maybe it's not her. It does sound pretty unlikely.'

'It does, doesn't it?'

'Why would a middle-class schoolteacher go to prison?'

'Exactly.'

Paula looked at her watch and grimaced. 'I have to go,' she said. 'Keep me posted on anything you discover?'

'I will.'

Looking harassed, she hurried out of my office, leaving me alone. I looked out of the window at the autumn sunshine. All my best thinking used to be done while I was out walking. And when Grant's actions made my whole life fall apart, I'd power my way round the commons of south London, working out solutions in my head. I'd go for a walk, I decided, and perhaps inspiration would strike.

As I left the school grounds, and pulled on my denim jacket though, I realised I was stumped. Back in London, I'd head to Wandsworth Common, or Tooting Common and follow the path round. But here in the countryside, I realised, I had no idea where to go. There was so much open space but I wasn't sure if I was allowed to walk there. Surely the fields all belonged to people? Were there footpaths across them? How would I know? What if there were animals? I wasn't keen on animals – I mostly just liked them from a distance. Especially scary ones like bulls.

Behind the playground was a patch of waste ground with the remains of a building on it and a broken fence. I'd seen teenagers out there in the evening, chatting and watching stuff on their phones, but it didn't look like somewhere I wanted to be.

Beyond that was a neatly hedged field. I eyed it suspiciously. I couldn't see a bull, but that didn't mean there wasn't one there.

Making up my mind, I crossed the road and headed instead to the park. It was only small, with a couple of football goals, and a little fenced-in play area, but I could walk round that without fear of being gored and hopefully clear my head a bit.

I'd only gone a little way round the edge of the park when my energy deserted me and I sat down on a bench, watching the kids running round the play area. I was at a loss about what to do for the best. The ideas we had were good but I wasn't stupid. I knew they were a drop in the ocean compared to our falling admissions and the squeeze on education budgets. It seemed like an impossible task to save Elm Heath Primary, but it also seemed really important.

The old me would have relished this challenge. She'd have swooped in like a super-teacher, told everyone what to do to improve results and foster a growth mindset in all the pupils, and then swooped off again. But my confidence in my own abilities had deserted me, and this was all just too . . . huge.

'You look like you have the weight of the world on your shoulders,' said a voice. I looked up to see Danny Kinsella smiling at me.

To my surprise, my heart jumped at the sight of him. Just a bit.

'School stuff,' I said.

He sat down next to me. 'Spill.'

'I can't.'

He pinched his lips together tight and made a zipping gesture. 'I'm the soul of discretion, me,' he said. 'And if there's anything I've learned over the years, it's that a problem shared really is a problem halved.'

I looked at him. 'You have to promise not to tell anyone,' I said. 'Not Cara and definitely not Sophie.'

'Sophie ignores everything I say anyway.'

'Promise,' I said.

Danny looked at me gravely and held out his little finger. 'Pinkie promise.'

'Danny . . .'

'It's the most binding promise there is, according to Cara.'

Feeling faintly ridiculous, I linked my little finger with his. His hands were warm and soft.

'There,' he said, shaking. 'Now you can tell me everything.'

And so I did. I told him all about Denise Deacon telling me the school would close unless we could do something to stop it, and about the ideas we'd had. It felt good to unburden.

'Those are all great plans,' he said. 'Sophie's the perfect person to run the after-school club.'

'It's not enough though, is it?'

He shrugged. 'Possibly not. But it's a start.'

'I also had the idea of proving the school was of historical interest, so I looked up Esther Watkins, who founded it back in 1912, and discovered she was a criminal.'

'What?' said Danny, delighted. But I wasn't happy.

'I feel like I've hit a brick wall,' I said. 'I can't tell the rest of the staff because they'll just look for other jobs and we'll be left with no one. Paula's devastated. And the one thing I thought might help – our history – is a non-starter.'

'It's weird, though, a woman like that going to prison,' Danny said. 'Are you sure it's the same Esther Watkins?'

I shrugged. 'I know it sounds crazy,' I said. 'I don't see what on earth she could have done to end up in jail.'

'Who's in jail?'

Cara was standing in front of us, chewing on the end of her pigtail.

'A lady from a long time ago,' Danny said. 'A hundred years ago.'

'Was she one of the ladies in that film?'

Danny and I looked at each other, confused, and then at Cara. 'Which film, sweetie?'

'The one you watched when Granny came to stay from Ireland When the ladies all were shouting and they had ribbons on them."

She looked at me and frowned. "I had to go to bed before it got good," she said. "But I saw them in *Horrible Histories*, too. Remember Daddy?'

She started marching up and down in front of us and Danny pointed at her and then at me, looking chuffed with himself.

'*Suffragette!*' he shouted in delight. 'She means the film, *Suffragette*.'

'I've not seen it,' I said blankly.

'When was your Esther in prison?'

I was bewildered, not following where any of this was going, but I told him the dates and he looked triumphant. 'Suffragette,' he said again.

'I've still not seen it.'

'I don't mean the film, I mean Esther,' he said. 'What if she was a suffragette? Loads of them went to prison.'

I stared at him, realising he could be on to something.

'A suffragette?' I said. 'Esther could have been a suffragette? Oh my God, this is amazing. Danny, I could kiss you!'

He leaned back against the park bench and grinned at me. 'Not in front of the kid, eh?' he said. 'But how about dinner?'

Giddy with excitement that our founder perhaps wasn't a hardened criminal after all, I grinned back.

'Dinner would be lovely,' I said.

Chapter 12

Lizzie

'A suffragette?' Paula said, when I arrived on her doorstep, slightly out of breath from running all the way from the park, and blurted out Danny's theory.

'I've not looked anything up yet, but it seems plausible, doesn't it? You said yourself how it didn't make sense for a woman like her to be in prison.'

Paula gripped my arm in delight. 'It makes perfect sense,' she said. 'Wonderful sense. Lizzie Armstrong, you could have stumbled on the thing that saves our school.'

'Well I'm not completely sure how we can use this to save the school, even if she was a suffragette,' I said. 'And it wasn't me who stumbled on it.'

'Who was it?' Paula hustled me down her hall and into the kitchen.

'It was Cara Kinsella, actually.'

'Never.'

I told her how Cara had overheard me talking to Danny and she beamed. 'She is bright as a button that little girl.'

'She is.'

Paula busied herself making tea. 'So you were with Danny were you?' she said ultra-casually.

'I went for a walk in the park and he was there with Cara.'

'Hmm.'

I felt a bit naughty, like I was keeping secrets. 'He asked me out for dinner,' I said.

'And what did you say?'

I shifted from one foot to the other. 'I said yes.'

'Hmm.'

I rolled my eyes at her back. What exactly did 'hmm' mean? 'I've not been out with anyone since Grant left,' I said.

Paula turned round to look at me. 'I'm not sure Danny should be the person to break your duck.'

'You said he'd stepped up,' I reminded her.

'He has,' she admitted. 'But as a dad, not necessarily as a boyfriend.'

'Oh give over.' Chris had wandered into the kitchen in search of tea and overheard. 'He's not a bad lad.'

Paula made a face. 'Think about how he was with Bella. And Sophie says . . .'

'Sophie is a bereaved mother who will always be angry that her daughter wasn't as happy as she might have been,' Chris said. 'Danny didn't treat Isabelle well but she didn't treat him well either and they were so young. People change.'

'Hmm,' said Paula again. 'Perhaps.'

'Maybe I shouldn't go.' My excitement had deserted me. 'I can't go on a date. I was just so pleased that we had an idea about why Esther might have been in prison, and I didn't really think about my answer.'

I sat down at the kitchen table, suddenly feeling gloomy. 'I don't want him to be my boyfriend,' I said honestly. 'I'm still getting over my marriage breakup. I guess I just thought it might be fun.'

Paula sat down next to me. 'Oh, Lizzie, I'm sorry,' she said. 'Of course it will be fun.'

'I don't want to wallow but it's been a while since I had any fun,' I said. 'The last year or so has been pretty disastrous.'

'Just go into this with your eyes open.'

I nodded. 'I'm really not going into anything. It's just dinner, not a wedding.'

'Hmm,' Paula said again. 'I've seen the way Danny looks at you. Just watch him.'

I grinned, cheered by her protectiveness. It was nice having someone looking out for me.

'I will,' I said. 'Don't worry. My eyes are wide open and I'm definitely not in the market for a serious romance. I'm just, well, a bit lonely I suppose.'

Paula gave me a quick squeeze with one arm, looking sheepish. 'Have dinner,' she said. 'Have fun.'

'Where's he taking you?' Chris asked. 'Somewhere nice?'

* * *

It was nice, actually. In fact, it was nicer than I'd thought it was going to be. I'd been in Elm Heath almost three months now but I was still underestimating rural living almost every day. I'd assumed Danny would take me for a curry or to the Three Kings – the pub in the village, which did good but pretty standard pub grub. So I'd not got myself particularly glammed up. Instead I'd thrown on a leopard-print dress that had once been my favourite but had now seen better days, black tights and flat ankle boots. My hair seemed to have developed an annoying kink so I pulled it into a twist on the back of my head and daubed on a bit of make-up.

But when Danny knocked at my door, on Friday evening, he had a cab waiting.

'Thought we'd go into Blyton,' he said. 'There's a cool Thai place that I like.'

It was pretty cool. All gold leaf and elephants with a pond in the middle of the room full of fish. Everyone was dressed up to the nines, in much more glamorous outfits than my tired old leopard print. Right in the middle of the restaurant was a table of very beautiful, very young people – who Danny told me were footballers for the local club and their girlfriends. Some of the other diners were taking sneaky photos of them. It was nothing like how I'd imagined our dinner date to be.

Danny steered me past the footballers, following the waiter as he took us to our table tucked in a corner.

'I don't like being near the pond because it always makes me need the loo,' Danny said and I wondered how often he came here and who with, but I just smiled and agreed it would do the same to me.

We ordered drinks and then Danny put down the menu and gave me his most charming smile. 'I bet Paula told you not to come tonight? Am I right?'

I started to protest and then gave up. 'You're right,' I admitted.

He nodded. 'She was a good friend of Isabelle's when things were pretty bad between us. She's not seen me at my best.' He smiled at me suddenly, making my heart jump again. 'And she's got a lot of time for Sophie, and Sophie is not my biggest fan.' He paused, playing with the corner of the padded cover on the menu. 'Mind you, she's got good reason not to think much of me.'

Disarmed by his honesty so early in the evening, I leaned forward. 'Paula told me your relationship with Cara's mum had ups and downs,' I said carefully.

'More downs than ups. And more my fault than Isabelle's.'

'Did you cheat?'

He looked at me, eyes narrowed. 'Is that what Paula said?'

'Not in so many words.'

The waiter brought our drinks – beer for both of us – and we ordered our food.

'So did you?' I said, when the waiter had gone again.

'Did I what?'

'Cheat on your wife?'

'We weren't married.'

'That's not the point.'

Danny gave me a sheepish grin. 'Yes and no.'

'And that's not an answer.'

'No, then.'

I raised an eyebrow.

'I thought I was too young to be settling down with a kid,' he said.

'Too young?'

I made a show of counting on my fingers. 'So Cara is eight and you're what? Late thirties? So how young were you?'

Danny looked down at the table.

'I was thirty-two,' he said.

'So young.' My voice dripped with sarcasm.

He shrugged. 'I can't excuse my behaviour,' he said. 'I was bored, staying in every night, so I'd go out and act like I was single.'

He looked up and met my eye, his own gaze level and honest.

'I never actually slept with anyone else though. So I suppose the answer is, no I didn't cheat on Isabelle.'

'But she left you anyway?'

'She did and I didn't blame her.'

He straightened his cutlery. 'And then she got ill, and she died and I came to live here so I could look after Cara.'

'Which proved you weren't too young to settle down.'

'I guess not.'

'But Sophie is finding it hard to forgive you for treating Isabelle badly?'

'She's still grieving,' he said. 'It's not easy for her.'

There was a pause and then he grinned at me. 'So that's my sorry tale. Now it's your turn.'

'There's not much to tell,' I said. 'Usual stuff. I thought my husband was one thing but he turned out to be someone else entirely.'

'Seeing another woman?'

'No, actually. At least, I don't think so.'

Again I waited as our food was put in front of us. The fragrance from my chicken satay wafted up and made my mouth water.

'Grant – my husband – was accused of doing something wrong. Really wrong.'

'Criminal?'

'No,' I said. 'But wrong professionally. It was unethical and just totally stupid. I stood by him, stuck up for him, and believed him when he swore to me he'd not done it.'

'So he had done it?'

I nodded, taking a bite of satay. 'He had.'

Danny made a face. 'So you felt like a fool for trusting him?'

'Yes, but it was more than that. His lies put my own job on the line, but he didn't do anything to protect me. Plus him lying about that made me wonder what else he'd lied about. He thought I was making a mountain out of a molehill, but in the end our marriage just wasn't strong enough.'

'It's always the secrets that get you in the end,' Danny said, biting into a spring roll. 'It's not the mistake, it's the cover-up.'

I nodded vigorously. 'That's it exactly,' I said. 'If Grant had fessed up to me right at the start I'd probably have forgiven him and we'd still be together. Or even better, if he'd come to me and said "I'm thinking of being a bit creative with these SATs results" before he'd done it, I'd have talked him out of it. It was the lies and the secrecy I couldn't live with. He destroyed all the faith I had in him and it was impossible to get it back.'

I paused.

'He's sorry now. He's apologised so often and he even sent me flowers when I started here. But it can't ever be like it was, not now.'

Danny had finished his starter. He pushed the plate to one side and leaned towards me, looking earnest. 'When Isabelle died, I felt so guilty. We weren't together when she got ill and I realise we wouldn't have worked anyway, but I still felt awful. I spent a lot of time going over the things I'd done wrong and wondering how I could have done things differently.'

'Go on,' I said.

'I swore to myself that if I ever managed to find someone new there was one thing I would definitely never do.'

'And what is that?' I leaned forward too, so our faces were quite close together.

'Keep secrets.'

I looked straight at him, wondering if he was spinning me a line. I was so close to him I could see the sprinkling of grey in the hairs at his temple and the flecks of amber in his brown eyes. The moment felt charged with energy, drawing me to Danny, and it took considerable willpower for me to sit back in my chair, pulling away from him.

'Well,' I said, trying to smile. 'That's good to know.'

Chapter 13

Esther

1910

I had taken to walking through the park every day. I was still weak from my prison stay, though I was getting stronger every day, and Agnes warned me not to do too much, but I told her the fresh air made me feel better.

'Just the fresh air that you're after, is it?' she'd said, teasing.

I'd turned away so she couldn't see me flush.

'Just the fresh air,' I'd assured her.

But of course it was Joseph I was interested in. Even though I knew my infatuation could come to nothing. Had to come to nothing. I looked out for him each time I wandered past the duck pond, and eventually my patience was rewarded when I saw him – wearing his own clothes this time, and strolling along the path.

'Miss Whitehouse,' he said, his face breaking into a wide smile when he recognised me.

I couldn't help but smile back. 'Constable Fairbanks.'

'Please call me Joseph,' he said. 'I'm off duty.'

'Then you must call me Esther.'

'Are you on your way anywhere in particular?'

'Just out for some air.'

'It's not really the weather for a walk,' he said, looking up at the grey sky. A fine drizzle was falling and I had no umbrella.

I met his eyes. 'And yet, you're out walking too.'

He let out a sudden guffaw of laughter, which made me laugh too.

'Why don't we sit for a while in the bandstand?' he said. 'If you have time?'

'That would be lovely. I am in no hurry.'

We climbed the steps to the bandstand and sat on the bench, grateful for the shelter it provided. I took off my hat and shook it, watching the drops of rain fly in all directions, and then wiped my damp face with my hand.

'You are rather pale,' Joseph said, sounding concerned. 'Are you cold?'

I was shivering. 'I've been ill,' I lied. Half-lied. For I supposed I had indeed been ill, even if it had been self-inflicted.

Joseph took off his coat and put it round my shoulders and I pulled it round me.

'Better?'

'Much, thank you. Shan't you be cold without it?'

'A big strong policeman like me?' he said, raising an eyebrow. 'Not a chance.'

I giggled, which surprised me slightly because I was not the sort of woman who giggled as a rule.

Joseph looked at me with fondness. 'So tell me about yourself, Miss Esther Whitehouse. What's your story?'

For the tiniest fraction of a second, I considered telling the truth.

'When my father died he left my mother with enormous debts and no way to pay,' I would say. 'I felt helpless and furious, and my mother was weak and resigned to her fate. I found a home with the WSPU who looked after me and made me see there was another path for women but I was arrested for breaking a window and taken to Holloway, where I went on hunger strike and was released early. I don't regret any of my actions and I would do it all again if I had to.'

'Esther?' Joseph snapped me out of my daydream, a concerned look on his face. 'Esther? Are you ill?'

I shook myself. 'I'm sorry, I was miles away,' I said. 'My story is rather dull, I'm afraid. My father died and my mother and I do not often see eye to eye, so I left my job as a schoolteacher and took the live-in position as governess for Agnes's children.'

'And do you enjoy it?'

'I do. The children are a delight. I find it endlessly fascinating to see the world through their eyes.'

Joseph smiled at me. 'I think you would make a wonderful mother one day.'

I bristled, slightly, at the suggestion. Was I not of value already, even though I wasn't a mother? I decided the best thing to do was change the subject. 'What about you, Constable Fairbanks? What made you join the police?'

Joseph looked thoughtful for a moment, then he smiled at me again and I had to admit, the way he gazed at me made my insides feel very peculiar – but in a pleasant way.

'I wanted to be noticed, I suppose,' he said. 'I'm the middle one in my family – two older brothers who are thick as thieves and two younger. I was always a bit lost.'

I nodded. 'Like Meg,' I said. 'I try to give her special attention because she's sometimes overlooked.'

'Lucky Meg,' Joseph said and I felt my cheeks burn again.

'It can't always be easy, being a copper,' I said, trying to cover my nerves.

He shook his head. 'It's definitely not easy. Sometimes it's messy, or even frightening.'

'Sometimes do you have to do things you don't want to do?'

'Like what?'

I shrugged. Really, I wanted him to say he was a passionate supporter of votes for women and he didn't like to arrest suffragettes but I wasn't going to admit that.

Joseph took a breath. 'Way I see it, is I don't make the laws. Some of them are right and some are probably wrong, but it's not my job to decide that. It's just my job to make sure everyone's doing right. It's the only way to make the world work as it should.'

Slowly I nodded, hoping that the laws he thought were wrong were the laws that said women couldn't vote. I should ask him, I knew that, but somehow I couldn't force the words out.

He reached out and took my hand and I let him, feeling as though it were completely normal to be sitting here, hand in hand, with a police officer who probably worked alongside those who'd arrested me. Who'd probably done his own fair share of arresting my WSPU friends. This was madness, surely? But then again, maybe he had a point when he said it was just his job to uphold the laws. Perhaps he wasn't the enemy?

I didn't pull my hand away.

'Esther you look dreadfully serious,' Joseph said, studying me. 'What on earth are you thinking about?'

I wasn't sure what to say, so I said nothing.

'Are you thinking about what you might have for dinner?' he guessed.

'Mrs Oliver has a cook,' I said, beginning to smile. 'So I just eat what I'm given.'

'Maybe you're secretly a music hall star and you're thinking about tonight's performance?'

'You've never heard me sing.'

'Bad?'

'Very bad.' I was giggling again. And Joseph was laughing too.

'Are you an engine driver and you're wondering which route you will have to take tomorrow?'

I rolled my eyes.

'That's it,' I said, laughing properly now. 'You've discovered my secret. I tuck all my hair into my cap and pretend to be a man named Ernest. You mustn't tell anyone you know the truth.'

'Your secret is safe with me,' he said.

I felt happier sitting there laughing with Joseph than I'd felt in years. I couldn't remember the last time I'd laughed properly and it felt nice.

'I have to go, Ernest,' Joseph said. 'Can we meet again tomorrow?'

'I can't tomorrow, I have the children all day and then . . .' I trailed off. I had a WSPU meeting in the evening. 'Mrs Oliver needs me after dinner.'

'The next day then?'

'I could do late afternoon? The children will be having their music lessons then.'

Joseph looked delighted.

'I will finish work at four o'clock so that would be perfect. If you give me Mrs Oliver's address, I can call for you. She might want to meet me?'

'No,' I almost shouted, and then checked myself. 'Mrs Oliver will not be at home, Mr Oliver will be at work, and the children will be busy. It's probably better if I meet you here.'

'Then that's what we'll do. We can have a stroll by the pond if the weather is good.'

'I'd like that,' I said, realising that I genuinely would. This funny, awkward, upstanding young man seemed to have wormed his way into my affections despite my trying to stop him.

Like a gentleman from a novel, Joseph lifted my hand and kissed it. I looked at him curiously and he laughed again.

'Is that not right?' he said. 'I've never done it before. I thought it would be nice.'

'It was nice.'

We looked at each other for a long moment, me feeling that squirming, liquid feeling in my stomach again, and wondering if he felt the same. Then he grinned.

'Got to go or I'll be in trouble with the inspector,' he said.

'Goodbye, Joseph.'

He blew me a kiss as he sauntered away, hands in pockets, looking very pleased with himself.

'Goodbye, Ernest,' he called.

Chapter 14

Esther

Agnes had organised the meeting of the WSPU the next evening to take place in her house because of the rats in the hall. Lots of the women – Agnes and I included – were jumpy about what had happened the other day and we didn't want to risk it. Having a meeting in a private house seemed easier to control and thankfully Agnes had enough space.

'It's so good that you volunteered to host the meeting,' I told her as we made the arrangements.

'If Mohammad cannot go to the mountain, the mountain must come to Mohammad.'

'I'm not sure Mrs Pankhurst will be pleased to be described as a mountain,' I said. But Agnes merely laughed and told me to help her shift a table.

'How many people are we expecting?'

She looked up to the ceiling thoughtfully. 'Hard to tell,' she said, tapping her chin. 'But not as many as at the last meeting. This is a more select gathering.'

'Select how?'

But the doorbell rang, announcing the first guests, and we were interrupted.

I made sure I was in the kitchen as people arrived because the police often trailed Mrs Pankhurst and others and I felt I didn't want to risk Joseph seeing me; I had no reason to think he would or wouldn't be sympathetic to we suffragettes, but I certainly knew him stumbling across me here would put him in a very awkward position. The chances were tiny, given he worked in East London, but I still didn't want to be seen when the door opened.

When everyone was in the lounge, perched on chair arms, sitting on the floor, and standing by the fireplace, I slid into the room and found myself a spot at the back, and to my absolute delight saw Minnie sitting on the sofa. She was still pale, but her cheeks were rounder.

'I was hoping you'd be here,' she said, throwing her arms round me. 'I didn't know how to get in touch because I didn't know where you were living.'

'I'm living here,' I said, enjoying her look of surprise. 'I'm the governess for Agnes Oliver's children.'

She clapped her hands in joy. 'Well, isn't that just perfect?'

'What about you?'

'Got my old job back, didn't I?' she said.

'Really? How wonderful.'

She preened a bit. 'I'm a very good shop girl,' she said. 'And the other staff all vouched for me. I think the boss has a soft spot for suffragettes, though he'd never admit it out loud.'

I gripped her hand tightly.

'It's so good to see you,' I said.

In fact, it was good to see everyone at this meeting. Because it was a more local gathering than the other day, I knew most of the women by sight, even if I didn't know everyone's name. A few came over to Minnie and me and said how pleased they were that we were back. We'd been given brooches to show we'd been inside, and many women admired them. It felt good to be back in the arms of my friends after the horror of jail, and the sadness of losing my job and leaving my mother. These women were my family now, I thought.

Mrs Pankhurst, who looked thin and pale, talked first about the Conciliation Bill that we hoped would soon be going through Parliament.

'As you know, we've agreed not to take any militant action for the time being,' she said. 'And while there is a possibility of the Conciliation Bill being approved, we need to adhere to the terms we agreed.'

Earlier in the year, Mrs Pankhurst, Millicent Fawcett and others had agreed to a draft Conciliation Bill drawn up by some MPs, which would give some women the right to vote. It wasn't perfect, but it was a good start – if it passed, which wasn't certain. But for now, we had to go along with the agreement Mrs Pankhurst had made, not to engage in any militancy while the bill was being discussed.

The women in the room all nodded and murmured in agreement as Mrs Pankhurst spoke, but no one seemed overly enthusiastic. It was a start, but would it happen at all?

Next to me, Minnie sighed. 'I don't trust them,' she muttered.

'Mrs Pankhurst?' I was surprised.

'No, the MPs, silly. I don't trust them.'

I shrugged. I wasn't sure I did either, but it was the best we had for now.

Minnie raised her voice above the crowd. 'Mrs Pankhurst, could I ask a question?'

'Go ahead.'

'Have the coppers been told about our agreement?'

Mrs Pankhurst made a face. 'I believe so.'

'Only I heard there were rats in a meeting, and it was the police that put them there.'

A swell of voices grew around me.

'There's no proof it was the police,' Mrs Pankhurst said, raising her hands for quiet. 'But I can speak to the MPs once more and urge them to remind the police that we are calming our activities.'

Minnie nodded. 'Do you think we'll win?'

There was a pause as all the eyes in the room turned to Mrs Pankhurst.

She nodded. 'I do think we'll win,' she said. 'Because if we don't win, then what was it all for?'

There was a moment's silence in the room and then everyone cheered and shouted their support. But I found I couldn't join in with the excitement. I was thinking about Joseph. Was he the type of copper who would let rats loose in a room of women? The memory of him kissing my hand arose and I smiled. He was a good, sweet man; he would not – could not – do things like that. I knew it.

Standing next to Minnie and me, leaning against the wall next to the sofa where we sat, was a younger girl, wide-eyed at everything going on around her.

'I've had a few run-ins with the police,' she said to me, nodding at the badge on my chest. 'Bet you have too.'

I nodded.

'I hate them,' she said with venom. 'Every one of them.'

'They're just doing their jobs,' I said, echoing what Joseph had said.

The girl stared at me in disgust. 'No they aren't,' she said. 'And if hurting women and stopping us from being part of society is their job then they should be ashamed of themselves.'

'I didn't mean that . . .' I began but my words sounded weak to my own ears.

The girl wasn't finished.

'They should do something else,' she said. 'Something worthwhile.'

She pushed herself up off the wall and went over to another group of women. I felt uneasy and out of sorts for the first time in all my days as a WSPU member. I was still convinced we were doing the right thing, and for the right reasons, but meeting Joseph had changed me. Made me question what I'd previously been sure of.

'Esther?' I looked round and found Mrs Pankhurst at my arm. 'How are you feeling?'

I smiled. 'Stronger,' I said. 'Better.'

She patted me gently on the hand. 'Good. Good.'

I swallowed. 'I told Agnes you'd mentioned the governess position to me, when you hadn't. I'm sorry.'

'I did wonder,' she said. 'I can understand why you did it and it has all worked out for the best.'

'It has.' I nodded. 'I'm very happy here.'

'Excellent.'

She made to walk away and I stopped her. 'Mrs Pankhurst, when we were in jail there was another woman with us who had taken terribly ill after being force-fed. Her name was Alice, I think. Alice Hudson. Do you know where she is? Or how she is recovering?'

She frowned. 'I'm so sorry, Esther, but I heard last week that Alice passed away. She was weak before she was arrested I believe – she suffered badly with her chest during winter and had been ill.'

I felt dizzy for a second. Poor Alice. What a dreadful thing we were dealing with here. I gritted my teeth.

'That is awful.'

Mrs Pankhurst nodded, genuine sadness in her eyes. 'It's like I said.' She glanced over to where the young woman who'd been so vocal about the police was talking to a group of older women, looking upset about something. 'We have to win, because otherwise what was it all for?'

I clenched my fists at my sides, thinking of Alice and all the other women I'd met in prison – and pushing away all thoughts of Joseph.

'We have to win,' I echoed. 'We have to win.'

Chapter 15

Lizzie

2019

I woke up the morning after my date with Danny with a slight hangover and a fizzing, excited feeling inside. It reminded me of waking up on my birthday when I was a kid and knowing something good was about to happen. It was Saturday and I didn't have to get up, so I lay in bed – alone – and stretched out, wriggling my toes. It had been a very nice evening. Fun, just like I'd told Paula I wanted. Danny was funny and smart, he obviously adored little Cara, and he was really interested in Esther Watkins and whatever her story was.

'Let me know what you find out about her,' he'd said as we neared Elm Heath in our cab home.

'I don't suppose you could call in a few favours and help us win?' I'd said. I was joking but Danny had looked startled.

'In what way?'

'I thought you financed public sector projects?'

Danny had started to explain how his job worked earlier in the evening, but then never finished because the waiter had interrupted us and we'd gone on to chat about something else.

But in the cab he'd nodded. 'Well, not me personally, but yes. We find private investors for public sector projects.'

'So you must know people at Blyton Council?'

He'd smiled. 'I do know people,' he'd said. 'And if I can help, I will. Keep me posted and I'll see what I can do.'

I'd felt a bit odd in the taxi home, remembering Uber trips with Grant back from nights out. When we went out, back when our lives were still fun, I always sat in the middle so we could hold hands in the back, or more often than not after a party, so I could rest my head on his shoulder and doze off. Danny and I had each sat by a window, an empty seat in between us, and the space seemed enormous. When the cab had pulled up at my house, he'd got out and come round to where I stood on the pavement, hands in pockets and my jacket pulled round me against the evening chill. He'd paid the driver and told him he'd walk from here and then he'd looked at me.

'I had a really nice time,' he'd said. 'I'd like to do it again.'

I'd smiled up at him, noticing how his eyes twinkled in the streetlights as though he was planning something mischievous. I'd twinkled back at him – it was infectious.

'I'll see if I can fit you in. I'm very busy doing head-teacher things.'

'Surely you've got a few spare evenings in among moulding young minds and saving Elm Heath Primary?'

I had nudged him with my shoulder. 'I reckon so,' I'd said.

There was the tiniest, awkward pause as I'd wondered whether I should invite him in for coffee. But though I'd enjoyed our meal together I wasn't ready to take things further. Not yet. Luckily Danny had realised I was hesitating and took charge.

'I'd better go because Cara is a devil for the early mornings,' he'd said, kissing me on the cheek. 'Night then.'

He'd sauntered off down the road towards his house, without looking back, and I'd let myself in to my little cottage feeling relieved and disappointed at the same time.

Now though, the morning after, I knew I'd done the right

thing. If – and it was a very big if – this thing with Danny was going to go anywhere, then I had to take it really slow. Not to mention the fact that Elm Heath was a small place and if Danny had so much as stepped foot across my doorstep it would have been all round the village by lunchtime that the new headmistress was inviting dads round for late-night shenanigans. That would hardly be professional.

I stretched again, then got out of bed and went downstairs in search of caffeine and my laptop. Then I took my coffee and the computer back to bed and fired up Google.

'Come on then, Esther Watkins,' I said to myself. 'What's your story?'

It took me a while and various different searches, but I found her eventually in a photograph. It was a picture of a row of women, marching along a road. They were all nicely dressed – one even had a fur stole round her shoulders – and wearing rather fetching hats. Each had a sandwich board across her front and back, some carrying the details of a meeting taking place on the Strand in November 1909, and others simply saying Votes for Women. The women's names were listed in the caption of the photograph and there, third in line, was Esther Watkins.

'Gotcha,' I said, delighted. I zoomed in on her face in the photograph and compared it with the portrait that hung on my wall – I'd snapped it on my phone the other day. She was younger in the picture in my office, but it was definitely her. Esther Watkins had been a suffragette.

'Clever girl, Cara,' I murmured as I screen-grabbed Esther and her Votes for Women placard. 'Clever, clever girl.'

I carried on searching and found Esther's photograph again. This time, though, she was standing at the back of rows of small children alongside two other women a similar age and one very stern-looking older woman. The caption read: 'Trinity Primary School, Wandsworth. 1909/10.'

I rummaged in the duvet for my phone, and rang Paula.

'I've found her,' I said when she answered. 'I've found Esther and she's fabulous.'

'Fabulous enough to save Elm Heath?'

I chewed my lip. 'Not sure yet,' I said. 'But she's definitely an interesting character. She was a suffragette and she was a teacher in London before she came here.'

'Just like you,' Paula said, sounding pleased. 'I wonder what brought her to Elm Heath?'

'No idea,' I said cheerfully. 'But I reckon we can find out. There's loads of stuff online about the suffragettes. We just need to do a bit of digging. And Danny even said he might be able to help.'

Paula scoffed. 'What does he know about the suffragettes?'

I shrugged, even though she couldn't see me. 'He knows people at the council.'

'How was your date?' Paula said the word "date" like she was putting air quotes round it.

'It was lovely, thank you.' I was deliberately misunderstanding what she wanted to know. 'We went for Thai in Blyton and the chicken satay was delicious. There was some footballer from Blyton Town, who I didn't recognise but Danny did.'

'And?'

'And nothing, it was just a nice evening. I told you, not that it's any of your business, that I'm not in the market for romance.'

'Okay.' Paula sounded prickly.

'I know you were Isabelle's friend . . .'

'I was.'

'Like Chris said, people make mistakes. Everyone deserves a second chance.'

'Except Grant?'

'I gave Grant a second, third and fourth chance and he blew them all,' I said. 'I just think Danny's not as bad as you and Sophie think he is. He knows he was shitty to Isabelle and he's sorry. He even seems keen to help with Elm Heath Primary and I think we should welcome his involvement.'

'Just be careful,' Paula said and I sighed loudly.

'If my experience with Grant has taught me anything it's to trust no one,' I said. Though as I said it, I felt uncomfortable, like I was lying.

Paula was silent for a moment. 'What shall we do with this Esther knowledge then?' she said, obviously realising she was getting nowhere warning me off Danny.

Suddenly deflated, I looked at the photograph on my laptop screen. 'Nothing, I suppose. What can we do? It's really cool that she was a suffragette but I'm not sure it's relevant to the school, is it? I can't imagine the bean counters at Blyton Borough Council suddenly finding extra cash, just because Esther believed women should have the vote.'

'Don't give up yet,' Paula said. 'Maybe we need to focus on why she ended up in Elm Heath, starting a school. Perhaps there's something in that?'

'Perhaps,' I said. 'Actually, perhaps this is where Danny could help? Maybe someone at the council knows more about the history of the school? He could introduce us.'

'Worth a try,' Paula said. 'Just . . .'

'I know, I will be careful.'

I ended the call and typed a message to Danny. 'Thanks for last night,' I began, hoping I was showing the right amount of casual interest. Enough to make him realise I liked spending time with him but not so much that he'd think I wanted to jump straight into a relationship. It was a long time since I'd dated anyone so it was a tricky business to choose the right words. 'I enjoyed it,' I added, then deleted it because it sounded formal and forced.

Instead I launched straight into my Esther news, saying she had definitely been a suffragette and did he know anyone at the council who could help us find out the history of the school? At the end I wrote: 'See you soon?' and then finished with an L and a kiss. I sent it before I could change my mind and then I got out of bed and went for a shower, leaving my phone in the bedroom so I couldn't keep checking for a reply.

'Loser,' I told myself as I got dressed. When I eventually allowed myself to look at my phone my heart jumped as I saw Danny's name on the screen.

'Leave it with me,' he'd written. 'Can you bunk off school early on Monday afternoon to go to the council office?'

'No worries,' I replied. 'The headmistress is a pushover.'

'Three p.m. at the council?'

'See you there.'

I sent my final reply and then scrolled back through the messages, rereading them and checking for any hidden meaning, but I couldn't find any.

Sighing, I threw my phone into my bag and then grabbed my car keys. If I was going to see important people at the council – and yes, Danny too – then I probably needed a new outfit.

Chapter 16

Lizzie

I spent most of the weekend reading everything I could find about the suffragettes, which was quite an eye-opener. I stared at the photograph of Esther and her friends, in their long skirts and fancy hats, and tried to make sense of them being proper bad-asses, setting fire to buildings, breaking windows and climbing the fences round the Houses of Parliament.

It was all pretty impressive, but I still couldn't see how it was going to help Elm Heath. After all, some of the things the suffragettes did were almost like terrorism today and I wasn't sure bigging up our association with jailbird Esther Watkins was going to swing it for the council.

On Sunday evening, with rain lashing the windows and the first dark evening after the clocks changed bringing gloom, I decided to brave the weather and treat myself to some chips for dinner. I put on boots and a raincoat, and found my umbrella, and headed out to the chippie.

It seemed half of Elm Heath had the same idea, as it was busy and I had to wait for my order. I sat at a table and leafed through a copy of *The Sun* that someone had left behind.

'Lizzie, how nice to see you.'

I looked up from a story about Ant and Dec's new game show to see Sophie standing by my table.

'Hi, Sophie,' I said. 'Great minds think alike, eh?'

She pulled out a chair and sat down. 'I would never admit it to my French friends but I just adore proper chip-shop chips,' she said. 'Especially on a miserable evening like this. Winter is just around the corner, eh?'

I chuckled.

'Your secret is safe with me.'

'Busy weekend?'

I shrugged. 'So, so,' I said. 'A bit of school stuff, and some research into the history of Elm Heath Primary.'

Sophie looked over my shoulder. 'Did you see much of Danny?' she said, ever so casual.

I smiled. 'No,' I said. 'I've not seen him since Friday.'

She relaxed. 'Great.'

'Is it?'

Sophie looked a bit shame-faced. 'Sorry, Lizzie,' she said. 'I know it's none of my business.'

'It's not,' I agreed. I fixed her with my best teacher stare. 'I know things were difficult between Danny and your daughter so I understand why you want to warn me off. But, Danny and I are just friends. And even if we weren't, I'm a grown-up and I've been through my own marriage break-up. I'm not some wide-eyed teenager and you don't need to look out for me.'

Sophie swallowed. 'You're right,' she said, looking down at her hands on the melamine table. 'I think I just feel guilty that I couldn't help Isabelle.'

'I understand.'

'I will butt out,' Sophie added and it sounded so funny in her French accent that I couldn't help but laugh.

As I walked home, clutching the warm paper package of chips to my chest, I thought about Sophie and Paula. They were both good people, I thought, and they both thought Danny wasn't someone I should trust. And yet, my gut was telling me to believe him when he said how bad he felt about Isabelle.

As though I'd summoned him with the power of my thoughts, Danny messaged just as I was tipping the chips on to a plate.

'All sorted for tomorrow,' he wrote. 'Still okay for three p.m.?'

'Looking forward to it,' I replied.

Danny had a meeting at the council office beforehand, so we arranged to meet in reception at three p.m. When I arrived, he was sitting on one of the low, grey sofas by the front desk talking urgently into his phone and looking harassed. I gave him a small wave to show him I was there, then signed in with the receptionist and clipped on the plastic pass she gave me.

Danny had finished his call and he came over to greet me.

'Everything okay?' I said.

A shadow passed across his face for a second, then he shook it off. 'Just work.' He gave the receptionist the full benefit of his smile. 'Lovely Lauren, can you let us through? We're heading to the archives.'

'I'm supposed to wait until someone comes down.'

He rolled his eyes. 'Claire knows we're coming and I know where to go. Save her a journey.'

Lauren grinned and pressed a button under her desk to open the barrier. 'Seeing as it's you,' she said.

Danny led the way into the lift and pressed for the basement.

'Lovely Lauren?' I said, raising an eyebrow.

'I am firmly of the opinion that it's best to be nice to everyone,' he said. 'Shop assistants, waiters, traffic wardens . . .'

'Teachers?'

He laughed. 'Yes, teachers too.'

The lift doors opened and we went out into a large room full of floor-to-ceiling metal shelves, stuffed with cardboard boxes and folders.

'Archives,' Danny said, spreading his arms out wide. 'Anything you want to know about the history of Elm Heath Primary will be in these boxes. Somewhere.'

I looked from one end of the room to the other, taking in just how many folders lined the shelves.

'I don't know where to start.'

'That's where Claire comes in,' he said. He tugged my hand and led me round to the left, past a pile of flattened boxes to a desk where a woman about my own age sat at a desk, tapping at a keyboard.

'Gorgeous Claire,' he said.

She looked up and beamed at him. 'Danny.'

'This is Lizzie, the head teacher of Elm Heath Primary. She's the one who wants to know more about the history of the school.'

Claire smiled at me. 'I can definitely help there.'

'Did you find those boxes I asked for?' Danny said.

She nodded. 'I sent the first lot up to Marcus in planning,' she said. 'He was furious, by the way.'

Danny chuckled. 'Good.'

'And the Elm Heath bits are all by Gloria's desk. She's on holiday this week so she's not around.' She gestured to the side of the desk opposite her.

'Have a root through, Lizzie. Take as long as you like.'

Danny touched the top of my arm gently. 'I need to pop in and see Marcus in planning, but I'll be back in a bit.'

Weirdly disappointed that he was leaving me, I nodded. 'He's furious with you,' I said. 'Be careful.'

'I'm always careful,' he said.

He disappeared off back to the lift, and I settled down at Gloria's desk and opened the first box.

It was a treasure trove of information. There were old photographs, programmes from school plays, newspaper reports on pupils winning awards for music or sport – and in one case a bravery award for pulling a dog out of a canal – but it was all from the 1960s and 70s, nothing earlier.

'Is there anything about the school being founded?' I asked Claire.

She barely glanced up from her screen; clearly me on my own wasn't nearly as interesting as me with Danny.

'The boxes are dated,' she said.

'Oh.' I looked at the side of the box I'd been rummaging through and right enough it said 1961–79.

With some effort I moved the piles around and finally found the one marked 1912–1925. Bingo.

It smelled dusty and old inside, but I got stuck in, pulling out the papers and laying them on the desk. This was more like it. I found more old school photographs, the original plans for the building, and lots of official correspondence from the education authority to Esther. Many of them were to do with building costs, and salaries, and while fascinating were not overly helpful. But then I found the letter giving Esther the go-ahead to open the school and let out a little yelp of joy. Claire tutted and I apologised, flattening the yellowed, ageing pages out on Gloria's desk.

'Dear Miss Watkins,' the letter read.

'I am writing to inform you that your plans to open a primary school in Elm Heath have been approved. As you know, I had some reservations about your character and whether it would be right to employ a woman with your history. However, the reference you provided from Sergeant Fairbanks of the Metropolitan Police assured me that your misdemeanours were youthful folly and would not be repeated. And your former employer, Mrs Agnes Oliver, provided a very positive character reference.

'I was also reassured by your aims for the school and the clear way you set them out in the letter you wrote me. You are obviously a teacher of talent and I am willing to take a chance on you. I need not remind you that any return to your previous behaviour would result in immediate dismissal . . .'

I breathed out slowly. This was more like it. Clipped to the back of the letter were the references mentioned. Mrs Agnes Oliver enthused about how well Esther had taught her three children and how much they would miss her, while Sergeant Fairbanks wrote in stilted police jargon about how much Miss Watkins 'regretted and apologised for her previous misdemeanour' and how she had 'learned a great deal from her time in Holloway'.

But what wasn't there, was the letter Esther had written that had convinced them to take the chance on her. The letter setting out her aims for Elm Heath Primary that would be absolutely and totally helpful for me, more than one hundred years later, trying to find a way to save the school. I tipped the box upside down, ignoring Claire's irritated sigh, and rifled through the papers but there was nothing there. Then I went through all the other boxes, looking for Esther's mission statement, as I was thinking of it, but it was nowhere to be found.

'Is this it?' I said to Claire. 'Nothing else on Elm Heath?'

'No, that's all of it,' she said. 'Is something missing?'

I showed her the letter from the council and explained the letter they mentioned wasn't there. She shrugged.

'Might have got filed in the wrong box,' she said. 'It happens. But it would be impossible to find it if so.'

'That's such a shame – it sounded like it would really have helped.'

Claire, to my surprise, looked interested. 'There are normally ways round these things,' she said. 'Can I see?'

I handed over the letter and the references and she scanned them, looking more cheerful than she had since Danny left. 'These people could be helpful,' she said, pointing to the names of Sergeant Fairbanks and Agnes Oliver. 'You've got an address for Agnes, and the police station where Fairbanks was based. You could try them.'

'They'll be dead, surely?'

She rolled her eyes at my stupidity. 'Well, obviously,' she said. 'But Agnes had three children who might have families, or there will be police records. It's something to follow up at least.'

I felt a tiny tug of excitement. 'It is,' I agreed. 'Thank you.'

Chapter 17

Lizzie

Claire copied the letters and references for me. While I was waiting I got a message from Danny to say he was waiting in reception and Claire glanced over, hopefully.

'Is Danny coming back?' she asked. I shook my head.

'He's done with his meeting so he's waiting for me upstairs.'

Clearly disappointed, she thrust the papers at me and sat down at her desk.

'I might need to come back sometime, if that's okay?'

'You're welcome any time,' she said, sounding as if she really meant the opposite.

I went back up to reception where Danny was standing, looking grim-faced.

'Everything okay?'

He gathered himself and gave me his most dazzling smile. 'All fine.'

'Was he furious?'

'Who?'

'Marcus in planning.'

He laughed, softly. 'Actually, no,' he said. 'For once Marcus and I are singing from the same hymn sheet. We're trying to find a solution to something, and it's my boss who's being difficult.'

We'd walked out of the council offices and paused by the car park.

'Do you need a lift home?' I asked.

'That would be great, if you don't mind. My colleague dropped me off earlier.'

On the drive home we chatted about the letter I'd found, and the references.

'The note from the council said they'd been impressed by a letter Esther had written, spelling out her aims for Elm Heath Primary, but that letter wasn't there.'

'That's annoying.'

'I know. I looked through every box but it wasn't anywhere to be found.'

'It would be fun to compare the aims of the school then with the aims now,' Danny commented.

'I know.' I indicated to turn off the dual carriageway on to the small side road that led to Elm Heath. 'But your friend Claire said it could be worth trying to find out more about the two people who wrote Esther's references.'

'Who were they?'

'One was some policeman. He sounds like a stuffed shirt. And the other was the woman who employed her as a governess.'

'Can I see the letter?'

'I've put my bag in the boot. I can get it when we stop.'

I glanced over at him. He was staring ahead through the windscreen, his jaw tight with tension and I wondered what had happened at the council to make him so stressed.

'Is Cara with Sophie?' I asked.

'Yes, she always does Monday evenings.'

'Then why don't you come back to mine. I can make us some dinner and open a bottle of wine. I'll show you the stuff I found today. You've obviously had a rotten day and it looks like you need to chill out.'

Danny leaned his head against the back of the car seat and smiled a tired smile.

'I can't tell you how nice that sounds,' he said. 'Yes please.'

The kitchen in my little cottage was small but Danny sat at the breakfast bar while I opened a bottle of red wine and put some pasta on to boil. It was still early for dinner, but as we'd chatted we'd realised we'd both skipped lunch and we were starving. I dug some garlic bread out of the freezer and put that on too.

'I love being with Cara,' Danny said. 'And I know I'm lucky to have Sophie round the corner because she helps out so much . . .'

'Despite her being so unpleasant to you?'

He grinned at me. 'I wouldn't say unpleasant,' he said. 'More, openly hostile.'

I chuckled and he carried on.

'But sometimes I get worn out always being the grown-up. Always being the one who's doing the looking-after, you know?' He paused. 'What I'm saying is, it's nice to be cooked for.'

'It's only pasta and pesto, so don't get too excited.'

He drank some wine, looking at me over the top of the glass. 'That's not the point and you know it.'

Our eyes met and the moment felt loaded, making the hairs on my neck tingle. I broke my gaze before he did, feeling my cheeks flush again.

'The bread should be ready,' I said, opening the oven door. 'Could you cut it up for me?'

I pulled out the tray but the hot glass door swung shut as I did so, hitting the back of my hand.

'Ouch, ouch, ouch,' I wailed.

Danny jumped from his stool and dashed over to me, taking my arm by the wrist and shoving my burnt hand under the cold water.

'It hurts,' I said, tears stinging my eyes. The back of my hand was red and forming a large angry blister. I tried to pull it out of the water and Danny held it in.

'Don't be a baby,' he said sternly. 'You need to cool it down.'

'But it hurts.'

'Not as much as it will hurt if you don't do this.'

He was standing behind me, one hand holding mine in the cold water, the other on my waist, keeping me steady. Danny wasn't a tall man, in fact we were a similar height, and it felt comfortable standing so close to him. I could feel the heat from his body on my back and his breath against my neck and I had to be honest, that was helping numb the pain from my burnt hand far more than the cold water was.

'How does it feel?' Danny said.

'Good,' I answered dreamily. I tilted back a fraction so I was leaning on him.

'Good? Really? It looks so painful.'

I realised what I'd said. 'Not good,' I gabbled. 'Not good. But it's getting better.'

He leaned over my shoulder to look at my hand, his face close to mine. If I turned my head the tiniest amount, our lips would touch. Did I dare?

'Oh shit, the pasta!' Danny let go of my hand and turned to rescue the pan from where it had boiled over the hob. 'Colander?'

'In the cupboard.'

He found it and I moved out of the way so he could drain the pasta, drying my hand carefully on a piece of kitchen towel.

'We should cover that,' he said, putting the drained pasta back in the pot. 'Do you have plasters?'

'I think there are some in the cupboard in the bathroom. I'll get them.'

'Nope,' he said, disappearing out of the kitchen. I heard him run up the stairs and then, after a few seconds, run back down again, with a large Elastoplast in his hand. I held out my wrist like a dog with a wounded paw and he gently covered the wound.

'There you go.'

'Now you're doing the looking-after again,' I pointed out.

'And yet funnily enough, I don't mind at all.'

I smiled goofily. He was really nice, despite what Sophie said.

'You sit down and I'll finish the dinner,' he said. I watched him stir the pesto into the pasta, cut up the bread, and top up my wine. My hand was still stinging but it was calming down now, and luckily it was my left hand and I was right-handed, so it didn't stop me picking up a fork. I grinned at Danny.

'Thank you,' I said.

'Lucky I was here.'

'It was.'

We smiled at each other for a second and then he tucked into his pasta and I did the same. We chatted about silly things Cara had said, and I shared some stories about kids at my old school, and then as I finished the last piece of garlic bread, I sighed.

'The kids at Elm Heath Primary are just as lovely as the ones from my old school. Lovelier even. Those corn dollies . . .'

I stopped, voice cracking as I remembered how overwhelmed I'd been.

'I hope I can do something to stop the council closing the school,' I said. 'But it feels like a massive ask at the moment.'

Danny looked down at his empty plate. 'In my experience, these decisions have sometimes been made by the people at the top long before anyone gets to hear about it.'

'Really?'

He shrugged. 'I just know how property works, that's all. It's a valuable site.'

I looked at him through narrowed eyes. 'Have you heard something?'

Avoiding my stare, he shifted on his stool. 'No,' he said.

'Danny?'

'I think it's amazing how much you care about Elm Heath,'

he said, finally looking up at me. 'You've only known us all of five minutes and here you are, trying your hardest for everyone.'

'I like it here.' It seemed obvious to me. 'Everyone is nice.'

Danny pushed his empty plate away and leaned towards me. 'Everyone?' he said. He reached over and brushed a strand of my hair over my shoulder and then, very softly he kissed me. A jolt of longing shot through me like an electric shock.

'Everyone,' I agreed, pulling him closer.

Chapter 18

Esther

1910

After my discussion about the police with the wide-eyed girl at the meeting, I worried all night about seeing Joseph so close to home. I barely slept and went down to breakfast hollow-eyed and pale, much to Agnes's worry. Fortunately, the children had their music lessons first thing, so she said she would take them and let me go back to bed.

Grateful, I snuggled back down under the blankets wondering what I should do. Joseph was coming from work, and I worried that he could be wearing his uniform. If Agnes, or one of the others saw, I'd have a hard time explaining. And if he discovered I was part of the WSPU – and more than that, a woman who'd been jailed for being a part of the WSPU – he'd almost definitely not want to spend time with me any more. But I didn't want to just not turn up, because short of going over to Whitechapel, to his police station, I couldn't get hold of him.

I sat up in bed as a thought occurred to me. I could go to Whitechapel. He said he finished work at four o'clock. I'd go at half past three and wait for him.

And so, that's what I did. I got the bus along to Whitechapel and found the police station, just as the clock on the nearby church was chiming the half-hour. In relief, I settled down on a bench opposite and waited for him to come out of the building. I was still nervous though. Perhaps he'd been working elsewhere today? Or maybe there was more than one police station in Whitechapel and I'd chosen the wrong one. By five past four, I was getting anxious. I stood up and paced back and forth across the pavement. And then I felt a hand on my shoulder and looked round to see Joseph's lovely face, his broad smile showing me how pleased he was that I was there.

'Esther?' he said. 'I thought we were meeting in Kennington?'

I couldn't help smiling back at him, despite my earlier worry. 'I fancied the fresh air,' I said.

'I'm pleased to hear it, since it means we get to meet earlier than I expected.'

He was not wearing his uniform, I noticed, but something about his demeanour still suggested copper to me. Maybe it was the way he held himself so upright, or how his eyes scanned the people around us. Or perhaps it was just because I knew he was a constable and I was imagining it. Whatever it was, I was glad that I'd made the trip east to Whitechapel instead of him coming to me.

'If you've already done your walking for today, what about we go for tea and cake?' Joseph was saying, still smiling.

'That sounds perfect.'

He offered me his arm and I took it, enjoying the feeling of his strong muscles beneath his jacket.

'Do you live in Whitechapel?' I asked, as we strolled. 'Why have I only seen you in Kennington?'

'I live in Whitechapel now. I have lodgings close to the police station. But my mother and father live in Kennington, and one of my brothers too, with his family, so I visit often.'

I tucked my hand into his arm a bit tighter. I loved the idea of a close family. My father had lied and tricked his way through my childhood and then Mother, well, she and I had little in common. I liked the thought of visiting parents on a Sunday, and playing with nieces and nephews in the park.

'That's nice,' I said. 'I would have liked to have a family. I see my charges with their grandparents and it makes my heart full. And the way they run to John when he comes home from work, barrelling down the stairs to tell him about their day, oh it's a sight to see.'

'You said your father died?'

I nodded as he guided me up the stairs to a teashop. 'He died five years ago.'

Joseph took off his hat and jacket and hung them on the rack by the door. 'I'm so sorry,' he said.

I shrugged. 'My father wasn't the man we thought he was. He wasn't as honest as he might have been.'

Joseph looked uncomfortable and I was quick to reassure him.

'He wasn't a criminal,' I said. No, the only criminal in our family, was me. 'He was bad with money and he gambled what he had – all in secret of course – and then he borrowed from some people he shouldn't have borrowed from. When he died, he left my mother to pick up the pieces.'

I felt my mood darken at the thoughts of my family, and shook myself. 'But let's not talk about them. I worked up a big appetite on my way over here. I fancy a big slice of Victoria sponge.'

I hoped I could eat cake. My stomach was still not as strong as it should be, after my time in jail, and sometimes rich food made me feel nauseous.

'What about you?'

Joseph grinned at me again. 'Ooh the same, I think. And a nice pot of tea.'

As we waited for our order to arrive, we chatted about the weather, and Joseph told me about his brother's children – twin boys who were a handful by the sound of it. It was all so normal, so calm and ordinary, that I felt myself relaxing and the knots in my stomach that had been there since Father died becoming less tight.

'I'd love for you to meet the kids,' Joseph said, beaming at me. 'I think they'd love you.'

'I'd like that too.'

He reached across the table and took my hand, and I froze, unsure how to react.

'Esther, I think you're marvellous,' he said. 'And I think it was fate that threw you in front of me that day.'

I chuckled. 'It was an uneven paving slab.'

'Oi! I'm trying to be romantic here.'

He stroked the back of my hand gently and my stomach twisted with a strange kind of hunger. I liked the way he was touching me. I wanted him to touch me more. I stared at him, not sure what I should say in case I said something wrong.

'I was trying to say that I know we've only just met, but I feel like we've known each other for years,' Joseph went on.

'I feel the same,' I managed to stutter. My voice sounded odd.

'Do you think I could persuade you to be my girl?' he said. 'Official, like?'

I couldn't be his girl. How on earth would that work? How could he introduce me to his friends at the police station? How could I bring him to meet Agnes and the WSPU? It was like we were Montagues and Capulets. And yet, I was smiling so broadly, I thought my cheeks would split.

'I would like that very much,' I found myself saying.

The waitress put our food down in front of us and Joseph let go of my hand. My fingers felt cold where he was no longer touching them.

In the end, I didn't find out if I could stomach the cake because my appetite had deserted me. All I could think about was Joseph, and the way his hand had felt on mine, and how his hands might feel on other parts of me. I was shocked at the way my mind was going, but I thought he was feeling the same because I felt his leg press up against mine under the table.

'I could walk you home?' he said, as we paid for our tea and left a sixpence under the plate for a tip for the waitress.

I shook my head vigorously.

'Too far,' I said. 'But to the bus stop, perhaps?'

He took my hand and we walked together, our bodies touching, back towards the police station where we'd met. But as we passed a small alleyway, Joseph ducked down it and pulled me with him.

'Joseph,' I said, laughing but also slightly nervous. 'What are you doing?'

He turned so he was facing me and gathered me into his arms.

'I'm doing this,' he said. He bent his head down and kissed my lips, softly at first then with more pressure.

I leaned back against the wall of the alley, light-headed and weak-legged with longing. So, this was what all the fuss was about? I thought. Finally I understood.

Joseph kissed my neck and I almost fainted with the sensation it gave me. My cheeks were hot.

'Esther Whitehouse,' he whispered into my ear, his breath ragged against my skin. I felt a twinge of guilt about him using my false name but I pushed it away as Joseph kissed me again. 'I believe I could fall in love with you,' he said.

Chapter 19

Esther

I felt as though I was walking on air all the way home. I almost wanted to dance as I hurried back to Agnes's house, because I was filled with such happiness I thought it might burst out of me at any time.

'Good afternoon,' I sang to people I passed. 'Hello, what a lovely day.'

As I approached home, practically skipping across the road, a hand grabbed my arm.

'Look at your grin,' Minnie said to me, peering at my face with something akin to suspicion. 'What are you looking so happy about?'

I tried to look aloof and mysterious but I couldn't help letting out a little bubble of laughter. Minnie gasped.

'Is it him? Your bloke? What's he done?'

Feeling like a giddy schoolgirl, which frankly was a welcome change from the last few months of feeling like a decrepit, world-weary criminal, I flung my arms round Minnie and squealed.

'He asked me to be his girl, officially,' I said.

'Did you say yes?'

'Of course, I did. He's perfect.'

Minnie squeezed me tightly. 'I'm coming to see Agnes. Let's walk and you can tell me everything.'

Arm in arm, we strolled along the street at a snail's pace, Minnie firing questions at me.

'What does he look like?'

'Strong,' I said in glee. 'Tall, broad shoulders . . .'

Minnie groaned in delight. 'Hair colour?'

'Sort of dark blond. Freckles. Blue eyes.'

'Your children will be so lovely.'

'Minnie,' I protested, but not too much. I'd already daydreamed about our future children, hoping they would inherit Joseph's looks and not my mousy hair and sludgy green eyes.

'I'm madly envious,' Minnie was saying. 'Who've I got wooing me? Just Gloomy Gilbert from the shop, who sees the bad side in everyone and everything.'

Poor Minnie was being romanced by one of the assistants in the shop where she worked. She said he had a way of seeing the world as a cross he had to bear and she had resisted his advances. But I secretly thought she talked about him a lot considering she wasn't interested in spending time with him.

'Joseph might have a friend who'd suit you,' I said as we climbed the steps to Agnes's front door. 'Someone just as strong and handsome as he is.'

Minnie clutched the doorframe dramatically. 'But what would Gloomy Gilbert think?' she gasped.

We were both giggling as John opened the door. He frowned at us with the sort of disapproval only a ten-year-old boy could provide.

'Mother was wondering where you'd got to,' he said. 'But I heard you coming along the street.'

'Were we too loud?' I teased, ruffling his hair as I went past. 'I know a boy who can be very noisy when he wants to be.'

John ducked away from my hand, making a pretend fierce face at me. 'I'll tell Mother you're here.'

'She can probably hear us,' said Minnie, and we both laughed some more.

Agnes appeared in the hall. 'Girls, I need you to take some leaflets,' she said, looking at us curiously. 'Are you up to mischief?'

I smiled. 'Not at all,' I said. 'Just letting off some steam. I'll take my coat upstairs and be with you in a minute.'

Winking at me over her shoulder, Minnie followed Agnes into the front room. I hugged my coat to me as I went up to my room, feeling like a new woman. I had more energy and vim than I'd had since long before I went to jail. Since before my father died, really. I had friends, and a family of sorts, and now I had Joseph. Things were good.

In the lounge, there was a hubbub of activity as Agnes co-ordinated the distribution of leaflets advertising a WSPU meeting at Caxton Hall. Minnie was looking sulky.

'I thought we weren't doing much now?' she said. 'Because of the bill.'

Agnes slapped her on the behind with a pile of papers.

'The fight is not won until it's won,' she said. 'I don't trust that slippery Mr Asquith as far as I can throw him.'

I grinned at her description of our prime minister, who was not a supporter of our efforts.

'We may have called a halt – a temporary halt – to our militant activities, but that does not mean we are staying quiet,' Agnes said, gesturing wildly with her hands. 'We are close, but not there yet. We must keep up the pressure.'

'Give them here, then,' I said, holding out my hands for a pile of leaflets. 'What are we doing?'

'Simply spreading the word, darling,' said Agnes. 'Spreading the word. Mrs P needs us to leaflet south of the river. She's keen to have a good turn-out at the meetings over the summer so everyone remembers we're still here.'

I nodded. South of the river was fine by me – I was happy as long as I didn't have to go east, towards Whitechapel where I could risk seeing Joseph.

I began sorting the leaflets into manageable piles, for women to take out, and tying the bundles with string, humming a little tune to myself as I did. This was a world away from the activities we'd done before. Breaking windows, like I'd done and been arrested for, or shouting at politicians, or causing trouble in all sorts of ways. It was calm. Nice. And, I couldn't help thinking, something the police could not object to.

If the bill was passed and some women were given the vote, as they were saying could happen, then maybe Joseph and I could be together. It might take a bit of persuasion for Minnie and the others to accept him. And no doubt my prison record could cause trouble with his friends. But perhaps they didn't need to know about that. A little voice at the back of my mind told me I'd already lied to him. I'd already given him a fake name. But I ignored that, drowning out the objections with memories of Joseph's kisses.

After a short while I realised Agnes and Minnie were both staring at me, nudging each other.

'What on earth has happened to her?' Agnes was saying, watching me work. 'Why is she so jolly?'

'Tell Agnes why you're so jolly, Esther,' Minnie said.

I felt my cheeks redden and Agnes pointed at me triumphantly.

'Is it the chap you met in the street?' she said. 'I knew something was going on there.'

'We met for tea and cake,' I admitted.

'And?'

'And I like him.'

Agnes clapped her hands. 'How gorgeous,' she said.

'He asked her to be his girl,' Minnie told her. 'Officially.'

Agnes raised her eyebrows at me. 'Do I hear wedding bells?'

'Oh stop,' I said, squirming in their attention, but laughing all the same. 'Stop it.'

'Is he sympathetic to the cause?' Agnes asked.

I reddened even more. 'I'm not sure exactly,' I spluttered.

'Have you talked about the WSPU?' Agnes was strident in her

support of we suffragettes and brought up the subject at any given opportunity. Minnie did too. We all did, because we believed so passionately in our cause. I was the same. Most of the time.

I froze, looking from one of them to the other. 'We mostly talked about other things,' I said quietly. 'About his family.'

'Did you tell him you were in Holloway?' Minnie said, all pretence of leaflet-sorting abandoned. 'What did he say? Was he impressed? Even Gloomy Gilbert showed a bit of emotion when he found out I'd been inside.'

I smiled, despite myself. 'You told him?'

'Thought it might put him off me,' she said, rolling her eyes. 'Fat bloody chance; He was actually rather impressed.'

Agnes prodded me and I jumped.

'Don't change the subject, Esther,' she scolded. 'I don't want to hear about Gloomy Gilbert, I want to hear about your chap. Your . . .?'

'Joseph,' I said, my grin broadening. 'He's called Joseph Fairbanks.'

'What does he do?'

I blinked at her. What should I say? Telling them he was a policeman wouldn't go down well, not if I just blurted it out. I needed to think about how to tell them. Outside the back of the house, I heard a train rattle by and breathed in relief. 'He works on the railway,' I lied hurriedly.

Agnes frowned. 'Not an engine driver?' She may have been a fervent supporter of women's votes, but she could still be a bit of a snob, my employer.

I shook my head. 'In an office,' I said. 'Not sure what he does exactly.'

'Pen pusher,' Minnie said in disdain, then she brightened up. 'Good prospects, though. To see you right.'

'I earn my own money,' I said, feeling prickly all of a sudden. 'Just as you do. We don't need Gilbert or Joseph to look after us.'

Agnes nodded her agreement. 'Well said, Esther.'

I turned my attention back to the leaflets.

'When can we meet him?' Minnie said. 'Your Joseph?'

I neatened a pile, not looking up. 'Meet Joseph?' I said. 'Oh, I'm not sure yet. It's still early days. Don't want to frighten him off.'

Agnes put her hand on top of the leaflets I was fiddling with and I looked up and met her gaze.

'We don't know this man,' she pointed out. 'It's not like when I was courting my John. I'd known him for years because my mother was friends with his mother. This Joseph may be handsome and charming but none of us know him from Adam.'

I opened my mouth to speak and assure her that Joseph was a fine, upstanding citizen, but she shushed me.

'Just be very careful, is all I'm saying, Esther,' she said. 'Tread carefully, because you know nothing about him yet.'

I nodded. 'I will,' I said. 'I promise.'

But, I thought, as I tied a loop of string round my pile. The real problem wasn't that I knew nothing about Joseph, it was rather that he knew nothing about me.

Chapter 20

Lizzie

2019

'How's your hand?' Danny asked me. We'd moved on to the sofa at some point, I wasn't completely sure when, but we'd not progressed past kissing, which was something of a relief, actually. I wasn't sure I was ready for anything more. Not yet.

'Is it still painful?'

The moment broken, I looked down at my hand in slight confusion. I'd actually forgotten about my burn.

'Much better,' I said. I shifted on the sofa awkwardly, suddenly feeling embarrassed to have been snogging like a teenager. Danny did the same, obviously having the same sense of being caught doing something naughty.

'Danny,' I began, just as he said: 'Lizzie.'

We both laughed.

'You first,' he said.

'No, you go first.'

We smiled at each other and Danny gently ran a finger down the side of my face. 'I like you, Lizzie,' he said. 'I think we could have something here.'

'But?'

He raised an eyebrow. 'There's a but?'

'Sounds like it,' I said. 'And, I think I have one too.'

'Cara is my but.'

I nodded.

'She has to come first,' Danny said. 'Lord knows I spent long enough not putting her – or her mother – first. I can't make the same mistake over and over.'

Once again I thought how badly Sophie seemed to have misjudged him. It made me like him even more.

'And there's work, which is . . .' He paused. 'A bit shit at the moment.'

I understand,' I said, though I wasn't sure I did. Was he saying this couldn't happen, even though he was the one who'd asked me out?

'What's yours?'

'Pardon?'

'Your but.'

I took a breath. 'I am still bruised from my divorce,' I said. 'Wounded. I need time. Not a lot,' I added hurriedly. 'But time.'

Danny looked relieved, which was odd. 'I thought you were going to say you didn't want to see me at all.'

'Is that not what you were saying?'

'God, no. I just meant we need to take things slowly.'

I couldn't help smiling. 'Brilliant,' I said. 'I thought you were dumping me.'

Danny took my hand – the one that wasn't burned. 'We'll do this the old-fashioned way. Dinners, walks, lots of talking. Get to know each other properly.'

'Sounds perfect.'

He looked away from me for a second, then back into my eyes. 'You've got a lot on, with school,' he said. 'And like I say, work is complicated. And I've got Cara and believe me, that girl has a very busy social life. I'm forever dropping her at trampolining, or picking her up from parties. She's like a Kardashian.'

'I'm not sure the Kardashians do much trampolining.'

'Oh, they do,' Danny said, wisely. 'Trust me.'

I laughed. 'The life of a single dad, eh?'

'It's a good life,' he said. 'Most of the time.' He stood up and picked up his jacket. 'I should go.'

I stood too, and he kissed me gently on the lips.

'It's been great. Thanks for feeding me.'

'Thanks for taking me to the council. It was really helpful.'

I showed him to the door and watched him walk off down the street. The family who lived opposite me were all walking up their path to the front door, teenage son trailing behind. The mother looked over at me curiously and I gave her a cheery wave. Then, to stop the inevitable gossip, I called after Danny: 'Thanks for dropping off that stuff.'

He looked round at me and shrugged, and the teenage son opposite turned to stare at me, then winked. What a cheek. Glad that it was dark now, so no one could see my blushes, I scurried back inside and shut the door. What a day.

* * *

I was at school early on Tuesday morning, at my desk with the photocopies of Esther's letters and references spread out in front of me. I'd done some admin after Danny had gone, watched an old episode of *Friends* and gone to bed early, feeling absurdly content. Then I'd woken up at the crack of dawn, full of energy. It seemed old-fashioned romance was good for me. I'd decided to use my time to have a think about what we could do with the information I'd uncovered the previous day.

'What were your aims for Elm Heath, Esther?' I asked her photograph. 'And where did you write them down?'

'She won't answer,' Paula said from my doorway. 'Believe me, I've spoken to her enough times over the years.'

I chuckled. 'Morning. You're here early?'

'I wanted to see how you got on yesterday.'

I thought of Danny and me on the sofa, and flushed. 'Yesterday?'

'At the council?'

'Oh, of course. The council.' I looked down at the papers in front of me. 'Come and see.'

I talked Paula through everything I'd found, showing her the plans for the original school building, the references and the letter from the authority giving her the permission to open Elm Heath.

'These are wonderful, you're so clever to have found them,' she said, her eyes gleaming with interest.

'It was Danny really,' I pointed out, eager to give him the credit I thought he deserved.

Paula shrugged. 'You did the hard work.' She picked up the letter from the authority.

'Where's the letter this is replying to?'

'Ah,' I said.

'Ah?'

'It wasn't there.'

Paula's shoulders slumped. 'Really? But that's the bit that would be most useful to us.'

'I know,' I wailed. 'The bit where she spells out her aims so brilliantly that it makes the council forget about her having been in prison, and hand over the cash to build the school.'

'If we had that, we could do a whole thing about our aims now and how they compare. Do a whole project on schooling now versus schooling then,' Paula said.

'I know it would be easier if we had the letter, but we could still do something along those lines,' I said. 'It might show the special historical interest we need.'

Paula clapped her hands. 'And prove how long Elm Heath has been important to the community.'

Struck by her enthusiasm, I started writing down what she said, scribbling as she spoke.

'We could get the kids to dress up and have a whole day of school like in the early 1900s,' she said. 'I bet the local papers would cover it.' Paula sorted through the papers on my desk until she found the old photos.

'Could we track down former pupils?' I asked.

'Well not those ones I don't imagine, because if they were five in 1912, they'd be well over one hundred now.' She chuckled.

'No, I suppose not. Maybe as far back as we can, though?'

'Worth a go.'

My spirits were lifted – slightly. Perhaps we had a chance here.

Emma, who'd come into the office without me noticing, stuck her head round my door.

'Denise Deacon from Blyton Council is on the phone for you,' she said. 'Shall I put her through?'

Straight away my spirits crashed into my boots again. 'Put her through,' I said.

Paula made to get up, but I stopped her.

'I'll tell you everything anyway,' I said, as my phone started ringing. 'May as well hear it all first hand.'

I picked up my phone and braced myself for bad news. I wasn't wrong.

'I wanted to tell you myself,' said Denise. 'That they've set a date for the education committee meeting where the decision is going to be made about the future of Elm Heath Primary.'

'When?'

'March 22nd.'

'That's really not long.' We were already into November and March seemed just round the corner.

'It's the latest we can leave it if we want to find the children other school places for September.'

'You won't need to find them other places, if Elm Heath stays open,' I growled, annoyed that it seemed to be a fait accompli.

'Of course,' she said mildly.

'Can I speak at the meeting? Put our case across?'

'If you want to.'

Obviously I wanted to. With great effort I managed not to growl again. 'Please,' I said.

'Then I'll make sure it's on the agenda.'

Through gritted teeth I said polite goodbyes, and then hung up.

Paula gazed at me, her eyes worried. 'It's official, then?'

'The education committee are meeting on March 22nd to make the final decision.'

'That's only a few months away,' Paula said in despair.

'Danny said that normally these decisions are made long before they're given the nod officially,' I said bitterly. 'And the way she mentioned finding alternative places for our kids really made it seem that way.'

'I'm going to ring Chris and see if he knows anything,' Paula said. Chris wasn't in property – he had his own accountancy firm in Blyton – but he seemed to know all of the important people locally and kept his ear to the ground.

She got up, but was stopped as Nate appeared at my office door, his hair dishevelled.

'Is it true?' he said.

'I'm not sure. Is what true?'

Nate glanced over his shoulder at Emma, edged his way inside my office and shut the door behind him.

'Marc just called me. Apparently, there's a council-approved developer drawing up plans for the site of the school. They want to convert the building into flats and they've asked Marc's firm to pitch for the contract.' He glared at me. 'Is that it, then? Are we closing?'

'No,' I said. 'Maybe. Hopefully not.'

Nate gave me a withering look. 'Sounds to me like the deal has been done.'

Chapter 21

Lizzie

The depth of my fury surprised me. After all, I'd only been at Elm Heath a couple of months and I hadn't been planning to hang around once I got myself back on track. But I felt part of something here now, and to hear that plans were already being drawn up to convert this beautiful school building into flats made my blood boil. I stood up and glared at Nate, who took a step backwards, flattening himself against the wall.

'What did you say?'

'I said the deal has been done,' he stuttered, his face reddening.

'No way,' I said. 'No bloody way. This is all kinds of wrong.'

Heartened to see I was on his side, Nate came closer again. 'Marc's firm aren't pitching,' he said quietly. 'But that doesn't mean others won't be.'

I nodded, biting my lip, my mind racing.

'I'm guessing at this meeting in March, they will look at all the options,' I said. 'That'll be why developers are seeing what they can do with the site. I expect they will present what they can do with the building, and we can speak about the school and the councillors will weigh up what's best.'

Paula's shoulders slumped. 'Then we're stuffed. We can't compete with money like that.'

I shook my head. 'No, we can't.'

But Nate wasn't giving up. 'Bollocks,' he said. 'Sorry.'

I managed a small smile.

'We can't compete financially but we can compete in other ways,' he said. 'We need to win hearts and minds.'

I blinked at him. 'How do we do that?'

'We need a proper campaign, with banners and marching and publicity.'

A little spark of interest grabbed me. 'Like the suffragettes,' I said.

'Erm, yes, I suppose so. No chaining ourselves to railings though.'

I waved my hand. 'They did loads of other stuff.' I was beginning to feel hopeful again. 'They were all about taking action. Obviously, I'm not saying break windows or that sort of thing, but we can definitely march, and wave banners.'

Nate nodded. 'Spread the word. Make everyone realise what we're up against.'

'Exactly.'

Paula squeezed my arm. 'This could be it,' she said. 'We can run a campaign inspired by the suffragettes to save the school that was founded by a suffragette.'

I clapped my hands. 'Brilliant.'

Nate looked relieved. 'So, we're going to fight this? It's just now we've got Leia, I can't risk losing my job.'

'I promise you we're going to fight,' I said.

'You need to tell everyone else.'

'I agree. Could you ask everyone to come to a very quick staff meeting after school?'

Nate agreed and headed off to his classroom, while Paula and I breathed a sigh of relief.

'Do you think we can do this?' she asked.

I shrugged. 'No idea,' I admitted. 'But I know we have to try. I think we owe it to Esther. She went to prison because she fought for what she believed in. We can wave a few banners.'

'So where do we start?'

'That I don't know.'

The school bell rang loudly in the outer office, making us both jump.

'Look,' I said. 'I'll take everything home this evening – all the stuff I found at the council offices, the admission data, everything – and see if I can come up with some sort of a plan. And maybe some of the others could have some good ideas, too.'

Paula nodded. 'I'd better get to my classroom,' she said. 'I'm glad you're here, Lizzie.'

'I'm glad I'm here too,' I said, realising, much to my surprise, that I meant it.

* * *

The staff meeting was difficult, especially when Emma burst into tears and didn't stop crying, but it was also encouraging. Nate boosted everyone's spirits, telling them he was determined to save the school so his little girl could come here one day, and I promised to fight as hard as I could.

'I'm going to work on a plan this evening,' I said. 'So if you come up with any ideas, message me, or call me, and I'll make sure everything's included.'

'Can you use your contacts?' Pippa said.

'Contacts?'

Celeste was perched on the arm of a sofa in the outer office, next to Pippa. Now they exchanged a glance that told me they'd discussed this already.

'You were kind of a celebrity teacher, weren't you? I saw you in the TES and whatnot.'

'Well, my husband was. My ex-husband.'

'But you knew people? People knew you. You've got a name.'

'I suppose . . .' I said warily.

She glanced at Pippa again.

'We think he owes you,' Pippa said. 'Your ex.'

'I beg your pardon?'

'He basically screwed everything up for you, left you without a job and with your reputation shot to pieces,' she said. I winced at the words, but she was right. 'And then got himself some high-flying consultancy role, right?'

I nodded.

'So we reckon he owes you.'

'He certainly does,' I snorted. 'But I'm not sure what that has to do with our campaign?'

'Get him involved,' Celeste said.

'But on the quiet,' Pippa added. 'I don't mean ask him to front the campaign or anything, because let's face it, he was a bit dodgy.'

'It's not as easy as that,' I said.

'It is.' Pippa looked earnest. 'He must know all sorts of people. Journalists, TV presenters, politicians. Get him to get in touch with them.'

Paula sat up straighter. 'Would you contact him?'

I bit my lip. 'Oh, Paula, I'm not sure . . .'

'Maybe you don't need to,' she said, thoughtfully. 'Maybe your name is enough. People will be interested to know what you're doing now.'

'You think?'

'Perhaps.' She didn't sound totally convinced, and I thought she was probably right. Grant was the one who knew people and he was the one who'd had the clout.

I chewed my lip. 'Let me think about it,' I said. I supposed they weren't wrong. Grant did owe me. And more importantly, I owed the kids. Perhaps it wasn't these children that I'd let down, but I still wanted to make amends. This might be the way to do it. 'Maybe when we've got a proper plan we can work out what publicity we need and I'll see what I can do.'

Pippa and Celeste nodded at each other.

But if the idea of going back to my old life was unwelcome, it was the coming up with a plan that had me really stumped.

Later that evening, I sat in front of the television, staring at my laptop, at the pictures of Esther as a suffragette, at the letters and references I'd found, and managed to come up with . . . precisely nothing.

A march was brilliant when it filled the streets of London, but I couldn't imagine a few teachers and a handful of kids could attract too much attention. And we could make as many banners as we wanted, but what would we do with them?

I ran my fingers through my hair in despair. Where should I start?

On the television they were showing a trailer for next week's episode of *Where Did You Come From?* featuring the breakfast presenter Sarah Sanderson. It gave me an idea. Claire at the council had recommended finding Agnes Oliver's family, or the family of the stuffed shirt Constable Fairbanks.

Maybe that was the best place to begin – if they could tell me any more about Esther's story, it might inspire me to come up with a campaign.

My phone beeped with a message. It was Nate.

'How about a rally on the village green?' he wrote. 'We could have banners, and speakers, and street food, and make it fun.'

'It's winter,' I wrote back.

'We'll get marquees.'

I sent him an emoji with dollar signs for eyes and he answered: 'It's fine. My dad knows someone who owes him a favour.'

I chuckled to myself. Village life really was easier in some ways.

'I'm adding it to the list,' I replied. Nate sent me a thumbs-up emoji.

I pulled my laptop closer to me and typed "genealogy" into the search bar, quite impressed that I spelled it right first time. It brought up a few options and I clicked on familyhistory.com, which was right at the top.

Tutting a tiny bit at the price for a subscription, I typed in my details and paid, and then logged in. I'd watched enough episodes of *Where Did You Come From?* to know people hunting for ancestors always started with a census, so I looked at the list of census years, chose 1911, and typed in Esther Watkins. There were no results. Strange. I tried Agnes Oliver. Again, nothing. Very odd.

I pulled out the copy of Agnes's reference, which named her husband as John, and tried him instead. Immediately it brought up an address in Kennington, London, which to my absolute delight matched the address on the letter.

Her husband John was listed as a banker with three children, another John, who was eleven, Margaret, who was nine, and Pearl, who was eight.

'Oh man, did Agnes die?' I muttered to myself, checking the date on the reference. Nope, she'd written that after April 1911. Strange.

Undeterred, I realised I now had the names of all her children, so I could track them down. I did a tiny fist bump and started typing.

Just an hour later, I'd found Agnes's granddaughter, who'd been born in 1928 to Margaret, and her great-granddaughter, born in 1955. The great-granddaughter's name was Fiona Willoughby and she was only a couple of years older than my own mum. I wondered if I had any suffragettes in my family tree and resolved to look up my ancestors when I had time.

A quick cup of tea, a chocolate hobnob and a bit more googling later, and I'd tracked Fiona down on Facebook.

'Boom,' I said, slightly stunned at how easy it was to find someone nowadays.

I picked up my phone and rang Paula. 'I've found Agnes's family,' I said.

'Already?' She sounded impressed.

'Her great-granddaughter is on Facebook; shall I message her?'

'Definitely. Do it now.'

'What shall I say?'

Paula thought for a moment. 'Explain who you are and why we need her help, and ask if we can meet up?'

I tried to balance the phone on my shoulder so I could type, then gave up and put Paula on speaker instead.

'My name is Lizzie Armstrong and I'm the head teacher at Elm Heath Primary,' I typed, saying the words out loud as I wrote. 'Our school is under threat of closure and we're trying to find out more about our founder, Esther Watkins, as part of our campaign to save it.'

'Nice,' said Paula approvingly.

'Your great-grandmother Agnes Oliver gave Esther a reference when she opened the school and we wondered if you can add any more to the story?'

'Perfect.'

I added my contact details to the bottom and pressed send. 'It's gone,' I told Paula.

'Well done,' she said. 'Let's hope it helps.'

Chapter 22

Esther

1910

We were leafletting in Camberwell the next afternoon, so I had the morning to myself. Agnes had taken the girls to their dancing class, while the two Johns – old and young – read the newspaper in the front room. I loved how young John mimicked his father and looked up to him. The older John was a good role model, I thought. Unlike my own father.

Because the sun was out and there was a strong breeze, I decided to strip my bed linen and wash it. But as I was shaking out a sheet in the back garden, I saw Joseph walk past – his head bobbing above the garden hedge. Worried he was going to spot me and realise which house I lived in, leading – no doubt – to him calling round whenever he wanted, I ducked behind the sheet that was billowing on the line, and edged back into the house. Then without even pausing to take my hat from the hook, I pulled on a shawl.

'I'm going for a walk in the park,' I called to the Johns.

Knowing Joseph could see me come out of the front door, I went out the back door, through the side gate and round on to the main road the long way. Just in case he was watching out for me.

Then I crossed the road to the park and found him by the duck pond.

'Esther,' he said with genuine pleasure when I approached. 'I found myself with nothing to do this morning so I decided to see if I could find you.'

'Then I found you,' I said, unable to keep the smile from my face. My efforts to keep Joseph away from my other life may have seemed ridiculous to the outside eye – not that there were any outside eyes – but I honestly felt they were worth it. The way my heart lifted when I saw him proved to me that I was right to do what I was doing.

'As I got to Kennington, I realised I didn't know where you live,' he said, rolling his eyes at his own stupidity.

Deliberately misunderstanding his leading question, I looped my arm through his. 'I'm here now,' I said. 'Shall we go for a walk? What an absolutely glorious day.'

We strolled round the duck pond, hand in hand, chatting about everything and nothing.

'I've no duties this morning,' I told him. 'The girls are dancing and John is being terribly grown up and reading the newspaper with his father.'

'What are you doing for the rest of the day?' he asked.

'Working.' It wasn't a complete lie, I thought. It was sort of work. 'I have some jobs to do for Agnes.'

He made a face. 'Me too. This evening, at least. I'm working overnight.'

'Are there lots more crimes during the night?'

He thought about it. 'Not always more crimes, but definitely different crimes.'

'Daring night-time bank raids, and grave robbing?' I joked.

He frowned. 'More like murders.'

I winced. I didn't remember the Whitechapel murders of course, but I knew the shadow they cast across that part of London was long.

'What about daytime crimes?' I asked hurriedly and then regretted it immediately as he frowned again.

'Theft,' he said. 'Lots of thefts.'

I nodded. I'd heard about the hardship of life in the East End from Mrs Pankhurst's daughter, Sylvia.

'Desperate people stealing to survive.'

He snorted. 'Sometimes, not always.'

Sensing we were on dangerous ground, I pointed out a mother duck with a trail of ducklings following after. 'Sweet.'

He smiled down at me and I sighed inwardly in relief.

'Joseph?'

A call from behind us made us turn round. Coming along the path was a constable in full uniform, beaming with pleasure at us.

'Joseph Fairbanks!' he shouted as he got closer.

'Alf Simpson!'

He and Joseph slapped each other on the back in a noisy, vigorous fashion.

'How have you been?' Joseph said. 'It's been ages.' He turned to me. 'Alf and I trained together,' he explained. 'But he was sent over to west London – Acton was it?'

Alf nodded. 'But I've been promoted,' he said, puffing his chest up with pride. 'Sergeant Simpson from Kennington Police Station at your service.'

'So, you'll be taking care of my girl,' Joseph said proudly. 'This is Esther Whitehouse.'

I wished I'd brought my hat so I could hide my face under it, but it was too late now. Keeping my eyes lowered, I shook Alf's outstretched hand. This was getting rather complicated and I didn't want to come across Alf at a march or a rally and have him recognise me. Imagine how awkward that would be for poor Joseph?

'Pleased to meet you,' I said.

'You're local, are you?'

I waved my hand vaguely in the direction of the main road. 'Close to Royal Road,' I said. I actually lived on Kennington Terrace, a few streets along, but I didn't want to give too much away.

'Joseph,' I said, tugging his hand. 'I have to be going. Agnes will need me to help with the children.'

'Really?' he said, disappointed.

'I'm afraid so.' I stood on tiptoes and kissed him gently on the cheek.

'Maybe we could meet tomorrow?'

He nodded. 'Late afternoon? At the tearoom on Camberwell New Road?'

I shook my head. 'No, don't come here, you'll be tired if you've worked all night. I'll come to Whitechapel. Same tearoom as before.'

He looked at Alf, pride in his eyes. 'See how she cares for me?'

Alf nodded. 'You're a lucky man.'

I blew Joseph a kiss as I scurried away, hoping my path wouldn't cross with Alf's again. I did not want to become friendly with local police sergeants, no matter how much they flattered me.

'In trouble?'

As I emerged from the park, I saw Minnie, leaning against a tree, watching me through narrowed eyes.

I stopped and looked round me, guiltily. 'What?'

'Saw you talking to a copper,' she said. 'You and another fella. Was that your Joseph? I'd have come over but then that bobby appeared and I thought I was best over here, out of your way.'

I wasn't sure what to say. I knew I'd been rumbled. Minnie's eyes were sharp and her mind was quick and I didn't think I could concoct a convincing lie fast enough.

'So what did he want? The copper?'

'He was an old friend of Joseph's,' I said. 'They knew each other a long time ago. But Alf – that's the copper's name – moved to Acton and they'd not caught up for a while.'

Minnie nodded. 'Did he recognise you?'

'No,' I said, prickly at the thought. 'They don't have photographs of us pinned up in every police station, you know.'

'They might,' Minnie said.

'There are too many of us, for a start.'

'Whatever you say.'

'We should go,' I said, hurrying along the pavement and hoping she'd follow. 'Agnes needs us to take the leaflets down to Camberwell.'

'Your Joseph going to help?'

'NO,' I said vehemently, and then caught myself. 'He's working tonight.'

'Overnight?'

I realised my mistake but I couldn't go back now.

'He works shifts.'

Minnie looked at me, thoughtfully. 'What did you say he does? Your Joseph?'

What had I said? 'Railways,' I muttered. 'Something on the railway.'

'Hmm.'

She took my hand and pulled me round so I was facing her.

'Esther, is your Joseph in the police?'

I wanted to lie, but I crumbled in the face of her piercing stare. 'Yes,' I admitted. 'He's a constable in Whitechapel.'

'Bloody hell, Esther.'

'I know,' I wailed. 'It's impossible. But I like him so much.'

Minnie steered me to a bench and pushed me down to sitting.

'This is lunacy,' she said. 'What on earth are you thinking?'

'I'm not thinking anything.'

'Obviously.'

'He's such a lovely bloke,' I said. 'I'm sure if I just told him, explained . . .'

Minnie groaned. 'Told him what exactly? That you've been inside? That you spend your weekends smashing windows and causing trouble?'

'It's over,' I protested weakly. 'We're finished with militant action. The bill will be passed in the autumn.'

'I'll believe it when I see it.'

'I thought if I could wait it out, keep quiet until then, it would all be all right,' I said. 'He's a good man, a clever man; he'll understand why we do what we do. I just don't want to make life difficult for him.'

Minnie shook her head. 'This is a war,' she said. 'You're an enemy sympathiser.'

'Oh for heaven's sake, Min, don't be so dramatic.'

But her face was stony. 'Remember the meeting the other day?' she said. 'With the rats?'

I shuddered. How could I forget?

'You heard the talk that it was coppers that released the rats into the room.'

'No,' I said. 'That's not true.' But as I said it, I remembered seeing the two policemen laughing at the women fleeing from the meeting, skirts hitched high. Was it true?

'They hate us,' Minnie said. 'And we hate them. There is no middle ground.'

'Well not now, but in a few months, perhaps?'

She shrugged. 'You really believe that?'

I slumped against the cold metal back of the bench, suddenly feeling utterly despairing. 'Yes,' I said. 'No. I just know that I like him, Minnie. He's funny and kind, and he makes me laugh and God knows I could do with a laugh every now and then. And he makes my chest swell, and my heart sing, and my head spin. I want to be with him – even though he's a copper – and he wants to be with me.'

'He don't know, though, that you're a suffragette?'

'No,' I admitted.

'Going to tell him?'

'No.'

'Going to tell Agnes and the others that your fella is a copper?'

'No.' I looked at her. 'Are you?'

Her steely glare softened. 'No,' she said. 'No, that's down to you, Esther.'

I nodded. 'I'll work out a way,' I said. 'It's going to be all right, I know it is.'

Minnie looked at a spot over my head and gave the tiniest of nods. 'If you say so,' she said. 'I just hope you're right.'

Chapter 23

Esther

I didn't get a chance to talk to Minnie about Joseph again, because we were kept busy gathering our leaflets and heading down to Camberwell. Agnes was coming with us, so we couldn't chat about anything other than WSPU business.

'You know the drill, girls,' she said, as shared out the bundles of leaflets. 'We're heading to the market at the bottom of Camberwell New Road. Stay together, hand out leaflets, we shouldn't have any trouble.'

She stood up, but staggered a little as she did so and sat down again quickly, hand to her forehead.

I rushed to her side, concerned. 'Agnes? Are you ill?'

She had a greenish tinge to her skin as she looked at me. 'I have just come over a little queasy,' she said.

'Minnie, could you fetch Agnes a glass of water?'

Minnie scurried off to the kitchen and I sat down on the arm of the settee where Agnes was and looked at her, sternly.

'Have you eaten properly today?'

She nodded. 'I'm fine, honestly. Maybe just tired.'

I frowned and she sighed. 'I think I'm pregnant,' she said. 'Again.'

'That's lovely news.'

She scowled at me. 'It will be lovely eventually. I suppose it will be lovely. But it always knocks me off at first.'

I patted her hand. 'Go upstairs and rest. Minnie and I can do the leaflets.'

'Really?'

'Of course.'

She looked as though she was going to argue, then changed her mind.

'You'll be all right?'

'You said yourself that there was nothing difficult about it. It's only leaflets.'

She nodded. 'Go on then.' She stood up, steadying herself with a hand on my shoulder and made for the door, taking the glass of water from Minnie who'd brought it as asked. 'Please don't mention anything to John yet.'

'My lips are sealed.'

She plodded off upstairs and I felt sorry for her. She obviously didn't think another baby was the blessing I thought it was. Still, she had me to help, and Meg was of an age now where she'd be more than happy to lend a hand. It would be fine.

'Come on then, if we're going.' Minnie gave me a shove and I wobbled off the arm of the settee, laughing.

'Let's go.'

We picked up our leaflets, and hoisted on our sandwich boards with the details of the meeting on them and slowly walked down Camberwell New Road towards the market. There would be lots of women there, buying supplies, and it was a good place to spread the word.

It was a warm day, and our sandwich boards were heavy so it took a while to walk there, but once we arrived we found a good spot close to the fruit and veg stall. We took off our boards and propped them up on the pavement for everyone to see.

'Votes for women!' we called as we handed out leaflets. 'Come to the meeting in Caxton Hall.'

'What's the bloody point?' one woman muttered as she hurried past. 'It's not for the likes of us.'

'It's for everyone,' I called after her hunched back. 'It's for all of us.'

'You'd do better if you stuck to the law,' a man shouted from near the fruit and veg stand.

Minnie narrowed her eyes. 'Laws mean nothing to me, because I'm not allowed to make them.'

'Yeah? Well you'll soon find out they mean something when they chuck you in Holloway.'

She gave him an impish smile and pointed to the badge on her lapel. 'Been there,' she said. She put her fists up, like a boxer. 'It's where I learned to fight.'

The crowd jeered, half supporting Minnie, half against her.

'Leave it, Min,' I said. I turned away to hand a leaflet to a woman walking by. Suddenly something hit me – splat – on the side of the face. I put my hand up and felt oozy rotten tomato running down my cheek.

'What?' I said, turning back as another tomato hit me square in the chest, leaving a large red stain on the front of my dress.

'That shut you up,' the man said in delight. He picked up another tomato from a box on the floor and threw it. This time it hit Minnie smack in the face, dripping down into her eyes.

'You sod,' she shouted, scraping it off and trying to throw it back.

And then suddenly, we were being pelted by all sorts of rotten fruit and veg. A potato hit me hard at the side of my eye and the oozy tomato stench was joined with the metallic smell of my blood as it trickled down my face. Minnie was whacked with stinking cabbage leaves, and then more tomatoes.

A woman – a bloody woman – threw mouldy strawberries at me, the juice stinging the cut by my eye.

'Stop that,' I shouted, grabbing the punnet from her and throwing the whole lot in her face. Behind me, someone pulled my hair, yanking my head back.

'Don't you treat my wife like that,' a man shouted. The woman smirked as he shoved a whole load of rotten berries into my face. I couldn't breathe as his big hand covered my nose and mouth and I kicked out, wriggling frantically to be free.

'Choke on this,' he said. Desperate I clamped my teeth into his finger and he reeled away, leaving me gasping for air.

'Minnie,' I panted, bent double as I caught my breath. 'We have to go.'

I looked up to see she was being pummelled by the man who'd started this. He was properly squaring up to her, fists raised, and her face was bruised already.

'Minnie,' I squeaked. I launched myself at the man, who'd just landed a punch on Minnie's purpling cheek, and I hung off his back, hitting him and trying to get him to stop.

'Stop it, you're hurting her, stop it,' I shrieked. 'Get off her.'

I heard police whistles and running feet and then hands pulled me off Minnie's attacker's back. I twisted and squirmed in their grip as they turned me round.

'Get off, let me go,' I said, furious that they'd got hold of me and not the man, who'd stopped hitting Minnie – thankfully – but who seemed to have disappeared. 'We're not the criminals here.'

'Calm down, Miss,' the policeman holding me said. 'No need to get hysterical.'

He yanked me round to face him and to my absolute horror, I recognised him. It was Joseph's friend Alf, from the park earlier. There was the tiniest moment when I thought he was going to recognise me, too, and I knew I couldn't possibly let that happen.

Minnie was to my right, breathing heavily, bleeding from her nose. I glanced at her. She was okay. We'd make it, I thought.

'Minnie?' I said.

She nodded. 'Esther.'

Breathing in deeply, I pulled my knee up and kicked Alf as hard as I could between his legs.

'RUN!' I bellowed and hitching up my skirt, I raced back towards the main road, hoping Minnie was following.

I could hear running behind me, and I glanced back to check it was Minnie. Thankfully it was. I could see Alf doubled over by the fruit and veg stall and felt a tiny glimmer of guilt – but not too much.

Minnie pulled my arm. 'Down here,' she said, ducking down an alley between two rows of houses.

I followed her along the passage, hearing distant shouts and whistles. 'They're coming,' I warned.

She shook her head. 'They won't know to look down here.'

'They might.'

She gave me one of her cheeky grins and pulled me faster along the narrow alleyway and out on to the next road, then quick as a flash she ducked into the front garden of the house on the corner and banged on the door.

'Minnie?' I was horrified at the noise, and the sheer brass neck of her. 'We can't just go into someone's house.'

'We can go into this one.'

The shouts were getting louder, and my heart was beating so hard I thought it might jump out of my chest.

Minnie knocked again and the door was flung open by a young man with a dour expression.

'Gilbert,' Minnie gasped. 'Can we come in?'

'In trouble again, Min?' he said, not sounding at all surprised.

'Not yet,' she said. 'But we will be if you don't let us in.'

To my utter relief, he stepped back and we both fell into the house, shutting the door firmly behind us.

I leaned against the front door, still breathing heavily, as Minnie threw her arms round Gloomy Gilbert, who looked pleased enough at the show of affection to make me wonder about the accuracy of his nickname.

'I thought we were toast,' she gasped. 'Gil, Esther kicked the constable in his you-know-whats.'

'Sergeant,' I said. 'He's a sergeant.'

'He's a poor sod is what he is,' said Gilbert, mildly.

But Minnie was looking at me, suspiciously. 'How do you know?'

'He's Joseph's friend – the one I met in the park earlier.'

'No!'

I nodded, feeling gloomier than Gilbert.

'Did he recognise you?'

'Not sure. Don't think so, but there's always a chance it'll come to him later, isn't there?'

Gilbert cleared his throat. 'I'm not completely sure what's going on here,' he said. 'In fact, I'm not sure I want to know. But I reckon we could all do with a cup of tea. Shall I put the kettle on?'

Chapter 24

Esther

Gilbert proved to be a surprisingly supportive ally. He poured the tea and listened as we told him what had happened. Then he gave us a bowl of warm water and flannels to wash off the rotten fruit juice.

'I'll clean up your cuts. Let me fetch the antiseptic.'

Ever so gently he cleaned the wound by my eye and then with a touch of tenderness, he bathed Minnie's cuts and bruises too.

'This makes me so angry,' he said as he dabbed at Min's grazed cheek. 'What bloody right has anyone to treat you like this? All you want is what you're due. Course women should have the vote. Of course.'

He shook his head at the ridiculousness of it all and I smiled. There were many men who supported us – Agnes's John for one – but it was always nice to meet another one. For the hundredth time I wondered if I should risk asking Joseph his opinion. Would he back our endeavours? I was afraid that if he didn't, it would be the end of the relationship we were developing.

'I'm going to see you home in the bus,' Gilbert went on. 'Because I'm not leaving you to be set upon again.'

'Oh Gilbert, there's no need . . .' I began but Minnie put her hand on mine and I stopped talking.

'Thank you,' she said.

He was as good as his word. He took us all the way to Agnes's house and waited until we were inside the front door, before he tipped his hat at us.

'Nice to meet you, Esther. See you at work tomorrow, Minnie,' he said and then he strolled off down the street in the direction of Camberwell.

'Well he is nothing like I expected,' I said in astonishment, staring at Minnie. She looked bashful.

'I think I might have made him sound worse than he is.'

'Girls!' Agnes came rushing out of the kitchen and wrapped her arms round us. 'Are you all right? Let me look at you. Where have you been? I've been so worried.'

'We're fine,' I said.

But she took one look at our faces and shrieked. 'What happened?'

She herded us into the living room and looked us over with an appraising eye.

'Someone cleaned you up?'

'Gloomy Gilbert,' Minnie said, with a hint of pride.

Agnes threw herself against the overstuffed back of the settee dramatically. 'Heavens above. I think you need to tell me everything.'

I began, telling her about the man shouting at Minnie, and her standing up for herself. And then the fruit and veg being thrown.

'It was all rotten,' I said, showing her the stains on my dress. 'It was horrible.'

'And painful,' Minnie added, gesturing to my eye, which was painful and puffy. 'Esther was hit with a potato.'

'Minnie was hit by a man,' I said. 'He gave her a right pummelling.'

Agnes reached over and took Minnie's chin in her fingers, carefully turning her face this way and that. 'Nasty,' she said. 'But it will heal.'

Minnie nodded, always the stoic.

'And did the police come?'

Ah. That was the question. Should we admit what had happened? While we were no strangers to militancy, the aim of the WSPU was always to damage property – not people. I wasn't sure how my attack on Alf would be received.

'I was sort of winded, with the bloke about to hit me again,' Minnie said, obviously seeing I wasn't about to talk. 'Esther, bless her, realised I was having a bad time, and she jumped at this fella. Hanging off his back like a monkey, she was. But then these coppers arrived and I was so relieved, because I thought we were in real trouble there and they'd help us.' She took a breath. 'But what they actually did was lift Esther off him and let him run off.'

'No,' said Agnes, shocked. 'They helped him and not you?'

'Exactly.'

'But they didn't arrest you?'

I exchanged a glance with Minnie and she gave me a tiny nod.

'I kicked him,' I muttered, staring at my shoes. 'I brought my knee up between his legs and while he was bent over, we legged it.'

There was a pause.

'You kicked a policeman?'

'A sergeant,' Minnie said proudly.

'I shouldn't have done it.'

Agnes nodded. 'You're right, you shouldn't have,' she said. Then she leaned over and squeezed my hand. 'But it sounds like you had absolutely no choice. If they could look at a man hitting a woman and side with the man, who knows what they would have done to you. Well done for being so brave, my darlings. I shall tell Mrs P how bold and daring you have been. She will be thrilled.'

'I thought she would be cross,' I said. 'She's so determined that we harm no one.'

'But you wouldn't have had to harm him, had he done his job right,' she said. 'He brought it upon himself.'

'I suppose.'

'And how does Gilbert fit into this story?' Agnes said, frowning. 'I thought he was your friend from the shop, Minnie?'

'He is,' she said. 'But he lives in Camberwell. When Esther ran I realised we were close to his house and I knew he'd help us.'

'What a good man he must be.'

'He is,' Minnie said. 'He didn't even hesitate when we turned up on his doorstep, battered and bleeding. He just let us in and patched us up.'

'How did you know where he lived?'

'I've been there a couple of times actually,' Minnie admitted. Was that a slight blush on her cheeks?

'Are you hungry? I can fetch some food for you.'

'I'm starving,' Minnie said. 'Bet Esther is too. We had some tea with Gilbert but nothing to eat. Lord, I really am hungry.'

Agnes hurried off to the kitchen and both Minnie and I breathed a sigh of relief.

'Sounds like we're off the hook with Mrs P, then,' she said.

I groaned. 'Now I just have to hope Alf didn't recognise me.'

'What are you going to do?'

I shook my head, at a loss. 'No idea,' I said. 'It will be so awkward for poor Joseph if word gets out that his girl is a suffragette.'

Minnie snorted. 'You think he'd still want to be your fella if he knew the truth?'

My stomach turned over. 'Yes,' I said, but my voice sounded uncertain to my own ears. 'He's such a kind man, Minnie. Clever and thoughtful. I'm sure he'd be on our side.'

Minnie made a face. 'Right. Why not ask him then? Why not tell him the truth?'

Why not indeed? Because I was frightened Minnie might be right, that was why. Wanting to move on, I forced a smile. 'So what's the story with you and Gilbert? I thought you weren't interested?'

Minnie gave me a shove. 'Don't change the subject,' she said. 'Gil and I are just mates, that's all. He's a miserable bugger but he's nice enough. I'm not all wide-eyed over him like you are with Joseph.'

I felt my heart plummet into my boots again as I imagined Alf announcing to a group of coppers that Joseph's new sweetheart was a violent suffragette, fresh out of Holloway.

I put my head in my hands. 'I don't know what to do,' I wailed. 'What if you're right? What if Joseph finds out who I really am and doesn't want anything more to do with me?'

'It would mean the end of his career in the police, if he stuck by you, I reckon.'

'For now,' I said, thinking. 'But I still think if I can keep it quiet until this bill goes through parliament then I'm home and dry.'

Minnie gave me a disbelieving look. 'I don't think Alf knew it was you,' she said. 'He only met you in the park, for a few minutes and I bet he didn't really pay too much attention to you. And don't forget, in Camberwell, you were wearing different clothes, your face was covered with rotten fruit, and he wouldn't have been expecting to see you. There's no reason to suppose he'd put two and two together.'

'Do you really think so?'

She nodded. 'I do. But, that doesn't mean this is over.'

'I know.'

'We don't know that the bill is going to happen, and even if it does, it won't be the end,' she said, telling me nothing I didn't already know.

I felt like I was going to cry, suddenly. It all seemed so hopeless.

Minnie took my hand. 'I hate to say this, Esther, but I think you're going to have to choose. The WSPU or Joseph. Because I don't think you're going to be able to have both.'

It was with real trepidation that I set off to meet Joseph the next day. There had been more than enough time for Alf to get in touch with him and reveal that I wasn't the girl he thought I was. I wished I shared Minnie's conviction that he wouldn't have recognised me.

'We all look the same to them,' she said with disdain. 'Stick a Votes for Women sash on and that's all they see.'

She had a point, but that didn't stop me approaching the tearoom with a slump to my shoulders and a tickling feeling at the back of my throat that warned tears weren't far away.

Joseph was there already, and the look of delight on his face when I walked in lifted my spirits slightly. He'd surely not seem so pleased if he knew?

He stood up as I got near the table and gripped my hands in his.

'Esther,' he said. 'You look lovely. Your hair is different. I like it.'

I'd arranged my hair to cover the cut to my brow but he'd obviously not noticed that bit. I almost swayed, because I was so light-headed with relief. He didn't know, my heart sang. He didn't know.

Trying desperately to act normally, I ordered tea and a cake, and asked Joseph about his day. He told me some funny stories about a drunk man he'd arrested, and I laughed uproariously. He looked delighted to have amused me, and told more silly tales about petty criminals he'd come across.

I watched him as he talked, delighting in the passion in his eyes. He loved his work, I thought. And I could love him, if only circumstances allowed me to.

Eventually, he paused. 'I'm talking too much,' he said. 'Look, I've not taken one bite of cake, nor drunk more than half a cup of tea. It's your turn. What did you do yesterday?'

I coughed as my mouthful of tea went down the wrong way. Was this a trap?

'Yesterday?' I said, pretending not to remember while I thought of something plausible I could have done. 'Yesterday?'

'You said you had chores to do for Agnes.'

'Oh, that's right. I had to deliver a package for her.'

'Exciting?'

If only he knew.

'Uneventful.'

'No rude drunken men?'

'Fortunately not.'

'And no cheeky widows stealing apples?'

I almost winced at the mention of apples, but managed to refrain. 'No cheeky widows. Just my friend Minnie, who tagged along.'

'I'd like to meet her,' Joseph said.

'She'd like to meet you,' I lied.

'I heard there was some trouble down your way, with suffragettes starting a fight.'

I froze, my teacup halfway to my mouth. 'Is that right?'

'Apparently they were causing trouble in the market, knocking over crates of fruit and veg.'

I put my cup down in case my shaking hand made me spill my tea, and put my trembling fingers on my lap so Joseph wouldn't notice.

'That doesn't sound like the suffragettes.'

Joseph laughed. 'No, you're right,' he said. 'Not their style.'

I looked at him. Now would be the perfect time to ask him what he thought. If he agreed that the lies he'd heard about what happened in Camberwell weren't the usual suffragette activity, he'd be bound to admit he believed in our fight. Surely? But I choked on the words, and instead – hating myself slightly – I told him all about Gilbert.

'Minnie is always complaining about him. She says he's miserable and she calls him Gloomy Gilbert. But I think she's sweet on him.'

Joseph chuckled. 'That's nice,' he said. 'Since I met you, Esther, I want everyone to find a sweetheart.'

I melted once more at his words. He was such a sweet man. Not afraid to show his feelings. So different from my father – which was a good thing, as far as I was concerned.

Feeling bold, I reached across the table and took his hand.

'It's strange isn't it, when you think what a short time we've known each other?'

He nodded. 'Just a matter of weeks. And yet I feel I've known you forever.'

'I feel the same,' I said. 'Like we belong together.'

Joseph laced his fingers through mine and I looked down at our interlinked hands.

'We belong together,' I said again.

But as I spoke, I remembered Minnie's warning and my happiness began to fade. Did I really have to choose between Joseph and the WSPU? I was afraid she might be right. It seemed an impossible choice – I had strong feelings for Joseph and wanted to spend all my time with him, but the WSPU were my family. They had stood by me when I needed them and they gave me a glimpse of a future where women wouldn't be forced to submit to men's rules. How would I ever make such a terrible decision?

Chapter 25

Lizzie

2019

I was strolling round the tiny Tesco in the village after school the next day, when I saw Danny and Cara.

'Hello, Miss Armstrong,' Cara said. 'We're buying biscuits for Brownies.'

'You should buy them brownies,' I said.

Cara frowned. 'I'm bringing biscuits. My name was on the list.'

Behind her, Danny laughed. The sound made my heart lift a little bit.

'You must never deviate from the Brownies list,' he said.

I was absurdly pleased to see him. 'Have you learned that to your cost?'

He leaned forward and checked behind him before he spoke, secret-agent-style. 'Once, we made small cakes instead of one big cake for the teddy bears' picnic. That's not a mistake I'll be making again.'

I laughed. 'So what's on your calendar for this evening?' he said, peering into my basket. 'Got a busy night planned?'

I was embarrassed. I had a bottle of wine, some more chocolate hobnobs, and a packet of stir-fry vegetables.

Danny looked up and met my eyes. 'I'm not sure this is a balanced meal,' he said. 'Perhaps we need to go out for dinner?'

Cara bounced up and down. 'Can we go to Nando's?'

Danny pulled one of her wonky bunches gently. 'You're going to Brownies to eat biscuits,' he said.

'And I have work to do,' I added, genuinely regretful.

'Really?'

I made a face. 'Really.' I tapped Cara on the shoulder. 'Cara, I've forgotten to get milk. Could you run and get me a small carton of the one with the green lid, please?'

'That's called semi-skimmed,' she said.

I hid my amusement. 'Is it?' I said. 'Then please could you get me a small carton of semi-skimmed?'

She skipped off and I pulled Danny to one side of the aisle so we couldn't be overheard.

'The council are making a final decision about Elm Heath Primary in March,' I said.

'Jesus.'

'Apparently there are already developers sniffing round.' A thought struck me. 'Could you find out what's going on? Use some of your contacts again? You must know people who do property stuff?'

Danny looked uncomfortable. 'Well, yes, but I'm not sure . . .'

'Just if you hear anything,' I said, not wanting to put him on the spot.

'So what's happening now?'

'We're launching a campaign to save the school,' I said quickly. 'We're going to follow in the footsteps of Esther Watkins and the other suffragettes. Deeds not words.'

'Okaaaay.'

Cara was coming back.

'I'll fill you in another time,' I said. 'Over a drink, perhaps?'

Danny grinned. 'Thursday? Cara's with Sophie.'

'Sounds great.'

He leaned over and kissed me on the cheek. I breathed in the smell of him, enjoying his closeness.

'Daddy, Brownies is starting now,' Cara said.

'So let's go.'

He gave me a last grin over his shoulder and let Cara lead him away towards the checkout, while I was left behind with a pint of milk I didn't need, feeling slightly deflated.

The feeling of mild disappointment stayed with me at home, while I made my sad stir-fry and drank a glass of wine. I did some school admin and flicked through Netflix without finding anything I wanted to watch. When my doorbell rang, I jumped to answer it, hoping it was Danny. But it was Nate.

'Sorry to bother you,' he said. 'I wondered if I could show you some ideas I've had for the rally? There never seems to be a good time at school.'

'Of course.' I stood back to let him into the hall and showed him into the living room.

'This is cute,' he said.

I felt a tiny swell of pride in my little – rented – cottage and nodded. 'I like it,' I agreed. 'Glass of wine?'

I poured us both a glass and we sat together on the sofa. Nate pulled out a folder and launched into an excited spiel about what he had planned.

'Like I said, I think the thing to do is win hearts and minds,' he said, his words tumbling over each other in his enthusiasm. 'If we can do that, get everyone on our side – locally and further afield – then the council won't want the bad publicity that will come from selling the building.'

'Perhaps. But times are tough, Nate. If they can get a load of cash for it . . .'

He waved away my concerns. 'Trust me,' he said. 'I really think this could work.'

I shrugged. 'I've got nothing else to offer, so go for it.'

With a grin, he opened his folder. 'I'm thinking a march round the village,' he said. 'Led by the kids, but we'll try to get everyone involved. We can make banners like the ones the suffragettes carried, and wear sashes.'

'Sashes?'

He showed me a beautiful drawing of a little girl – who looked a bit like Cara – wearing a green and purple sash.

'Marc drew this,' he said proudly. 'It's based on the Votes for Women sashes you see in the photos of suffragettes, but instead of Votes for Women they say Save Elm Heath.'

'Okaaay,' I said.

'So we'll all march to the park and we'll have stalls and an old-fashioned fair, and maybe games and stuff, and you can do a speech.'

'Nate, it's going to be cold and probably raining,' I said.

'My dad's mate is going to sort us out with a load of marquees and tents. It'll be fine,' he said. 'We'll all wear coats. And if we do it at the beginning of March it'll be warmer anyway.'

I registered what else he'd said. 'A speech?'

'About how important the school is and talking about the history and about Esther and what she wanted from Elm Heath.'

I made a face. 'I still don't know.'

'You'll find out though. You're not exactly someone who gives up at the first sign of trouble, are you?'

I looked at him curiously. 'What do you mean?'

'You had a rotten time of it, with your husband and that, didn't you?'

I couldn't argue with that. I nodded, still not sure where he was going.

'But you just picked yourself up and kept going.'

From where I was sitting, it looked like I'd run away and hidden, but I supposed to some people it could seem as though I'd kept going.

'Nate,' I began, but he wasn't finished.

'We all think you're brilliant,' he said. 'And we reckon if anyone can do this, you can.'

There was nothing like a bit of flattery to win a woman over. I smiled, despite my misgivings.

'I suppose it's worth a try.'

Nate clapped his hands. 'It's definitely worth a try. We've got nothing to lose.' He paused. 'I will sort the rally,' he said. 'I'll do all the organisation and drumming up the support and stuff, if you . . .'

'Yes?' I was suspicious about what he wanted.

'If you get your husband to use his contacts and get us some publicity.'

'Ex-husband.'

'He owes you,' Nate said. 'Pippa was right about that.'

'It's awkward.'

Nate's expression softened. 'I know.' He reached out and patted my hand gently. 'But we really need you to do this. It could make all the difference. The kids from Elm Heath will be so grateful.'

'Ooh that's cheap,' I said. 'Using the kids as leverage.'

'I'm shameless,' he said cheerfully. 'But you know I'm right.'

I winced. He was right. The kids were more important than my wounded pride.

'Fine,' I said. 'I'll email him and see if he can help.'

Nate shut his folder with a snap and drained his wine glass. 'Then we're good to go,' he said.

Feeling a bit browbeaten, I showed him out, and then thinking I had to do it before I changed my mind I found my laptop and emailed Grant.

I wrote a quick explanation of the school ('so welcoming,' I gushed) and the problems it was facing ('the usual perfect storm of budget cuts and falling pupil numbers,' I wrote airily as though it was no biggie). Then I outlined the 'amazing and incredibly inspiring' history of Esther Watkins and how she'd founded the school, and I wrote a bit about what we had planned to fight for Elm Heath.

'We need publicity for this to really make a difference,' I typed. 'Can you help?'

I paused, tapping my fingers lightly on the keys as I thought about how to write 'you owe me, you lying sod', without actually writing 'you owe me, you lying sod'.

'I'm so pleased that with all the water that's gone under the bridge, we can still be there for each other,' I wrote. Then I changed the bit about being there to 'help each other out'. That was better – less emotionally charged, I thought.

'Hope all is good with you,' I added, finishing with an L and a kiss. Which I also deleted. He didn't deserve my kisses, virtual or not. But I didn't send the message – not yet. I still wanted to make sure it was absolutely the right thing to do. So instead, I saved it into my draft folder. I'd send it in the next couple of days, I thought.

To distract myself I checked my Facebook messages and with a thrill realised Fiona Willoughby had replied.

'Happy to help,' she'd written. 'I have some boxes of papers, and other bits and pieces that belonged to Agnes. Would you like to come and have a look?'

Grinning to myself, I replied that I would love to visit if possible, and gave her my phone number so we could arrange it.

With a sense of achievement I put the wine glasses in the dishwasher and turned it on, then I went upstairs to bed, thinking perhaps all was not lost after all.

Chapter 26

Lizzie

'When are you going to meet her?' Danny asked, as he put my drink down in front of me. It was Thursday – finally – and we were in the pub for our date. I'd been filling him in on Nate's plans for the rally and my correspondence with Fiona Willoughby. I'd not mentioned writing the email to Grant, but then I'd not sent it yet anyway. Maybe I'd send it tomorrow.

Now I smiled at Danny and straightened my wine glass on the beer mat.

'Paula and I are going on Saturday,' I said. 'She lives in Sussex so we can easily be there and back in a day.'

'And she's got information about Esther Watkins?'

'Well, information about Agnes Oliver and her involvement with the suffragettes. And we know Esther was the governess for Agnes's children, so I'm hoping it's all relevant.'

'You're putting a lot of work into this.'

'Not just me. Nate's working hard, and Paula. Everyone really. It's worth it.'

Danny nodded. 'Sounds great,' he said. I looked at him carefully. He didn't sound like he thought it was great.

'Are you okay?'

'Just tired,' he said, running his fingers through his hair. He did look a bit rough round the edges, with smudges under his eyes and more stubble than I'd ever seen him with. He wore it well, though. He was really very nice to look at.

'Lizzie?'

I jumped and, realising I was staring, I squinted at a picture behind Danny on the wall of the pub instead of at his lovely face.

'Isn't that a wonderful painting,' I said in a hurry. It was an abstract canvas covered in red and orange swirls. 'I love the energy in it.'

Danny looked behind him. 'Do you?' He raised an eyebrow. 'Really?'

'Oh I do,' I said. I felt my cheeks reddening. 'Who painted that?' I asked the barmaid who was cleaning glasses from the table next to us. 'Do you know where it's from?'

She gave me a disdainful look. 'It's from IKEA,' she said.

Ah. Maybe I should just admit I was looking at Danny next time. Might be less embarrassing.

'Is the art appreciation class over?' Danny said. His eyes crinkled in amusement and I looked down into my glass to stop myself drifting off again.

'I do really like it,' I muttered, knowing I should just let it go. If I didn't stop, I'd end up with a violent orange canvas on my cottage wall by the end of the week.

'Marc's firm isn't pitching for the development, then?' Danny said.

'No, Nate said they'd turned it down.'

Danny nodded.

'Do you ever work with him?' I asked. 'Marc? Remind me what it is you do exactly?'

'Marc's an architect so I don't work directly with him. But sometimes our paths cross. I work for a company that secures private finance for public sector projects. Mostly big stuff like hospitals and roads. The occasional new public transport scheme, like the new railway line by the coast.'

I studied him over the top of my glass. 'Schools?'

He nodded – I thought reluctantly.

'Sometimes schools. I really only deal with the finance.'

I remembered his cross exchange of words with Chris at the barbecue back at the end of the summer.

'Is that how you know Chris?'

Danny grinned. 'Chris knows everyone.'

Under the table he put his hand on my knee. It felt nice there.

'Let's not talk about work,' he said. 'Let's talk about fun stuff.'

'Like what?'

'Christmas. It's only a few weeks away.'

I shuddered. 'Oh don't,' I said.

'You're not one of those people are you?' Danny said, darkly. 'The "it's just one day" brigade?'

I laughed. 'Actually, no I'm not,' I said. 'I like Christmas but I'll be at my mother's in my teenage bedroom. It feels like a backwards step, you know?'

'Just you and her?'

I gave a grim smile. 'Oh heavens no. My perfect brother and his perfect fiancée will be there for a while. And I'm sure various other family members will drop in. It's just not how I expected to be spending Christmases in my late thirties.'

Danny squeezed my knee sympathetically and I felt a surge of attraction towards him.

'What about you?' I squeaked. 'Where will you be?'

'Ireland. It's my family's turn to host us this year. Cara loves seeing my parents and I always find Irish Christmases a bit easier than when we do the day with Sophie.'

'Is it hard to spend so much time with Sophie?' I said.

He shrugged. 'No, not really. I'm being unfair. She's wonderful with Cara. And I have to be honest, I can't blame her for being cautious because I was a bugger when I was younger.' His face softened. 'Cara loves her so much, she adores Cara, and they're really good for each other. You know she's taught Cara to speak French?'

'She has?'

'They chat away to each other. Drives me up the wall. I'm always sure they're talking about me.'

'They probably are,' I said.

Danny rolled his eyes. 'Probably.'

'Sophie's going to run our after-school club for us,' I told him. 'She was thrilled when we asked her and she's got lots of plans already. And Paula's daughter Chloe is busy recruiting sixth-formers to help out too. She's found some sporty types to run football and netball sessions, and one of her friends is doing music A Level and she said she'd like to start a school choir for part of her assessment. I might get Sophie to throw in some French lessons too.'

'Sounds brilliant,' Danny said. 'I've signed Cara up for a couple of afternoons a week.'

I grinned. I knew that. 'We've got a waiting list already,' I said. 'It's very popular.'

'It was a great idea,' Danny said.

'I hope it works.'

We chatted for a bit longer and ordered more drinks and some chips to share. I went to the loo before the food arrived and sat in the cubicle for a moment, grateful to have some time out.

Danny was a lovely man, I thought. He was funny and attentive and caring – I loved the way he was so devoted to Cara. He was really handsome and the way he smiled at me made my head spin.

And yet I still had that niggle about Paula, and Sophie and Isabelle.

It was good that we were taking things slowly, I thought. Although, it was easier to think about taking things slowly when I was locked in a toilet cubicle, than when I was sitting next to him. When I could see the way his eyes darkened as he looked at me, and feel the warmth of his hand on my leg, and smell his skin, and . . .

'Stop it, Lizzie,' I said out loud.

'Everything all right in there?' a voice said from the cubicle next to me. I'd not realised there was anyone else in the loo.

Embarrassed – again – I cleared my throat. 'All fine, thanks,' I said. 'Thought there was no loo roll but I've found some.'

I waited for the woman in the other cubicle to flush the loo, listened as she washed her hands and then opened the door back to the bar, and then I finally went back to Danny.

Our chips were on the table in front of him.

'You were a while,' he commented, pushing the bowl towards me. 'I've almost eaten them all.'

I shoved a chip in my mouth so I didn't come up with some rubbish excuse, or worse blurt out that I'd been thinking about him, and smiled.

Danny leaned back in his seat, and watched me. 'You're something, Lizzie Armstrong.'

I swallowed the last bit of chip. 'What does something mean?' I said. 'Clueless about art?'

He shook his head. 'Determined. Focused. Brave.'

I felt heat in my cheeks. 'I'm not any of those things.'

'Ah, look at how you've got the bit between your teeth now. Researching your Esther Watkins, and organising rallies.'

I looked down at the table. 'I don't have anything else to do,' I admitted. 'It's not like I've got a family or a husband demanding my time.'

Danny put his hand back on my knee. 'I'm demanding a bit of it.'

I looked up and met his gaze.

'I like you, Lizzie,' he said.

'I like you too.'

The moment felt charged as we looked at each other, and then he looked away.

'I need to go,' he said. He did sound genuinely regretful, which was something. I looked at my watch – it was almost ten o'clock.

'Me too,' I said. 'Busy day tomorrow.'

We both stood up and Danny helped me on with my coat in a very gentlemanly way.

'I'll walk you home,' he said.

I opened my mouth to say there was no need, because we lived in opposite directions from the pub, but then I thought it meant spending more time with him and I nodded.

We strolled down the main street, close together. We weren't holding hands but our fingers brushed as we walked.

At my front door, Danny turned to me. 'I had a lovely evening,' he said. 'Can we do it again next week?'

'I'd like that.'

He kissed me on the lips, softly at first, and then as I relaxed into it, more firmly. My head was spinning with wine and longing, but I was also not nearly drunk enough to forget that snogging in the street was not a good look for a head teacher, so I pulled away.

'Night,' I said.

Chapter 27

Lizzie

Fiona Willoughby was an energetic woman in her late sixties. She lived in a large house that was full of family memories. I liked her immediately. She showed us into the kitchen and made tea. In the garden, an older man with shaggy grey hair – her husband I assumed – was planting bulbs with a small boy wearing wellies, while a slightly bigger boy dribbled a football round the two trees at the bottom.

'We're on grandparent duty today,' she said fondly, following my gaze out of the kitchen window. 'Do you have children?'

'I've got a hundred of them,' I joked to deflect any questions from my personal life.

'Of course, you're a teacher – you mentioned that in your messages.'

She handed me a mug of tea, and then gave one to Paula.

'We both work at Elm Heath Primary – it's the school that was founded by Esther Watkins,' I said. 'But like I explained, the council are planning to close us down and we think the school should stay open.'

'We're desperate for it to stay open,' Paula said.

Fiona nodded.

'We're trying to find out as much as we can about Esther so we can prove the school is of special historical interest.'

'Well, I've dug out all the bits and pieces I've got about the suffragettes,' Fiona said. 'It's all in the lounge – come through and I'll show you.'

We followed her into the large lounge that ran the length of the house. Two faded but pretty sofas, a coffee table and the television, were at the front end of the room, while the other end was lined with groaning bookshelves. There was a wooden dining table, with several boxes stacked on it and that's where Fiona took us, gesturing that we should sit.

I pulled out a chair and sat down opposite her, with Paula next to me.

'Agnes was my great-grandmother,' Fiona began. 'I don't remember her unfortunately but my mother was close to her and she told me stories.'

'About the suffragettes?'

'About everything, but the suffragettes in particular.'

Paula leaned forward. 'We're organising a rally,' she said. 'We've been inspired by the action they took and we decided we weren't just going to sit around talking.'

'Perfect,' Fiona said. 'Deeds not words.'

'Exactly.' I was pleased she understood.

I pulled out my own bundle of research.

'We found lots of information about Esther starting the school,' I said, laying out some papers on the table. 'She'd been to prison, I discovered, so obviously the education authority weren't keen to let her open a school. I imagine they didn't think she was a very good role model. But she gave them references from your Agnes, and from a policeman called Joseph Fairbanks, and she also wrote what sounds to be a visionary letter, spelling out her aims for the school, and she won them over.'

Fiona smiled. 'How clever.'

'We really want to find that letter,' I said. 'But it wasn't in the council archive.'

'I can't imagine it'll be here, but we can have a look,' Fiona said. 'Shall we get stuck in?'

She pushed one of the boxes towards Paula and me, and stood up to open the one nearest to her. I copied, standing up and opening the cardboard lid. The box was full of treasures – papers, books, newspapers, posters – and I gasped in delight.

'Oh, this is amazing,' I said.

Paula clapped her hands, as I carefully tipped everything out on to the table and put the box down on the carpet.

'Let's get cracking,' she said.

As we waded through the reams of memories, it became clear that Agnes was an amazing woman. She'd been involved with the WSPU from its early days and had got stuck right in, marching, organising, helping with the newspaper and generally making a nuisance of herself.

'Her husband, John, was active too,' Fiona said, showing me some photos of the couple together. 'He was very in favour of women's suffrage.'

Paula had sorted out anything about rallies and marches, and was busy taking photos on her phone.

'We can use these posters advertising marches as the template for our own posters,' she said. 'My Chloe is very arty. I'm sure she can come up with something that looks right.'

'What a good idea,' I said. I was pleased she was finding it inspiring, but I was disappointed not to have found any mention of Esther yet.

'Nothing in your pile?' Fiona said, realising I was looking glum.

'Lots of incredible stuff but nothing about Esther,' I said.

'When was she living with Agnes?'

I pulled out the reference and looked at it again.

'I suppose it wasn't that long really,' I said, showing Fiona. 'The spring of 1910 until the end of the year, as far as I can see. Then she moved to Elm Heath, and began trying to start the school towards the end of 1911.'

Fiona nodded. 'The year 1910 was a funny one for the WSPU,' she said. 'The summer was very quiet and then it all kicked off in the autumn. Let me find it, hang on . . .'

She started leafing through her box and Paula and I exchanged an excited glance. Things kicking off sounded fairly thrilling. I said as much to Fiona and she grimaced.

'Well, yes and no,' she said, pulling out a newspaper. 'Look at this.'

I took the newspaper carefully. Its pages were brittle and yellow. On the front page was a photograph of a small woman with a marvellous hat, lying on the ground protecting her face with her hands. Above, a policeman towered over her his truncheon raised. The headline read: *Violent scenes at Westminster.*

'Jesus,' I breathed.

'It was called Black Friday,' Fiona said. 'I can't remember all the details exactly but I'm sure you can find out.'

I nodded eagerly. I was really enjoying the research and having more to do pleased me.

Fiona carried on: 'From what I know, the suffragettes marched on Westminster. But when they got there, the police and the crowds turned on them.'

I looked at the shocking picture on the newspaper. 'They were hurt?' I asked.

'Some were. They were beaten, sexually assaulted, and generally treated very badly. And then lots of them were arrested.'

Paula tutted. 'That's awful.'

I was looking at the date on the paper. 'Esther moved to Elm Heath in December 1910,' I said. 'That would have been just a couple of weeks after all this happened.'

'Maybe it's related?' Fiona was looking through the box once more. 'Perhaps she ran away because she didn't want to go back to prison,' she suggested. 'I've read some reports of how the women were treated in jail, and it wasn't pleasant.'

'That makes sense,' Paula said. 'Why Elm Heath, though?'

Fiona looked up. 'Is Elm Heath in Kent?'

Paula looked pleased. 'It is,' she said. 'No one ever knows where it is.'

'I've got letters,' Fiona said. 'From Agnes to John in early 1911. I remember reading them a few years ago. She was recovering from some sort of an illness at a convalescent home there.'

'That posh hotel on the Blyton road used to be a convalescent home,' Paula said.

I sat up a bit straighter. 'Perhaps Agnes was hurt in this march on Parliament,' I said, gesturing to the newspaper. 'Maybe she was badly hurt and needed time to recover.'

Fiona screwed her nose up. 'Maybe. I had an idea it was some sort of woman's illness but I'll find the letters and we can check.'

I waved my hand.

'It doesn't really matter actually. We know she was there, away from the trouble in London. It's a link to Elm Heath at least. I think perhaps Esther went to visit her, perhaps to escape any risk of being sent to prison again, and thought Elm Heath was a nice sort of place to stay?'

'It was actually really, really poor,' Paula said. 'Rural community, kids working all hours despite the laws that had been passed to stop that.'

'So Esther saw a need and wanted to help?' Fiona said.

'Think how amazing this would all be – Esther took her passion for campaigning from London to this small village where she realised the children needed her. I imagine starting a school would have made a huge difference to the whole community.'

Paula nodded. 'Changed lives,' she said.

'But we don't know for sure,' I said with a groan. 'This all sounds so plausible but we're just guessing aren't we? This must be what she said in the letter.'

Fiona frowned. 'I don't think that matters,' she said.

I looked up at her, confused. 'Really?'

'You do know she did it,' Fiona said. 'You know she went to

172

Elm Heath and she started a school. It doesn't really matter why. Focus on what she did, rather than why she did it.'

Paula and I looked at each other.

'You're right,' Paula said. 'What do you think, Lizzie?'

I chewed my lip. 'I think we've been so busy looking for this letter, we've forgotten what really matters,' I said. 'We don't need the letter, Fiona's right. We can use all this history and tell stories around it. The fact she set up the school is enough.'

I looked at Fiona. 'It's your family's story,' I said. 'Do you mind if I tell the council about Agnes being ill and give them the background about how Esther came to be in Elm Heath?'

'Not in the slightest,' she said cheerfully. 'Strikes me that Agnes would be thrilled to be campaigning again.'

I grinned at her. 'So that's what we'll do,' I said.

Chapter 28

Lizzie

'I'm feeling much more positive,' Paula said when we were in the car and heading home. 'What about you?'

I nodded. 'Positive, but overwhelmed,' I admitted. 'There's such a lot to do.'

'We've got time, though. The meeting's not until March, and the rally's only a couple of weeks before.'

'But Christmas is looming, and that always stops everything,' I said. 'I need to start planning what to say at the meeting. We need to finalise all the arrangements for the rally and get everyone on board.'

'And you need to drum up some publicity,' Paula said.

I groaned. 'I know. I know. I drafted an email to Grant but I didn't send it.'

Paula was driving, but she glanced at me quickly. 'Why not?'

'A million reasons,' I said. 'I hate admitting I don't know how to do something for starters. But when we were in London, he dealt with all the press stuff – I never paid attention. I didn't think I'd have to.'

'That's fair enough, but don't feel bad about that. I wouldn't have a clue where to start with all this. We're lucky to have you.'

I grinned. It was nice to be needed, even if I didn't think I lived up to their expectations.

'What else?'

'What?'

'What were the other million reasons?'

'Because I don't want to ask him for anything,' I said. 'Because I don't want to speak to him, or communicate with him in any way, and risk feeling as bad as I did back then just when I'm starting to feel better. Our break-up made me feel silly. Because I thought our marriage was one thing and it turned out to be another. I felt stupid.'

'You shouldn't feel stupid. You didn't make a mistake – he did. He was the one who let you down. You can't blame yourself for that.'

'I guess not.' I paused. 'Plus there's . . .'

I trailed off and Paula looked at me again. I deliberately avoided her glance.

'There's?'

'Nothing, that's it.'

'Danny?'

'No.'

'Really?'

I sighed. 'Perhaps a bit.'

'What's the latest with you two?' Paula asked casually, like she didn't remotely care what my answer was. But I knew she was desperate to know really.

'I feel weird talking to you about it,' I said.

'Why?'

'Because you were Isabelle's friend.'

Paula didn't speak for a minute. I waited as she changed gear to go round a bend, then changed back up again. Then, finally, she said: 'I was Isabelle's friend.'

'So it's strange to chat about going on dates with her bloke.'

It was Paula's turn to sigh. 'Isabelle and Danny weren't exactly love's young dream you know,' she said. 'Isabelle gave as good as she got.'

'Sophie said . . .'

'Chris nailed it when she said Sophie is grieving for her daughter, and she wants someone to blame,' Paula said. She drummed her fingers on the steering wheel, searching for the right words. 'Bella was brilliant. She was funny and full of energy, she was so, so kind to everyone, she adored Cara. I loved her, and I miss her.'

She took a deep breath, staring straight ahead through the windscreen.

'But the fact is, Lizzie, she wasn't easy to live with. She had a terrible temper. She was impulsive, and she was crap with money, and she and Danny were an awful couple.'

'Really?'

'Oh God, totally. He was horrible to her – that's completely true.'

'He told me that.' I felt prickly, as though Paula was being unfair to Danny, even though I knew she wasn't really.

'The thing is, until Cara arrived, Danny and Bella had split up more times than I can remember. They were always having huge rows and breaking up. Once, they fell out on holiday and she left him in Tenerife and came home on her own. They were even apart for about two years at one stage, then they got back together just before Bella found out she was pregnant.'

This was all news to me.

'Danny made out he was the bad guy.'

'He was,' Paula said bluntly. 'He was shit when Cara was born. He kept disappearing and even staying out all night without telling Bella where he was. I couldn't blame Bella one bit when she came home – it was definitely the right thing to do.'

'But?'

'But what I'm saying is, it wasn't all one-sided. It's not like Bella spent her last years weeping over Danny and he ruined her short life, no matter what Sophie might have you believe.'

That was exactly what I'd thought. What I'd feared.

176

'Bella was happy,' Paula said, her voice catching. 'She loved the drama of being with Danny. She always loved a bit of drama. And yes, she found things tough when Cara was born, but she was brave enough to admit she was struggling, pack up, and come home, which was the best thing to do for everyone.'

'That is brave,' I said. 'She sounds really brave altogether.'

'She was.'

There was silence in the car as we both thought about Isabelle.

'She knew Danny would step up, you know,' Paula said. 'Before she died, she made sure he was a part of Cara's life, and that he was ready to take over. She always believed he would prove himself to be a good dad.'

'She was right.'

Paula nodded, slowing down as we approached the edge of Elm Heath. 'About the only time she was right.'

I chewed my lip.

'I like Danny, and I think he likes me,' I said. 'But it's really complicated.'

'I know,' Paula said. She patted my leg. 'Just don't dismiss it altogether. These things can be tricky, but I reckon the best things always are.'

We'd reached my house. She pulled over and I eyed her suspiciously.

'You've been with Chris since school?' I said.

'Yes.' She was proud.

'So how do you know so much about relationships?'

She shrugged. 'I read a lot of romance novels.'

I chuckled. 'I read a lot of crime,' I said. 'Perhaps that's where I'm going wrong.'

As I opened the door I impulsively leaned over and kissed Paula's cheek. 'Thanks for driving,' I said. 'And thanks for telling me about Isabelle.'

She squeezed my hand. 'Just think about what I said.'

The rest of the weekend passed without any incident. I spent

Saturday afternoon in Elm Heath library looking up local history books, and then most of Sunday reading about the convalescent home and what the village was like in the early twentieth century. Paula was right. It had been so poor, it took my breath away a bit. And the worst thing was, I knew there were still pupils at the school who were living in poverty, even nowadays. Esther had done an amazing thing, starting Elm Heath Primary and I felt the heavy burden of carrying on her work.

On Sunday evening, there was a knock on my door and I skipped to open it, hoping it would be Danny. I'd not heard from him all weekend and I was keen to see him. But instead a woman in her fifties stood there, wrapped up in a thick winter coat, with a woolly hat pulled down over her forehead.

'Can I help you?'

'Are you Lizzie Armstrong?'

'Yes?' I was cautious. 'And you are?'

'I'm Denise Deacon, from the council. We spoke on the phone?'

I was startled. What on earth was the woman from the council doing on my doorstep on a Sunday evening?

'Do you want to come in?' I said. 'What's going on? Is something wrong?'

She shook her head. 'I won't stay. I just wanted to let you know something I'd heard and I realise I'm probably being stupid, after all this is just a school, it's not James bloody Bond, but I didn't want to email or phone in case anyone overheard.'

I blinked at her. I had absolutely no idea what she was talking about.

'Sorry, get me, going off on a tangent. I always do that. My son takes the mickey. He's always saying, "Mum, stay on topic." He makes me laugh.'

'Denise?' I said gently, desperate to know what had brought her to my door. 'Why are you here?'

She took a breath. 'I wanted you to know that things are moving with Elm Heath,' she said. 'I know you've got the meeting in your diary, and you're working on the assumption that the decision won't be made until after you've had your chance to put your point across. But I've seen that they've got developers on board, so frankly it's looking like a done deal.'

I nodded, pinching my lips together grimly. 'I've heard.'

'You have?' Denise looked a bit disappointed that her sneaky visit was for nothing.

'One of my staff is married to an architect.'

Denise leaned against the doorframe. 'Are you planning to fight it?'

'We are.' I looked at her. 'Do you reckon we stand a chance?'

She shrugged. 'It's always worth a try, but money talks. It's the only thing they listen to, really.' She stood up straighter as she thought of something. 'Well, not the only thing.'

I felt a glimmer of hope. 'What else?'

'Bad press,' she said. 'They're always terrified of looking like the bad guys.'

'We're planning a big protest march, and a rally,' I said. 'What about if I can get the newspapers involved?'

Denise curled her lip. '*The Blyton Advertiser*?' she said. 'I'm not sure many people read that any more.'

'Well, yes, but not only them. I mean national newspapers, the BBC, all sorts. It's such a good story with the history of the school. We think our founder started the school to help poor kids achieve more. It's a perfect message of social mobility and altruism.'

Denise frowned. 'How would you get them to know about it?' she said. 'We've got a press team, but I can't get them to do it – it's a big conflict of interest for them.'

'I've got contacts,' I half-lied. 'From my old job. I can call in some favours.'

'I think you'd better call in every favour you can,' Denise said. 'Because the way things are looking at the moment, Elm Heath Primary will be closing in the summer.'

179

Chapter 29

Lizzie

When Denise left, skulking down the garden path like Tom Cruise in *Mission: Impossible*, I curled up on the sofa with my laptop and opened the draft email to Grant. Should I send it? The brutal truth was the kids at Elm Heath were more important than my stupid pride, I thought. I had to just woman up and press send. I hovered the cursor over the send button, took a deep breath, and jumped as the doorbell rang again. Denise must have remembered some other top-secret info she had to tell me. Not that I wasn't grateful for her input, but it just made everything seem so much harder.

Putting my laptop to one side – email still unsent – I flung open the door and gasped in surprise to see Danny. He was holding a bottle of wine and a slightly fraught expression.

'Busy?' he said.

I looked down at my scruffy jogging bottoms, slouchy jumper and slippers. 'Just on my way out actually,' I said. 'Going to a party.'

'Shame.' He gave me one of his cheeky smiles and I felt myself melting even though to my appraising eye, he seemed a bit out of sorts. 'I was at a loose end and I thought you might fancy a drink?'

'No Cara?'

'Impromptu sleepover with her friend Shari. I dropped her school bag and uniform round for the morning, and saw your light was on.'

'Quite the detective.'

Danny hunched down in his coat. 'I don't want to presume but it's really cold, so if you're going to invite me in, do you think we could skip the flirty banter and move straight to the bit where I'm sitting on your sofa in the warm? I could really use a shoulder.'

I laughed, standing aside to let him in and shutting the door behind him. 'What's up?'

'Sophie's ill. She's in Blyton Hospital.'

I looked at his drawn face and felt my stomach lurch in panic. 'What's happened? Is she okay?'

'She's fine now,' he said. 'It was scary though. She's got a chest infection and she's asthmatic anyway and she couldn't breathe.'

'Were you with her?'

'I called an ambulance,' he said. 'I thought she was going to die, Lizzie.'

I pulled him into a hug. 'You did the right thing,' I said. 'And she's okay now?'

'She's doing well. She's on antibiotics and she's coming home tomorrow. She's fine. It just got me thinking, you know? That I'm all Cara has if Sophie isn't around.'

He looked so stricken I hugged him again.

'Have you eaten?'

Danny shook his head. 'I was working and time got away with me.'

'Takeaway and a film?'

He grinned and I grinned back. It was good to see him smile again.

'Is that your version of Netflix and chill?'

I whacked him on the arm, gently. 'Oi,' I said. 'Don't get any ideas.' Although actually my own head was full of those kind of ideas. Brimming with them, in fact.

'Sounds good.'

We ordered food, then got comfy on the sofa, bottle of wine in front of us. I chose a film at random from Netflix, and put it on, and we mostly ignored it as we ate and chatted.

I told him all about what we'd discovered when we visited Fiona.

'We didn't find the letter Esther wrote, which is disappointing,' I explained. 'But we think she saw a need for the school in Elm Heath back in 1910 or 11. And I think there is still that need.'

Danny frowned. 'Can't that need be met by the schools in Blyton?'

'On paper, yes, but not on a practical level – there aren't enough regular buses to Blyton so the kids would all have to be driven for starters. And in terms of community, it's so important to have a local school.'

Danny was watching me, with an unreadable expression on his face. 'This is really important to you,' he said.

'I know.' I felt a bit embarrassed suddenly. 'I can't lie, I wasn't planning on staying in Elm Heath. When I took the job, I saw it more as a stop-gap than anything else; a way to reset my career and prove myself before going back to London. But now . . . Well, I can just really see how much the village needs the school.'

'And how much you need a project?'

I felt my cheeks flush. 'Perhaps,' I admitted.

'To keep your mind off your ex?'

I took a slurp of wine to give myself time to think. 'Not him as such,' I said slowly. 'More the whole situation. I don't really think of him at all now.'

Danny didn't speak, his eyes fixed on my face.

'Well, I think about him sometimes,' I said. 'But he wasn't the man I thought he was. Or at least, he wasn't the husband I thought he was, and I wasn't the wife he wanted.'

'It's tough when someone lets you down,' Danny said.

I looked away. 'It is.'

There was a slightly awkward pause.

'Paula was talking about Isabelle today,' I said to break the silence, mentally kicking myself for bringing up his ex when we'd just stopped talking about mine. I should have told him about Denise Deacon's mysterious visit instead, I thought. What an idiot I was.

'Paula was talking about Isabelle?' Danny was guarded.

I sat back against the sofa cushion, looking down into my glass. 'She said she can't have always been easy to live with.'

Danny laughed. 'That's an understatement.'

'And she said your relationship wasn't always easy either.'

'It was either completely amazing or utterly hell,' Danny said. 'There was never any middle ground. It was exhausting – for both of us. I think, if she'd not got pregnant when she did, we'd probably have gone our separate ways for good long before she got sick.'

He took a breath.

'But I let her down, when she really needed me. And I have to live with that.'

I took his hand. 'And then you stepped up when she needed you.'

He looked up at me, his face close to mine, and then suddenly we were kissing, urgently. His hands were pulling at my tatty old sweatshirt, so I tugged it off over my head, and did the same with his T-shirt.

Was this a good idea? I thought, as his hands roamed downwards. Probably not. But I didn't really care.

* * *

It was still dark when I woke up the next morning, after not much sleep. I glanced at the clock – it was only six a.m. – but Danny was sitting on the edge of the bed, pulling on his jeans. I ran my hand over his back and he turned to me.

'Hey, I didn't mean to wake you.'

'You didn't.'

He leaned over and kissed me softly. 'I need to go before it gets light. I don't want to sully your reputation.'

I made a face, but I knew he was right.

'I'm picking Cara up from school today so I'll catch you then.' He smiled at me, and I felt my insides turn to liquid.

'Okay,' I said. I pulled him down towards me for another kiss.

'Was this a mistake?' I said.

'Almost certainly.'

'Should we stop?'

'Definitely not.' He gave me another kiss. 'I'll call you.'

I watched him go, happily stretching my toes like a contented cat. Then I slid out of bed and into the shower to get ready for school, singing Christmas songs loudly.

My good mood carried me through the whole morning – rehearsals for the nativity, and reams of admin, and covering year one because Pippa was off sick. I didn't have time to think about Esther, or the rally, or anything Denise Deacon had said, because I was so busy, but I didn't even mind.

Then, at lunchtime, I was on playground duty watching a group of year-five girls choreograph what seemed to be a fairly inappropriate dance and wondering when I should step in, when I saw Danny. He was standing outside the school, the other side of the railings to me, by the main entrance. He was on his phone with his body turned away from me so I couldn't see his expression.

At once, my heart lifted as I admired him from a distance – he'd not seen me so it was a good chance to really take him in. He was wearing a suit so he'd obviously been home before work to change and he wore it very well. He was one of those men who looked gloriously scruffy in jeans and a T-shirt, but effortlessly glamorous as soon as he stuck a tie on.

Leaving the year fives to their gyrating, I casually sauntered over towards where he stood. I was close enough to hear him talking as I approached but he'd still not seen me.

'I'm in an impossible position, and I'm not happy about it,' he was saying. 'It's complicated.'

I paused in my sauntering, realising he was obviously in the middle of a difficult phone call. Was it work? His job sounded tricky and he'd said he was having a bit of a hard time at the moment. I must ask him to explain what was going on, I thought. I should show an interest.

'I've said yes,' he hissed down the phone. I noticed his Irish accent was more pronounced when he got angry. I liked that he had no affectations, unlike Grant whose carefully honed pronunciation gave no clue to his Midlands roots. 'I just think you're asking too much of me.'

I should go, I thought. He was obviously busy and I didn't want to interrupt.

Danny was running his fingers through his hair in exasperation and I turned to go back and check on the year-five version of the Pussycat Dolls.

'Vanessa,' Danny said, his tone changing from frustrated to more affectionate. I stopped mid-turn and gave him my attention again. Who was Vanessa?

'You know I adore you . . .'

Wait. What?

'But you're not being fair here, sweetheart,' he carried on.

My heart lurched at the cutesy way he said 'sweetheart' and suddenly I wasn't sure what to do. Should I stay here, listening to his phone call and possibly hear something I didn't want to hear? Should I confront him? Or should I sneak away and pretend it never happened? I could have the wrong end of the stick, after all.

I'd tiptoe away, I decided. Give him the benefit of the doubt. But just as I took a step backwards, the year-five girls ran up.

'Miss Armstrong,' they all bellowed. 'Come and watch our dance.'

I watched in horror as Danny turned round, phone stuck to his ear, staring at me through the railings.

'Lizzie,' he said. 'Sorry, Ness, can I call you back?'

'Go and get set up, girls,' I told my year fives. 'I just need a quick chat with Mr Kinsella.'

He ended the call and we looked at each other through the bars of the school fence. I didn't speak.

'Shit, Lizzie,' Danny said. 'What did you hear?'

'Enough.'

Had I?

'I'm sorry,' he said. He reached through the railings and squeezed my arm but I pulled away.

Danny's eyes were wild, and he looked half furious, half devastated. I had no idea what was going on. Was he seeing someone else? What was this?

'Danny,' I began. 'Is this . . .?'

'Lizzie, I'm so sorry. I'm going to sort this,' he said. 'I promise.'

Then without saying goodbye, he turned and walked away.

Chapter 30

Lizzie

Numbly, I watched Danny walk quickly down the road, get into his car and start the engine. He obviously wasn't planning on coming back to explain anything. I had no idea what I'd heard – not really – but he was obviously up to something or he'd not have reacted as he did. Who was Vanessa? Was he seeing her? I'd never explicitly asked if he was single; I'd just assumed. Surely Paula or Sophie would have said if he wasn't? If they knew.

In a daze, I let the year-five girls perform their Ariana-Grande-inspired dance and applauded wildly, though I did manage to get my head together enough to gently suggest it probably wasn't a good idea to rework the nativity to include their performance.

As the bell rang, I marched back to my office and shut the door. I wanted some time to myself to think about what had happened.

I had been so stupid to sleep with Danny, I thought. What sort of idiot was I exactly? I hadn't even made him work for it. All he'd offered was a bottle of wine and a cheeky grin, and I was inviting him in.

'Bloody hell, Lizzie,' I groaned aloud, putting my head in my hands. 'Bloody, bloody hell.'

I sat like that for a while and then I straightened up again, looking at the picture of Esther.

'Bet you'd never go so giddy over a man, Esther,' I said. 'Of course not. You were too busy supporting your sister suffragettes and starting schools. And now it's up to me to finish what you started.'

I pushed my shoulders back and opened my emails, scrolling until I found the draft I'd written to Grant. With a flourish, I pressed send and listened in satisfaction to the little "whoop" noise it made as it went.

'I'm going to take a leaf out of your book, Miss Watkins,' I said. 'I'm going to start focusing on what's important instead of on stinky boys.'

'Ahem.'

I looked up and saw the caretaker, Jeff, standing at my office door, holding a box.

'Emma said it was okay to come in,' he said, looking slightly sheepish.

Style it out, I thought to myself. I flashed him a dazzling smile.

'Of course,' I sang. 'Come on in. It's really lovely to see you.'

Perhaps that was a bit too much.

'What can I do for you?'

'I've got good news and bad news,' he said, coming into the office properly and sitting down at my desk as I'd gestured. 'Bad news first?'

'Hit me,' I said, grimacing.

'There's been surveyors round, over the weekend,' he said. 'Checking out the structure of the building and making sure it's all sound. For a developer. I know we knew they were sniffing around but this seemed really official, you know? A few of them in high-vis vests, measuring bits.'

'Son of a bitch.'

Jeff winced.

'Sorry,' I said. 'Bit of a shock, that's all.'

'I know. I wasn't happy when they turned up. I tried ringing you and Paula to check what to do but there was no answer, so I had to let him in.'

I thought of us driving through the remote country lanes to Fiona's house and nodded.

'It's fine,' I said. 'It's not your fault.'

My mind was racing. Denise had obviously been right when she said things were moving faster than we'd anticipated.

'Do you want the good news?'

'Pardon?'

'There is some good news.'

'Please,' I said, desperate for any tiny crumb he could give me.

'I took one of them up into the attic,' he said. 'Not been up there in yonks. He was poking around the beams and whatnot and so I had a look at what else was in there and I found this.'

Triumphantly, he picked up the dusty box that he'd been holding on his lap and thumped it down on to my desk in a cloud of cobwebs.

I coughed. 'What is it?'

'Have a look.'

Not overly keen to touch the filthy box, I stood up and gingerly pulled open the top. Inside was a pile of paper.

I looked up at Jeff and he beamed at me.

'It's all stuff belonging to your Esther,' he said. 'I've not looked at all of it, but I reckon it could help with your campaign.'

'Oh my God,' I breathed. 'It could be the letter.'

He shrugged. 'There's all sorts in there. Photos, letters, notes, accounts books. It's a real find I reckon. Have a dig about and see what you can find. I'll leave you to it.'

'Thanks so much,' I said. 'This might be just what we need.'

I pulled out a bundle of papers and dumped them on to my desk. My heart was thumping. Could the missing letter be in here somewhere?

I leafed through two accounts books, smiling as I saw the cost of pens and ink, and of school dinners. Tucked inside one page devoted to food, was a page torn from a notepad on which someone – Esther I assumed – had written: 'It is of the utmost importance that these children are given proper food at lunchtime and I will not countenance any suggestion otherwise.'

'Whoa,' I said to my silent friend in the photograph. 'You were a feisty one.'

Under the accounts books was a bundle of pamphlets, magazines and newsletters, all dedicated to the subject of Votes for Women and all dated after Esther had started Elm Heath Primary.

Intrigued I flicked through the pages. She'd obviously not abandoned the fight altogether, I thought. Perhaps she'd kept up with what was happening with her friends in the suffragettes, or perhaps she'd even been writing for these magazines.

I picked up one and tried to find a mention of her name, but couldn't see any Esther anywhere. I did, however, find several articles written by someone called Enid Whitehouse, both focusing on the importance of taking the suffragette cause into schools and getting the message about women's rights to the younger generation.

'Hmm,' I said aloud. 'Are you Enid? Were you spending your days at school and your evenings writing revolutionary literature under a pen-name, Esther?'

There was a bundle of photographs in the box, which I glanced through and set aside to look at properly another time, a folder containing what seemed to be job applications from potential teachers, all beautifully written in the most gorgeous copper-plate handwriting. I thought about the struggle to teach cursive to reluctant year twos and admired the teachers' teachers for getting them to write such lovely script.

The bell rang for the end of the day, and I ignored it, so caught up in this glimpse into the history of Elm Heath, was I. I was getting a real sense of how exciting it was for Esther and her staff to start something new, and to feel like they were making a difference.

At the bottom of the box was a brown folder, tied with a faded red cord. I tried to untie the knot but couldn't, so I snipped it with some scissors and opened it out, gasping in sheer delight as I realised what was inside.

It was all of Esther's notes and plans for Elm Heath Primary. There were notes about the local children she'd observed, a rough hand-drawn map of the local area marking the other schools nearby – there weren't many, sums and guesstimates about how many pupils they could expect and how many staff they would need, and there were several sheets of paper, each covered in lots of crossings-out and corrections, that were Esther's draft of the missing letter. The letter she'd written to the council that had convinced them Elm Heath Primary was worthy of their support.

I smoothed out the papers and started to read. It was inspiring stuff – I could see why it won everyone over. She talked about how she'd spent six months supporting a friend who was recovering from an illness.

'*I was very kindly put up on Orchard Farm and there got to know the local children. They were bright and attentive, and eager to learn, but there were no schools close enough and no one cared if they attended or not. I came to realise they were in desperate need of education and more than that, I realised they wanted an education.*

'*I began teaching lessons round the kitchen table in Orchard Farm and slowly the children were joined by friends, and their friends, and even their parents on occasion. There is a genuine and desperate need for a school in Elm Heath.*'

I felt my eyes filling up as I got a glimpse into a world before everyone got to go to school. I thought about the kids I taught, who didn't always want to be in the classroom, but always got something out of school eventually.

'*I believe passionately in giving everyone – be they men, women, of high birth or low – the opportunity to better themselves,*' Esther wrote.

I nodded. This was great stuff.

'*This is a time of change,*' Esther had written. '*I think preparing our children for the world they will one day be running is the most rewarding job there is.'*

I wiped my eyes, taken aback at how much the words of a long-ago teacher had affected me. I could see how Esther had won over the bean counters at the council. If I could channel a fraction of that passion, I'd be laughing.

I tapped my chin, thoughtfully. Nate was determined to get me to speak at the rally, though I'd not been sure what to say. Until now. Seeing Esther's plan spelled out so clearly, I wondered if I could simply read what she'd written.

'Perfect,' I muttered.

Somewhere under the piles of papers on my desk, my phone rang. I jumped, not just because I wasn't expecting a call, but because the ringtone was Uptown Funk. It was the ringtone I'd assigned to Grant's number because it reminded me of our wedding.

'Shit,' I said. I found my phone tucked inside one of the accounts books and paused with my finger hovering over the cancel button. I didn't want to speak to him; that was why I'd emailed. Typical bloody Grant, always going one better.

But then I glanced out of my window at the school railings, where earlier I'd heard Danny smooth-talking Vanessa, and I changed my mind. I jabbed the answer button violently and put the phone to my ear.

'Hi, Grant,' I said, like we'd only seen each other that morning.

'Queenie,' he said. No one else called me that silly nickname. I was Lizzie to everyone – even my mother – and Elizabeth on official documents. But like I said, he always went one better.

'I've missed you.'

Chapter 31

Esther

Autumn 1910

It had been a strange summer. The weather was terrible, which meant it didn't really feel like summer, given we had to wrap up in raincoats and hats every time we went outside. And there was a general feeling of expectation in the air. Things were just – slow. It was as though we were all waiting for something to happen. Which, I supposed, we were.

Agnes was blooming. Finally. Her stomach had swelled and her sickness had lessened and she had some colour back in her cheeks. She'd been so quiet and sad after she'd first found out she was expecting that Minnie and I had been really worried. John, too. She'd not even told him for ages, thinking he'd not be pleased at the prospect of another child under foot. But John was delighted and eventually, some of his enthusiasm rubbed off on Agnes.

'You've got me,' I told her over and over. 'I'll take care of the big ones and you can concentrate on the baby. It'll be so lovely having a little one in the house.'

We found all the pieces of Pearl's old crib, and all her baby clothes and I washed them all and hung them out in the garden when there was a gap between rain showers. The children were thrilled at the idea of having another sibling and argued endlessly over what the baby should be named.

'George,' John declared at the dinner table. 'After the new king. Or Edward after the old king.'

Agnes rolled her eyes. 'It might be a girl,' she said, smoothing her dress over her stomach. 'I think it's a girl. I felt worse with Pearl and Meg than I felt with you, John, just like I was with this one.'

John threw his head back dramatically. 'I can't bear it,' he wailed. 'I can't possibly be expected to put up with another sister.'

His father smiled at him indulgently. 'You'll be away at school soon and then you shall be complaining that you're missing out on all the cuddles with the new baby.'

'What do you think we should call the baby, Esther?' Meg said. 'It's so hard to decide, don't you think?'

'Maybe we should call her Esther?' Agnes said.

'That could get confusing.'

'Or Agnes,' Pearl suggested.

'Even worse,' her mother said, laughing. 'If I had my chance again I'd call John something different. It's so silly having two people with the same name in one family.'

John almost fell off his chair in outrage. 'Don't you dare think about changing my name now,' he said. 'I'm far too old to get used to something new.'

Everyone laughed and I joined in, relieved that Agnes was happy about being pregnant.

'You could call her Emmeline,' I suggested.

Agnes nodded. 'I might.'

It wasn't just the baby we were waiting for. The WSPU had all but stopped its activities because we had been promised that things were changing. We held one glorious rally in Hyde Park and marched occasionally, but generally things were quiet. We were hoping that the Conciliation Bill would pass when Parliament reassembled, which would give some women the right to vote. It would be a victory – of sorts. But as the autumn arrived, the weather cooled, and Agnes's baby's arrival drew closer, it began to feel we were waiting for something that would never come.

'I don't trust that bloody Mr Asquith,' Minnie said one evening as we waited for Mrs Pankhurst to speak at a meeting. 'I don't trust him one bit. He doesn't care about us and he's never been a supporter of the cause. He's got other priorities.'

'We have to give him a chance to see this bill through,' I said. 'There's no point worrying it's not going to happen until the MPs come back.'

Minnie looked at me through narrowed eyes. 'You like this waiting around,' she said. 'You're enjoying this.'

'I'm not.'

She snorted. 'Bloody well are. Makes your life much easier, don't it? Makes your romance with Joseph much easier.'

I flushed. 'Well, yes,' I admitted.

Joseph and I had had the most wonderful summer. John and Agnes had taken the children to Pevensey Bay for two weeks in August. They'd asked if I'd wanted to go along, but I'd said that I would rather stay in London and enjoy the peace and quiet. Not that I'd had much peace and quiet, because I'd actually spent every spare minute with Joseph. We'd been to the theatre, for tea, walked along the river, been dancing – it was all so perfect.

We even had some stolen evenings in his lodgings because his landlady had gone to Southend for the summer. I was certain he was the one for me so I felt no shame when we took our romance further than the kisses we'd shared until then. We loved each other, I told myself. We were going to be together for our whole lives. It just felt right.

And with there being no WSPU activities happening I wasn't worried about being forced to choose between my love for Joseph and my political convictions. In fact, I thought if the Conciliation Bill passed, then I wouldn't ever have to choose. Things would calm down, and Joseph and I could be together. We'd already talked about getting married, though I did manage to change the subject whenever he brought up meeting my family. I knew if he met my mother she would undoubtedly – and gleefully – spill the beans about what exactly I'd been doing with my life up until now. But still, I daydreamed about waking up each morning with Joseph at my side, and us making a home together.

Now I glanced over to where Agnes sat, uncomfortable on the hard, wooden chair, legs slightly spread to accommodate her growing bump, but still looking peaceful and content as she rested her hand on her belly tenderly. Maybe Joseph and I would have a baby as soon as we were married. A little boy who looked like his dad. Or a baby girl who would grow up not knowing that women were once seen as second-class citizens.

Mrs Pankhurst got up to speak and I tried to snap out of my daydreams and concentrate on what she was saying.

'Mr Asquith is no fan of the fight for women's suffrage,' she said.

Beside me, Minnie hissed: 'What did I say?'

I ignored her. I couldn't stand to think that this would fail.

'Parliament returns in one week and I propose we act then to remind the men at Westminster just how important this is,' Mrs Pankhurst said.

I drifted off again, dreaming of white lace and veils, and tiny baby girls, and only half-listening as Mrs Pankhurst told us what would happen.

'I propose a Women's Parliament to meet at Caxton Hall at the same time as the men arrive in Westminster,' she said. 'If for any reason, Mr Asquith lets us down on that first day, we can march to the House of Commons and demand an audience.'

The women around me cheered. I felt a flicker of unease.

'Will we be allowed in?' someone asked.

Mrs Pankhurst raised her chin. 'Perhaps not all of us, but when they see they strength of feeling, I imagine it would be a very foolish PM who keeps me shut out.'

Everyone cheered again. Minnie and I exchanged a glance.

'He'd never let her in,' she hissed at me under her breath. 'Not in a million years. This is going to be chaos.'

I was still determined to look on the bright side. 'It might be fine. The Conciliation Bill could pass and then everything will be all right.'

Minnie glared at me. 'You can't trust any of them,' she said. 'They'll just let you down again and again.'

'I trust Joseph.'

She tutted. 'Then you're more stupid than I thought.'

I bristled at the suggestion my feelings for Joseph were stupid. 'You trust Gil.'

Minnie's face softened, just a bit, at the mention of Gloomy Gilbert. 'Well, he's one of us, isn't he? Like John is. But Joseph isn't. He's one of them.'

I'd heard enough. Around us, the excited chatter was growing louder as people planned for next week's Women's Parliament and my head was beginning to ache. I stood up.

'I'm not stupid, I'm hopeful,' I said. 'And you, Minnie, are as gloomy as your bloody Gilbert. This is it, don't you see? This is where all our hard work pays off. Remember in Holloway, how you'd lie in bed, planning revenge on them all – the men who made the laws and who put us behind bars?'

Minnie looked up at me, sulky but listening. She nodded.

'This is the best revenge we've got. We're going to win this fight, Minnie. And once we've won this bit, we'll keep fighting until every woman has the vote.'

'I hope you're right,' Minnie said. 'Because from where I'm sitting it still looks like it could all be snatched away from us at the last minute.'

'It's always darkest before the dawn.'

Impulsively, I reached down and gave her a hug.

'We've done it, Minnie. We've won. Things are going to be so much better from now on. You'll see.'

Chapter 32

Esther

There was a strange atmosphere as we gathered back at Caxton Hall on the Friday. Feverish. Excitable. And with a good smattering of nerves, too.

We crowded into the room. The chairs were all taken but Minnie glared at a woman sitting near us until she stood to let Agnes sit down, and then we waited for news.

Minnie and I bickered gently with each other. She was still convinced Mr Asquith would do something – anything – that would mean the bill didn't happen. I was – foolishly, perhaps – desperate to believe that it would.

'It passed its second reading,' I said.

Minnie rolled her eyes. 'Means nothing.'

I bent down and addressed Agnes. 'What do you think? Do you think we've won?'

She shrugged. 'I hope so, but I'm not holding my breath,' she said. 'We've been here before. Close enough to taste it and then it all falls apart.'

I sighed and Agnes took my hand.

'We're strong enough to keep fighting,' she said.

She didn't know, of course, why I was so keen to see an end to this battle. Couldn't for one minute imagine that I wanted to put my militant days behind me and settle down with a policeman.

I gave her a thin-lipped smile as Mrs Pankhurst and the other leaders climbed on to the stage and the crowd cheered. But Mrs Pankhurst was grim-faced and the others looked similarly stern.

Minnie felt for my hand and I squeezed her fingers. I was still holding Agnes's hand, so we made a chain of three, all hoping for good news.

The hall fell silent as Mrs Pankhurst stood at the front of the stage.

'My friends,' she said. 'It is with heavy heart that I give you the news that Mr Asquith has let us down. The Conciliation Bill is to be shelved.'

I had been holding my breath. Now I let it out in a gasp. Minnie squeezed my hand harder. Beside us on her chair, Agnes sat up straighter as Mrs Pankhurst began to outline her plan.

'Mr Asquith has called a general election. This means Parliament will be dissolved and there will be no time for the Bill to be approved.'

There were shouts and jeers as we all realised our hopes had been dashed.

'What will we do?' someone in the front of the crowd shouted.

Mrs Pankhurst raised her chin in defiance. 'I propose we send a deputation to Mr Asquith, straight away,' she said. 'We have some banners and placards here ready.'

A murmur of agreement spread around the hall.

'Will we all go?' one woman called.

Mrs Pankhurst and Mrs Garrett Anderson, who was on the stage next to her, spoke to each other for a moment. Then they both consulted the other women sharing their platform who all nodded as they spoke. Then Mrs Pankhurst raised her hand for silence.

'Our aim is to reach the House of Commons,' she said. 'So we propose we split into smaller groups of ten or twelve women. If we leave here at intervals of a few minutes, it will give us a better chance of getting to the entrance.'

We all nodded. I was impressed at the leaders' strategy. They were right, I thought. There would be police at the Houses of Parliament; that wasn't in doubt. They would be expecting us. And a large group of women would surely be easier to stop than smaller deputations.

'She's right,' Minnie whispered to me. 'She's so clever.'

'We will go first,' Mrs Pankhurst announced. Minnie and I stared at the group of leaders, gathering their banners and placards.

'Some of them are old,' Minnie breathed into my ear. 'Will it be dangerous? I don't think they should go first.'

She had a point. One of the women on stage was in her seventies, and Mrs Garrett Anderson and Mrs Pankhurst were hardly youngsters.

I shook my head. 'It won't be dangerous,' I assured her, though I was really trying to convince myself. 'I don't think so anyway.'

We both looked at Agnes, who was heaving herself to her feet.

I turned to the side slightly and whispered in Minnie's ear. 'Should Agnes stay behind?'

She gave the tiniest nod. 'I reckon so. She shouldn't be marching anywhere, in her condition.'

'Rubbish,' Agnes said behind us. We both started, guilty at being caught out talking about her. 'I can walk.'

'Agnes,' I began. 'What if it's dangerous?'

She glared at me. 'Why would it be dangerous?'

'Well, there's bound to be a crowd.'

She shrugged. 'I'm not an invalid, Esther. I've been pregnant before and I know what I'm doing. I admit, I might be a bit slow, and I accept I might get jostled if it's busy. But you girls can stand either side of me and protect this one.' She hugged her stomach and smiled at us.

I chewed my lip. 'If you're sure?'

Agnes glanced round at the groups of women sorting themselves out, holding placards, and readying to leave. 'Perhaps we'll go in one of the last groups,' she said. 'That way, the women ahead of us will have cleared the way, and we can walk straight up to St Stephen's Gate.'

I was pleased she was being sensible.

'We'll look after you,' Minnie said. 'Right, shall we find ourselves some people to tag along with?'

We found a few other women milling around and within minutes, Agnes had taken charge and sorted us into a group.

Mrs Pankhurst and the others in the first band of protesters were ready to go. We cheered them off and they headed towards Westminster, banners and placards held aloft.

'I hope Mr Asquith is amenable,' Agnes said, watching them go. 'He's so stubborn.'

My stomach was churning with nerves. 'I can't imagine what we'll do if he doesn't agree to speak to Mrs Pankhurst.'

Agnes patted me on the shoulder. 'I told you, we'll carry on fighting,' she said.

Exhausted at the mere thought of juggling my two lives for longer, I felt tears well up in my eyes. Agnes put her arm around me, as though she was my mother. For a moment I rested my head on her shoulder and took comfort from her warmth.

'Darling Esther, I know it's not been easy for you,' she said, stroking my hair. 'Your time in Holloway was awful, and you stayed firm despite it all. But you're a soldier, my girl. A brave warrior. And we will win this war. Remember why we're doing this. Remember why we fight.'

I buried my head in her shoulder, taking strength from her words and then with a deep breath I straightened up. I believed so passionately in what we were doing that it equalled my feelings for Joseph. Seeing my mother suffer because of my father's actions, and having no way to right those wrongs had just been the beginning of my fervent belief in women being equal to men. Once my eyes had been opened, I saw inequality and closed doors everywhere and I was determined to fight. However tiring it was to be involved in the WSPU, and spending time with Joseph, I couldn't give up now.

'You're right,' I said. 'Let's find some placards.'

Minnie had found some paint and some blank boards and was crouched on the floor, merrily painting slogans alongside some other women doing the same.

'*Where there's a Bill there's a way*,' she wrote in her neat hand. I grinned. 'That's nice.'

'I copied it off that one over there.' She pointed with her paintbrush to where a group of young suffragettes were standing ready to leave. 'Come on, we need to get ready. We don't want to be left behind.'

Altogether there were about twenty-five groups of women, I estimated, so it took well over an hour from when Mrs Pankhurst's band of protesters had left Caxton Hall before it was our turn to go. We were one of the last groups to march, and the febrile atmosphere at the hall had calmed down a lot by the time we got going. I felt my heart rate slow and began to almost look forward to whatever was going to happen. I enjoyed taking action; it felt like I was doing something – being mistress of my own destiny – rather than sitting around waiting for a man to tell me how to act.

'Ready?' Agnes said, as we lined up by the entrance. We all nodded and murmured our agreement. 'Then let's go and show Mr Asquith exactly what we think of his bloody general election.'

Chapter 33

Esther

We could hear the trouble before we saw it. Feel it before we heard it. It was like a rumble, rolling over Parliament Square as we approached. Minnie clutched my arm.

'What's that?' she said.

We'd been marching determinedly from Caxton Hall, but now our pace slowed as we all listened.

'Shouting,' I said.

But it was more than just shouting. We could hear bellows, that was true, but there were also cries and screams. We all looked at each other nervously.

Agnes tilted her head, all senses on alert as she listened. 'It sounds like trouble.'

'Some sort of riot?' Minnie bit her lip in worry, but there was a gleam in her eye, too. I knew how she felt. I was scared, of course, but I could feel the adrenaline flooding into me and my heart pumping faster.

'Should we carry on?' one of our group asked. She was very young – I guessed maybe around sixteen – and jumping at every roar or screech that we heard. 'I think we should go back.'

'Absolutely not,' Minnie said, drawing herself up to her full height. Which wasn't much but still managed to look impressive. 'We came here to do a job and we're not going until it's done.'

'But . . .' the girl began and then stopped speaking as Agnes took her shoulders.

'What's your name?' she asked.

The girl took a shuddery breath. 'Hannah.'

'Hannah, you go if you want to,' Agnes said. 'But we are here to support Mrs Pankhurst, Mrs Garrett Anderson and the rest. They're up there now, facing down whatever's waiting for them. And we should be there to stand shoulder to shoulder with them.'

'Miss Heligan is almost eighty and she's there,' Minnie added. I stayed quiet because though I completely agreed with Agnes, and while there was no way I was even considering turning back, I did feel that perhaps Agnes should head home while she still could.

'I'm scared,' Hannah whispered.

Agnes nodded. 'We're all scared,' she said. 'But this is what makes it worthwhile. And it's nothing we've not seen before, right girls?'

She looked at Minnie and me and we both grinned.

'We're battle-worn,' Minnie said. 'Got the scars to prove it.'

'Fine,' Hannah said.

I looped my arm through hers. 'Come on then.'

But we'd not taken five steps when a suffragette appeared in front of us, hurrying away from Parliament Square.

As she got closer, we could see she was bleeding from her nose and her dress was torn, almost to the waist. She was blotchy and tear-stained and dripping blood on to the pavement.

'It's worse than I ever saw,' said the bleeding woman.

I let go of Hannah and caught the woman, who stumbled as she passed us.

'Stop,' I said. 'Sit down. Catch your breath.'

Hannah and I bundled her on to a nearby step and she slumped against the railings. Agnes pulled out a handkerchief and gently mopped the blood from her nose and we all gathered round, staring at her.

'Step back,' Minnie shouted. 'Give her some air.' She looked down at the woman. 'What's happening? Who did this to you? Should we get a policeman?'

The woman looked fearfully down the street towards Parliament Square and shuddered. 'No,' she said. She let out a sob and tried to swallow it down. 'The police did this.'

Next to me, Hannah gasped. 'Are you sure?' she said.

But Minnie and I exchanged a glance. We knew from our own bitter experience that the police couldn't always be relied on but we'd never seen such blatant evidence of their cruelty.

Agnes took charge – as always. 'Hannah,' she said. 'Until we know what's happening, you should go back to Caxton Hall. Take the others with you and stop anyone else who's coming along for now. I think there were only one or two groups left. Minnie, Esther and I will stay with . . . what's your name?'

The bloodied suffragette looked up. 'Nelly,' she said.

'We'll stay with Nelly, make sure she is all right, and find out what's going on.'

Looking relieved, Hannah rounded up the rest of our little group and they all turned back in the direction we'd come, towards Caxton Hall.

Carefully, Agnes lowered herself down on the step next to Nelly. 'Now, tell us exactly what happened.'

Nelly looked alarmed at Agnes's bossiness but she started to talk, faltering at first, then more confidently. 'I've been to loads of rallies and that,' she said. 'But I've not seen anything like this. It feels different this time.'

'How so?'

'I was in one of the first groups, just behind Mrs Pankhurst and the others. So when we arrived in the square we were expecting a bit of trouble. We knew there would be police and it wasn't like we thought they'd just wave us in . . .'

She paused.

'But there were so many police. Loads of them. Far more than you'd normally see round here.'

'Really?' Minnie said. 'Do you think they were expecting us?'

'Definitely,' Nelly said. She leaned forward. 'Someone said they weren't the usual coppers that patrol round here. It can't have been, 'cause there were far too many. And, I reckon there were police in the crowds too. Not in uniform. Because I recognised a few faces.'

'Why would they do that?' Agnes asked, frowning. 'Why have police in the crowd, too? Are they arresting lots of our girls?'

Nelly shook her head. 'That's the thing. I didn't see them arresting anyone. The police were just grabbing women and chucking them into the crowd and letting them do what they wanted to them.'

We all stared at her, horrified.

'I got punched by someone, and one of them pulled my skirts right up.'

Her strength wavered, just a bit, and her voice trembled.

'They're not all police, in the crowd. There's day-trippers and other people. The man who punched me looked like he was on his way to work. But his eyes were black – you know how they get?'

Agnes looked grave. 'How many were police?'

'Dunno. I just know there were a lot of them. Same girl who told me about the ones in the crowd said there were police from all over.'

I stiffened. 'Where? Where is all over?'

Nelly shrugged. 'Up East, I think. Whitechapel. But someone else said there were some from south of the river, too. And someone else said north. So who knows.'

I felt icy cold suddenly. Joseph was working today – I knew that. What if he was among the police that had been drafted in from Whitechapel? I could hardly deny being a part of the WSPU now, given I was wearing a Votes for Women sash and carrying a placard.

'This is a disgrace,' Agnes said. 'How dare they! How dare they do this. We have been let down and all we want to do is express how we feel.'

'I'm furious,' said Nelly. 'The whole thing's a mess. It's like one huge fight.' She stood up. 'Shall we go?'

Agnes nodded firmly. 'Shoulder to shoulder.'

I looked down past them towards Parliament Square. The shouts were still echoing round the buildings. Was Joseph there somewhere?

'I don't think we should go,' I said desperately. 'I think we should go back to Caxton Hall.'

'You have got to be joking,' Minnie said. She looked furious. 'You want to run away? What's wrong with you?'

'Not run away. Just, take a moment.' I pulled her arm and we stepped away from Agnes and Nelly.

'I don't think Agnes should get involved in this. She's pregnant, Min.'

Minnie screwed her nose up. 'I suppose.'

She watched me carefully. 'Where's your Joseph based?'

I swallowed. 'He's not working today,' I lied. 'Doesn't matter.'

'Right.'

'He's not working, honest.'

'Hmm,' Minnie said. 'So you're telling me that you, brave Esther Watkins, devotee of the WSPU cause, former Holloway inmate, who just a few months ago fought off a handy copper, are suggesting we run away from this protest because . . .?'

'Because of Agnes.'

'And not because you're scared you might spot your fella in the crowd?'

'No,' I said, but my protests sounded weak, even to my own ears.

'Anyway we're too late,' Minnie said. 'Look.'

I turned to see Agnes, arm in arm with Nelly, walking towards Parliament Square.

'Bugger,' I breathed. 'Looks like we're doing it.'

'Sure?'

I looked at Agnes, seven months pregnant and still willing to add her voice to the others, and Nelly, bloodied and tear-stained and going back for more, and felt ashamed of my cowardice.

I nodded. 'I'm sure,' I said.

Minnie reached up and pulled my hat down over my eyes.

'He won't see you, even if he is there,' she said. 'All they see is the sashes and the banners.'

I straightened my hat again and lifted my chin. 'I'm not ashamed,' I said. 'This is who I am. If Joseph sees me, then I'll deal with it.'

Minnie picked up our placards and handed me one, then we clasped our hands together.

'Wait for us,' I shouted after Agnes and Nelly. 'We're coming.'

Chapter 34

Esther

It was chaos in Parliament Square. There were people everywhere; women shouting, crying, screaming.

'Where are we heading?' I said, trying to see through the crowds to the Houses of Parliament.

'St Stephen's.' Nelly gestured with her placard. 'They shut the gates and women were climbing them.'

She sounded proud and I wasn't surprised. The resilience of the women I called my friends never stopped impressing me.

'Did they get through?'

'Police grabbed them first.'

Minnie stood on her tiptoes to see better. 'They're still going,' she said in delight. 'I can see people trying to get over.'

Agnes was watching the crowds in front of us. 'I think if we can go round the back here, we can skirt the edge of the grass,' she said. 'I can see a route where there are fewer people.'

I looked where she was pointing and nodded in agreement. But I was still worried about the crush of bodies, because brave as she was, Agnes had a baby to think about.

'Agnes, you go in the middle of us,' I said. 'We'll shield you.'

She nodded, grateful. 'Thank you.'

We arranged ourselves with me in front of Agnes, and Minnie and Nelly either side, and with our heads up and our shoulders back, I led the way round to the right of where we stood towards the huge black gates of Parliament.

We walked confidently, but cautiously, because around us were scenes of sheer horror. I saw one woman dragged along the ground by two policemen. Her legs were kicking but they were much stronger than she. They left her in a heap on the grass, like an old piece of rubbish, and she lay there for a moment.

'Should we help her?' I said to Minnie, but as I spoke, the woman stood up – shakily – and started towards the gates once more.

'Let's just keep going,' Minnie said. She looked pale in the wintry sunshine and I knew the fear I could see in her eyes was reflected in my own. 'We just need to get to the gate.'

But as we started to walk again, a large policeman barred our way. He didn't speak but he grabbed the placards we were holding. Mine had a rough edge that cut into my hand as he yanked it and I cried out in pain. The policeman threw the placards on the ground and snapped them, standing on one end and pulling up the handles. As he snapped mine, the jagged edge cut his hand too and he cried out in pain – and anger – as I'd done.

Another policeman stopped to see what was happening. 'Did they do that?' he said.

The first man nodded. 'Slashed me.'

'Oh rubbish, you caught your hand on our placard,' I said. 'I did the same thing.'

The first policeman didn't speak; instead he just pulled my arm.

'Search her,' he said, pushing me towards the other man. 'She must have a knife.'

'I don't have a knife, don't be ridiculous.'

He started to pat me down, though it was less patting and more grabbing. His hands seemed to be all over me, clutching at my breasts. I squirmed away and he shouted at me to stay still, so I did. I wanted to cry as his thick fingers probed under my skirts but I kept my head up, trying not to flinch as he pushed his hand in between my legs. My cheeks flushed with humiliation, and I tried not to think about what he was doing.

'She's got nothing,' he called, slowly removing his hand.

I stared him right in the eyes, meeting his gaze with defiance, though my inner thighs felt bruised from his assault.

'As I told you.'

He shoved me back towards the group. 'Go home,' he said in a mocking tone. 'Ladies.'

We stayed where we were, still and watchful, as he and the first policeman continued on their way, laughing with each other, and then I took a deep breath.

'Are you all right?' Minnie asked, her brow furrowed.

I nodded. 'Let's keep going.'

We stepped over the broken remains of our placards and carried on towards the gates. As we drew nearer, it seemed things were getting more out of hand. Women were being pulled from the gates, but instead of being arrested as you'd expect, they were being thrown back to the crowds that had gathered, just as Nelly had said.

'See?'

'I do see,' Agnes said. 'I do.'

'Agnes,' I said urgently. 'I know you are bold but I really think it's time for you to go back. Take yourself to safety.'

Minnie nodded.

'She's right, Agnes. This is no place for a pregnant woman.'

Agnes looked up at the women being grabbed from the gates and slowly she nodded too.

'I think you're speaking sense,' she said. 'I'll go back to Caxton Hall and wait for you there.'

I put my hand on Nelly's shoulder. 'Would you go with her?' I asked. 'I think you need a sit-down too and probably someone should have a look at your injuries.'

Nelly's face was turning purple on one side, her eye was almost swollen shut and she was swaying slightly.

'I suppose,' she said. 'Come on, Agnes.'

She offered her arm to Agnes, but as she did, a man in a smart suit and woollen overcoat walked by and without warning, kicked out at Nelly. He took her legs from under her and she crashed to the ground, taking him with her, which he'd obviously not intended to happen. He looked shocked to be sprawled on the pavement and he glared at Nelly.

'Officer!' he shouted. 'This woman attacked me.'

At once, we were surrounded by three or four policemen, all bellowing at us. I was filled with fury – and frustration – as I tried to explain what had happened. But they weren't listening. One grabbed Minnie by the shoulders as she was trying to help Nelly up, and held her arms behind her back, rendering her helpless. Another gave poor Nelly a whack with his truncheon simply for raising her head, and she slumped back on the ground, looking frighteningly limp. The man who'd tripped her was back on his feet, and he gave her another strike with his foot for good measure.

'Stop!' I screamed.

Agnes, who was closer to Nelly than I was, turned on the nearest policeman in anger.

'What are you doing?' she shouted into his face, standing on her toes so she could better match his height. 'How dare you? She's just a girl and she's done nothing wrong.'

And that's when it happened. The policeman, not wanting Agnes so close to him, gave her a huge shove. She stepped backwards but tripped over the kerb and landed on the road on her side.

'Agnes,' I screamed. 'Help her. She's pregnant.'

But the policeman with the truncheon was angry, and as Agnes started to get up, he whacked her on the head, once, twice, and she fell back down.

I tried to get past him but his back was so broad and the crowd so suffocating, I couldn't get to Agnes. Instead I pulled at his arm, wanting him to stop hitting her.

'She's pregnant,' I shouted. 'She's pregnant, you idiot.'

He looked round at me, and I recognised him – again. Once more I was in a struggle with Joseph's friend, Alf. He didn't know me; that was obvious. He just tried to shake me off his arm.

'Alf,' I said, hoping to get through to him, to make him stop. 'It's me, Esther. We met in the park?'

He didn't hear – or didn't listen – as he kicked Agnes in the small of her back and sent her sprawling on the pavement once more – right on to her round belly. She made a horrible sound, a wail of sheer despair, and I felt a rush of blinding fury rise up inside me. What had Alf done?

Making an animal-like roar, I used all my strength to pull Alf's arm back and he dropped his truncheon.

Quick as a flash, I bent and picked it up. Its handle was warm, and the weight of the weapon soothed me. I looped the leather strap round my wrist, held on tight and raised the truncheon above my head, then I brought it down with all my might, on to Alf's face as he looked round at me.

There was a crunch as the truncheon met his nose and I watched in satisfaction as blood splattered across his face.

'Esther,' Minnie shouted, but it sounded as though she was a long, long way away as I raised the truncheon again and once more brought it down on to Alf's head. He swore at me, trying to shield himself from my blows.

'I told you she was pregnant,' I said, as I hit him over and over. 'I told you, but you attacked her anyway. Her baby's blood is on your hands.'

'Get her off me,' he shouted at his colleagues. 'She's a bloody madwoman. Get her off me.'

I kept hitting him, wildly lashing out, until someone grabbed my arms from behind and twisted my wrist. I felt the bones crunch, agonisingly, and I dropped the truncheon as I cried out.

'Oh, you're in big, big, trouble, Miss,' said a voice behind me. 'Big, bloody trouble.'

Roughly, I was pulled round to face the man holding me. And there, looking down at me, with an ugly sneer on his face, was Joseph.

Chapter 35

Lizzie

2019

Grant came. Of course he came. Even though I'd specifically told him not to.

'I'll come,' he'd said on the phone. 'I'm between contracts and I could do with a project to get my teeth into.'

I'd bristled. 'It's fine,' I said. 'I'm fine.'

He'd carried on as though I'd not even spoken. 'It'll be great. Something new. Good for the old CV.'

'Grant, listen to me. All I need is for you to let me have some of your media contacts. I can do the rest on my own.'

There had been a pause. 'Oh, Queenie,' he said. 'Where's the fun in that?'

That had been more than a week ago and I'd begun to think that I was off the hook. Perhaps he'd got another contract and his time was too precious to waste on a little school like Elm Heath. Or perhaps he'd – for once – listened to what I'd said.

Then, as I sat at home one evening, going over the budgets for the after-school club and working out to my immense pride and pleasure that it was making a profit, I heard the familiar roar of Grant's motorbike. Or, as I liked to call it, his mid-life crisis.

'No,' I said out loud, tilting my head so I could hear better. 'He wouldn't.'

But he would and he did. The engine stopped and I heard footsteps on my path and then a loud knock at the door.

I could pretend I'm not here, I thought. But my curtains were open to show off my, fairly pitiful admittedly, Christmas tree and my lights were on. There was no avoiding this one.

Resentfully, I plodded to the door, wishing I'd not changed out of the dress I'd worn to school as soon as I got home. Instead I was wearing an oversized jumper that I thought might once have belonged to my brother, and faded leggings along with some thick socks and novelty slippers in the shape of yellow Minions.

'Hello, Grant,' I said, as I opened the door. 'What a surprise.'

Grant flashed me his best smile. 'You don't sound very surprised,' he said. He bent and kissed me on the cheek, and the smell of his aftershave and the memories it triggered made me dizzy. I steadied myself against the wall. I'd loved him once and despite everything I was pleased to see him. Sort of.

'You're looking good.' I was telling the truth. Grant had always been handsome, but he was the kind of man who got better-looking with every year that passed. His hair was properly salt and pepper now, and he'd grown a beard, which suited him.

'So are you,' he said. 'Love the feet.'

'I wasn't expecting company.'

'Busy?'

'Doing some budgets.'

'Can I come in?'

I rolled my eyes but of course I was always going to let him in. I was weak where Grant was concerned. Always had been. He beckoned and I followed, without ever asking where we were going. It had taken all my strength to leave him, and even more strength to stay away. And now he was here, filling my hallway and looking at me in that same indulgent and slightly patronising way.

216

'Are you annoyed with me?' he said.

I flopped down on the sofa, leaving all my budget notes and my laptop next to me so he'd have to sit in the chair.

'Not with you,' I said. 'More with myself for imagining you'd listen to me, or trust me to do this on my own.'

'Queenie,' he said. He picked up my notes and my laptop and put them on the coffee table and sat down next to me. So much for that plan. 'This isn't about your little project. I wanted to see you.'

'It's not a little project. It's a campaign to save a very important school.'

Grant nodded. 'You're right, I'm sorry. It's just that to me, it's not as important as you are.'

'Balls.'

He snorted with laughter. 'There she is,' he said. 'My Queenie. Sweet-talking never worked with you, did it?'

I smiled, despite myself. 'No. And don't call me Queenie.'

Grant put his hand on my knee and I looked down at it and then up at him.

'Grant,' I said, warning him off. He, predictably, ignored me.

'I miss you, Liz,' he said glumly.

'Right, like the women aren't queuing up for you,' I said. Because despite his flaws, Grant was a proper charmer. He was funny, and good-looking, and really clever. And when he fixed his eyes on you, you felt like you were the only person in the whole room – the whole world almost – that he was interested in. He had charisma. Chutzpah. Big Dick Energy. Whatever you wanted to call it. And women loved it. I couldn't blame them – I'd been the same once.

Now he shrugged. 'There's no one special,' he said. 'And it's Christmas. Our first Christmas apart, Queenie.'

I glared at him. 'It's our second Christmas apart,' I said. 'Last Christmas I was living with my mother, listening to her tell me for the millionth time about how well my bloody brother's career

217

was going, worrying I was never going to work again and crying every time I thought about how many lies you'd told me.'

Grant did, at least, have the grace to look slightly embarrassed. 'Second Christmas,' he said. 'Of course it is.'

He shifted on the sofa.

'Last year was a bit of a blur, if I'm honest.'

I felt a sudden – and very small – flash of sympathy for him. He'd done things totally wrong, and he'd made everything about himself when it should have been about the kids at his school, but he wasn't a bad man. Not really. At least, not completely.

I patted his hand. 'Drink?'

'I thought you'd never ask.'

I gave him the first genuine smile I'd managed since he'd turned up. 'I've got nothing here, but there's a pub just down the road,' I said. 'Why don't you head on down there, and get the drinks in, and I'll get changed and be there in five.'

It was what we always used to do when I was being slow at getting ready for a night out.

Grant grinned at me. 'Gin and slim?'

'Please.'

Wasn't it funny how quickly you just slotted back into old habits?

I took Grant to the front door and pointed him in the direction of the pub, then I took the stairs two at a time up to my bedroom. I didn't want to take too long getting ready because I knew if I did, Grant would have made friends with everyone in the pub – that was the sort of man he was.

I yanked off my scruffy sweater and leggings, pulled on the dress I'd worn to work, pulled it off again because it looked too head-teachery, and instead went for black jeans and a soft, slim-fitting, black jumper. My hair was wild but I didn't have time to tame it, so I pulled it into a bun and added some sparkly earrings to stop me looking like a Russian spy. I squirted myself with perfume to disguise the smell of school dinners, whacked on some mascara and took a deep breath.

'Stay strong, Lizzie,' I said to myself. 'He is not good for you. Get what you need and then send him on his way.'

Despite my lightning-fast makeover, by the time I got to the Three Kings, Grant was standing at the bar, surrounded by people, telling a story that was making everyone – even bloody Nev the grumpy barman – laugh.

I paused for a minute by the door, to gather myself and to roll my eyes without anyone seeing, and then went over.

'Lizzie!' Paula's husband Chris was in the group surrounding Grant. 'Grant was just telling us you were on your way.'

'You know me, Chris,' I said through a forced smile. 'I'm never one to miss out on a drink.'

Grant reached over and handed me my gin. 'Shall we grab a table?' he said. He shook Chris by the hand, jovially. 'Great to chat, Chris,' he said. 'Let me know about that round of golf. And Phil –' he turned to another man who I'd seen around but never spoken to '– keep me posted on how your wife's getting on, won't you?'

I raised my eyebrows at him as he slid into the chair opposite me.

'Wife's got cancer, poor git,' he said. 'But apparently the treatment's going well.'

'You're something else,' I said. 'You've been here five minutes and you know everyone better than I do.'

He smiled. 'That's not true,' he said. 'They were all singing your praises.'

I was pleased. 'Really?'

'They said you've done wonders already and that you're planning some big rally?'

I nodded. 'That's what we need publicity for,' I explained. 'It's a really good story. The woman who founded the school was a suffragette, so we're drawing inspiration from her, doing a march and a rally, and trying to show the council how important the school is.' I took a slug of gin. 'Will you help?'

Grant leaned forward across the table, his eyes gleaming. He loved a challenge. 'Tell me everything.'

It took a while but I filled him in on how lovely the children were, and how much everyone wanted to keep Elm Heath Primary open. And I told him about the developers sniffing round, and that the surveyor had been to visit, and he frowned.

'It doesn't sound good, Liz.'

I lifted my chin. 'I know, but it's not fair that they're just acting as if the Elm Heath kids don't matter. They're such a lovely bunch and for all the fancy big houses there are round here, there are a lot of vulnerable kids too. I don't want them to have to schlep into Blyton every day, where no one knows them.'

Grant was staring at me.

'What?'

'Just, you,' he said. 'I always loved how much you cared about the kids.'

I looked down into my empty glass, embarrassed by the affection I could see in his eyes. 'Don't,' I said. This was already too complicated. Keen to deflect his attention away from me, I pushed back my chair, and stood up. 'Another drink?'

Grant nodded. 'Same again, please.'

I picked up our empties and weaved through the tables to the bar. I'd just ordered when I felt a hand on my back and turned, expecting to see Grant. But it was Danny.

'Lizzie,' he said. 'How are you?'

I looked up at him. What to say? That I'd spent a week berating myself for sleeping with him when he was obviously seeing someone else? That I had seen him around the village a few times and deliberately gone the other way to avoid a situation just like this one? That my ex-husband had just rocked up and was making it quite clear that if I fancied rekindling things, he'd be up for it? Instead I said nothing. I just smiled.

'Listen,' Danny said. 'I'm sorry.'

'What for?'

Our hands were next to each other on the bar, my left hand close to his right. He stretched out his little finger and hooked it round mine. The touch of his skin on mine had an immediate effect on me, sending heat rushing to my face – and elsewhere.

'I've fucked everything up, but I'm sorting it, Lizzie,' he said. 'Trust me?'

I pulled my hand away from his. 'How can I trust you now?'

I felt his eyes on my back as I took the drinks Nev handed me and headed back to the table, slopping some of Grant's beer as I plonked down the glasses.

'Easy,' Grant said. He leaned back in his chair and looked at me carefully. 'Are you okay?' he said.

'I'm fine.' I forced a smile.

'Who was that you were speaking to at the bar?'

I pretended not to remember. 'Speaking to? Erm . . .'

Glancing round, making out I was checking to see who'd been there, I accidentally caught Danny's eye. He was still watching me, though he was chatting to Phil and Chris.

Quickly I looked away. 'Oh that's Danny,' I said casually. 'Just a parent.'

Grant narrowed his eyes. 'Just a parent?' he said. 'No one special?'

I swallowed. 'No,' I said. 'No one special.'

Chapter 36

Lizzie

Grant didn't stay with me. I was weak when it came to him, but not that weak. Instead he made himself comfy in a room above the Three Kings and arranged to come into school at lunchtime the following day to meet the staff.

I'd not even taken my coat off the next morning when Paula arrived in my office.

'Tell me everything,' she demanded, handing me a coffee. 'Chris says your Grant was in the pub?'

I hung my coat up, and sat down at my desk, groaning. 'He turned up on my doorstep with no warning,' I said. 'I knew it was a mistake telling him about Elm Heath. He's like a dog with a bone, that man. He loves a challenge.'

'Is he going to help?'

'He thinks it's difficult but he didn't say no. He's coming into school at lunchtime to meet you all.'

Paula looked thrilled. 'Chris says he's really nice.'

'Yes, well, he is,' I said bluntly. 'Just don't marry him.'

She leaned forward across my desk. 'Is it tricky, seeing him again?'

I sighed. 'You know the expression "rubbing salt in the wound"? Let's just say I'm living it.'

'That bad?' Paula grimaced. 'What about Danny? Have you seen him?'

I'd not told Paula anything about me and Danny since our trip to visit Fiona. I'd not told her about him spending the night, nor about me overhearing him on the phone – it just all seemed a bit embarrassing. Now I looked away from her enquiring gaze.

'He was in the pub last night, actually,' I said. 'But I don't think that's going to work out, you know. We've both got a lot on . . .'

'Hmm,' said Paula.

'What does that mean?'

She looked at me, head tilted to one side. 'It means, I don't think you're telling me the whole truth,' she said. 'Either you're hiding something about Danny, or you're still in love with Grant. Or both.'

I felt my cheeks colour. 'Not true,' I said. 'I'm definitely not still in love with Grant.'

'Really?'

I nodded, more firmly than I felt. 'Him being around is strange, and unsettling, and yes he knows how to push my buttons,' I said. 'But honestly, that ship has sailed.'

I thought about the electricity that had zinged through me when Danny touched his little finger to mine, and felt my cheeks glowing again. 'That ship has sailed,' I said again.

'And what about Danny's ship?'

I shrugged, not knowing where to begin with Danny.

Paula opened her mouth to talk, just as the bell rang. 'Saved,' she said.

I laughed in relief, glad I'd avoided an interrogation. 'Go,' I said. 'But come to my office at lunchtime. I'll introduce Grant to everyone.'

The morning flew by. Because it was the last week of term, school was crazy. It was the nativity that week and I was really excited about seeing all the kids show their parents how hard

223

they'd been practising. There was a festive feel to the whole place with decorations in all the classrooms and the children just one notch away from being totally out of control. I was really loving it.

I was just writing a list of local dignitaries we wanted to invite to the nativity when Grant appeared in my office. He always came into a room like he was expecting a fanfare. I'd forgotten how annoying it was.

'Morning,' I said, glancing up from my list. 'Have a seat, I just need to finish this.'

I added the name of the chair of governors even though we'd emailed his invitation weeks ago, then wrote "another name, and another name, and another one" at the bottom, just to stretch out the time I was taking. And then I finally looked up. Grant was sitting opposite me, watching me and smiling.

'Nativity plans?' he said.

'Local bigwigs who we should invite.'

'Let's have a look.' He reached out for my notepad and I whisked it away before he could see the fake names I'd written, dropping it into my drawer and slamming it shut.

'Won't mean anything to you.'

Grant leaned back in his – my – chair and surveyed the room. 'It's a nice school,' he said. 'Tiny.'

'It's a lovely school.'

'Kids seem well-behaved.'

'They are.'

'What about the staff?'

'They're well-behaved too.'

He grinned and I softened.

'They're all coming to meet you.' I checked my watch. 'Any minute, actually.'

Right on cue, Paula knocked on my doorframe. 'Knock, knock,' she called, even though the door was open and she had also actually knocked.

'Paula,' I said. 'Come in. Grant, this is my deputy, Paula. You met her husband Chris last night. She teaches reception.'

'Jesus,' said Grant, standing up and giving Paula his best smile. 'You're a better person than I am. Is it all potty training and phonics?'

I knew for a fact that Paula hated when people reduced teaching reception to sounding out letters, so I braced myself for a rude comment from her, but instead she beamed at Grant.

'Luckily I've got a TA for the toilet trips,' she said.

'Wise woman,' Grant said. 'So, your husband was saying that your daughter is doing her A Levels . . .'

Paula started talking about Chloe and I smiled. Grant knew how to get someone chatting, that was for sure. He was good at asking questions and being genuinely interested in other people's lives. It was why he was so popular with the kids and staff at the schools he'd worked in, and why they all adored him. It was just a shame he got carried away with all that hero-worship and started firstly to believe his own hype and then to push things to the limit to stay on his pedestal.

There was a flurry of activity as Nate, Celeste and the others all arrived in my office at once. It was a bit of a squeeze but everyone eventually found a space and looked up at me expectantly.

'Everyone, this is my, erm, my . . . This is Grant Mansfield.'

There was a murmur of interest and Nate glared at Grant.

'I contacted Grant because he has a lot of experience dealing with the media and I thought he could help with our campaign to save Elm Heath,' I said. 'He had a bit of free time so he decided to come up and see for himself.'

'Well, aren't we the lucky ones,' said Nate sarcastically. I frowned at him and he made a face at me. I let it go. It was sweet that he was being protective of me.

Celeste looked Grant up and down and he shifted in his chair under the weight of her stare. Amused to see him uncomfortable, I waited for her to speak. 'What can you do for us?' she said eventually.

Grant seemed slightly nonplussed by my team's indifferent welcome. I'd never seen him like that before. He paused for a second and then recovered his composure.

'Actually,' he said. 'I've got a few things up my sleeve.'

'Go on,' Nate said.

'I was chatting with a friend who works for the BBC,' Grant said. 'I wanted to see if we could get a news crew to cover the story. And then he said it was more of a human-interest thing, and anyway the long and short of it is, *The One Show* are totally on board and they're coming to film the nativity and do a little piece on your campaign.'

There was a stunned silence in my office.

'Oh, and,' Grant went on. He was enjoying this, the bugger. 'A couple of the Sunday newspapers are interested, and the *Guardian* wants a profile on you, Queenie, erm, Lizzie.'

We all stared at him. Never in our wildest dreams had we imagined things would happen this way. Never.

'That's incredible,' Nate stammered. 'Amazing.'

I forced myself to speak. 'It is,' I said. 'Thanks, Grant.'

Paula was looking stunned. 'We need to do some juggling,' she said. 'We've got some vulnerable kids who can't be on camera, a couple are adopted and one family need to be kept away from an abusive relative.'

'We'll need to make sure all the parents are on board, too,' I said. 'We can't just stick kids on TV without permission.'

'We've got three days,' Grant said, as if it was all the time in the world. 'Let's make it happen.'

And, true to his word, he did. Paula and I sorted out parental permission for the kids involved, which wasn't hard because everyone wanted to be on telly. And we spoke to the producer about the kids who absolutely couldn't be in shot – and explained to the children, who were luckily old enough to understand, why it had to happen this way.

Grant, who was an old hand at interviews, gave Nate some

media coaching so he could handle all the questions about the campaign.

'I'm not sure I'm the right person,' he said, but Grant waved away his protests.

'You are absolutely the right person. You're so passionate about Elm Heath and Liz said the rally is all your idea,' he said, and Nate went away preening like a peacock.

I was so busy getting everything ready that I didn't even have time to think about Danny, which was a blessing. Grant and I fell back into the easy working relationship we'd had for years as we rushed around sorting scenery, and preparing the children.

The camera crew arrived on the morning of the nativity with the kids all in a frenzy of excitement, the parents hanging round the school gates dolled up to the nines, and the teachers barely holding it together because we were so nervous.

I was pacing my office, trying to remember two or three pithy facts about Esther and her involvement in the school, in case anyone asked, when Grant appeared at my door.

'I'm going to take off,' he said.

I stopped pacing and stared at him. 'What?'

'I'm going back to London.'

I ducked behind him and closed the door. 'Now?' I said in horror. 'Today?'

He grinned. 'I've done my bit, Queenie. This is your campaign.'

I grimaced. He was right, actually. After all, I'd not wanted him there in the first place, and his interference had been more than a little annoying. But it had also been brilliant; we'd never be on *The One Show* without him.

'We need you here,' I whined.

He took me by the shoulders and looked straight at me. 'You don't. You've done all this on your own, Queenie. The campaign, and the rally, and the whole school being part of this nativity – it's all you.'

I looked at his handsome face in wonder. 'Two years ago,

you'd have taken all the credit for this,' I said. 'You'd never have stepped aside.'

Grant smiled. 'Two years ago I was a very different person.'

We looked at each other and, gently, he kissed me on the lips.

'Grant, I . . .' I began, but he stopped me by kissing me again. I relaxed into his embrace for a second – it was so familiar and so easy – and then pulled away.

'Sorry,' he said, looking anything but. 'I couldn't resist.'

'S'fine.' I pushed my hair back from my face.

'I'm just going to go,' Grant said. He took one of my curls in his finger and tugged it lightly. 'You know where I am, Queenie.'

He headed out of the door and I heard him saying goodbye to Emma in the office.

I looked up at Esther's picture on the wall. 'Don't say a word,' I said.

* * *

The nativity was a huge success. The children sang their little socks off, Mary only dropped Baby Jesus once, and Paula swooped in to break up the fight between the shepherds before there were any serious injuries.

And, of course, thanks to Grant working his magic, the publicity we got for our campaign was incredible. *The One Show* aired the day after the nativity – the last day of term – and there were articles in the Sunday papers a few days later, too.

It was exciting, and exhilarating and exhausting.

On the Sunday, I bumped into Danny when I was buying the papers. We stood awkwardly in the street, me peering at him over a pile of Sunday supplements.

'You've done brilliantly,' he said, nodding to the newspapers. 'Loads of publicity for the school.'

'I hope it's enough.'

The corners of his eyes crinkled, just a bit. 'I'd say you've made life difficult for the council. The kids were all so great in the play that the council will look like utter bastards if they shut the school now.'

Despite myself, I smiled. 'Fingers crossed.'

There was a pause.

'So Grant went home?'

I nodded. 'He's a busy man.'

'Sorry to see him go?' Danny sounded off-hand but I wondered if he was digging.

I swerved the question. 'He really helped.'

Danny nodded.

'Where's Cara?'

'With Sophie,' he said. 'They're doing a sort of pretend Christmas Day because we're off to Ireland tomorrow.'

'Is Sophie feeling better?'

'Right as rain,' he said. 'Thankfully.'

'Good.'

There was a small, awkward pause.

'Are you busy? Fancy a drink?'

I looked at my watch. 'It's ten-thirty, Danny.'

He rolled his eyes. 'Cara was up early because she was so excited,' he said. 'It feels like dinnertime. A coffee then?'

I was tempted, but as I wavered as I remembered him talking to Vanessa on the phone outside school, and instead I shook my head. 'Not a good idea.'

He looked satisfyingly disappointed. 'Look, things are all just a bit tricky with Christmas right now,' he said. 'You know how everything gets ignored when people are out at parties and carol singing and whatnot. I'm sorting it, honestly.'

I'd heard enough. 'I have to go.' I hoisted the pile of newspapers up my arm to a more comfortable position. 'Have a good time in Ireland. Wish Cara merry Christmas from me.'

Danny leaned over and kissed me on the cheek. 'Merry Christmas yourself,' he said. 'See you in the new year.'

I marched home without looking back, and later that day I did what I always did when times got tough.

I ran away.

Mum had invited me to spend Christmas with her, and I'd been planning to go up on Christmas Eve. But knackered from the excitement of the nativity and all the press attention, and with thoughts of Danny and Grant whirling round my head, I decided I should go sooner so I packed the car with presents and stopped off at the big Tesco near Blyton to buy booze, and headed up north to my mum's house.

We had a really quiet festive season. A decidedly non-festive festive season, I supposed. My brother Oli and his perfect fiancé Norah came on Christmas Day, en route to Norah's parents' house, full of wedding planning excitement. Norah kept asking me questions about my wedding, which was uncomfortable at best.

'What was the best thing about the day?' she said. We'd had dinner and now we were chilling out in the lounge watching rubbish TV. Norah was sitting on the floor, rooting about in the Celebrations tin for a Twix while Oli and I lazed on the sofa.

'What would you say was your absolute essential for a wedding?'

I grimaced. 'I'd say making sure the man you're marrying doesn't turn out to be a liar is fairly essential.'

Oli stretched his leg out and kicked me. 'Elizabeth,' he said. 'Be nice. Norah's excited.'

'Sorry.' I took the chocolate tin she was offering. 'It's just hard to look back on the day because it was lovely, and then it all went to shit.'

Norah patted my knee sympathetically. 'You'll meet someone new,' she said. 'It's not too late.'

I opened my mouth and Oli shot me a warning glance.

'Nice,' he hissed.

I rolled my eyes but I stayed quiet.

The rest of the time at Mum's was just the two of us. I barely left the house, pottering round in scruffy clothes, with my hair piled on top of my head. Mum didn't live in the house we'd grown up in any more, but I found my old childhood books in a box in the spare bedroom and spent the days rereading *Anne of Green Gables, Little House on the Prairie,* and all my old *Baby-Sitters Club* books. I ate loads of chocolate, drank quite a lot of wine, didn't turn my phone on for days on end, and basically checked out.

At least, I would have, had it not been for Mum.

She came into my room one evening, in that weird time between Christmas and New Year. I'd had a bath and I was sitting on the bed in my dressing gown, reading *Anne of Avonlea.*

I looked up. 'What on earth's that?'

Mum was wrestling a large flat present, wrapped in Christmas paper. 'It's for you,' she said, putting it down on my bed ceremonially. 'I didn't have time to do it before Christmas.'

'Did you make it?' I was pleased. Mum was retired now, but she'd been a teacher too – an art teacher. She was very creative.

'It's for your office wall.'

I pulled the paper off and discovered she'd collected all the press cuttings about our campaign, printed them out in various different sizes so they all fit perfectly into a large frame, and trimmed it in suffragette purple and green, with her own version of our campaign sashes – the ones designed by Nate saying Save Our School – across one corner. I was genuinely moved.

'Mum, this is beautiful.'

She sat down on the bed next to me and crumpled up the discarded wrapping paper. 'I wanted you to know how proud I am. You're working so hard on this campaign.'

I felt my eyes prickle with tears. 'I'm not sure it's going to do much good,' I said. 'And . . .'

'Was it hard seeing Grant?'

I nodded. 'I knew it was a mistake to contact him, but I did it anyway.'

231

'You did it for Elm Heath.'

I gave her a small smile. 'And me,' I admitted. 'I sort of wanted to see him.'

I rubbed my thumb along the smooth edge of the picture frame.

'He says he's changed, and that I know where he is.'

I felt Mum's eyes on me.

'Do you think he's changed?'

'He went home before the press arrived.'

Mum raised her eyebrows in surprise, but I shook my head.

'It's not enough, Mum. There's too much history, and . . .' I paused. Mum and I got on well enough, but we'd never really had the kind of relationship where I told her about my love life, or – God forbid – she told me about hers. But suddenly I really wanted to talk about Danny.

'I met someone else,' I said.

'But?'

'What?'

'It sounded like there's more to this than just meeting someone else,' Mum said. 'Has it gone wrong? Is it because of Grant?'

'Actually, no. This is something I can't blame Grant for.'

Mum arranged herself on my bed more comfortably. 'Tell me everything.'

So I did. I explained about our evening in the restaurant where – I'd thought – we'd been totally honest with each other, about his candour when he talked about Isabelle and their relationship, and about how I reacted whenever he was near me. And then I told her what had happened when I overheard him on the phone to Vanessa.

Mum frowned. 'What did he say?'

'He said he adored her.'

'And what did he say to you?'

'That he was sorting it. He said that twice actually. Once at school, and then again when I saw him at the pub.'

'Oh, Lizzie.'

I threw my head back in despair. 'Have I got it all wrong again, Mum? Have I done the same thing with Danny as I did with Grant? Thinking he was one thing and finding out he was someone else entirely? How can I be so stupid?'

Mum squeezed my arm. 'You're not stupid.'

'What should I do?'

'I think you need to speak to Danny and find out what is going on. Ask him straight out. Does he want to be with you? And if so, who is this Vanessa?'

'I don't want to. What if he says she's the one he wants to be with.'

She gave me a stern look. 'If there's one thing I know about you, Elizabeth Armstrong, it's that you're not a scaredy-cat. You have never been one to run away from a tricky situation.'

I barked a laugh. 'That's absolutely not true,' I said. 'I ran away when things went wrong in London, and I'm literally running away right now.'

'Is that what you think?'

'It's what I know.'

'The way I see it, is things in London couldn't continue,' Mum said. 'And you could have given up teaching. Or you could have stood by Grant and gone down with him. Either of those options would have been easier. But instead you faced the worst, found out exactly what had gone wrong, and you brushed yourself off and came back.'

'Hmm.'

'And now, things are tricky with Elm Heath but you're not rolling over and letting it happen; you're fighting for the school you've only worked at for a term.'

'I suppose.'

'So I think you need to message Danny and ask him to meet up. You need to know exactly what's going on, because you can't keep tormenting yourself like this. If you know the truth it'll

233

make you feel better. Even if it's not what you want to hear, you can deal with it.'

She took my phone from my bedside table and handed it to me. 'Do it now.'

Reluctantly, I took the phone and turned it on. It took a few seconds to connect, and then suddenly flashed into life, beeping as message after message came through.

'What's going on?' I said in surprise, staring at the screen. I had ten missed calls from Paula, four from an unknown number and two from Blyton Council. I pressed to listen to my voicemail. Paula was first.

'Lizzie, please call me back,' she said breathlessly. 'Things are happening.'

I had no idea what that meant. I shrugged my shoulders at Mum and listened to the next message. It was from the unknown number – who turned out to be Denise at the education department.

'Please call me,' she hissed. 'The bigwigs are rattled.'

I had no idea what that meant either.

'It's like they're talking in code,' I said to Mum. I pressed to listen to the next message, which was from the council.

'This is a message for Elizabeth Armstrong,' the voice said. 'Just to let you know, in the light of recent publicity, we've decided to hold a preliminary meeting regarding the future of Elm Heath Primary School, on Thursday 2nd of January at eleven a.m. I'm going to email you the details. Please could you confirm your attendance ASAP?'

I ended the call and grinned at Mum. 'The council want a meeting,' I said. 'The publicity is working.'

'What's happening . . .' Mum began, but she was cut off as my phone rang. It was Paula. I snatched it up and answered.

'Finally,' she said. 'Do you know what's happening?'

'I do now. I've just waded through all the messages.'

'This is brilliant. Where are you? Can we meet up to go through everything?'

'I'm at my mum's but I'll come as soon as I can. We don't have long until the meeting.'

'We're having a New Year's Eve party tomorrow,' Paula said. 'Come home and come to the party.'

Suddenly, I really wanted to be back in Elm Heath, working on the campaign and seeing in the new year with my new friends.

'Okay,' I said. 'I'll come home.'

Chapter 37

Lizzie

In all the excitement, and the rush to get back to Elm Heath in time for Paula and Chris's party, I never got round to calling Danny.

'Will Danny be at the party?' Mum asked as she helped me put my bags in the car.

I had been wondering that too, but I'd not wanted to ask Paula in case I came across as too needy.

'I'm actually not sure,' I said. 'He was taking his little girl to Ireland for Christmas to see his parents.'

'He's got a daughter? Is he divorced?'

'His partner died.'

Mum made a face. 'Sounds tricky.'

'I know, but Cara is wonderful, and Danny and Isabelle had a rocky relationship before she passed away.'

I gave her a hug and she squeezed me tightly then pulled back and looked straight at me.

'Just be cautious,' she said. She put her hand on my chest. 'Your heart is healing but I think it's still bruised.'

'I will.'

I hadn't lied to Mum about being cautious, but it wasn't forefront of my mind when I got dressed to go to Paula's party later. I'd bought a new top in the sales, which was black and sparkly and low cut. Too low cut? I wondered looking at myself in the mirror as I pulled it on at home. Hmm, maybe a bit, but it was New Year's Eve. I teamed it with skinny jeans and sparkly stilettoes that I couldn't walk in, and swept the front of my hair back with a diamante slide. I didn't scrub up too badly, I thought, admiring my reflection. I hoped Danny would agree. If he was there.

But he wasn't.

Paula and Chris's house was full when I arrived. People were everywhere, chatting in the lounge and the kitchen, and the conservatory was filled with unbelievably glamorous teenage girls, who I assumed were all Chloe's friends, along with two gawky and awkward-looking teen boys wearing jeans so tight they couldn't sit down.

'Lizzie,' Paula said, grabbing me as I made my way through the crowd of people in the lounge, looking for a familiar face. 'Everyone, Lizzie's here.'

At once, I was surrounded by party-goers. Some I knew – like Nate and Pippa – others were strangers or only vaguely familiar, but they were all firing questions at me, telling me how pleased they were that the school was saved, and asking to get me a drink.

'We're not out of the woods yet,' I kept saying. 'It's not a done deal.'

It felt nice to be adored, and for a little while I had a glimpse into how Grant must have felt back when everything was going well. I could almost – almost – see how he'd got carried away with it all.

Someone handed me a glass of Prosecco, and Nate asked me about my Christmas, and made me laugh telling me stories about his family, and I felt part of something special. Later, I took off my painful shoes and danced in the lounge with Pippa and Emma, and laughed a lot with Paula, and ate delicious nibbly food, and eventually as midnight drew closer, I grabbed my coat and went out into the garden to ring Mum before the celebrations began.

We chatted for a minute or two, but she was at a party as well and I didn't want to keep her from her friends, so we wished each other a happy new year, and I ended the call. I sat for a moment on Paula's garden bench, looking out into the dark garden and listening to the sounds of happy conversation, muffled music and bursts of laughter from the party behind me.

It was strange how content I felt. Mum was right: I was still bruised from my marriage break-up. And trying to save a school from closing, despite all the odds being against us, and feeling pretty betrayed from sleeping with Danny only to have him let me down almost immediately. It hadn't been easy. And yet, as I sat there, I was happy. And a bit drunk. But mostly happy.

'Lizzie?'

I jumped as someone came up behind me.

'Danny! Have you been here the whole time?'

'Just arrived. Can I sit?'

I nodded and he sat down next to me.

'So cool, turning up to a party at the last minute.'

'We were having dinner with Sophie,' he said. I raised my eyebrows and he grinned. 'My new year's resolution is to start being nicer to her, so I thought I'd start as I meant to go on. But Cara fell asleep so she said I should come here.'

'I'm glad you did,' I said.

I took a breath, emboldened by Prosecco and mini burgers.

'Talking of starting as we mean to go on. I wanted to ask you something.'

'Yes?'

'When I saw you on the phone, at school, I overheard you saying you adored the woman you were talking to.'

Danny looked startled. 'That's not what I expected you to say.'

'I heard you say you adored her, and then when you saw me, you were worried I'd overheard and you said you'd sort it. Then you said it again in the pub.'

Danny wasn't smiling now; he looked kind of grim-faced and determined.

'I just need to know, Danny, if there's someone else. Are you seeing someone else? Because I am battered from Grant and everything, and I can't put myself through that sort of thing again.'

Danny leaned back against the garden bench and sighed heavily. My heart lurched. Was he about to tell me he was indeed seeing someone else?

But no, he sat up again and took my hand. 'Lizzie, I absolutely promise you that this is not what you think,' he said. I snorted. 'God, I know that sounds like the most awful cliché, but honestly, I'm not seeing anyone else. There is no one else.'

'Oh come on, women fall over themselves to be near you,' I said, thinking of Claire at the council.

He shrugged. 'I know I'm a bit of a flirt, but I've only been on one date in years and that was with you.'

'Really?'

'Really. I swear to you that I'm not seeing anyone else.'

He looked straight at me, his eyes honest and clear. I believed him. Even though Grant had taught me that people could lie to your face without so much as a flicker of guilt, I believed what Danny was telling me.

Danny opened his mouth to carry on, just as Paula's back door opened and Pippa, Emma and Nate tumbled out festooned with streamers.

'She's here, I said she was here,' squealed Pippa. 'It's almost midnight – you have to come inside for the countdown.'

They all wobbled round to where Danny and I sat.

'Danny!' Nate exclaimed, struggling to focus on Danny's face. 'Mate!' He tumbled forwards and gave Danny a clumsy hug.

'Come inside,' he said. 'It's time for the new year to begin.'

'Lizzie and I were just having a chat,' Danny said, peeling Nate off himself.

Emma blew a party hooter at us and I laughed.

'It's fine, Danny,' I said. 'Let's talk about this later.'

'Are you sure?'

'I'm sure.'

I let Emma and Pippa drag me to my feet.

'We put the telly on so we can see the countdown,' Emma slurred. 'And Paula's got more Prosecco ready to pop.'

'I'm not sure you need any more Prosecco,' I said, but I was giggling as they bustled me in through the patio doors. It was warm inside so I shrugged off my coat and threw it on to the back of the sofa, just as the countdown began.

'Wow,' said Danny. 'You look great.'

I smiled, slightly embarrassed. 'Thank you.'

'TEN!' roared the party-goers around us. Danny put his hand on my waist.

'Nine!'

My heart began to beat a bit faster.

'Eight!'

I took a step towards him and looked up into his eyes.

'Seven!'

'I really like you, Lizzie,' he said.

'Six!'

'I don't want to make a mess of things.'

'Five!'

'You won't,' I said. 'I won't let you.'

'Four!'

I put my arm round him and pulled him closer to me, our bodies almost touching.

'Three!'

'It's going to be a good year,' I said.

'Two!'

Danny bent his head down and our lips touched, as Big Ben's bongs rang out accompanied by a flurry of party poppers.

'Happy new year!'

Chapter 38

Lizzie

2020

I welcomed 2020 with a thumping hangover and an absolute inability to move from my sofa. Danny had gone back to Sophie's after our midnight kiss, saying he had to get back for Cara. Giddy with the feeling of his lips on mine – and too much Prosecco – I'd carried on partying with Nate and the others until the small hours, then staggered back to my little cottage and collapsed fully clothed on the bed and slept until lunchtime.

At about six p.m., I finally dragged myself downstairs with my duvet, made beans on toast, and stayed hunched under the blankets watching rubbish telly and going over my notes for the council meeting the next day.

It was hard to prepare because I didn't really know what was going to be discussed. Denise had said it was a preliminary meeting. I decided to write some notes about how important Elm Heath was to the community – referring to the publicity we'd had obviously, and mentioning all the things we'd put in place, like the after-school club, the plans we had for the afternoon teas, and using quotes from Esther's letter about the need for a local school in Elm Heath.

I'd not heard from Danny, except a message sent while I was

241

still asleep to say he and Cara were off to catch up with some friends and go for a walk on the beach to blow away the cobwebs. I had no idea which beach. He finished with a kiss, which I liked. I replied, simply saying: 'Have fun!' grateful he'd managed to avoid any morning-after weirdness.

The next day was Thursday, back-to-school day and council meeting day. I woke up – thankfully – without any trace of lingering hangover, and bounced out of bed, eager to greet the kids as they arrived and then race to Blyton for the meeting.

I got to school super-early and rewrote all the notes I'd written the day before, making them snappier, more confident and adding details, and putting them all into a presentation so I could show everyone at the meeting – I wasn't exactly sure who would be there – just what we'd achieved in only a term.

Nate, bless him, had emailed me his own notes about the rally he was planning, so I added those in, along with clips from *The One Show*, and some of the things I'd learned about Esther Watkins.

'Esther wasn't from Elm Heath, but she fell in love with the area,' I wrote. 'She saw there was a real need for a community school and she made it happen. That need still exists, and as someone who has also fallen in love with Elm Heath, I am determined to keep this school open.'

Was that too bolshie? I read it over again. No, I didn't think so. I felt like we needed to play hard ball if this was going to work.

'All set?' Paula appeared in my office, clutching two mugs of tea. She handed me one and I wrapped my hands round it. The school was cold first thing in the morning.

'Nervous.'

'Not surprised. Do you want to go over what you're saying?'

I nodded and she sat down, looking at me expectantly. 'Hit me.'

'My name is Lizzie Armstrong and I'm the head teacher of Elm Heath Primary,' I began.

My presentation lasted four minutes – Paula timed it – not including a three-minute clip from *The One Show*.

'Is it too long?' I asked, worried everyone would zone out.

Paula looked thoughtful. 'Ordinarily, I'd say yes, but the clip is great with all the kids talking and that nice chap who was on *Strictly* summing it all up at the end. And your bit is very good.'

'Really?'

She grinned. 'Really.'

I started gathering all my notes together and putting them and my laptop in my bag. 'I'm going to see all the children arrive, and then head off,' I said. 'The meeting's at ten and I don't want to be late.'

'Make sure you take your phone and ring me as soon as you're done,' Paula said.

I felt in my trouser pocket for my phone and pulled it out. 'Urgh, it's only on ten per cent,' I said.

'Take your charger.'

'I've not got it.'

Paula rolled her eyes. 'I'll see if I've got mine. Or run home and get yours?'

But already I could hear kids' voices outside as the playground filled up.

'No time,' I said, draining my tea. 'It's fine. There might be one in my car, or I'm sure someone at the meeting will have a charger.'

I spent a happy fifteen minutes greeting all the children, and listening as they told me all about their Christmas presents, their excited chatter creating little puffs of breath in the cold air.

When the bell rang I waved to Paula, who was seeing them all inside, and headed off to my car to drive to Blyton.

The traffic wasn't bad – I guessed lots of people with normal jobs had decided to take today and tomorrow off and start back on Monday, lucky sods – so I got to the council offices early.

I parked and decided to read through my notes one last time before I went inside.

As I got to the bit about the rally, my phone rang. I found it, tucked inside one of my folders in my bag, and was pleased to see it was Danny.

'Wish me luck,' I said as I answered. 'It's the big council meeting this morning. I'm just waiting in the car park. Hello, by the way.'

'Hello,' he said. 'And good luck.' He sounded amused and something else that I couldn't quite identify. His voice was odd.

'Are you driving?' I said. 'Are you on hands free?'

'I am.'

Maybe that was it. He sounded distant.

'Listen, Lizzie,' he said. 'I need to—'

My phone went dead. I took it away from my ear and looked at the screen. The battery had gone flat.

'Bugger,' I said. Oh well, at least he'd called. I'd catch up with him afterwards, once I'd found a charger. Time was ticking on, so I took a deep breath, shoved my laptop and my dead phone in my bag, and went inside.

Denise came to meet me from reception. She was wearing a suit and had her hair pulled back and she looked like something out of *The Good Wife*. Her heels clicked on the council-issued hard floor as we walked to the lifts. I was wearing black trousers, flat ankle boots – I'd learned the hard way not to wear heels when I was on my feet all day at work – and a green fine-knit jumper. I suddenly felt under-dressed, like a sixth-former on work experience.

'Who's going to be at the meeting?' I asked, walking into the lift and waiting for Denise to press the floor. My voice was a little trembly and I suddenly realised that was how Danny had sounded – he'd sounded nervous. Bless him, I thought, being nervous about calling me. What a sweetheart.

Denise was reeling off job titles and names.

'And the developer, and I think their finance bod,' she added.

I blinked. 'The developer?'

'You've done an amazing job,' she said quickly watching the floor numbers light up as we rose up. 'The profile of the school has never been higher, and there's no denying the bigwigs are worried about closing it and losing all that goodwill.'

'But?'

She sighed. 'But the building is old and knackered, and expensive to run. It's on prime land and the council's been running a loss for years. They could make a lot of money if they sell it. Even more money if they sell it with planning approved already.'

I was shocked. 'Are they allowed to do that?'

She shrugged as the lift dinged and the doors opened. 'I guess we'll find out in the meeting.'

'But there won't be a decision today?'

She shook her head, opening the door to a large meeting room where about five middle-aged men in suits were helping themselves to coffee and pastries from a trolley.

'Ah, Denise,' one of them said. 'Come on in.'

'This is Lizzie Armstrong,' she said. 'Head teacher of Elm Heath.'

The man regarded me with what I thought looked like pity, and then stuck out his hand and introduced himself. The others followed, though I didn't completely keep up with all the job titles. Someone was from the education department, someone else from finance, another from policy.

I refused a pastry because I didn't want to get bits of croissant stuck in my teeth, but accepted a coffee and sat down.

'We'll get going in a few minutes, just waiting for one or two more to arrive,' the man who'd welcomed us said. He seemed to be in charge and I knew I should have paid more attention to his name. I was just so nervous; all I could think about was making a good job of my presentation. He smiled at me kindly. 'We take any potential closure of a school very seriously,' he said. 'It's not something we do on a whim, and we have to make sure it's the correct decision for everyone involved.'

I nodded.

'Today's meeting is just so we can all hear where things stand at the moment, ahead of the final meeting in March. It helps us keep track.'

I nodded again.

'Once everyone's here, I'll do a quick welcome, then I'll hear from you, Miss Armstrong, and the representative from the developer.'

'It's Ms,' I said.

He looked at me blankly.

I swallowed. My mouth felt dry with nerves so I took a swig of coffee.

'And I believe Maurice has a quick presentation too,' the man carried on.

Maurice – one of the suited chaps to my right – nodded. 'I've got a breakdown of school places across the district, a few budget bits, and some other figures,' he said. I groaned inwardly. Not only did that sound terribly dull, they were the sort of stone-cold facts that could finish Elm Heath. All the hearts and flowers and Esther Watkins stuff was lovely, but could it compete with statistics? I wasn't sure.

Behind me, the door to the meeting room opened.

'Good,' said the chairman. 'Here are the developers now. Lizzie, this is Vanessa Morgan from the council's favoured contractors, Texo.'

Vanessa? I turned in my chair to see a well-groomed older woman, in her fifties. And behind her . . .

'And she's brought along her financial consultant today from Vanir Investments. This is Daniel Kinsella.'

. . . behind her was Danny.

246

Chapter 39

Esther

1910

It took him a moment to recognise me, my Joseph. My love. The man I'd dreamed of a future with. It took a moment for his brain to catch up with what his eyes were seeing and when he realised that the woman who was attacking the policeman in front of him was me, his face crumpled. Just for a second, but it was long enough for me to realise that his heart had shattered into a thousand pieces right there in Parliament Square. And then the anger was back and he squeezed my arms even tighter.

I couldn't speak. I just stared at him as he yanked me away from Alf, who was covered in blood, and pushed me on to another, younger police constable nearby.

'Arrest her and take her to the station,' he said. 'I'll get help for Alf.'

Around me, the shouts and screams continued, but it seemed that we were in a quiet pocket of shock. I looked round at the scene, as though it were a renaissance painting on the walls of the National Gallery. In front of me, Alf was slumped on the kerb, cradling his bloodied nose. The front of his uniform was drenched with dark red stains and Joseph was standing next to him, a steadying hand on his shoulder.

A little way away, Agnes lay, sobbing, on the grass, curled up around her stomach. Her position was mirroring the baby inside her. The baby that I prayed would survive today's violence. Prostrate next to her was Nelly, worryingly still. And Minnie stood by, her face frozen in horror, unable to decide where to go or what to do.

And then suddenly, the noise and the chaos was back.

'Take her away,' Joseph bellowed to the young constable and he dragged me away. Over my shoulder I looked round and my eyes met Joseph's.

'Please,' I managed to shout. 'Please . . .'

He looked away and instead I focused on Minnie.

'. . . help Agnes,' I screamed. 'Help them both.'

Like I'd woken her from a nightmare – into a worse nightmare – Minnie jumped and immediately crouched down in between Agnes and Nelly. I watched as she gently touched Agnes's shoulder, and with the other hand, reached out to find a pulse on Nelly's wrist. Confident she was doing all she could, and unable to see another course of action, I allowed myself to be pulled across the square by the young constable.

He gripped my hands behind my back, said something that I didn't listen to, and took me to a small police station somewhere near Whitehall. It was full of women. Some were hurt, some were scared or upset, others were angry. The sergeant at the desk looked weary and cross.

'Not another bloody suffragette,' he said as the young constable entered, pushing me ahead of him. 'We're running out of room. I keep telling your lot to take them up to Bow Street.'

The constable shrugged. 'She's dangerous,' he said. 'She attacked one of ours, took his truncheon off him and leathered him.'

The desk sergeant eyed me doubtfully.

I lifted my head and met his suspicious stare dead-on.

'Cell four,' he said. 'There's two others in there already. They'll have to share the bed. But they like that, don't they? That type.'

He gave a lascivious bark of laughter and the constable sniggered like a schoolboy as he shoved me along the corridor.

The cell was tiny, just like the one I'd been in when I'd been arrested before. It had bare walls and a hard bench on one side – the "bed" the sergeant had mentioned. In the corner was a bucket with the stench of urine soaking into the room, and hunched together on the bench were two young suffragettes.

'Enjoy yourself, ladies,' the constable said. He pushed me into the room and locked the door behind me.

* * *

I knew Joseph would come eventually. At least, I hoped he would come. But in my mind's eye I kept seeing his face crumple, and his furious expression, and I wondered if he'd leave me here. If that was it. The end of everything we'd had. I knew it was my fault, that I should have told him my story from the start. But that didn't make it easier.

The two other suffragettes and I spent an uncomfortable night in the small cell. We took off our coats and laid two of them on the bench to make it softer, and shared the other to cover ourselves with because the only blanket was itchy and smelled of vomit. It was cold in there and got more so as the night wore on, so we huddled together under the coat, arms and legs intertwined. It felt odd to be so intimate with two strangers, but I'd been there before – in Holloway – and I found reserves of resilience that I'd forgotten I had.

The other two women also proved stronger than I'd expected. There were no tears overnight, just flashes of anger, worries about our friends, and – in my case – huge spasms of guilt that I hid from my cellmates. We chatted quietly about our experiences in the WSPU. We slept fitfully, and I woke early, cold and stiff.

With pins and needles in my foot, I awkwardly slid off the bench and walked round the tiny room, trying to bring the feeling back into my limbs. The other two women were lying, eyes closed, on the heap of coats. One was moaning softly as she slept. I tried to shake my legs to get the blood flowing again, wrapping my arms round myself to keep warm.

I thought something would have happened by now. That we'd have been charged, or released. Mind you, I wasn't sure I would be released. I'd done something awful, hitting Alf like that. I remembered the way his nose had crunched and I shuddered. I'd seen red, when I'd heard Agnes wail in that tortured, animalistic way. But he'd done something awful too, attacking poor Agnes like that. I knew I'd be going back to Holloway, and I couldn't bear to imagine where Agnes was now or how she was feeling. But I had a sick feeling that Alf would be free to don his uniform once more.

A noise outside the cell made me stop my pacing. I could hear voices and I thought, perhaps, that one of the men talking in the corridor was Joseph. I needed to see him, to explain why I'd done what I did – not just with the lying and the keeping my life as a suffragette secret – but with Alf and the truncheon. I needed to make him understand.

I looked up hopefully as the cell door swung open and almost wept with relief as I saw Joseph standing there. His uniform was clean and his hair neat. He'd obviously been home after yesterday's events.

'Joseph,' I breathed.

He looked at me, no affection in his gaze. 'I'm afraid I don't know your name.'

I winced. 'It's Esther,' I assured him. Then, eyes downcast, I added: 'Watkins. Esther Watkins.'

He looked down at the sheet of paper he was holding. 'Strange,' he said. 'I was under the impression you were called Esther Whitehouse. Someone must have made a mistake.'

'I think so.'

There was a pause as we looked at each other.

'I'm to interview you,' he said eventually. 'I don't work here but as I was on the scene, I offered to hear your version of events.'

I nodded, pleased he wanted to listen to what I had to say.

'Come with me.'

I took a step towards the bench, planning to retrieve my coat, then changed my mind. Those two needed it more than I did. Instead I walked to Joseph. He gripped my upper arm tightly. Too tightly. And walked me briskly down the corridor back towards the front of the police station.

'The interview rooms are on the other side of the building, so we have to walk past the front desks,' Joseph explained. 'I don't want to use force on you, Miss Watkins.' He spat out the name. 'But if you so much as think about trying to run for it, I won't hesitate.'

'I won't run,' I said. 'I want to speak to you, to explain . . .'

He pulled my arm and I stopped talking. As we crossed behind the front desk where a different sergeant was on duty, I heard my name shouted. And there, sitting on a wooden chair looking dirty and tear-stained, was Minnie.

'Esther, stop,' she called. 'Please. I need to tell you . . .'

I paused and when Joseph squeezed his fingers into my arm, I wriggled away from his grip.

'I just want to hear what she has to say,' I said. 'Please, Joseph. She might have news of Agnes.'

But he simply grabbed me again, harder this time. 'Come on,' he said.

Minnie stood up and leaned over the front desk to see where we were going.

'Stand back, Miss,' the sergeant said, but she didn't.

'Esther,' she called to me as Joseph dragged me along the corridor. 'Agnes wanted me to tell you . . .'

Her shout ended in a sob and she took a breath and then tried again. 'She had the baby,' she said. 'Agnes had the baby. But it was too soon.'

I stopped walking, despite Joseph's efforts and his annoyed grunt, and I turned to see Minnie as she leaned over the desk.

'Tell me,' I said.

Minnie looked stricken. 'It was too soon,' she repeated. 'Too soon for the little girl.'

'Is she . . .?'

Minnie nodded. 'She never took a breath. Agnes's baby is dead.'

Chapter 40

Esther

My legs buckled and I stumbled as the enormity of Minnie's news hit me. Joseph pulled me upright and before I could ask any more questions, he bundled me through a door and into another bare room. This one had a large wooden desk and two chairs. I dropped into the chair nearest me.

'Did you hear her?' I said. 'Did you hear what happened?'

Joseph nodded, but he didn't speak.

'Agnes's baby is dead.'

'I'm sorry to hear that. As a mother she should have been more responsible. That was no place for a pregnant woman.'

I stared at him. 'This wasn't her fault,' I said. 'It was Alf.'

Joseph looked back at me. 'We were just doing our jobs.'

He was like a stranger; I couldn't believe I ever thought I could spend my life with him. I felt drained of all fight and I slumped on to the desk.

'Sit up,' Joseph said. He pulled out the other chair and sat down. 'You need to explain this to me. You owe me that much.'

He was right, I supposed. I dragged my heavy head up and met his gaze.

'I'm sorry I lied to you,' I said. 'I'm sorry I didn't tell you my real name. And I'm sorry I didn't tell you that I'm a suffragette.'

His lip curled in a sneer. 'I looked up your file this morning.

It was easy once I knew your actual name. You've been in Holloway. You're a criminal. Are you sorry about that, too?'

'Political prisoner,' I said. Perhaps I'd not quite lost all my fight.

He put both his hands on to the desk with a thump, but I didn't flinch.

'Tell me this,' he said. 'Was it worth it? Was this crusade worth the violence and the dead baby?'

Now I flinched. But deep inside I felt a spark ignite my fury once more. 'Not yet.'

He sat back in his chair, looking triumphant.

'But it will be.'

Joseph snorted. 'You are a disgrace. And you're deluded.'

'How so?'

'Women aren't capable of leadership. They can't make decisions about politics. Imagine a woman making the decision to go to war? It's ludicrous.'

I went to speak but he'd not finished. Instead his face softened.

'It's not your fault,' he said. 'You've just misunderstood. Men and women each have jobs to do, and you've got confused. Women are nurturers, carers. Men are protectors.'

The rage was back. 'Really? I didn't see much protection going on in Parliament Square yesterday.'

He snorted, but it was my time to carry on.

'I saw women being attacked. Assaulted. One police officer put his hands under my skirts and squeezed my breasts. I'll show you my bruises if you want.'

Joseph looked away. 'It's true,' I said. 'And worst of all, one policeman – your friend . . .' I spat out the name. 'Alf, attacked Agnes and pushed her on to the ground, when it was obvious to anyone with eyes that she was pregnant.'

'She was wearing a large coat,' Joseph said. 'Perhaps he couldn't see.'

I looked straight at him. 'Did you see it?' I said. 'Did you see what happened?'

He nodded and I felt a huge flood of relief.

'Then you know that we were screaming at him to stop. We were telling him over and over that she was expecting.'

Joseph didn't speak.

'Don't tell me that men are supposed to protect us,' I said. 'Don't you dare tell me that. Because from where I'm standing, it seems men are hurting us, and touching us, and murdering our children, just because they're scared that we might get to hold a tiny fraction of the power they've been holding for generations.'

There was a pause. Joseph sat up a bit straighter. 'No one murdered anyone,' he said. 'You're being hysterical.'

I forced myself to speak calmly. 'Here's what I saw,' I said, looking at the point where the ceiling met the wall. There was a large damp patch and I stared at it so I didn't have to look at Joseph. 'I saw chaos and panic. We were with a young woman called Nelly and she was pushed over by a man – a passer-by – and then hit by a policeman. We were surrounded by policemen. I saw Agnes get cross and try to defend Nelly, and I saw one of the men shove her and she fell. Then as she tried to get up, another policeman hit her, over and over. We tried to stop him, but he was so angry.'

Despite my best efforts, my voice cracked with a sob.

'He was so angry,' I said again. 'And he wouldn't listen and he wouldn't stop. I pulled his arm, and I recognised him as Alf, but it was as though he didn't see me. His face was twisted in anger, Joseph. He was like an animal.'

'Go on.'

I wiped away a tear and carried on looking at the ceiling. 'He kicked her in the back, and she fell forwards on to her stomach and she cried out.'

Now I lowered my gaze from the ceiling and looked straight at him.

'And I lost my temper. I admit it. But I was just trying to get him to stop. You must see that?'

Joseph had a piece of paper in front of him, and a pencil, but he'd not written anything down.

'You must see?'

'I saw you screaming like a banshee, lashing out,' he said calmly. 'I saw you steal Alf's truncheon and hit him with it, without stopping, even when his nose splattered all over his face.'

'I did do that,' I whispered.

'His nose is broken, of course, and he is in a great deal of pain. He has lost a few teeth, and he has a black eye.'

I was ashamed. 'Mrs Pankhurst says we aren't to harm anyone.'

'That might be the only sensible thing that woman has ever said.' He sighed.

'The truth is, Esther, that what you did was a crime. A terrible crime. And being as you already have a criminal record, you're going to be back in Holloway by the end of the week. And this time you'll stay there much longer.'

'I know,' I whispered.

'And don't expect any special treatment,' he went on. 'This wasn't one of your political acts; it was violence, pure and simple. You'll be in with the normal prisoners.'

I wanted to cry, but I stared at the damp patch and blinked the tears away. I'd made a mess of everything – my romance with Joseph, my involvement with the WSPU. I'd thrown away my relationship with my mother and lost my job, and all just to end up back in jail.

'What will happen to Alf?' I said quietly. 'Will he have to leave the police?'

Joseph looked bewildered. 'No. Of course not. Why would he?'

'Because he attacked Agnes.' It seemed obvious to me.

'He was doing his job.'

And there was the fury again. 'He and the others were attacking a pregnant woman, whose baby then died,' I said. 'They killed her baby girl, Joseph. I accept that I should be punished for what I did. But they should be held to account, too.'

Joseph gave an exasperated laugh. 'Esther, you can't go around accusing good people of murder. The fact is Agnes put herself and her unborn baby in harm's way. She did something no mother should ever do. And she is suffering the consequences.'

I opened my mouth to argue, but stopped as the door to the room opened and a large police officer entered.

'Constable Fairbanks,' he said.

Joseph scrambled to his feet. 'Inspector Ford.'

The big inspector gave me a look of utter disgust. 'This one of them?'

Joseph nodded. 'Esther Watkins,' he said. He looked at me pointedly as he said my surname.

'Word is the Home Secretary is going to release them all,' Ford said.

Joseph's eyes widened. 'Really?'

Ford grimaced. 'Reports of some officers going too far. This morning's *Daily Mirror* has a photograph of an officer about to hit an old woman on its front page. It's not making us look good.'

I felt a glimmer of hope. Ford looked at a list he was holding in his meaty hands. 'Watkins, you said?'

'Esther Watkins.'

Ford nodded slowly, then he gave me a horrible smile. 'You're not going anywhere, sweetheart.'

My stomach plummeted into my shoes. 'You said Mr Churchill was going to release us all.'

'All the suffragettes,' he said. 'But not you.'

'I'm a suffragette.'

'Says here you attacked Sergeant Alfred Simpson.'

'I was trying to stop him hurting my friend.'

Ford looked down at his papers again and shook his head. The flesh under his chin wobbled with the movement. 'No, all it says here is you attacked Sergeant Simpson. Unprovoked.'

'That's not what happened,' I growled. 'He was hitting my

friend Agnes Oliver. She was pregnant and he attacked her. I was trying to get him to stop.'

Ford looked distinctly uninterested.

'She was pregnant and now she's not,' I said, my voice shaking with emotion. 'She had her baby but the baby died. Joseph – Constable Fairbanks – he was there. He saw Sergeant Simpson hit Agnes. He was a witness.'

Now I had Ford's attention.

'You're saying Simpson was violent first?'

'That's exactly what I'm saying.' I was frustrated.

'And you're saying Constable Fairbanks saw what happened?'

'Yes.'

Ford looked at Joseph. 'Did you see Sergeant Simpson lash out?'

Joseph shrugged. 'It was chaos,' he said. 'I was there, that's true enough, but I didn't see him do anything.'

Devastated, I slumped in my seat. That was it, then.

But Ford was shaking his head again. 'Simpson says he can't identify the woman who hit him,' he told Joseph. 'He says they all look the same. With Churchill on the warpath, we're going to need a proper witness to identify the attacker or we'll have to let her go with the rest of them.'

Joseph opened his mouth and closed it again without speaking. I could see his dilemma written all over his face. He wanted me punished for everything I'd done – attacking Alf certainly, but also betraying Joseph, lying, and pretending to be someone I wasn't. But if he admitted to being there and seeing me hit Alf, he'd have to confess that he saw Alf attack Agnes first. Although, I thought, this new Joseph could lie. This cold, vengeful Joseph might not hesitate to tell Ford that he'd arrived on the scene to see me brandishing the truncheon and hadn't seen what went before.

Ford wrote something on the paper he was holding and then waved it at Joseph. 'You've got until lunchtime to find a witness or we'll have to let her go with the rest of them.'

Without even glancing in my direction, Ford backed out of the room and slammed the door shut.

As soon as I heard his heavy footsteps recede, I looked at Joseph. 'Please, Joseph,' I said. 'Please don't tell him it was me.'

To my surprise, Joseph crumpled. He sank down in his wooden chair, looking a shadow of the man he'd been moments before.

'I loved you,' he said. 'I was going to ask you to marry me. I thought we could have a Christmas wedding with candles in the church.'

I pinched my lips together to stop the sobs that were threatening to burst out.

'When I go home to my lodgings after my shift, I imagine going home to you. I imagine coming home to our house, and seeing you in the kitchen getting my dinner ready. The kids running out in the street to welcome me in, and you there, all warm, kissing me and asking about my day.'

I stared at him. I'd certainly dreamed of spending my life with him but my imaginings hadn't involved him being out all day while I cooked and looked after the children. In that instant, I realised how naïve I'd been. What choice would I have if I married Joseph? I couldn't have a job, and a family. I couldn't be a copper's wife and a suffragette. What had I been thinking? But seeing the sadness etched on Joseph's face made me feel terrible.

'You have betrayed me and you have broken my heart,' he said.

'I'm sorry,' I whispered. 'I'm so sorry.'

He took a breath. 'I wrote that crime report, you know. On Ford's form? I was the one who reported that you'd attacked Alf.'

He sighed. 'But he doesn't know it was me. And I'm not going to tell him that I saw you hit Alf,' he said.

'You're not?'

'No.'

I felt weak with relief.

'But you need to leave.'

'Leave?'

'I want you to go, leave London.'

'Where will I go?'

'I don't care. Go to Glasgow. Manchester. Plymouth. I don't care. I just want to get on with my life knowing I won't see you around every corner. And I want to know that you won't be causing more trouble because I will inform the police stations in every city that you are dangerous and if you are seen to be involved in suffragette activity you are to be arrested.'

I stared at him. 'I can't just leave.'

'You can and you will. And if you don't, I will tell Ford that I saw you attack Alf, for no reason. That I didn't see Agnes there, I just saw you screeching like a thing possessed and violently lashing out.'

I felt sick.

'He'll believe me, you know he will,' Joseph said. 'You leave London, or you'll spend the next ten years in Holloway.'

I raised my weary head and nodded slowly. 'Fine,' I said. 'I'll go. Can you give me a few days to make arrangements?'

'I'll give you until Monday evening. I want you gone by then. I will check.'

My mind was racing. It was Saturday morning. I didn't have much time. But how could I say no?

'Monday evening.' I looked directly at him. 'I'm sorry I broke your heart,' I said. 'But I want you to know that you have broken mine too.'

Chapter 41

Esther

I was released that afternoon. Joseph left me in the airless room with the bare desk while he went to find out if Mr Churchill had decided to free everyone arrested the day before. He never came back. Instead a young constable arrived and stood nervously at the door as though I were a circus lion about to pounce.

'You're to go,' he said, twisting his hat in his long fingers. 'Constable Fairbanks said to tell you to remember the deal.'

I stood up on legs that shook beneath me. 'Where is Constable Fairbanks?'

The lad shrugged. 'He's gone.'

I didn't know it then but I would never see Joseph again; never again see the man I once dreamed of marrying. But now I simply straightened my dusty skirt and thanked the young constable. He showed me out of the police station most politely and I emerged into the dull grey November afternoon with a raging thirst, a ravenous hunger, no coat and absolutely no money.

It was a long walk to Camberwell, so I decided to take a chance and hope someone would be home if I hailed a taxi.

It took me three attempts to get a cabbie to take me and I realised I must look dreadful. My blouse was splattered with blood – Alf's blood I assumed – and I couldn't cover myself because my coat was still in the cell where I'd slept. My boots, stockings and skirt were filthy, my hair was dishevelled and hanging down at the back, and my face was mucky. I must have been such a sight that I couldn't blame the cabbies for slowing down as I stuck my hand out, then yanking the reins of their horse to speed up past me.

Eventually, though, I reached Agnes's house where the curtains were all drawn – whether against the gloom of the day outside or the gloom of the occupants I wasn't sure. I asked the cabbie to wait and ran up the steps to the front door.

John answered, his face drawn and pale.

'Oh, Esther, thank the Lord,' he said, gathering me into his arms. 'We didn't know what was happening.'

'I am so sorry to ask but could you possibly pay for my cab?' I said, hating myself for being so useless. 'I had no money and no coat and I couldn't walk from the West End.'

'Of course,' John said. He patted his pockets and then plodded down the front stairs – looking ten or even twenty years older than he had done when I last saw him. 'Go on inside,' he called over his shoulder. 'Agnes is in bed. She'll be glad to see you.'

'I will wash first,' I told him as he approached the driver, patting his pockets again.

Slowly I went up to my little room. It felt like hundreds of years since I'd last been here. Was it really only one night I'd been away? There was a jug of water on my dresser so I stripped off my clothes and washed myself all over, put on clean undergarments and a dress, then I brushed my hair out and pinned it up again neatly. And then, feeling much better, I went down one floor to Agnes and John's bedroom.

Taking a deep breath I knocked gently on the door and heard Agnes calling for me to come in. As I went inside, she was struggling to sit up and I rushed over to aid her.

'Careful there,' I said, putting my arm round her to help. 'Don't hurt yourself.'

She rested her head on my shoulder for a second. 'Oh, Esther,' she said. 'Esther.'

I gripped her tightly and stroked her hair. 'I know. I'm so sorry, Agnes. So sorry about your baby.'

We sat there together for a while and I felt her tears and mine mingle and trickle down on to my neck.

'We named her Emmeline,' she said eventually, wiping her face and sitting back against her pillow. 'She was so small, but she was perfect.'

I was glad Agnes had got to see her baby. I'd heard other women talk of their babies being taken away before they'd even got to know if they were a boy or a girl.

'She is to be buried at St Mark's,' she said, speaking slowly and deliberately as though it were hard for her to say the words. 'John gave the sexton some money and asked him to arrange it. She will be buried close to the wall and the sexton is to tell us where.'

I nodded. It seemed so cruel that little Emmeline would be laid to rest without her parents in attendance but I was glad she would at least be in the churchyard.

'How do you feel?' I said. 'Are you in pain?'

Agnes shook her head. 'I am numb. I feel nothing but guilt.'

'Oh, no,' I said. 'This wasn't your fault.

'I didn't want to be pregnant,' she said, folding the bedclothes into pleats in between her fingers. 'I was horrified when I realised I was expecting and I didn't want another baby. I told you that, didn't I? I said those very words to you and Minnie?'

'Well, yes,' I admitted, reluctantly. 'But that didn't mean . . .'

'I wished her away,' she said. 'I lay in bed night after night and wished I wasn't pregnant. And now all I can do is wish that I was.'

A tear snaked its way down her cheek. 'I want my baby,' she said.

I reached out and took her hand. It was cold. 'Agnes, my love,' I began, not sure what I could say that would make her feel better. 'This wasn't your doing.'

She looked at me with hollow eyes, but she didn't argue so I carried on.

'I know it was a shock to discover you were expecting. Heaven knows, there's barely a woman in London who's not been caught unawares at some time. You weren't the first and you're definitely not the last.'

As I spoke, I was counting days in my head, wondering if I was one of them and hoping against hope that I was not. No, I was safe, thank goodness.

I sighed. Agnes was watching me expectantly and I wanted so much to ease her pain, that I cast around for the right words.

'You may not have been enthusiastic at first, but I was here and I saw how you grew to love that baby,' I said. 'How you felt her little kicks, and debated names with the family, and planned her nursery. I know how much you loved her already.'

Agnes nodded, tears streaming now. 'But I went along to Parliament Square, even though you tried to stop me,' she whispered. 'I put her in danger.'

'No,' I said. 'No. We went to Caxton Hall for a meeting, and we walked to Parliament. We had no way of knowing what would happen when we got there. It was impossible to predict that the police would react as they did.'

'But . . .'

'No,' I said again. 'You were attacked, Agnes. You were attacked and the only person to blame for your baby's death is the policeman who kicked you to the ground on to your stomach.'

She blinked, as though remembering, and then grasped my hand tightly. 'What did they do to you?' she said. 'You were arrested. I thought you would go to jail.'

I tried to smile reassuringly, but found I couldn't quite muster the strength necessary. 'Mr Churchill set us all free,' I said. 'All the suffragettes.'

She frowned. 'Minnie told me about your sweetheart,' she said. 'That he was a copper and he was there.'

So much for my brave face.

'He was,' I said. 'And he saw me lashing out at the policeman who hurt you.'

'You were bold and daring and I was so proud,' Agnes said.

'I was foolish and angry.'

'But you're free now. No harm done. Except to that copper's nose.'

Again I tried to laugh at her weak joke but my laughter turned into a sob. 'I have to leave,' I said. 'I have to leave London.'

'What?'

Falteringly, I explained the deal I'd made with Joseph, telling her how serious my crime was and spelling out just how hurt Joseph was, and how vengeful.

'I broke his heart,' I said. 'I can't blame him for being angry. I just don't know where to go or what to do now.'

Agnes looked devastated and I felt awful for piling my problems on to hers when she was in no state to cope with more upheaval.

'What will I do without you?' she said. Helpless, I shrugged. I was at a total loss. I had some savings but the little money I'd put aside from my salary wouldn't last long. I had no friends elsewhere – I'd lived in London my whole life.

'I wondered perhaps if the WSPU might help? I know there are branches everywhere. But Joseph made it clear that if I stay involved with any sort of suffragette activity then he will find out about it.'

I felt bone-tired. Weary to my very soul. I put my head on to Agnes's counterpane, unable to think or plan for a moment longer.

I felt her hand on my head, stroking my hair as I'd stroked hers, and then she paused.

'I have an idea,' she said.

I forced myself upright and looked at her.

'I lost quite a lot of blood when I had the baby,' she said. No wonder she was so pale. 'I am weak and I am heartsick. So John is downstairs, trying to find a convalescent home where I can go for a few weeks. Months, even. Somewhere quiet in the country-side where John and the children can visit, but where I can get my strength back.'

'That sounds like a very good idea,' I said, pleased John was so sensible. Agnes was such a restless, busy woman that I feared left to her own devices she would try to get back to normal too soon and make herself ill in body and mind.

'Come with me.'

'What?'

'There are a few different places John is trying. Two down in Kent – one is by the sea in Margate, and another in a small town called Blyton, and there is another further away in the Derbyshire hills. But wherever he finds me a spot, why don't you come with me?'

'I can't go to a convalescent home,' I said. 'I'm not poorly.'

Agnes waved her hand. 'I don't mean that you should stay in the home. Just find a room nearby and a job, perhaps? There is bound to be a local school, wherever we go.'

I sat up a bit straighter. 'I can travel with you and look after you, make sure you're settled in the convalescent home.'

'Indeed.'

'And if there is no school, there are all sorts of jobs I can do. I'm not frightened of hard work.'

'I can give you a reference.'

Flooded with relief, I squeezed Agnes's hand.

'Will it be soon enough? Joseph made it clear he wanted me gone as soon as possible.'

'I was planning to travel on Monday.'

I smiled at her, the first genuine smile I'd smiled in days.

'Thank you,' I said.

Chapter 42

Lizzie

2020

The meeting was awful. Awful. I couldn't look at Danny, couldn't bear to think about what he'd done to me – and to Elm Heath. How could he have said all the things he'd said at New Year, knowing he was part of the team plotting to redevelop the school site? How could he sleep easily at night and then sit opposite little Cara every day at breakfast when all along he was responsible for closing the school she loved and sending her elsewhere?

I knew I was being dramatic, but that was just how I felt. I was furious, upset, betrayed, humiliated all at once. And worst of all, I'd been here before. The emotions I was feeling were horribly familiar because they were just how I'd felt when I'd discovered what Grant had been doing.

I sat numbly, barely listening as Maurice went through his presentation, full of dull and gloomy facts about why keeping Elm Heath open was financial lunacy.

'Miss Armstrong, would you like to speak now?' the man in charge asked. I did not want to speak. I wanted to go home and hide under my duvet, or run back to Mum's, or go anywhere apart from this stuffy room, with everyone looking at me, and the expectations of the Elm Heath kids weighing heavily on my shoulders, and the stench of Danny's betrayal in the air.

But obviously I didn't say that. Instead I nodded, and stood up.

'My name is Lizzie Armstrong and I'm the head teacher of Elm Heath Primary. I've only been a part of Elm Heath's story for a few months,' I said in a shaky voice. 'But I'd like to tell you about that story and why I think it's so important to keep the school open.'

My presentation went like clockwork. I had some history about Esther and how she'd seen the need for a community school, I had some anecdotes about why the need was still there more than one hundred years later, and I had the clip from *The One Show*. It was impressive and I knew it well and didn't so much as stumble over a word. But I felt like I was just going through the motions. I focused on Denise, and the man in charge, and carefully avoided looking in Danny's direction.

When I sat down again, it was Vanessa's turn. She gave the room a sweet smile and turned to Danny. 'You know me,' she said, beaming at the men who were making the decision like they were old friends. Which it seemed they were. 'So it won't surprise you all to hear that I've delegated the hard work on this. Danny's my money man, so he's going to take you through the figures.'

I couldn't help looking up as Danny stood to deliver his presentation. I was slightly heartened to see he looked completely wretched. Like a broken man. I looked away again as his eyes met mine.

I'd expected Danny's figures to be as boring as Maurice's but actually they were mind-blowing – and not in a good way. He explained the council owned the land and the building that the school was on. He said they could sell it as it was, and earn an amount that made me blink in surprise at how large it was. Or, they could sell it with planning permission for development and make an even larger amount. Or – and this was where it all started to get slightly complicated and, to my mind, a bit murky – they could let Vanir secure investment, hire Texo to develop the site – for a large cut of the profits, natch – then sell it, and make even more wonga.

As Danny went through projections and costings, I felt sick. The whole thing was obviously cut and dried. Vanessa and Danny knew all the right people at the council, Elm Heath was a money pit, and the cash Texo and Vanir could make from the site didn't talk so much as bellow.

I'd failed to save Elm Heath, and I'd been humiliated by Danny. I was done.

Danny finished talking and the man in charge gushed his thanks.

'It's been extremely useful to hear all the options,' he said. I snorted and had to pretend to blow my nose. There were no options – that was clear. With budget cuts and belt-tightening everywhere, no council in the country would turn down the chance to make money just to save a few kids a longer journey to school. Would they?

I gathered my papers and stuffed everything back in my bag, eager to leave. And as soon as the man wrapped up the meeting, I murmured thanks to Denise and legged it down the corridor and into the lift, jabbing the button frantically to shut the doors before Danny could emerge from the meeting room.

When I was safely on the ground floor, I virtually threw my security pass at the receptionist and charged out of the door.

'You need to sign out . . .' she called after me, but I ignored her as I raced across the car park and into my car. As I drove towards the exit, Danny appeared in between two parked cars and stood in front of the barrier, blocking my way.

I wound down my window. 'I need to go back to school,' I said. 'Please move.' I half expected the windows to frost over, so icy was my tone.

'Lizzie, I want to explain.'

I pushed my foot down on the accelerator slightly so the engine revved. Danny didn't flinch.

'Please, Lizzie.'

'Move.'

I revved again and moved the car forward, just a fraction.

'I thought you'd overheard me talking to Vanessa,' Danny said, his words tumbling over each other in his eagerness to fill me in on the whole sorry story. 'I thought you'd put two and two together and realised what was happening.'

I glared at him through the windscreen. 'I thought you were seeing someone else. Not that you were busy dismantling all the hard work we were putting into saving Elm Heath.'

Danny looked like he wanted to cry. 'I didn't have a choice, Lizzie. I need the money. I'm a single parent, remember.'

'Well your difficult single-parent life is about to get harder, isn't it? When you have to cart Cara to school in Blyton every day.'

'Blyton Primary's actually right by my office,' he said.

I banged my palms on the steering wheel. 'Oh so you're all right and the rest of us can just go to hell?'

'No. That's not it at all. Look, can we go somewhere and talk?'

'No way. Absolutely not. I don't want to talk. What is there to say? That you've let me down and humiliated me in the same exact way as my sodding ex-husband did? Only this time it's almost worse because I told you how much he'd hurt me and you went and did it anyway?'

'Lizzie . . .'

'Or that you've sat and watched while Nate, and Paula, and the people who are meant to be your friends, Danny, have worked their socks off coming up with new and creative ways to try to save the school, knowing all the time that it's pointless?'

'No, that's not what's been happening,' he said. I pushed my foot down again and the engine growled.

'Did you get close to me just so I'd give you insider info on what we were planning?' I said, raising my voice so he'd hear me over the sound of the car. 'Were you some sort of industrial spy? Recruited for your good looks? How many other women have you seduced just so Texo can make a quick buck, eh?'

I was starting to sound hysterical, and Danny looked bewildered.

'I didn't want to take on this project,' he said helplessly. 'But they wanted me because of my local knowledge, and my boss agreed. I have been trying to get out of it – that's what you overheard on the phone. That's all this is, Lizzie. Bad luck.'

'No,' I said. 'What was bad luck was me getting involved with you in the first place, and me trusting you to be the good person that you pretended to be. And, actually, what was also a bad idea was me thinking the kids and staff at Elm Heath, and even Esther bloody Watkins, meant anything to the stinking bean counters at the council. Because it's become very clear that none of it counts for anything.'

'Lizzie,' Danny said. 'Lizzie, please stop shouting and get out of the car.'

'No, I won't. It may be the end of Elm Heath, but those kids still need me to work. So I'm going back to school now and if you won't move, then I'll drive right over you.'

I revved the engine and pulled forward enough so I could put my ticket into the machine. Behind Danny the barrier lifted.

'Goodbye, Danny,' I said. I put my foot on the pedal and accelerated – possibly a bit too much – out of the car park.

Danny dived out of the way just in time.

Chapter 43

Lizzie

I was still shaking when I got back to school. I parked on the road and skulked round the back, hoping that as it was lunchtime I could sneak into my office without seeing anyone. I couldn't face Paula's enthusiasm at the moment, and winced at the thought of having to let everyone down.

'How was it?' Paula's cheery voice stopped me in my tracks as I crept along the corridor.

I turned towards her, and she took one look at my face and lost her smile.

'Oh bloody hell,' she said. She took my arm and steered me into my office, sat me down at the desk, and shut the door.

'Spill.'

'I honestly don't know where to start.'

'Was it that bad?'

I let out a mirthless laugh. 'However bad you think it was, multiply it by ten and you're getting close.'

She leaned across the desk and took my hand. 'Tell me, or I can't help.'

'I don't want to,' I groaned. 'I don't want to have to say the words.'

'Let's go step by step,' she said. 'You arrived?'

'It was fine when I arrived,' I began. I took her through the beginning of the meeting, right up until the Texo team came in, along with someone from the company handling the investment.

'What?' Paula demanded. 'What did they do?'

'It wasn't what they did, but who they were.'

'Who were they?'

'A woman called Vanessa from Texo,' I said. Paula looked blank. 'And Danny.'

It was vaguely gratifying to see Paula looked almost as shocked as I had done.

'Danny?'

I nodded, lips pinched together tightly. 'Danny.'

'Why was he there?'

'His company is finding investors for the development of the school site.'

Paula's jaw dropped.

'And let me tell you,' I carried on, getting into my stride. 'He's very good at his job. Excellent, in fact. His financial projections for the money the council can make from developing this ramshackle building are eye-watering. There's no doubt that he's signed Elm Heath's death warrant.'

'Shit, Lizzie,' Paula said. 'You didn't know?'

'Of course I didn't know. He did half-heartedly attempt to tell me something at your party the other day, and he rang me just as I was going into the meeting, but he didn't try very hard to confess.' I put my head in my hands. 'I feel like such a bloody fool.'

'It's not your fault,' Paula said. But she didn't sound very sure.

'I don't know what to do next.'

Paula shrugged. 'We carry on.'

'What's the point?'

'It's not a done deal yet, is it? You said they weren't making the decision until March.'

'No, but Paula, the money involved is crazy. I just don't see how they can turn it down.'

'It's not all about money.'

'But it is. In the end, it always comes down to money. We can't compete with that.'

I felt exhausted at the thought of even trying.

'Did you speak to Danny?'

'Ha, no,' I said. 'He chased after me in the car park but I wouldn't stop.'

I dropped my head into my hands again and looked at Paula through my fingers.

'I almost drove over him.'

She smiled. 'Sounds like he deserved it.'

I smiled back. 'He did.'

'But seriously, Lizzie. Danny's not a bad guy. You should talk to him.'

'You've changed your tune. It wasn't so long ago you were warning me off him.'

'I just think there's probably more to it.'

'He said he was only doing his job,' I said. 'Which is exactly what Grant said when he was found to have faked SATs results, and tweaked budgets, and whatever else he was up to.'

'Ah.'

'What?'

'Do you think you're projecting a bit?'

'No. What does that even mean?'

'I mean maybe you were so hurt by Grant that a whiff of Danny doing something similar and you go off on one.'

I sighed. 'That would make sense. And I wish it was what happened. But the horrible truth is that Danny is right in the heart of the team that's going to ruin all our hard work. He's working out all the finances that are going to make it impossible for Blyton Council to keep Elm Heath open. And he did all that while he was pretending to have feelings for me.'

'I don't think he was pretending about that,' Paula said. 'I saw him at New Year. He's smitten with you.'

'Doesn't matter, though, does it? Because even if he's totally in love with me, he's ruined it by lying. I can't be with him now.'

Paula shook her head. 'I suppose not. God, Lizzie, what a mess. Are you going to be okay, seeing him round the village?'

Up until then, I'd mostly been angry. Furious, in fact; feeling a sort of impotent rage. But now, at the thought of carrying on with my life around Elm Heath for the few months until the school closed, seeing Danny every day, I simply dissolved. I just crumpled right there at my desk, into loud, gasping sobs.

Paula looked horrified. 'Oh my goodness,' she said. She leapt up from her chair, crouched down next to me and gathered me into her arms.

I laid my head on her soft shoulder and cried into her baby-pink cardigan.

'It's going to be fine,' she soothed. 'It's all going to be fine.'

Eventually, after an embarrassingly long time, I managed to get myself together, or at least control the huge honking sobs so they were more just hiccups.

'Sorry,' I said, blowing my nose. 'I'm so sorry.'

Paula stood up, putting her hand on her lower back as she did. 'Ooh, that's not as easy as it used to be,' she said. She put her hand on my arm. 'You've got through worse than this before. You'll do it again. We just do what we have to do, don't we?'

Like the clouds had cleared and the sun had come out, I had a sudden realisation. I didn't have to do anything.

I looked at Paula. 'I'm going to resign,' I said.

She gasped, theatrically, putting her hand to her mouth. 'No, Lizzie.'

'It's the only thing I can do, Paula. You said yourself, it's not going to be easy seeing Danny around every day.'

I nodded, mind made up.

'It's so early in the term, I bet I could hand my notice in now and still be allowed to leave at half-term. You can take over until the summer. It's right that you take charge for the end of Elm Heath.'

'Oh, Lizzie, that's not what I meant at all. What about the rally? And the final meeting of the council?'

'You should still go ahead with the rally,' I said. 'It's a fitting celebration of the school.'

'Please don't make any decisions today. You're understandably upset and angry, and you shouldn't act without thinking about it for longer.'

I opened my mouth to argue, then shut it again. Paula was right.

'I'll sleep on it,' I agreed.

The bell rang and I winced. 'Shit, I've got to go and watch year three's assembly,' I said. 'Do I look awful?'

Paula screwed her nose up. 'Bit blotchy and tear-stained,' she said. 'I'll do the assembly if you like. I'll take the reception kids along – they'll enjoy it. You wash your face and get yourself together. Have a think about what you want to do next.'

I nodded, grateful, and Paula headed for the door.

'For what it's worth, I think you should stay and fight. But I'll understand if you decide to go. I'll be sorry, but I'll understand.'

She headed out and closed the door behind her, leaving me in silence. I sat for a moment, drumming my fingers on my desk. Then I got up and wandered round my office, looking at my corn dollies on the shelf and the framed picture Mum had made me.

Esther Watkins gazed at me as I paced. I looked at her.

'What would you do, Esther?' I said, knowing full well that someone who was willing to go to prison for a cause she believed in wouldn't run away at the first sign of trouble. I walked over to the wall and studied the portrait, noticing for the first time that the frame was cracked along one side.

'I should get that replaced before I go,' I murmured. I reached up and unhooked the frame from the wall. It was heavier than I'd expected and as I braced my arms under its weight a shriek from the playground made me jump. The picture overbalanced and toppled face down on to the floor, and I heard the glass smash.

276

'Oh bloody hell,' I said.

I bent down and carefully plucked the frame from among the broken shards. The back board came off in my hands. Gently I laid the pieces of wooden frame and the back on to my desk and peeled the photograph away so it didn't get damaged. And to my surprise, underneath was an envelope, yellowed round the edges but still in good condition. It had no name on the front but I could feel it had something inside. Intrigued, I left the broken glass on the carpet, and sat down at my desk. I slid my finger under the seal and carefully pulled out the paper inside, smoothing out the pages, and I took a sharp breath as I realised the address at the top was Orchard Farm, where Esther had stayed and where she'd had the inspiration to start Elm Heath Primary.

'Dear Joseph,' the letter began.

Chapter 44

Esther

1910

I liked this time of the day most of all. As the sun was beginning to set and I could hear the men shouting to each other outside, while they settled the animals down for the night. I'd been surprised to discover how much work there was to do on a farm even in the depths of winter, but Kenneth had assured me that his was a year-round job.

I had been in Blyton for a month now and every day I was surprised anew, and filled with gratitude, at how welcome Kenneth and Mary had made me. They'd welcomed me into their home and I felt like part of the family already.

John had found me the lodgings at Orchard Farm. He'd contacted a friend of a friend of a friend – people like him knew everyone I'd realised – who knew Kenneth and Mary had been struggling a little, and could use the extra income a lodger would bring. And it was all arranged in what felt like an instant. Before I could even really think about everything that had happened, Agnes and I were on a train – John too, because he didn't want to leave Agnes's side until he knew she was all right – and travelling down towards Canterbury.

Agnes was doing well. The convalescent home was warm and

cosy, and the staff were caring. There were other women there whose babies had died, a few who'd been ill and were recovering, some who had trouble with eating, and others who were just sad – I didn't know why. It was calm and quiet, and Agnes was – I thought – beginning to come to terms with what had happened.

I was coming to terms with everything too. I was surprisingly happy in the countryside, for a girl who'd never left London. Kenneth and Mary had two children – George and Harriet – who were bright sparks, full of energy. They were both quick with numbers and though he was only ten, George already helped his father with the farm's accounts. Interested in their abilities, I had questioned their mother about how much education they'd had.

'Not much.' She had shrugged. 'There's no school nearby and no one checks. I do what I can with them, but they're sharper than me already. Harriet's almost twelve anyway so she's too old for school now. She'll be looking for a position next year.'

Unable to resist, I'd started giving the children little challenges. Setting George sums to do in his head disguised as questions about milk yields or the price of apples at market, or asking Harriet what she thought of ethical dilemmas – she had a way of seeing solutions in problems that I found inspiring.

And just this week, they'd cornered me one morning, after they'd done their early chores on the farm, both of them gripping old-fashioned school slates.

'We thought if you're not too busy you could give us some work to do?' Harriet had said, her bright eyes shining. 'Proper work. Not just pretending you're chatting or telling us stories.'

I'd looked at them both, standing there eagerly, seeing through my silly attempts to trick them into schoolwork, and thought of Agnes's children happily going to dance classes, and music lessons and complaining about me giving them sums that were too hard. I adored those children of course, and they were always a joy to teach, but there was something about Harriet and George that fired me up inside, just as the WSPU had done.

'Let's sit down,' I'd said.

And so we'd sat together and I'd given them some lessons, with Mary watching, and then the next day another boy with a shock of red hair and an ear for poetry had joined them, and then yesterday there were two more boys – both friends of George and red-headed Lester – and today Harriet, fed up with being the only girl in my makeshift schoolroom, arrived with a skinny child named Delia in tow.

'Seems like there's a call for a schoolteacher round here,' Mary had said to me afterwards, nudging me gently. 'There are children running wild all round Elm Heath village, with no one to teach them.'

'I'm not staying,' I'd said at the time. But that was several hours ago, and since then I'd been thinking, wondering what I would do when Agnes had recovered enough to go home. Christmas was just a few days away and she was returning to her family for the day, or maybe even two, depending on how she felt. I knew it wouldn't be long before she wanted to go back to London for good. And then what would I do? I couldn't go home, Joseph had made that very clear. So why shouldn't I stay in Elm Heath?

I'd been quiet as I'd visited Agnes that afternoon, mulling over my options. I'd assumed I'd go to Manchester or another city, and join the WSPU fight there instead of London, hoping that Joseph hadn't really spread the word about me to other police forces.

But could I give up the fight for women's suffrage altogether and instead devote my life to teaching? Would I even be allowed to teach again, given my criminal past?

'You're in an odd humour today,' Agnes had commented, so I'd told her what was on my mind. She'd nodded thoughtfully. 'You might not have to give up entirely,' she'd said. I'd seen a glint in her eye that I'd not seen since the terrible events in Parliament Square.

I'd leaned forward. 'How do you mean?'

'We always need writers, for the newspaper and for pamphlets.

You're forever scribbling your thoughts down in that notebook you carry round. Scribble for the suffragettes instead. You could write under a pen-name.'

'Esther Whitehouse,' I'd said immediately. 'That was the false name I gave Joseph.'

Agnes had looked almost disappointed. 'Really?' she'd said. 'I thought you were more creative than that.'

'I was thinking on my feet.'

She'd snorted, and I'd smiled to see the old Agnes emerging.

'Enid Whitehouse,' she'd suggested.

I'd shrugged. 'Matters not one bit to me.'

'It does matter,' Agnes had said. 'It means Esther Watkins can stay here and teach the next generation, while Enid writes revolutionary literature.' She'd looked at me carefully. 'If, of course, you want to stay here?'

I'd examined my emotions, testing myself to see how I'd feel to leave Elm Heath and start new in Manchester or Glasgow. It did not seem to be a tempting proposition. Then I'd thought about staying with Kenneth and Mary, perhaps running my own school, getting to know Lester, and Delia, and the others. And I'd smiled.

'I think I do want to stay,' I'd said. 'There are some wonderful children here, who need proper teaching. I want to be the one to do it.'

'It won't be easy, starting a school,' Agnes had warned. 'It's going to be a fight.'

'That's one thing I'm most definitely not afraid of.'

Now, sitting by my window, watching the sun drop behind the barn and listening to the men's calls as they shut up the cows for the evening, I realised I was happy. I had a plan, and I had some fire in my belly – and I hadn't left the WSPU behind after all. There was just one thing I still had to do, to draw a line under this whole episode, I thought. I needed to write to Joseph and tell him exactly how I felt.

Agnes was right that I scribbled in my notebook all the time. Ever since I had been a young girl, I'd found writing was the best way to manage my feelings and make sense of things that happened to me. I'd written letters to my father when he died, getting out all of my anger on to the page and then burning the pages when I felt better. I'd written about my experiences in prison for the WSPU, and when I met Joseph I'd written him love notes. And now I was going to tell him what I thought of what I had done. What he'd done. What we'd done to each other. I knew I'd probably never send the letter, but I knew it was worth writing.

With the light in my room beginning to fade, I lit a candle, and then I pulled my notepaper towards me, and began to write.

Dear Joseph, I began.

I have lived many lives in my twenty-one years in this world. I have been a daughter, a teacher, a criminal and a lover. But above all, Joseph, I am a fighter.

I don't mean fighting with fists, or sticks, or weapons; I know that's wrong. I know I should never have lashed out at Alf the way I did, and I hope you can tell him that I am sorry.

What I do mean is fighting with all my heart for whatever I believe in.

I have fought tooth and nail for the right of women to vote and though you have made it clear I cannot continue, I will not stop fighting in my heart. I have fought to defend my friends when they are in trouble. And I can see now that my future will be fighting to give children an education. All children, not just the privileged few.

But part of knowing when to fight is knowing when it's just not worth the battle. Joseph, it's clear that you didn't think our love was worth fighting for. And, I have to admit that I didn't think it was worth the fight either.

I loved you, Joseph, and I think we could have been happy together. We'd have lived a simple life with no conflict. But what's the point in that? Sometimes the fight is part of the fun.

Goodbye, Joseph. I'm sorry for any hurt I caused you. I hope you can look back on our time together one day and smile. And I hope sometime soon you find a girl who is worth fighting for.

Fond regards,

Esther.

Chapter 45

Lizzie

2020

I read Esther's letter over and over. It was inspiring and sad in equal measure. I wondered if she'd ever met anyone else after Joseph. It seemed not, as I knew she'd never married.

A knock on my door made me look up. It was Cara Kinsella, looking very worried.

'Are you okay, Cara?'

'Miss,' Cara said. 'I've done something bad.'

I doubted that. She was such a sweet little girl. But I nodded seriously.

'Take a seat and tell me all about it. But come round that way because I dropped something.'

Cara looked at the broken glass on the floor.

'Ooh careful, Miss. Someone could cut themselves. Maybe you.'

I smiled. 'I know, I'll clear it up after we've had a chat.'

Cara sat down. She looked very small and sad and my heart ached for her.

She took a breath. 'I pushed Stevie in my class and he landed on his bum and now he's crying,' she said in a hurry.

'Okay. That's not like you, Cara.'

She bit her lip. 'I wanted him to stop.'

'Stop what?'

'Well, you know Mia in year three?'

'I do.'

'Well, I was sad, because my mum died. And sometimes I feel sad, but no one minds. They just let me be sad for a while and then I am happy again.'

I blinked in surprise. Kids were amazingly astute.

'Right,' I said. 'So, you were sad, Cara?'

'Stevie was being annoying and asking me why I was sad. And Mia said he should just let me be sad because what difference did it make to Stevie, and she said Stevie was lucky to have a mum.'

'Good girl, Mia,' I said under my breath. 'Is that why you pushed him?'

'No,' Cara said witheringly. 'I pushed him because instead of leaving us all alone, he started being really annoying and saying horrible things about Mia's mummy like how she would die soon too and then Mia would be sad as well.'

She swallowed a sob and I felt awful for her.

'And I got even more upset and Mia was upset too, and I told Stevie to shut up but he didn't, so I shoved him.'

She looked down at her knees.

'And I know we're not allowed to hurt each other, but Stevie was hurting Mia.'

'You should have told one of the teachers.'

'I know but Maisy Cooper fell off the wall and her head was all bleeding so Mr Welsh was busy, Miss.'

I gave her a stern look. 'Cara, I can't condone violence. Do you understand what that means?'

'No, Miss.'

'Condone means to allow something and give it approval.'

'Right, Miss.'

'So, I can't condone what you did.'

Cara looked sad but there was a glint of defiance in her eyes that I liked.

'But?'

I couldn't hide my smile. 'But you were defending a friend and I'm not going to punish you. This time.'

'Thank you, Miss.'

'I'll have a word with Mia and Stevie too.'

Cara was staring at my shelf. 'You kept the corn dollies,' she said.

'Of course I did.'

'Are they working? Are they bringing you good luck?'

I tried not to grimace and instead forced a smile. 'I hope so.'

'That's good. That's what we wanted to happen. Because we all like you.'

This time my smile was genuine. 'I like you all too. You can go back to class now.'

Cara jumped to her feet, obviously relieved to have got off scot-free and I looked down at Esther's letter.

'Some things are worth fighting for,' I said, as Cara left. She gave me a look that suggested she thought I was losing my marbles and scampered off down the corridor. But, I thought, getting up and going to the window, I wasn't losing my marbles at all. In fact, I was finding them. If that was a thing. Cara's little story, and Esther's letter, had made me realise that sometimes you did have to fight for what you believed in.

Grant hadn't fought for me – he'd chosen his career instead of our marriage. And it looked like Danny had done the same, picking his contract with Texo ahead of Elm Heath and our budding romance. So there was no reason why I couldn't fight for what I wanted too. I felt a spark of determination deep inside. What I wanted was to save Elm Heath. I wanted Cara to go to a school where her friends would understand that she had sad times and that was okay. I wanted the kids to believe that their corn dollies had done the trick. I wanted to fight for this little school and, I had to admit, I wanted to rub bloody Danny's nose in it too. I wanted to show everyone that money and financial projections weren't as important as giving kids a chance, and building on history.

I stared down at the empty playground. The sky was heavy and grey and I thought it might snow.

'Some things are worth fighting for,' I said again, out loud. Danny wasn't worth the fight. But Elm Heath most definitely was.

'Talking to yourself?' Paula was by my side. 'Looks like it might snow,' she said.

'I know. I hope it does. We can get the kids out on the village green, building snowmen and having snowball fights, and then take loads of photos. They'll look great on the website.'

She studied me, amusement in her eyes. 'What do you care?'

I took a breath. 'I'm going to stay,' I said. 'I'll see this through.'

Paula shrieked in a manner most unbecoming to a deputy head, and threw her arms around me. 'Thank God. We'd be lost without you.'

'It's not going to be easy,' I warned.

'Well, as I always tell Chloe, if it's worth doing, it's probably going to be difficult.'

I grinned. 'Sometimes the fight is part of the fun.'

'Wise words indeed.'

'Esther wrote them.' I showed her the letter I'd found.

'Where did you get this?'

'It was behind the photograph in the frame,' I said. 'I was looking at her picture, feeling a bit gloomy and I noticed the frame was cracked. So I took it down, thinking I'd get it reframed but I dropped it. And the letter was inside. She must have hidden it, I guess.'

Paula was reading the letter already, tears filling her eyes.

'It's really sad, isn't it? That she was let down by the man she loved.'

I snorted. 'We are kindred spirits, Esther and me.'

Paula chuckled.

'It's inspiring too, though don't you think?' I continued. 'She had such a vision of what this school was going to be. I don't think we can let her down.'

'It's like a message from beyond the grave, or a warning from history,' Paula said dramatically.

'It's a reminder that things aren't always straightforward.'

Paula rolled her eyes. 'So what's the plan?' she asked, carefully laying the letter down on my desk.

'We've got two months to turn things round, which isn't long. But Nate's done a great job with the rally, and I'll make sure all the journalists know about it. It would be brilliant if we could get some more press coverage.'

I'd probably have to get in touch with Grant again, I thought. But it would be worth it.

'I think we're doing really well with the PR side. But It's the money side of things we need to work on,' Paula said. 'I can speak to Chris, see if he's got any bright ideas? We need to get the school making some proper cash.'

'The breakfast and after-school clubs are doing well.'

'Yes, but we need more. Ways to get the building earning money outside of school hours, I think. Maybe we could brainstorm some ideas?'

I smiled at her. 'I'd like that,' I said.

'Come round for dinner?'

I knew that she was only asking me so I didn't stay at home by myself and mope about Danny, but somehow I didn't mind. I was lucky to have her, I thought.

'Thanks, Paula,' I said.

She patted my arm. 'Any time.' Then she frowned. 'Now, I hate to come over all health and safety, but are you aware you've got a load of broken glass on the floor of your office?'

I nodded. 'It's from Esther's photograph. I suppose I should clean it up.'

'I'll get the dustpan and brush.'

Chapter 46

Lizzie

The rally was a triumph. It was a joy from start to finish. We were really lucky with the weather, which had been wet and wild the week before but cleared just in time and revealed a beautiful, if a bit blowy, spring day.

We all gathered in the school in the morning as Nate took us through the plan for the day.

'I'm expecting about a hundred people,' he said. 'Perhaps a few more. I've got banners ready, and Pippa's made the sashes.'

He gestured to a table by the door where the props were piled. As before, he'd based them all on the now-familiar suffragette banners and sashes but they read Save Elm Heath instead of Votes for Women.

'I've also blown up the photograph of Esther Watkins and used that on some banners,' Nate added and I smiled at the thought of Esther continuing to campaign, fifty years after her death.

'So we're going to gather in the playground then march along the main road through the village to the big roundabout. Then we'll march round the roundabout, and back to the school,' he said. 'I've got some of the kids ready with drums to lead the parade and we've got the big banner to hold at the front. When we get back to school, there's a makeshift stage set up round the back where Miss Armstrong is going to make a speech . . .'

'This is brilliant,' I said to Paula. 'He's worked so hard.'

'Everyone's worked hard,' she said. 'Especially you.'

She was right, I supposed. In a desperate effort to stop myself brooding over Danny, I'd thrown myself into working every evening on the campaign to save Elm Heath. I'd helped Nate with the preparation for the rally, organising the closure of the road and finding people to man stalls. And I'd spent hours poring over figures and budgets, trying to find a way to make the school building pay. I'd discovered that the patch of waste ground behind the school belonged to us, too. I had wondered if we could sell it for development but Paula's husband, Chris, said he thought it was too small.

'You could build an extension to the school, though,' he said.

I'd snorted. 'Ah yes, with all the extra money there is lying around.'

But he'd given me an idea.

'Maybe we could do some sort of partnership,' I said, thinking of how Danny's firm operated. 'Get a company to build something – a sports hall perhaps or a music centre – and then we can use it for the kids, and rent it out to organisations, and the builders can take a cut of the profits.'

Chris had reacted so favourably that I knew it was a good plan. But though I'd drawn up a list of ideas about what we could build, I was a teacher, not a business guru. I had no idea how to get investment or how to start pitching ideas.

Apart from that, I'd budgeted a plan for expanding the breakfast and after-school clubs into holiday clubs, and for renting out parts of the school at weekends. I'd found a netball club that wanted to use our courts one evening a week, and a painting group that had expressed an interest in meeting in our hall.

But while it was all very encouraging, I wasn't sure it was enough to compete with the big fat luxury-flat-shaped carrot Texo were dangling in front of Blyton Council.

For now, though, I was determined to be positive, as Nate clapped his hands together.

'Today couldn't have happened without you guys – the staff and the PTA of Elm Heath,' he said, sounding a bit choked up. 'Your efforts have shown us all that this school is worth the fight we're all putting up. I think people are beginning to gather in the playground ready to march, so grab yourself a banner, and a sash, and let's get going.'

There was a small cheer from the gathered group of teachers and other staff. Paula and I followed them all out into the playground and stopped in astonishment at the sight that greeted us. The playground was full of children, parents, local people and people I'd never seen before. Some of them were in Edwardian dress like mini suffragettes. Others were decked out in purple and green. There were so many people that no one else could fit into the school grounds and the crowds were beginning to snake down the road.

'Oh my God,' I breathed. Paula grasped my hand and we exchanged startled glances.

'I never for one minute expected this,' she said into my ear above the buzz of voices.

'Neither did I.'

She squeezed my fingers. 'This is all your doing,' she said.

'It's everyone.'

I felt really emotional as I looked across the heads of everyone gathered. I noticed there were several photographers snapping away, as well as a couple of camera crews. I'd emailed Grant – a bright, breezy message – and asked him to work his magic again and he'd obviously come up trumps. I'd have to message him again and say thank you, I thought, grudgingly. Because for all his faults, he knew what he was doing when it came to publicity.

In the end, it was less of a march and more of a parade. There were the drummers at the front, lots of people with tambourines and other things to bash and crash, and the school's tiny windband – led by Celeste – had been practising walking and playing at the same time so they put on a good show too. There were some children with pompoms doing jumps and cheers, lots of little ones on scooters, and a real party atmosphere. Even the police who were supervising the road closure that Nate had organised were joining in, dancing to the music and high-fiving the kids.

When we looped round the roundabout and made our way back to school, there were still marchers at the back just leaving the playground. It was an astonishing turnout and when I climbed on to the little rickety stage to make my speech, I felt really nervous.

I waited for the crowd to quiet and then I began by saying how amazed I was to see so many supporters and how over-whelmed we all were by the love everyone had for Elm Heath.

'The founder of Elm Heath Primary was a woman called Esther Watkins, who you've all heard a lot about recently,' I said. 'She was so passionate about fighting for what she believed in that she even ended up in prison.'

I smiled at the children who'd wriggled their way to the front of the crowd.

'Now, I'm not suggesting we all get locked up, but I do think we can learn from Esther's story. We need to fight hard for what we believe. And what we believe is that Elm Heath needs this school. And more than that, it deserves this school.'

I looked out into the crowd and saw, with a shock, that Grant was there. He was standing slightly to the side of the mass of people and he was looking at me with pride. He'd never looked at me like that before.

Faltering, I took a second to compose myself and carried on.

'When Esther was setting up this school, she wrote to the local education authority and told them why she thought Elm Heath was needed. She wrote that "preparing our children for the world they will one day be running is the most rewarding job there is" and I agree. Today, children, you have proved that you're going to be running the world brilliantly one day. Far better than we grown-ups have managed. And I'm proud that I – and Elm Heath – have played a tiny part in this. I just hope we're allowed to carry on.'

I felt tears welling up again and decided that was a good place to stop. I blew a kiss to the children and went to leave the stage. As I made my way down the steps at the side, I saw Danny. He was standing on the opposite side from Grant, but he was also slightly detached from the crowd and he was also watching me closely. I couldn't read the expression on his face, though. My heart thumped loudly in my chest as I looked at him. I'd barely seen him since I tried to run him over. I'd blocked his number and avoided him in the playground, only catching a glimpse of him at a distance as he collected Cara from school or drove through the village.

I'd thought, foolishly as was obvious now, that I was getting over him. But from the way I had such a physical reaction to his presence, I'd clearly just squashed my feelings down and ignored them. I was still staring at him and he at me, and as our eyes met, he gave me a tiny smile. I felt the corners of my mouth turn up in response, and quickly looked away to where Grant stood, weaving my way through the crowd to him instead.

'You were amazing,' he said, giving me a hug. I stood stiffly, arms by my side, and let him embrace me without responding.

'Thank you.' I pulled away and gave him a genuine smile. 'And thanks for getting all the press here. I really appreciate it.'

He shrugged. 'They all had it in their diaries anyway,' he said. 'It's a great story. When's the final decision?'

'Monday,' I said, feeling nauseous at the thought. 'In the evening. Full council meeting with reports from all sorts. I don't fancy our chances.'

'Never say die.' He gave me another hug and this time I did respond. I was pleased he'd come.

'Fancy a drink? I saw a beer stall over in the corner.'

'That would be great.'

We wandered round the edge of the playground towards the awning where the pub landlord had put up his stall.

'You never called me,' Grant said casually, as we walked. I tried to pretend I'd not heard but he took my hand and stopped, tugging me so I turned to face him.

'I want you back, Queenie. I made such a mistake letting you go.'

Back when our marriage had first gone wrong, I'd have done anything to hear him say those words. But now, I smiled at him, looking at his handsome face, and winning smile, and slowly shook my head. 'It won't work, Grant.'

'But we had a good marriage.'

'We did, and I loved you,' I said. 'But when things got tough we didn't fight, did we? In the end, we didn't fight hard enough to stay together.'

Grant looked surprised, like he'd never thought of that before. 'I've always thought if something's right, you don't need to fight,' he said.

'Sometimes the fight is part of the fun.'

There was a second while we both looked at each other and then he smiled again. 'For what it's worth, I'm sorry,' he said.

I squeezed his arm. 'Thank you. I'm sorry too.'

'Shall we get that beer then?'

'Lead the way.'

As we made our way over to the temporary pub, I looked round for Danny, but I couldn't see him anywhere.

Chapter 47

Lizzie

I was strangely calm when Monday dawned. It reminded me of when I had an important exam at university, and I knew I'd done all I could do to prepare. Like being in the eye of a hurricane.

But as the day went on, my nerves resurfaced and I was twitchy and distracted at school, desperate to get it all over with so we could celebrate or drown our sorrows.

The meeting was at seven p.m. so by six p.m. I was in the town hall, pacing the corridor, waiting for the doors of the main hall to be opened. And by half past, I was surrounded by supporters – many wearing Save Elm Heath sashes from the rally. I found Paula in the group and gave her a grateful hug.

'So nice of everyone to come.'

'Wouldn't have missed it.'

Up ahead there was a thud as someone inside the hall unlocked the large wooden doors. The crowd all shuffled back to let them be thrown open and fastened back, and then we all filed inside.

'This is it,' Paula said. 'Good luck.'

I saw Denise at the front of the room in her *Good Wife* outfit and waved to her. She came over, smiling broadly.

'Brilliant turnout,' she said. 'This is looking better than I could have hoped.'

'How is this going to work?' I knew really, because she'd gone through it already, but I wanted to hear her say it again.

'We're item three on the agenda,' Denise said. 'James, the committee chair, will share some opening remarks, just summing up where we're at. Then the council will hear all the submissions.'

'So that's me and the developers?'

Denise frowned, glancing down at the sheet of paper she held in her hand.

'Yes,' she said. 'But on the agenda there is another submission, too. From a company called Watkins & Co. Heard of them?'

I shook my head. 'Watkins? As in Esther?' I said. 'How strange. Could it be a rival developer?'

'Perhaps. But that's unusual at this stage. I guess we'll find out soon enough.'

'So once we've all done our bit, what happens?'

'The councillors will discuss it. Beware, that can drag on. And then they'll vote.'

'And that's it?'

'That's it.'

I felt sick and excited and full of dread all at once.

'People tend to sit in groups,' Denise was saying. I forced myself to pay attention. 'If you encourage all your supporters to fill the left side of the hall, and up into the balcony if necessary, then I'll tell the Texo people – and this Watkins & Co – to go to the right.'

'Like a wedding,' I said.

Denise looked dubious. 'Not really. I just thought that way it's going to be very clear that Elm Heath has loads of support locally, while the Texo plan has none.'

She leaned towards me and spoke in a whisper. 'Just don't tell anyone I told you. Because I'm supposed to be impartial.'

I grinned at her, fighting my nerves, and went to tell everyone where to sit.

Once the meeting got underway, I looked round. Denise had

been spot-on when she told us to organise ourselves the way we had. The large, wooden-clad council chamber had a huge oval table at the far end, round which the councillors were seated. There was a desk to one side for the press, and while Denise said often there was no one there at all, today there were several reporters squeezed round the table.

The room was divided into two blocks of seating and the Elm Heath support filled every chair on their side. There were people standing in the aisle by the windows, and at the back, and more supporters sitting upstairs in the viewing gallery at the back. It was a wonderful sight, especially when you looked at the empty chairs on the other side of the room. There were a few journalists perched on that side, taking advantage of the space, and a couple of other people who I didn't recognise.

At the front, on her own, was Vanessa from Texo. There was no sign of Danny and I couldn't decide if I was relieved or disappointed that he wasn't there.

I was twitchy throughout the first two items on the agenda. Something about a supermarket car park, and something else about waste management. I passed the time looking over my notes again and again. I was basically making the same pitch I'd made in January, with the added budgets and some photos and a bit of film from the rally at the weekend. And I was going first this time, which I thought was good. Or was it bad? Was it better to be first and get your arguments in early, or last and stay in people's minds while they debated? I had no idea.

I fidgeted in my chair, waiting for my chance to speak. Sitting next to me was Paula and beside her was her husband Chris who'd helped me with the budgets, and behind us were the other teachers from Elm Heath. It felt good to know that while I was the one who had to get up and speak, I wasn't doing it alone.

'Item three on your agenda, is the future of Elm Heath Primary School,' the council leader was saying. 'James is going to explain the vote.'

The man from the first meeting, whose name I couldn't remember that time, stood up. I wrote James down on my notes, in case I needed to address him later. He briefly ran through the two viewpoints and then introduced me. With trembling legs I walked to the front of the room and began my presentation.

'My name is Lizzie Armstrong,' I said.

Again, everything went smoothly. I'd practised so often that I knew it all off by heart and even the financial bits that I'd been nervous about tripped off my tongue. The photos from the march looked wonderful and as I sat down I felt confident I'd done everything I could. The supporters all whooped, their cheers echoing round the old room and I beamed with relief and hope that it was all going to be okay.

Next, it was Vanessa's turn. She stood up and straightened her skirt, then she plugged a memory stick into the laptop and clicked on her own presentation. But as she began to talk she was inter-rupted as the doors at the back opened with a clatter. Everyone turned to look, including me, and I was surprised to see Danny hurrying down the aisle like someone turning up to stop a wedding.

'Sorry,' he said in a stage whisper. 'Sorry, was waiting for an email.' He waved his phone at the disapproving councillors. 'I have it all now. Sorry.'

I expected him to go right, to the empty seats but instead he hesitated in the middle of the aisle, looking at the Elm Heath contingent. Vanessa glared at him and Danny gave her the tiniest shake of his head.

'Sorry,' he said again.

Then in one quick, bewildering and almost rehearsed, move, Paula's Chris got up from his seat and went to the side where other spectators were standing, Paula slid sideways into the seat her husband had vacated and Danny plonked himself down next to me, right in the middle of the Elm Heath supporters.

There was a pause as Vanessa waited for the hubbub to settle down and then she began her presentation.

As she started talking I gripped Danny's arm. 'What the actual FUCK are you doing here?' I hissed.

He kept his eyes fixed on Vanessa. 'Shhh,' he said. 'I'm trying to listen.'

Vanessa was showing the rapt councillors a graph of how much money her development would give them. I couldn't decide whether to focus on her or on Danny.

Danny won.

'What are you doing? Shouldn't you be doing the Texo presentation?' I muttered.

He still didn't look at me.

'I don't work for Vanir any more,' he said.

I had no words.

Up at the front, Vanessa was wrapping things up. I could see the councillors all scribbling furiously like Peter Jones in *Dragons' Den*.

I turned to Danny again. 'What's going on? Where do you work?'

'I've started my own company,' he said, finally turning to me and giving me the benefit of his mega-watt smile. 'It's called Watkins & Co.'

Vanessa had sat down and the council leader was speaking again.

'Finally, could we have the submission from Watkins & Co, please?'

Danny stood up, gripping his laptop, and I watched in amazement as he went to the front of the room.

'I'm Danny Kinsella and I represent Watkins & Co,' he said. 'I think we can all agree that we've heard some convincing arguments here today. The money speaks for itself, doesn't it? Texo are a great company and they know what they're doing. They know how to make a profit and they do it well.'

I grimaced. What was he up to?

'But where Texo's plans for the Elm Heath site have failed is not taking into account the human side of the argument,' Danny continued. He wasn't looking at notes as he spoke. He was natural and warm, and everyone in the room was paying attention. Me included.

'Because the human side of this argument is, I think, the most important part of today's decision.'

He clicked to move the presentation on and Cara's little face beamed out from the large screen.

'This is my daughter, Cara,' he said. 'She goes to Elm Heath Primary and the staff . . .' he nodded to us and we all sat up a bit straighter. 'The staff are like a second family.'

He paused.

'Cara lost her mum a few years back, and it's not been easy for her. But I know at Elm Heath she's in good hands.'

He looked down at the floor for a second, then seemed to gather himself. I had absolutely no doubt that he was speaking from his heart; he was so genuine and I could see everyone in the room was listening carefully as he spoke. But I still didn't understand what he was doing.

'My point is, every child at Elm Heath has their own individual story and their own needs. School – and Elm Heath Primary in particular – is an important part of all their lives. But more than that, it's an important part of the village. Like our wonderful head teacher, Miss Armstrong said . . .'

Was I imagining it, or did he emphasise the "Miss"? I met his gaze for a second and he looked back, eyes wide and innocent.

'Miss Armstrong quoted our founder Esther Watkins when she said there was a need for this school in the village. Not just for the children but for everyone.'

There was a murmur of approval from my side of the room. I didn't join in. I didn't understand where Danny was going with this. I knew what he was saying was true, but what was the point of him saying it?

'But I also understand that times are tough and we need to

make everything – even a school with credentials like Elm Heath – pay. So I've come up with a plan.'

My jaw dropped as Danny outlined how his new company was planning to develop the waste ground at the back of the school, just as I'd tried to do.

He put up a slide showing the structure of the new business, with himself at the top and various consultants listed. Paula's Chris was up there as part of the finance team, which explained why he'd been expecting Danny's arrival. And Nate's partner, Marc, was also one of the names. I looked round and caught Nate's eye. He looked as startled as I did. Startled and very, very pleased.

'I knew he was up to something,' he whispered loudly. 'I thought he was planning my birthday party.'

At the front of the room, Danny was outlining the plan that I'd tried to formulate but not managed. His company had secured investment to build a multi-use centre at the back of the school.

'We'll have to come up with a better name than that,' he said ruefully as he put up the plans. 'We can't call it a MUC.'

The centre would have a large hall, which could be used for fitness classes, parties, shows and concerts. There would be sound-proofed music rooms for lessons. A teaching kitchen. The Elm Heath library, which was currently housed in a tumbledown building at the edge of the village, would move into the centre too and there would be a café and space for book groups and other clubs to meet. And at the back it would have one all-weather tennis court and one astro-turfed football pitch.

'The aim is to build something all the children will benefit from at school,' Danny continued. 'But also something that will be in use every evening, at weekends and during the school holidays – and bringing in a considerable income.'

He grinned at the councillors.

'And if it works at Elm Heath, I'm hoping we can do similar projects at other local schools. I'd like to make them into proper hubs for the area, putting the schools right at the heart of the communities they serve.

'Of course, the Elm Heath multi-use centre won't be as profitable immediately as developing the site along the lines proposed by Texo would be. But it's a long-term scheme and I like to think that with this plan, everyone wins.'

He looked across at me and I felt my stomach twist with emotion. It took everything I had not to jump up from my chair and run over to him, and throw my arms round him.

'Everyone wins,' I said.

Chapter 48

Lizzie

There had to be a vote, of course, but Danny's proposal had won the council over and it was just a formality. The motion to allow Watkins & Co to develop the waste ground was carried and just like that, Elm Heath was saved.

The whole room erupted in a huge cheer. Nate, Pippa, Celeste and the others all bundled around me and squished me in the middle of a huge group hug. Paula wiggled into the middle and joined in.

'We did it,' I said. I couldn't quite believe I was saying the words. It felt like a wonderful dream. 'We actually did it.'

'Thanks to you,' said Nate, but I shook my head.

'Absolutely not. This was everyone.'

With a bit of difficulty, I untangled my arms from the bundle of limbs, beaming from ear to ear.

'Who fancies a drink?'

There was another big cheer.

'Three Kings in an hour?'

'See you there,' Nate said. 'Are you okay for getting back?'

'I've got my car.'

He blew me a kiss and he and the other staff all headed off. The councillors were packing up and the crowds were thinning now. I grabbed Paula as she was sneaking out of the door with Chris.

'Don't you dare go without explaining what just happened.'

She grinned. 'I promise I only found out about it all this afternoon,' she said. 'Chris has been seeing quite a lot of Danny but he said he was just stopping him moping over you. I didn't question it.'

She bounced up and down on the balls of her feet.

'Brilliant, isn't it?'

'I'm overwhelmed.'

'It was your idea,' Paula said. 'Tell her, Chris.'

Chris had been talking to Denise, but now he turned round and nodded. 'Totally your idea. I mentioned it to Danny . . .' He looked a bit sheepish. 'And by mention, I mean forwarded all the emails you sent me asking questions about how to find investment for your ideas. He picked it up and he ran with it.'

I let out a tiny squeak of joy. 'Are you coming to the pub to celebrate?' I asked Chris.

'Wouldn't miss it.'

'Great.'

I looked round. 'Where is Danny?'

He'd disappeared somewhere in the throng of people that had rushed to me after the vote. I felt deflated as I realised I'd not seen him since his presentation, but as I looked across the room, one of the councillors moved aside and there, behind him, was Danny. He was grinning at me across the room and I felt my heart soar at the sight of his smile.

'We'll leave you to it,' Paula said. 'See you in the pub.'

Danny walked towards me and the rest of the room fell away as I gazed at him.

'Hi, Lizzie,' he said. 'Can I ask you something?'

'Anything.' I couldn't stop smiling.

'You couldn't give me a lift home, could you? My car's in the garage.'

I stared at him for a second then laughed. 'Course I can,' I said. 'Come on.'

We didn't talk as we made our way downstairs and out into the street. Just exchanged smiles.

'This is safe, isn't it?' Danny said as I led the way to my car. 'Only the last time I was in a car park with you, you tried to run me over.'

'You deserved it,' I said mildly, beeping to unlock the door. 'Get in.'

Once we were out of Blyton and on the road to Elm Heath, I glanced at him.

'So, what on earth happened? I'm thrilled, obviously, but you owe me an explanation.'

Danny sighed. 'You happened, Lizzie. It was you.'

I frowned as I indicated to turn off towards Elm Heath. 'What do you mean?'

'I felt awful after that last meeting. Fucking awful. I've done some shit things in my time, but not telling you I was working with Texo on the development was right up there with the worst.'

'Got that right.'

I shot him a quick glance.

'How did it happen? Your company was involved in the investment?'

Danny adopted a sort of fake modest expression.

'Texo were trying to get me to join the school development project,' he said. 'Because like I said, I had the local knowledge, and the truth is, Liz, I'm really good at what I do.'

A sudden memory popped into my head. 'Was that what you were arguing with Chris about at the barbecue?'

'You saw that?'

'I was watching you.'

He raised an eyebrow at me and I chuckled.

'I'm going to park at mine and we can walk round to the pub,' I said, though I was a bit sad the journey was almost over. I was enjoying having Danny to myself.

'Sounds good.'

'So, Texo wanted you and you went?'

'It wasn't that simple,' he said. 'They wanted me for this particular project because of my contacts and whatnot. Obviously, I said no at first, more than once in fact. But Texo are a big company and Vanir is fairly small. If there was a whiff of them going elsewhere, it'd have been big trouble. My boss put pressure on me, and when I didn't respond, he offered me a lot more money.'

'So it was just about the money?'

'Yes and no,' he said. 'It all happened when Sophie was in hospital. I was in a bit of a state, thinking about how I'm all Cara has, you know? I need to make sure she's okay, Liz. It was hard to say no to.'

I pulled up outside my little cottage and turned off the engine.

'I understand that,' I said honestly. 'But it was a shitty thing to say yes to.'

Danny leaned his head against the headrest. 'I know that. And when we got together, it seemed even shittier. Especially when you explained what had happened with Grant. I knew I had to tell you but . . .'

'But?'

'I was really falling for you and I didn't want to ruin it.'

I rolled my eyes.

'I know,' he groaned. 'You can't make me feel any worse than I do.'

He reached over the gearstick and took my hand. I let him, enjoying the feeling of my fingers in his. They were a perfect fit.

'At first, I thought I could wriggle out of it, and you'd never know the truth, then you overheard my conversation with Vanessa.'

'Except I jumped to totally the wrong conclusion,' I said. 'But what about New Year? Why did you let me think everything was okay?'

'Because it was, as far as I was concerned. I'd gone back to my boss and virtually threatened to hand in my notice if he didn't take me off the project. I thought I was home and dry. But then they found a clause in my contract that meant I had to be at the meeting.'

'That was really awful,' I said. 'I felt like you'd pulled my heart out of my chest and stamped on it.'

'Can you forgive me?'

I gave him a small smile. 'I'm working on it.'

Danny ran his thumb over the back of my hand. 'It was Cara who made me realise I had to act,' he said.

'Really?' We'd been careful not to let the little girl get wind of our romance so far.

'She came home from school and told me about how some lad had been annoying her, teasing her about not having a mum . . .'

'Stevie. I remember.'

'She said you'd told her some things are worth fighting for. And I realised in that second that you were one of the things that I should fight for but my job wasn't.'

I smiled more broadly this time. 'That was the same time I decided Elm Heath was worth the fight and you weren't.'

Danny laughed. 'You were right. Totally right.'

'But what about Watkins & Co?' I said. 'How did that happen? Chris said it was my idea.'

'It was your idea.'

I raised an eyebrow. 'Really?'

'Honestly. I had a beer with Chris one night and he told me you'd come up with this idea to use the waste ground but you were struggling to find investors. He said, half as a joke really, that you could use my help, forwarded me the emails you'd sent him outlining your ideas, and that was it. I put out some feelers, Chris agreed to help and I got Marc on board to sort out the designs.'

'You're incredible,' I said, shaking my head in disbelief. 'And infuriating.'

'What did you say? Sometimes the fight is part of the fun?'

'It was Esther who said that.'

Danny shifted in his seat so he was closer to me. 'She knew what she was talking about.'

His lips touched mine gently.

'Nope,' I said, staying close to him. 'I'm done fighting.'

'We've got lots of fights to win still. First of all, I need to persuade you that I'm sorry for all the shit I've caused. How is that fight going, by the way?'

I smiled. 'I think you can safely assume you've won that one.'

Danny did an air-punch and I laughed.

'Then we need to sort out the MUC.'

'And come up with a better name.'

'Definitely, and we need to make sure it's doing what we need it to do.'

'Okay.'

'We need to win Sophie's approval, which frankly could be easier said than done.'

'True.'

'And,' he said. 'At some stage I'm probably going to need to persuade you to move in with Cara and me, and maybe even convince you to say yes when I propose.'

'I don't want to get married again.'

'See? That's something worth fighting for, right there.'

We both laughed and then we were kissing again, and I was wishing we'd not agreed to go to the pub with everyone. My heart was pounding and the blood rushed round my body making my ears ring. Unless . . .

'Someone's banging on the window,' Danny said against my lips.

'What?'

'Someone's banging on the window of the car.'

We broke apart and sure enough there were Nate and Paula banging on the window of the passenger side door. I turned my head and saw Chris on the other side, waving gaily.

'Come on, lovebirds,' Paula shouted. 'There's enough time for that later. We need to celebrate.'

Danny gave me another quick kiss and we undid our seatbelts and got out of the car.

'I'll get the first round,' Paula called. 'Come on!'

Danny and I grinned at each other, and hand in hand we followed our friends into the pub.

Epilogue

Esther

1971

I slept a lot these days. So much that I couldn't always tell the difference between my memories and my dreams, as I drifted in and out of sleep.

Agnes's daughter Meg was with me most of the time, bustling around my bedroom. She was grown-up now, an old lady herself, with lines around her eyes and grey in her hair, but sometimes I still saw her as the little girl I'd met all those years before when I moved in with her family. I'd never felt sad about not having my own children because I'd had Meg, John and Pearl in my life.

I sighed, pulling the sheets up around my shoulders, and felt my eyes closing again. Some people might have thought of me as a lonely old spinster but I'd never been sorry that I hadn't married or become a mother. And I'd never been alone. Not really.

I had a lot of time to remember, now. Lots of hours spent with my thoughts. I wasn't sorry about that, either. It was nice, going back through my memories – as though I was reading a book someone had written especially for me. I thought about Elm Heath Primary and all the children I'd seen come and go.

I was so proud of the school and the pupils and even though it had been a long time since I'd been a teacher, I loved when they invited me in to watch plays or hear the choir sing.

I thought about the suffragettes too. I thought about them a lot. The friends I'd made back then, the strength the women had showed and the support we'd shared. The fight we'd put up, the violence we'd suffered, and the victories we'd won. It really had been the best of times and the worst. Their fight had made me the woman I'd become.

Sometimes I thought about Joseph and what my life could have been like if we'd married. But it was all such a long time ago and I found I couldn't imagine being a wife. Being his wife. Because that wasn't who I was at all.

'I'm a fighter,' I murmured. Meg was sitting next to my bed, reading, and she looked up as I spoke.

'What are you saying, Esther?'

I felt a rush of affection for her and her siblings and I reached out my hand to her from under the blanket.

'I was so sad about the baby,' I said as Meg squeezed my fingers gently. 'So sad about the baby.'

'I know, Esther,' she said.

I squinted at her. She was silhouetted in the light from the window and I couldn't see her face properly. For a moment I thought she was Agnes, sitting there.

'Agnes?' I said. 'Oh, Agnes, I do miss you.'

Agnes – or was it Meg? – patted my hand softly.

'Is Minnie coming?' I said. 'I'd like to see her.'

'She can't come because it's too far for her and she's not strong enough for the journey now. But she has been on the phone and she sent a card. Remember?'

I didn't remember. I found it hard to remember things from today or yesterday. I couldn't remember the names of the nurses or how old I was, or if I'd had breakfast.

Instead I remembered things from long ago, like Minnie and

Gilbert coming to live with me in Elm Heath during the war and helping with the evacuees. I organised them all coming to the country, and arranged their billets, and gave them somewhere to go when they were homesick or scared. I loved that, just as I loved teaching. Every child who'd passed through my school held a special place in my heart.

I remembered Minnie's heartbreak when her son Percy died in France. And I remembered Agnes's terror when John was called up in the Great War and her joy when he came home safely. I remembered those fights, which now didn't seem worth all the devastation and the fights that did. Like our fight for women's rights.

'A battle still not won,' I breathed.

I remembered all that so clearly but I couldn't remember if the woman sitting by my bed was my friend Agnes or her daughter.

I blinked at her, once, twice, and her face swam into view. It was Agnes. She was young again. So young. And she was smiling at me. In her arms was a bundle wrapped in a blanket, and she gazed down at her precious baby in wonder. Behind her was Gilbert, hand in hand with Percy, and my pupils who'd been lost in the wars were gathering – there was Lester Jacobs, who'd been one of my first ever students at Elm Heath, and who'd died in a trench in Belgium. And there was Jilly Atkins who'd been killed in an air raid on a day trip to London to buy fabric for her wedding dress.

With them was Mrs Pankhurst, regal in her fur stole, and Christabel, looking just as she had that day when she'd leaned out of a window to speak to a crowd and introduced me to the suffragettes. I could see Nelly who we'd met on that awful day in Westminster, but who'd become a good friend until she passed away last year. Oh it was so wonderful to see them again. So wonderful.

Agnes reached out to take my hand and I felt her fingers clasp mine. I closed my eyes. And everything was still.

If Esther and Lizzie's story had you cheering them on, you won't want to miss Kerry Barrett's moving and unputdownable *The Girl in the Picture*. When lonely Violet Hargreaves meets the mysterious and handsome Edwin on the beach, a chain of terrible events begins to unfold . . .

Acknowledgements

I immersed myself in the world of the suffragettes while I was researching Esther's story. The Museum of London was a wonderful resource. I visited their suffragette exhibit, and went on a very illuminating guided walk round London with one of their staff. The museum staff also helped me find newspaper reports of Black Friday from which I shamelessly plundered lots of the stories that made it into my novel. The women being thrown to the crowds is true. Esther's placard cutting the policeman's hand actually happened to a suffragette on the day, as did the invasive searches that some of the police were carrying out. Agnes's sad experience on the day is, thankfully, fiction.

While I was living Esther's story, I suddenly realised I knew nothing about the day-to-day role of a head teacher in 2019. So I need to thank the fabulous Sally Weeks, head teacher at Poverest Primary School, who took time out of her busy day (and believe me, it's busy!) to speak to me and fill me in on everything she does. Many of the ideas that Lizzie and Paula come up with to save Elm Heath were copied from Sally's great work at Poverest.

A huge thank you to my fabulous agent, Felicity, and my editors at HQ, Abi, Belinda and Dom. Also to my fellow writers who are always there to offer help, advice or simply a sympathetic ear, especially Aimee, Kath, Annie and Andi. And of course, to all my readers. Thanks for everything and I hope you enjoy this one!

Keep reading for an excerpt from
The Girl in the Picture

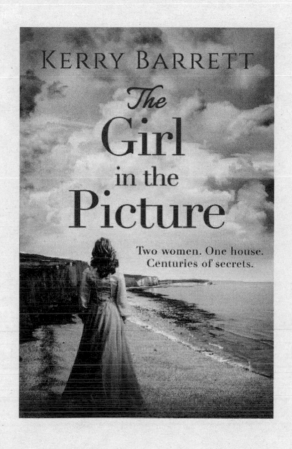

Present day

Ella

'It's perfect,' Ben said. 'It's the perfect house for us.'

I smiled at the excitement in his voice.

'What's it like?' I asked. I was in bed because I was getting over a sickness bug but suddenly I felt much better. I sat up against the headboard and looked out of the window into the grey London street. It was threatening to rain and the sky was dark even though it was still the afternoon.

'I'll send you some pictures,' Ben said. 'You'll love it. Sea view, of course, quiet but not isolated . . .' He paused. 'And . . .' He made an odd noise that I thought was supposed to be a trumpet fanfare.

'What?' I said, giggling. 'What else does it have?'

Ben was triumphant. 'Only a room in the attic.'

'No,' I said in delight. 'No way. So it could be a study?'

'Yes way,' said Ben. 'See? It's made for us.'

I glanced over at my laptop, balanced on the edge of my dressing table that doubled as a desk, which in turn was squeezed into the corner of our bedroom. We'd been happy here in this poky terraced house. Our boys had been born here. It was safe here. But this was a new adventure for us, no matter how terrifying I found the thought. And just imagine the luxury of having space to write. I looked at my notes for my next book, which were scattered over the floor, and smiled to myself.

'What do the boys think?' I asked.

'They're asleep,' Ben said. 'It's pissing down with rain and we're all in the car. I rang the estate agent and he's on his way, so I'll wake the boys up in a minute.'

'Ring me back when he arrives,' I said. 'FaceTime me, in fact. I want to see the house when you do.'

'Okay,' Ben said. 'Shouldn't be long.'

I ended the call and leaned back against my pillow. I was definitely beginning to feel much better now and I'd not thrown up for a few hours, but I was glad I'd not gone down to Sussex with Ben because I was still a bit queasy.

I picked up my glass of water from the bedside table and held it against my hot forehead while I thought about the house. It had been back in the spring when we'd spotted it, on a spontaneous weekend away. Ben had a job interview at a football club in Brighton. Not just any job interview. THE job interview. His dream role as chief physio for a professional sports team – the job he'd been working towards since he qualified. Great money, amazing opportunities.

The boys and I had gone along with him at the last minute and while Ben was at the interview, I'd wandered the narrow lanes of Brighton with Stanley in his buggy and Oscar scooting along beside me. I had marvelled at the happy families I saw around me and how my mood had lifted when I saw the sea, twinkling in the sunshine at the end of each road I passed. That day I felt like anything was possible, like I should grab every chance of happiness because I knew so well how fleeting it could be.

The next day – after Ben had been offered the job – we'd driven to a secluded beach, a little way along the coast, and sat on the shingle as the boys ran backwards and forwards to the surf.

'I love it here,' I said, shifting so I could lie down with my head resting on Ben's thigh and looking up at the low cliffs that edged the beach. I could see the tops of the village houses that overlooked the sea and, on the cliff top, a slightly skew-whiff To Let sign.

'I wish we could live here,' I said, pointing at the sign. 'Up there. Let's rent that house.'

Ben squinted at me through the spring sunshine. 'Yeah, right,' he said. 'Isn't that a bit spontaneous for you?'

I smiled. He was right. I'd never been one for taking risks. I was a planner. A checker. A researcher. I'd never done anything on a whim in my entire life. But suddenly I realized I was serious.

'I nearly died when Stanley was born,' I said, sitting up and looking at him. 'And so did Stanley.'

Ben looked like he was going to be sick. 'I know, Ella,' he said gently. 'I know. But you didn't – and Stan is here and he's perfect.'

We both looked at the edge of the sea where Stanley, who was now a sturdy almost-three-year-old, was digging a hole and watching it fill with water.

'He's perfect,' Ben said again.

I took his hand, desperate to get him to understand what I was trying to say. 'I know you know this,' I said. 'But because of what happened to my mum I've always been frightened to do anything too risky – I've always just gone for the safe option.'

Ben was beginning to look worried. 'Ella,' he said. 'What is this? Where's it come from?'

'Listen,' I said. 'Just listen. We've lived in the same house for ten years. I don't go on the tube in rush hour. I wouldn't hire jet skis on our honeymoon. I'm a tax accountant for heaven's sake. I don't take any risks. Ever. And suddenly I see that it's crazy to live that way. Because if life has taught me anything it's that even when you're trying to stay safe, bad things happen. I did everything right, when I was pregnant. No booze, no soft cheese – I even stopped having my highlights done although that's clearly ridiculous. And despite all that, I almost died. Oscar almost lost his mum, just like I lost mine. And you almost lost your wife. And our little Stanley.'

'So what? Three years later, you're suddenly a risk taker?' Ben said.

I grimaced. 'No,' I said. 'Still no jet skis. But I can see that some risks are worth taking.' I pointed up at the house on the cliff. 'Like this one.'

'Really?' Ben said. I could see he was excited and trying not to show it in case I changed my mind. 'Wouldn't you miss London?'

I thought about it. 'No,' I said, slowly. 'I don't think I would. Brighton's buzzy enough for when we need a bit of city life, and the rest of the time I'd be happy somewhere where the pace of life is more relaxed.'

I paused. 'Can we afford for me to give up work?'

'I reckon so,' Ben said. 'My new job pays well, and . . .'

'I've got my writing,' I finished for him. Alongside my deathly dull career in tax accountancy, I wrote novels. They were about a private investigator called Tessa Gilroy who did all the exciting, dangerous things I was too frightened to do in my own life. My first one had been a small hit – enough to create a bit of a buzz. My second sold fairly well. And that was it. Since I'd had Stan, I'd barely written anything at all. My deadlines had passed and my editor was getting tetchy.

'Maybe a change of scenery would help,' I said, suddenly feeling less desperate when it came to my writing. 'Maybe leaving work, and leaving London, is just what I need to unblock this writer.'

That was the beginning.

Ben started his job at the football club, commuting down to Sussex every day until we moved, and I handed in my notice at work. Well, it was less a formal handing in of my notice and more a walking out of a meeting, but the result was the same. I was swapping the dull world of tax accountancy for writing. I hoped.

My phone rang again, jolting me out of my memories.

'Ready?' Ben said, smiling at me from the screen.

'I'm nervous,' I said. 'What if we hate it?'

'Then we'll find something else,' said Ben. 'No biggie.'

I heard him talking to another man, I guessed the estate agent, and I chuckled as the boys' tousled heads darted by.

It wasn't the best view, of course, on my phone's tiny screen, but as Ben walked round the house I could see enough to know it was, indeed, perfect. The rooms were big; there was a huge kitchen, a nice garden that led down to the beach where we'd sat all those months before, and a lounge with a stunning view of the sea.

'Show me upstairs,' I said, eager to see the attic room.

But the signal was patchy and though I could hear Ben as he climbed the stairs I couldn't see him any more.

'Three big bedrooms and a smaller one,' Ben told me. 'A slightly old-fashioned bathroom with a very fetching peach suite . . .'

I made a face, but we were renting – I wasn't prepared to risk selling our London place until we knew we were settled in Sussex – so I knew I couldn't be too fussy about the décor.

'. . . and upstairs the attic is a bare, white-painted room with built-in cupboards, huge windows overlooking the sea, and stripped floorboards,' Ben said. 'It's perfect for your study.'

I couldn't speak for a minute – couldn't believe everything was working out so beautifully.

'Really?' I said. 'My attic study?'

'Really,' said Ben.

'Do the boys like it?'

'They want to get a dog,' Ben said.

I laughed with delight. 'Of course we'll get a dog,' I said.

'They've already chosen their bedrooms and they've both run round the garden so many times that they're bound to be asleep as soon as we're back in the car.'

'Then do it,' I said. 'Sign whatever you have to sign. Let's do it.'

'Don't you want to see the house yourself?' Ben said carefully. 'Check out schools. Make sure things are the way you want them?'

Once I would have, but not now. Now I just wanted to move on with our new life.

'Do you want to talk to your dad?'

'No.' I was adamant that wasn't a good idea because I knew he'd definitely try to talk us out of it. I'd not told him anything about our move yet. He didn't even know I'd handed in my notice at work – as far as he was aware, Ben was going to stick with commuting and I'd carry on exactly as I'd been doing up until now.

I got my cautious approach to life from my dad and I spent my whole time trying very hard not to do anything he wouldn't approve of. I'd never had a teenage rebellion, sneaked into a pub under age, or stayed out five minutes past my curfew. I'd chosen my law degree according to his advice – he was a solicitor – and then followed his recommendations for my career.

This move was the nearest I'd ever got to rebelling and I knew Dad would be horrified about me giving up my safe job, about Oscar changing schools, and us renting out our house. And even though moving to Sussex would mean we lived much nearer him, I thought that the less he knew of our plans, the better.

'We could come down again next weekend,' Ben was saying. 'When you're feeling well?'

'No,' I said, making my mind up on the spot. 'I don't want to risk losing the house. We were lucky enough that it's been empty this long, let's not tempt fate. Sign.'

'Sure?' Ben said.

'I'm sure.'

'Brilliant,' he said, and I heard the excitement in his voice again, along with something else – relief perhaps. He would be pleased to leave London.

'Ella?'

'Yes?'

'I've been really happy,' he said softly. 'Really happy. In London, with you, and the boys. But this is going to be even better. I promise. It's a leap of faith, and I know it's scary and I know it's all a bit spontaneous, but if we're all together it'll be fine.'

I felt the sudden threat of tears. 'Yes,' I said.

'We're strong, you and me,' Ben said. 'And Oscar and Stan. This is the right thing for us to do.'

'I know,' I said. 'We're going to be very happy there.'

**Want to find out what happens next between Ella and Ben?
Order *The Girl in the Picture* now!**

Dear Reader,

We hope you enjoyed reading this book. If you did, we'd be so appreciative if you left a review. It really helps us and the author to bring more books like this to you.

Here at HQ Digital we are dedicated to publishing fiction that will keep you turning the pages into the early hours. Don't want to miss a thing? To find out more about our books, promotions, discover exclusive content and enter competitions you can keep in touch in the following ways:

JOIN OUR COMMUNITY:
Sign up to our new email newsletter: po.st/HQSignUp
Read our new blog www.hqstories.co.uk
🐦 https://twitter.com/HQDigitalUK
f www.facebook.com/HQStories

BUDDING WRITER?
We're also looking for authors to join the HQ Digital family!
Please submit your manuscript to:
HQDigital@harpercollins.co.uk
Thanks for reading, from the HQ Digital team

If you enjoyed *The Secret Letter*, then why not try another unputdownable historical read from HQ Digital?

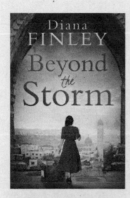